MURDER
IN
STONY CROSSING

Murder in Stony Crossing is a work of fiction. Any resemblance to actual events or parsons appearing herein is entirely coincidental.

Copyright© 2003 by Donald D. Huddle
All rights reserved

ISBN: 0-9748394-1-8
LCCN: 2004090002

Printed in the United Stated of America
Graphics by Larry Holloway Design

Douglas Publishing LLC
Box 326
Plymouth, IN 46563
Website: www.stonycrossing.com

A sequel to *Murder In Stony Crossing* titled *Justice in Stony Crossing* is scheduled for publication in 2005. A brief excerpt appears at the end of this book

Acknowledgments

Thanks for contributions and/or support to the following: Liza Ahrendt, Valerie Allison, Lynne Barden, Jay Blanding, Sylvia Bieghler, Lieutenant Commander William Bushnell, Ida Chipman, Robin Cupka, Dr. Randy Coulter, Jeanne Dams, Dr. Dave Detamore, Jackie Guernsey, Phil Harris, Chuck Jackson, Pody Kaiser, Anne Liechty, Dale Mitchell, Cathi Norton and John Wraight.

This book is dedicated to Grace Mary, naturally, who often refrained from committing justifiable homicide while the draft of this book was written in a corner of her kitchen.

Stony Crossing

In the late 1820's, surveyors dispatched from Washington to map a route for the proposed National Road across the United States arrived at a tiny Indiana settlement during a record drought. The river at its eastern edge was at a particularly low level, revealing many large boulders requiring much labor to remove. Consequently, the recommendation was for the new road to pass five miles to the south. The only legacy of the surveying party's visit was the name they inked on their map—*STONY CROSSING.*

Although not meeting the approval of many long-time residents, the old town is experiencing a rebirth of sorts. Newcomers have discovered an *Our Town, Grover's Corners*, kind of place with its ancient buildings, wide tree-lined streets, river, and large park. They can find peace and security within a few minutes of malls in Wayne City, the county seat fifteen miles distant, or downtown Indianapolis—an easy one-hour drive.

Happily for new bed-and-breakfast entrepreneurs, tourist business is growing by leaps and bounds. For shoppers and souvenir hunters, a variety of merchandise and "authentic" craft items are available in newly opened boutiques. Out on Oak Road, the aged HARRY HILLER'S WOOD SHOP sign is no more, replaced by one lettered in ersatz-hayseed, **HILLBILLY HARRY'S,** another beneath it advertising **ANTEEK ROKKERS MADE EVER DAY**. Hungry? Sweet tooth? Eat at the Country Kitchen or stop in 𝔇𝔢 𝔒𝔩𝔡𝔢 𝔗𝔬𝔣𝔣𝔢𝔢 𝔚𝔬𝔯𝔨𝔢𝔰 on Sycamore Street for a bag of taffy (formerly SMITH'S CANDIES). Building restorations and a housing development are also evidence of growth.

Yes, Stony Crossing is indeed changing—even if it makes the long-timers a bit uncomfortable.

1

In August, Ezekial Amos (Zeke) Tanner traveled east through Kansas toward Indiana along a boring I-70, his only companion an ancient Chevy Blazer, "Ol' Emmy." (Short for "Emphysema.") He was leaving the coaching life after nearly 20 years, thankful for inheriting sufficient means to be forever free of football and basketball in sports hotbeds the likes of Buffalo Branch and Fort Hogg. From now on, it's the big city for him.

His bequest includes a house and acreage in Stony Crossing. In his letter, Uncle John's attorney said he'd be glad to handle probating the will and selling the property. After swinging by the old hometown to sign the papers and visit his long-time buddy, Police Chief DeVon Bookman, it would be, "Hello, city life" for Mr. Ezekial Tanner. Oh yeah!

Zeke climbed rutted wooden stairs to the second-story office of Nathanial Newfield Nesbit, widely known as "Nickel-Nabber" Nesbit.

One glance confirmed he was the same old miser—shiny three-piece blue-serge suit, string tie, thin as a rail with lips to match. He put on what passed for a smile and extended a bony hand. "Ezekial, my boy, please do come in."

Zeke sat in a decrepit wooden chair, and they passed the usual amenities before he got down to business. "Your letter said you could see to probating Uncle John's will and selling the property."

"Probatin's only a formality. Been to see the place yet?"

"No, but I plan to stop by on my way out of town."

"Well, you'll soon see several little things that need fixin' so the place'll sell better."

"You know everyone around here. Can you hire someone?"

"Price'a labor's gotten so high, it'd cost a pretty penny. Hafta charge for my time, too. You could do what's needed in a couple weeks, no more'n three at the most."

"Guess I could take a look."

"That's good. That's good. By the way, you don't need to check on that storage buildin' out beyond the orchard. You'll find locks on it, and I don't have a key. Took the liberty'a rentin' it to a party from over at the county seat. Lucky for you, they paid a year in advance. The three hundred dollars about covers your cost'a what I've done on your uncle's estate so far. You know—for filin' paperwork and tendin' to some upkeep, n'all."

"I see." *(Never miss a trick for a dollar, do you?)*

"OK then, I'll talk to you later."

When Zeke saw the knee-deep grass in the yard, he was more than a little irritated with the old attorney. *(Three hundred dollars and he didn't even have the lawn mowed!)* Worse still, Nickel-Nabber was correct—some "fixin" was indeed needed, including painting trim and replacing several pickets in the fence.

The property, typical of those described by real estate hucksters as a "gentleman farmer's dream," was situated at the edge of town, fronting east on Newmarket Street and extending nearly 300 feet west to

Jacob Waggoner's farm. Beginning at Vine Street half a block north of the house, it stretched 400 feet south to the nearest neighbor.

An apple orchard covered much of the area. Halfway along the fence between the orchard and Waggoner's on the western property line stood the storage building Nesbit rented out. Empty and unused for twenty years, its driveway, shielded from view by a row of thick evergreens all the way to Vine Street, made it a favorite parking spot for countless high school kids.

Zeke walked up the four steps to the front porch of the house the same real estate peddlers might list as "vintage fieldstone." Passing through the small entryway, he entered what he remembered as its best feature, the beamed-ceiling living room with a huge fireplace. On through the kitchen greatly in need of painting and onto the back porch, he discovered several additional repair jobs his Uncle John's advancing years no longer permitted him to do. In Zeke's opinion, no mortal man could finish them in Nesbit's estimate of "...a couple weeks, no more'n three at the most." He'd tell the old miser to find a handyman or sell the property as it was.

Returning to the kitchen, Zeke heard a vehicle crunch to a stop in the drive. A glance through the front window told it all. There was no mistaking the 6 foot-9 figure of DeVon Bookman, "Dee" or "Stretch" to those well acquainted. He's served as Stony Crossing's chief of police approaching two decades. In elementary school, Zeke and Dee became inseparable, and the bond grew even stronger in high school when Zeke was either lofting a jump shot or dishing off to Dee for a lay-up or hook. They were so tight some suggested they must've been twins separated at birth. However, that didn't hold up too well in light of their statures. With Zeke's height at 5 foot-10, weight a shade under 180, and hair in the process of receding slowly to a half-halo, the comparison to the tall, lanky and fully haired Bookman made twinship unlikely.

Using the name his high school coach gave Zeke after a poor performance, Bookman inquired in his best John Wayne, "Just come in on the stage, Gertrude? Must'a—that bucket'a rusty bolts sittin' over there would'a never made it all the way here. When you gonna get rid'a that thing? Gotta be older'n baseball."

Invoking the coach's name for DeVon after the same godawful game, Zeke responded, "Out without a keeper, Ethel? Don't you badmouth Ol' Emmy—she's been my true friend far too long to desert now. What're you doing here, anyway? Slow day for jaywalkers? Wear out the papers you push around all day?"

"Pilgrim, my official duties include seein' to it that public disgraces like this yard are tended to and rollin' junk piles get hauled away. In our town, podner, we lock up violators such as yourself. Put your hands behind you."

After a few more rounds of the customary insults between two great pals, Bookman suggested, "What say we harvest this hayfield, then go to the diner for supper?"

"OK, but don't forget I need to get back to Nickel-Nabber's office before being on my way to the city."

The chief sighed. "Yeah, yeah, yeah. You been harpin' on the same bull for the last gazillion years. Now let's get the mower and rakes out'a my pickup."

After reducing the overgrown lawn to stubble, it was too late for Zeke to return to the attorney's office. They feasted on grilled T-bones at Lurinda Beatty's chintz-curtained diner, the Country Kitchen, before returning to Zeke's. After many arguments about the merits of city life versus small towns, DeVon departed. At least Zeke would stay the night, and tomorrow would be another day.

Early next morning, Bookman returned. As they sat on the porch sipping coffee, he raised the subject. "Still hell-bent on leavin' the fixin' up to old skinflint Nesbit, are you? Big mistake. Say he finds somebody to repair things, who's gonna check on 'em? You'll wind up with both of 'em stealin' you blind. And knowin' Nickel-Nabber, he'll stop tryin' to sell the property and offer a pittance, then sell it at a big profit for himself."

Zeke frowned. Dee was probably right, but he wasn't going to give up on his plans. "Suppose I could advertise for help and check them out. But, I'm staying only long enough to be sure the repairs are going to be done right, then I'm out of here."

"Whatever." Driving away, DeVon was smiling to himself over Zeke's decision to remain, however brief the stay might be.

The only respondents to Zeke's ad were two still hung-over drunks and one shifty-eyed character with a "gotta-report-weekly-to-my-parole-officer" look. While waiting for a suitable repairman, he busied himself with painting and refurbishing. Another week passed, then two more. No more applicants appeared. He kept fixing and painting—his vows to live in a big city growing ever more sporadic.

Zeke fell into a comfortable pattern. Up early, he fed the dogs (two strays with a keen eye for a soft touch), and went downtown for the newspaper and breakfast with Dee at the diner. Soon, the locals, many remembering his high school basketball heroics, began including him in their ribbing sessions. He installed his stereo so he could get his daily dose of classics and jazz. For mental stimulation, he solved tough cryptograms, a hobby developed after spending three years in a Navy decoding unit.

Hearing Zeke was in Stony Crossing, Jim Henry, editor of the *Wayne City Tribune*, phoned to welcome him, then offered a proposition. "Your Uncle John was our Stony Crossing stringer for years. You'd be a natural to do the same job. How about it?"

There was no way he wanted any part of it, declining each time Henry phoned. The editor persisted, pestering Zeke until he finally agreed to try it. The paper only needed material every week or so, and he could quit any time. It wasn't long before the job became enjoyable. He even contemplated trying a weekly column. The only serious flap occurred when the name of the canned-pickles winner at the Fall Harvest Festival, Edna Mae Zook, appeared under a photo of the prize heifer.

Nickel-Nabber Nesbit sent a prospective buyer or two, but their offers were ridiculously low. The winey air of late autumn arrived with apples to pick. Sometime after Thanksgiving, his already diminished resolve to leave virtually disappeared.

There were a few annoyances, of course. During the week prior to New Years Day, one appeared in the pompous person of H. Charles "Call-me-Charlie" Ackerman, the gaunt, blue-veined, hawked-beaked lay evangelist of the local fundamentalist church. Its membership doesn't believe in having a full-time minister, so Preacher Ackerman works full-time at a local grocery. He's a fire-and-brimstone pulpit pounder of the first order. Lately, he's gained a measure of regional notoriety with his Sunday afternoon program, *The Best of God Hour,* broadcast at a Wayne City FM station.

One evening after the Christmas holidays, Zeke was relaxing before the fireplace when the preacher showed up. "I just happened to see you drive by today, and it reminded me to drop over and give you a special invitation to the annual New Year's Day service, you bein' my neighbor, n'all. It's our turn to hold it, y'know."

By tradition, everyone in town was expected to attend ecumenical services on New Year's Day. This year, it fell on Sunday, but there was always a New Year's Day service, no matter on what day of the week it occurred. Zeke was unable to manufacture a quick evasion, so he was hooked.

After a night of revelry followed by too few hours of sleep, folks stumbled into the morning service. Zeke took a seat in the last row and fought nodding off along with the others while preacher Ackerman droned on and on. Finally the sleep-inducing homily mercifully ended. Delbert Dove, the preacher's head gofer, whacked his tuning fork and led the congregation in a quick a Capella verse of *When the Roll is Called Up Yonder,* after which Ackerman concluded with a Guinness-record benediction. Thankful for rear pews, Zeke bolted for the door ahead of the tidal-surge of escapees. Had he known what was transpiring at a mansion up in Wilshire Heights, he probably would've left much earlier.

*****

Alan Bannister, snappish retired millionaire owner of Bannister Paper Company, sat reading, sipping his "early-on" brandy, and occasionally responding to Mrs. Bannister's nervous chattering about her dog. He despised the mouthy critter, referring to him as a black hole into which money was poured. "I'm telling you, that dumbbell will come home of his own accord. He's only been gone half an hour."

"But it's so cold! What *were* you thinking when you let him out? Besides being out in this freezing weather, he's so valuable anyone who knows the slightest thing about dogs might steal him."

"No one with a grain of sense will steal a ten-pound excuse for a *real* dog."

Accustomed as she was to tuning out her husband's grousing about her precious pet, she didn't continue the sparring, instead moved from window to window anxiously looking for "Tinkerbell," her name for Champion Sir Brotherington of Bostwich.

Her husband only half heard her sudden squeal of delight and doggie-prattle. "Oh, there comes my darling Tinkerbell now! What's this—you brought me another present? How thoughtful!"

Alan Bannister caught enough of her usual claptrap to know he'll no doubt be forced to take whatever the mongrel brought home and garbage it. *(Damned dog's always dragging in a dead something or other. Ah well, a little more brandy first.)*

Maybe he was conscious of only one-quarter of his wife's gibberish, but the first near primal scream wiped away any alcoholic fuzz, rammed through each temple, collided head-on, and flamed down his spine. Elizabeth Bannister stood mesmerized, eyes wide and riveted on Sir Brotherington's offering as her screaming echoed throughout. It was a human hand.

2

Zeke was half way down the church steps when the silver stretch-Benz skidded to a stop. As did everyone, He knew it belonged to Alan Bannister, harsh critic of Chief of Police Bookman. He first aroused Alan Bannister's ire by refusing to overlook a case of staggering-drunk-and-disorderly on the part of Bannister's favorite nephew. This following the kid's successful attempt to moon the customers leaving Waggoner's True Bible Bookstore.

In retaliation, as president of the Stony Crossing town council, Bannister tried to cut the police budget, but Bookman won the battle. He also refused Bannister's repeated requests to fix traffic tickets for his country club cronies and ordered two of them jailed for ignoring them. Later, one of DeVon's officers nabbed the nephew again, this time for DUI.

These and other sword-crossings with Bookman added fuel for the town's richest citizen's acid-tongued campaign against the police department in general and its chief in particular.

A split second after Zeke reached the sidewalk, a hyper-excited Bannister grabbed him by the lapels and stridently demanded to know, *"IZATJACKASSBOOKMANINCHURCHTODAY?"*

"Say again?"

More slowly this time, but just as loud, Bannister clipped off each word, *"DAMMIT, YOU DEAF! I SAID, IS THAT JACKASS BOOKMAN IN CHURCH?"*

"Chief Bookman didn't attend today."

"WHERE'NHELLIZE?"

Zeke thought he knew where DeVon Bookman was, but he wasn't about to disclose the whereabouts of the chief, who was probably getting ready to dive into Sunday brunch prepared by the owner of the Country Kitchen. Nothing wrong with eating at the diner, of course. However, it was closed on Sundays, and about this time, Lurinda Beatty would be waiting to prepare the shirred eggs in her own kitchen up on Ivy Street while DeVon toweled off upstairs after his shower.

Bannister continued geysering forth, part of which Zeke was having trouble deciphering. Something or other about a dog and Mrs. Bannister ending with, *"Get me to him right this minute, or you'll be the sorriest sumbitch in history!"*

Zeke dealt with some powerfully sorry alumni sumbitches during his coaching career and wasn't much bothered by this threat, but he decided to humor him. "Follow me, and we'll take a look around. He could be anyplace, though." Bannister calmed down enough so that his words were coming out a bit more normally. "I'm not tagging around behind your heap. Get in my car and take me to him."

"We better try the station first. If he's not there, maybe the deskman will know where he is."

"Already checked there!"

Torturing tires, Bannister careened around the corner heading for downtown. "Don't screw around trying to cover up for him. I don't give a flea's fart who he's rubbing uglies with—just get me to wherever he is!"

A siren wailed behind them, and Zeke was nearly pitched into the windshield when Bannister slammed on the brakes. "Maybe that fool knows where Bookman's hiding out."

That "fool" was Chief DeVon E. Bookman himself. Lurinda ran short on bacon and dispatched the town's finest to the diner's refrigerator to fetch another couple rashers. Bannister had ignored the four-way stop at Sycamore Street as DeVon's squad car approached on East Main. He sat for a moment behind the violator, taking his time, enjoying every minute. Other drivers were already slowing and gawking.

The chief's enjoyable anticipation was short-circuited by Bannister rushing back and snarling, "For once in your life, you could be in the right place at the right time!"

Bookman pushed open his door, shoving his critic aside, and stepped out. "What was that you just now said?" (In a tone suggesting, "You're already under arrest, wanna make it worse?")

Ignoring the chief's question, the meagerly built 5 foot-7 Bannister grabbed the chief's arm and tried to drag him toward the Benz's trunk. "Take a look in there!"

The chief shook free. "More'n happy to if you're a mind to open it first."

Bannister whirled, dashed to his car and jerked the trunk's release lever. "OK, big shot, now look."

It was empty except for a paper sack. "Not much in there, Alan."

"*Inthesack! In the sack!*"

Bookman opened the bag, and glimpsed Sir Brotherington of Bostwich's gift to his mistress. Without a word he folded the sack tightly closed and slammed the trunk lid, then rapped on the back window, beckoning Zeke to join them. He complied, and the chief began issuing very cop-like orders. "Alan, give Tanner your keys and get in my car. Zeke, drive Bannister's car and lead the way around back of the station into the garage. I'll be right on your bumper. Take it slow. I don't want any other vehicles gettin' 'twixt us."

Bannister opened his mouth to protest, but Bookman's manner caused him to hand the keys to Zeke. It didn't sound as if it were a good time to voice his reluctance, either. Shrugging, he walked to the Mercedes and slid under the wheel.

As ordered, Zeke led the snail-paced two-car parade. Enroute, Bannister told Bookman the story of the dog bringing home the hand. Inside the garage on the lower level at the rear of the station, the chief took out a two-quart plastic food bag with a diagonal yellow stripe labeled *EVIDENCE*. Saying nothing, he held out his hand to Zeke for Bannister's keys and opened the big car's trunk. Keeping the paper bag closed, he carefully put it into the evidence bag and thumb-nailed it shut. Zeke still had no idea what it contained.

Bookman led the way upstairs to a room doing double duty as an examination site for the coroner and a small morgue consisting of two cold-storage compartments with slide out body trays. However, there was so rarely even one victim that they usually only contained all sorts of perishables stashed there by department personnel. The chief sat at a small table, placed the evidence bag before him and punched an intercom button. "Phone the coroner and ask him to get right over here. Then tell Benson to come in and bring the camera and recorder."

Zeke's spine tingled at the mention of the coroner. "So sorry, Great Chief, but I do believe I'll take this opportunity to depart."

"Siddown, will you? Call it a favor. I'll explain later."

Bannister demanded of the chief, "Exactly why'd you bring me here, anyway? All I did was throw a handkerchief over that thing and drop it in a sack, then bring it to you. There's nothing more I can offer. I'm leaving."

"Don't get all swole up, Alan. I wanted you here as a good citizen who's gotta give a statement. I also wanted to ask you to go home and talk over everthing with your wife that she remembers about her dog bringin' home the hand."

Zeke stopped dead in his tracks. *(Hand! Did he say **hand**! I'm out of here.)* He started for the door.

The chief flagged him down. "Hold on, hold on! You're gonna hafta give a statement. Besides, your experience and that curiosity'a yours could be'a help later on."

"*Experience*? *What* experience? *Curiosity*? What've they got to do with anything, Dee? I don't..."

Bannister interrupted, "Bookman, you said I should talk to Elizabeth. "Isn't that your job?"

"I'm askin' for your cooperation 'cause she's more likely to simmer down sooner if you do it. Later on, I'll probly wanna talk to her, too, then see whether anything might'a slipped *your* mind."

"All right, all right, but while I'm doing *your* job, what are you going to do—sit here and wait for the killer to walk in and tell you where the body is?"

"What makes you so all-fired sure there *is* a killer? Or a body, for that matter? Hell, for all we know, we're dealin' with a med-school kids's stunt or some kook's doin'."

"Of course there's a body! If there's a hand, there's a body!"

"Alan..."

"Oh all right. I'll talk to her, but she won't have anything new."

"Fine, I'll check with you later. Now, why don'tcha just step on down the hall and give your statement to the sergeant." Bannister left, grousing about cops with heads too big for their hats.

Officer Hollis Benson entered. Benson occasionally showed signs of good police work, but more often skated on the thin ice of a three-day suspension. He fancied himself something of a soldier of fortune—wanna-be mustache and tattoos included. On his right forearm a war eagle flew. On the left, an armored fist threatened, **DEATH TO TRAITORS**. He was involved in church activities, but was known to be a bit shaky in practicing what was preached. Members who called attention to his misdeeds were discouraged from pursuing the issue when informed by Preacher Ackerman that Benson was repentant—*and*, rumor mongering was a sin—*and*, folks with skeletons in their own closets should take care to keep the doors closed—if they caught his drift.

Horatio Churchill Forsyth, MD, came chugging in. In spite of a 5 foot-4, 125-pound, little-engine-that-could demeanor, he was known for his expertise in analyzing forensic evidence. The chief waited patiently through the coroner's routine. He carefully hung his camel hair topcoat on the rack, centered his pork-pie hat over it, then placed boots directly beneath them, pointing outward. Next came sitting and attending to creases, cuffs, and tie. After smoothing his goatee and pencil-line mustache, he interlaced his fingers and inquired of bookman, "What business is there for the coroner?"

"Doctor, in this sack is a human hand brought in by Alan Bannister. Nobody's had a close look at it. Benson'll put it in a lab tray, and we'll listen to your comments while you're makin' your preliminary examination." He handed the sack to Benson.

The coroner sat on one side of the table, Bookman and Zeke on the other. Benson took the evidence across the room to a counter atop a cabinet containing lab equipment. His back to the others, he stood speechless after dumping the hand into a tray.

"Come on, Benson, you've seen lots worse," the chief admonished. "Get it on over here for the coroner."

In spite of steeling himself, Zeke was shocked at the sight. Springing to his feet, he simultaneously plotted his escape route. *(Curiosity or no curiosity, I'm gone!)*

DeVon put a hand on his friend's shoulder. "This won't take long." Still flight-ready, Zeke sat. However, Dr. Forsyth's voice soon penetrated, and he found himself becoming interested in spite of his unwillingness to remain.

The coroner continued, "...Caucasian male...between 50 and 60 years of age...larger than average hand...muscular...no anatomical anomalies visible on the back...no evidence of decomposition. It's a right hand on which the person probably wore a ring of greater than average width for some time. See the slight indentation in the flesh and the untanned strip?"

Forsythe inspected a thermometer. "Current outer temperature of the severed member is fifty-two degrees, but it has been inside for some time. Later on, I'll make some incisions and tests which will tell me more, but I'd guess this hand was severed no more than twenty-four hours ago."

Zeke gathered himself for take-off. *(Bookman be damned, I'm out of here before the incisioning starts*!) He relaxed when the coroner began using medical terminology about skin tension, lividity and other forensic analysis, which Zeke couldn't interpret but was happy to see surgery wasn't imminent. Forsythe turned the hand palm-up and straightened the fingers. "Hello! What's this?"

What appeared to be an irregular circle more than two inches across was drawn on the palm with a black marker of some kind. Inside, also in black, was the number 70, with a line boldly slashed diagonally across it. It looked like some sort of traffic sign to Zeke. Below the circle was 1 5 3 0, also in black.

Simultaneously:

"*Whataya make'a that!*"—Bookman

"*Holy Toledo!*"—Zeke

"Well, now."—Forsythe

The chief spoke. "Doctor, leave it right there for a minute, will you please? Hollis, start takin' pictures."

When Benson finished, the doctor resumed his examination and comments. "It looks reasonably clear that this hand was disarticulated by a person or persons using sharp instruments. In other words, there is no evidence of sloppy hacking or tearing." Forsyth paused to reposition the hand. "There's no damage as might have occurred in an altercation. The fingernails have been well cared for. I will remove a scraping from beneath each nail for analysis, but there are no visible signs of unusual material under any of them."

Taking a small reading glass from his pocket, the coroner peered at several areas of the palm. "A black chemical, probably indelible ink, was used to draw the shape, the numbers, and the line crossing out the large number above them. All were probably applied after the hand was severed. At first, the drawing appeared to be a crude attempt to make a regular circle or perhaps a traffic sign. However, it's a rather carefully drawn heptagon, which is not the easiest thing to do, especially on the uneven surface of a human hand. It appears someone's gone to considerable trouble."

Bookman growled, "All right, all right, somebody tell us poor ignorant folk what a hecta-whatever is."

Zeke scolded, "Dee, you should've paid more attention to Mr. Lestin in geometry class. A heptagon is a seven-sided figure with seven angles."

"You mean a seven-sided circle."

"No, but you're close enough."

One more inspection and Forsyth prepared to go. "Gentlemen, those are my initial findings. I promised Jake Pettibone I'd drop by, He was extremely anxious to ask a very important favor while his wife's away. Can't imagine what it could be. The only favor he ever asked was how to win a ruckus with his Mrs. They've been married more than 50 years and at each other most of it. Shouldn't take long—I shall return as soon as possible. For now, please have Officer Benson remove foodstuffs from a cold storage compartment and replace them with this evidence. Please also have him lock it and place the key in my custody."

Bookman turned to Benson. "Do it, Hollis."

Benson complied, walked over to Doctor Forsyth, and announced in a peeved tone, "Everbody please witness I'm placin' the key in the coroner's hand. And, you might wanna check to see if the compartment's locked. It's number two."

Bookman responded, "Don't go gettin' a knot in your knickers, Benson. You wouldn't wanna be responsible if anything happened to that thing, would you? By the way, can you have those photos ready in an hour?" Benson's silence answered for him as he left.

Doctor Forsyth departed and Bookman turned to Zeke. "Let's step into my office."

3

They walked into an office containing only an ancient scarred desk, an equally beat-up storage cabinet, a minimum number of chairs, and a seldom used black-and-white TV isolated in a far corner. Three walls were barren of the usual collection of photographs and professional membership documents found in most counterparts' offices. Only on the fourth was there a display of sorts. Several marksmanship trophies surrounded a framed sign announcing:

I STILL MISS MY EX
(But My Aim Is Getting Better)

Bookman's attire reflected his Spartan view of life. Few could remember when he was seen in anything except jeans, denim jacket, cowboy boots, and what is known in western lingo as a cattle-buyers silver-belly Stetson. Arctic blue eyes, handlebar mustache and height were personal features of note—not counting the occasionally garbled words, phrases and quotes. Since grade school, Zeke was forever correcting him. Since grade school, it did no good.

DeVon enjoyed a special relationship with the town's citizens. In his long tenure as chief of police, he collected enough dirty linen to fill several closets, but knew how to keep his mouth shut. Alan Bannister aside, only a few chronic petty gripers among town councilmen made occasional attempts to interfere with how he did his job.

DeVon sat as his desk and began filling a grungy Calabash Meerschaum with mangy-looking tobacco as he began working on Zeke. "We can forget your statement for now. I wanna talk about some things you can help with."

Zeke stretched his arms upward and waved. "Time out! Stop right there! I've already gone farther than I should with this business. Doggone it Dee, it's ridiculous! What do I know about criminal investigation, anyway?"

Bookman sighed deeply. "All right, Gertrude, if I must take the time. I got some real good reasons for wantin' you underfoot. To start with, it'd be nice to have somebody I trusted to check ideas with or talk about certain people's stories. You've even had police experience. Right?"

"Some *experience*! Two three-month summer stints filling in for cops on vacation."

"There you are—two hundred percent more'n most. Zeke, there's other reasons I wantcha underfoot. The stuff on the hand must mean *somethin'*. Could be we're into some spooky-do about cults. Lots'a cult crap goin' around in the country. You surely must'a learned at least a little about it durin' your teachin' jobs. Another thing—there's bound to be a slew'a press hounds stickin' their big bazoos into everthing. I need somebody to handle 'em that won't get as riled as me. Also need somebody to write a press release now and then. Over the years, the department's not had too much luck gettin' things put down right. What's more natural than the local reporter for the county newspaper coverin' department doins'? Jim Henry'd be tickled to death."

Zeke thought it over but still wasn't ready to buy in. "Assuming there's an ounce of ore in what you say, how are you going to explain my working in the department?"

"Don't hafta explain nothin' to nobody. I'm authorized to use anybody I want for special jobs—mostly voluntary help, a'course. Somethin' I got from the skinflint town council instead of 'em approvin' hirin' another regular officer. We'll call you the Special Assistant for Press Relatin'."

After more arguments, Zeke decided he'd do it, but first have some fun. "You silver-tongued rascal, say 'pretty please,' and I'll think about it."

Chief of Police Bookman's face began to redden, and he pushed back his Stetson—a habit when irritated. "Confound it, Tanner! I'm not listenin' to any more'a your tongue-draggin'. Forget the BS, you're in!"

"Well, it might be interesting to see how a real high class detective goes about solving the case of the century. Guess I could give it a short try."

"*Finally*! Slow but sure. Let's get started. First thing, give your statement to the sergeant. While you're doin' that, I gotta get started on organizin' a search for tomorrow mornin' out around the Bannisters'. Long shot, but maybe we'll stumble over a body. When we get done here, there'll still be time enough before dark for us to take a ride out there. Wanna get a good fix on the lay'a the land."

Zeke finished his statement while DeVon started the search wheels turning. He returned and directed. "C'mon, let's get a move on—can't keep the bad guys waitin'."

They got into Bookman's unmarked Ford and started for Wilshire Heights, the nicely wooded hilly section north of town. When Zeke was a kid, roads with descriptive if unofficial names crisscrossed the area—names the likes of Horse Hockey Road and Bumpy Butt (Horse Hockey, so coined by earlier citizens who were walking to Bailey's Stables—Bumpy Butt for being the roughest road in the county). Years later, the region was developed to build homes sold mostly to Bannister

Paper Company executives. Naturally they couldn't list return address as "1274 Bumpy Butt" or "72034 Horse Hockey Road." An obliging town council voted to allow the developer to use names deemed more appropriate.

Name them they did, opting mostly for cutesy bird names ending with Lane, Trace, Place, Way or Trail. They began with the ubiquitous "Mockingbird Lane," closely followed by the obligatory "Meadowlark Way." Horse Hockey Road was now "Warbler Drive," "Bumpy Butt," Oriole Way. Townsfolk refused to use the new names and immediately branded Wilshire Heights "Birdland" as much for the types who lived there as for the street names.

Warbler Drive) bordered Bird land on the south, separating it from Bramblewood Park (the natives' "Make-Out Woods"). County roads were the north and east boundaries, a boulder-strewn river the western. (Called what? Right—Rocky River" by the long-timers, "Flagstone Flow" by the come-latelys.)

A stone's throw west of Rocky River, Sycamore Street paralleled it and continued south roughly a half-mile to become Stony Crossing's main north-south street. Plans to rename Sycamore Street "Titmouse Trace," fell through when townsfolk heard about it and "rared up" against having a "sissy-britches" name for their main drag.)

DeVon turned east from Sycamore onto Horse Hockey and stopped to set aside one of the Street Department barricades put there during snowy weather to block the approach to Bailey Bridge, the ancient covered wooden span over Rocky River. He thought better of moving it and drove on out Sycamore. "Some hawk-eyed hoity-toity hoot owl is sure to see us and raise a stink. We'll go on up Sycamore—cross over the iron bridge on Bumpy Butt into Birdland."

Bookman and his "Special Assistant" spent considerable time cruising the area. Occasionally, the chief stopped to take a long look at a ravine or secluded area. "If there's a body around somewhere to match the hand, it'll be tough to spot. Sure lots'a places in these thickets to hide one."

They drove down Hummingbird Trail (Moonshine Ridge) and onto Wood Thrush Lane (Slip'n Slide). At the end of the winding street they stopped in front of the Bannisters' mansion on the hill overlooking Make-Out Woods. Zeke was amazed. "Holy Pete, just look at the view from up here! Since they cleaned out the brush, you can see all of the covered bridge and beyond it clear to Sycamore where Horse Hockey meets it. Halfway through Make-Out Woods, too."

"Yeah, it's pretty, all right, but if you gotta be an Alan Bannister to get this view, I can do without. Let's go—gotta see if the coroner's been back."

Forsythe hadn't been, and Devon offered, "C'mon, I'll drive you to that rust pile you call transportation."

"No thanks, I'll walk. I don't ride with folks who insult great ladies. Later, Ethel."

"Later, Gertrude."

In the January cold, a pale sun was trying hard to fool folks into believing it was a fine mid-summer afternoon. It wasn't working.

The telephone was ringing when Zeke walked onto his porch. He took his time about shaking off the snow and keying the lock, hoping the caller would give up. No such luck. He went into the kitchen and picked up the phone. "Hello."

It was Jim Henry, editor of the *Wayne City Tribune*. "That you, Zeke?"

"If it sounds like a Zeke, it must be a Zeke."

Henry sounded more enthusiastic than was called for by hearing his out-county stringer's voice. "I just got a call on my cell that a human hand with some strange drawings on it was brought into the police station over there. You're tight with DeVon Bookman. Give him a shout to see what you can dig up. Don't need to write it up. Phone it to the rewrite man and he'll do the rest."

"Jim, how did you find out about this?"

"Oh, it doesn't matter. Just try to get more details."

"I'll talk to DeVon."

"OK, but phone the rewrite desk as soon as you learn anything at all."

Zeke sat and thought about how Jim Henry obtained the information about the hand. *(Better phone Dee.)*

"Stony Crossin' Police." Zeke thought he recognized Hollis Benson's voice.

"Give me Chief Bookman, will you please."

He came on the line. "Doc came back in. You might wanna know somethin' interestin' he said."

"I do, but it can wait until I get there. Something we need to talk about—wanted to see if you were in." He had an idea who made the call to the paper, and wasn't about to pass it along over the phone.

When he told the chief about Jim Henry's call, he exploded, "*Dammit!* What's Henry tryin' to pull—buyin' tips right out'a my police station!"

"Sure it came from here?"

"Could'a only come from here! Could'a only been Benson! Not the first time somethin's leaked. I've had my suspicions, but couldn't pin down the faucet-mouth doin' the leakin'. The Bannisters wouldn't know about the hand's markin's—he covered it up as soon as he saw it and put it in a sack—besides, the fingers were half-way closed. The coroner wouldn't spill nothin'—that leaves only Benson. He'd do anything for a buck, the no good prevert."

Silently, Zeke agreed but asked, "Sure it couldn't be anyone else? His partner, maybe? And the word is *per*vert, not *pre*vert."

"Whatever, correction policeman, whatever. To answer your question, it wouldn't be Anders. They're cut out'a the same stripe, but Benson wouldn't share a dollar with anybody if his life depended on it. Nope, it's him, all right. This is as good a time as any." He jabbed the intercom. "Benson, get in here!"

Hollis Benson entered, sullen-faced from the chief's abrupt order. "Yeah, Chief?" He stood, unblinking, trying to look unconcerned.

For several seconds, Bookman just sat, eyes boring into his subordinate. That's all it took for Benson to break off any attempt to win a stare-down. Eyes straying side to side, he shifted from foot to foot.

The chief growled, "Let's save lots'a time. I got the total skinny on you. How much did Jim Henry pay for spillin' your guts to his paper?"

Benson tried mightily to regain some eye contact, but it was no use—each time his eyes sought a different compass point. He couldn't speak either—there he stood, a pillar of guilt.

Bookman added, "I hope it was enough to pay your wages for the next three days. Get out'a here, and don't even come *near* the station before talkin' to me!" Uttering not a word of denial, Benson fled.

DeVon worked on his pipe and cooled down enough to report the coroner's interesting finding and tomorrow's search plans. "Doc wants to do more tests, but he came in long enough to work on a few things. Said the hand was most likely carved off before the owner was dead. How about that!"

"Wow! That is something interesting, all right. What do you make of it?"

"Nothin' yet. Could mean somethin' when we get more to go on."

"Incidentally, Dee, I'm curious—did Dr. Forsythe mention the big favor Jake Pettibone wanted?"

"Don't hafta tell me you're curious—you're *always* curious. Yeah, I meant to tell you about Jake—funnier'n heck. He wanted Doc to prescribe some Viagra for him."

"Viagra! Jake must be at past 85."

"Oh yeah. Way Doc told it, Jake said he was seven years older'n his 'she-devil' wife and expected he'd die sooner. Said he'd figured how to fix her good so he could die happy. He was gonna take out about half'a the Viagra pills and hide the rest somewhere she'd find 'em after he died when she was goin' through his stuff lookin' for anything to sell. Said he could go a really happy man thinkin' about her stewin' over what woman he had over when she was out'a town."

"That's hilarious! Did the doctor prescribe the pills?"

"Nah. Said he didn't wanna get 'twixt Jake and his Mrs."

After their chuckles, DeVon returned to business "About the search—hell of it is, a body could be anywhere in the county or the state for all we know, but we're gonna start at Birdland. Accordin' to the weather-guesser, there's gonna be very little snow tonight. If he's right, it might help, but there's already on the ground, we'll be dog-lucky to stumble onto anything."

The chief turned to another topic. "Jim Henry's call makes me think we oughta give some thought to how we're gonna handle gettin' stuff to the news noses. How about phonin' Henry and givin' him the bare skeletons. Tell him there's been a hand found and turned over to the police. Tell him the coroner's workin' on it, and the police are treatin' it like any other investigation. Tell him nobody's releasin' any more information. Whataya think?"

"If you don't want every newsperson pestering you on the phone and putting their own spin on things, you better give all of them the same information and let them know how the game's going to be played. I suggest telling them there'll be one statement now and an occasional follow-up or news conference when there's something to add. I can type a paragraph or two to give to all of them."

"Good idea, podner—knew you'd be earnin' your keep."

The intercom interrupted. "Chief, Captain Bill Mickner from the State Police post returnin' your call."

""Bill, you old snakehead, thanks for phonin' back."

"What's the burr under your saddle, Chief?"

"Remember we talked about cults a couple weeks ago? I know it sounds goofy, but we may have some sign'a one operatin' right here in Stony Crossing." He brought the captain up to date and added, "With your fat budget, I know you won't mind sparin' a dozen troopers to help out in a body search tomorrow out to Birdland."

"Depends on how sweetly they're going to be treated. Cake and ice cream would be a good start. The men are so busy making vacation plans for Bermuda, I don't see how I dare ask any more than one or two. You're welcome to them—if they choose to volunteer, that is."

"Your outfit's eatin' high on the taxpayer's hog, all right. We kick off at nine o'clock Try to see to it they're halfway sober when they get here."

No sooner did Bookman hang up than Sheriff Leon Laddis was on the phone. Laddis, with his immensely more than ample proportions, was known far and wide as "Lardass" Laddis. Running on the right ticket with Wayne City's political-party backing kept getting him elected. Some said other little things such as blackmailing, terrorizing area residents, and overlooking after-hours-joint violations also helped. Sheriff department arrests were higher than average, but the caliber of criminals slung into his slammer didn't go much beyond speeders who couldn't recognize a bribery opportunity when it smacked them in the mouth. Then too, there were the good ol' boys who started out to celebrate Friday evening with a full paycheck, swilled a couple six-packs, and sobered up dead broke in the sheriff's drunk tank. Oddly, most couldn't remember spending the whole check.

Bookman loathed the sheriff and his methods and didn't care who knew it. However, he felt it necessary to advise him of developments. Not that he wanted help from the sheriff's shiftless deputies, but there was no telling where the body was. If the searchers didn't find it in that part of Birdland in his jurisdiction or in town, there was a good chance it was somewhere out in the county. DeVon would then be obliged to work with the sheriff, so he decided to touch bases without actually asking for help.

Laddis was his usual officious, malicious, suspicious, and obnoxious self. "Must be pretty damned important, else ya wouldn't be botherin' a man to phone back on a Sunday afternoon. My department's run so's we don't have much to do on the Sabbath."

(Why, you hypocritical sumbitch!) Bookman would have dearly loved to say it aloud, but his voice didn't betray him. "Sheriff, I wanted to be the first to tell you we got maybe a body-part crime here in town, and we're gonna start lookin' for the rest tomorrow mornin'. I know

you'd be happy to volunteer some'a your best men, but I think we're pretty well fixed. Bill Mickner offered to help. *(That'll frost the old goat.)* If there's anything else you wanna know, just phone."

"If ya got that sissy and his tootsies on the job, I reckon we'll pass. Doubt I'll need any information, but if I do, we kin dig it up ourselves in short order."

Bookman was smiling as he hung up. "Takes care'a that degener-right."

Zeke didn't bother to correct him. He left to type his first press release, later returning to Bookman's office to toss a copy on his desk. "Take a look at your first pack of lies. If it's OK, I'll give it to the deskman to phone to Jim Henry's paper and other media."

DeVon read through it. "It's good not to say nothin' about the markin's on the hand." He leaned back in his chair and stretched. "Looks like maybe you're gonna be all right—with my coachin', a'course. There's not much more to do today. I'll be done pretty soon. Diner's closed Sunday, a'course, but we can grab a bite at Jim's Truck Stop."

"You couldn't coach me to a two-pointer if I were standing on a ladder. Forget grabbing a bite at Jim's House of Heartburn. I hope I *never* get that hungry. See you, Ethel."

"Never gonna make it as a party animal, Gertrude."

Home once again and hungrier still, Zeke headed for the kitchen and put together an appetizer sandwich before settling into his watching chair. He plugged channel eight with his quick-draw remote to see what was left of the Pacers game, and was only a bite into his sandwich when the phone rang.

(Wouldn't you know it!)

A vaguely familiar voice began squawking into what must've been a speakerphone. "This is Elmer Jones. I want to talk about the hand the police found over there this morning."

Zeke knew of Elmer Jones, the know-it-all, overblown, self-aggrandizing TV investigative newscaster in Indianapolis and easily one of the most disliked men in the state. Bookman always referred to him as "that damned newsfarter."

"I'm afraid I've never heard of you, Mr. Jones. Are you affiliated with a law enforcement agency?"

A snicker came from the background. "My Lord, they're *really* out in the sticks!"

Jones asked, "Do you ever watch television?"

"Exactly what I'm trying to do if the phone would stop interrupting."

"Listen here, a public servant on the taxpayer's dole might think about doing his job and answering my questions."

"How did you get this number, Mr. Jones, and what leads you to believe I'm employed by the taxpayers?"

"Your own police gave my secretary your number and told her you were handling all press matters."

Zeke didn't respond while craning around attempting to see the final seconds of the game. He had to get rid of this pest.

"Hello!...Hello!" Jones could not abide dead air.

"Mr. Jones, please refer to the press release. There is no more information available at this time. Good afternoon."

Leaving the receiver off the hook, Zeke returned to his game-watching too late to see it, but the Pacers lost. He dolefully finished eating and sat holding the plate, not even clicking off the national network's never-was and his verbose has-been side-kick analyzing the loss. Finally, he rose, struck a match to the makings in the fireplace, and mixed a Snake Bite, two ounces of hundred-proof Yukon Jack liquor and a splash of Rose's lime juice. Many swore it would pacify an enraged rattler. He began to mellow out. True, it hadn't been the best of days, what with the business about the hand and the Pacers' loss, but it *was* cozy here. Soon, his dogs began gently reminding him it was time to eat.

A few weeks after arriving in town, Zeke came home one morning to see this beautiful black Lab sitting on his porch as if he always belonged there. An ad in the *Lost and Found* produced not one response, so Ace became a member of the household. Apparently, the word got around dogdom about a new sucker in Stony Crossing to be had. A week later, a half-starved Siberian Husky stray showed up, ripped open the chow sack on the back porch, and helped himself. Through his robber-mask, he fixed piercing azure eyes on Zeke, daring him to chase away this new freeloader. Another ad in the *Lost and Found* again resulted in no reply, so now there were two dogs. With a face so marked, there could be no other name for this newest human manipulator but "Bandit."

When Zeke opened the gate leading to the orchard and their houses, they started the dog dances common to those knowing they're going to get attention and food from their best friend. As usual, they were faced with the tough decision of whether to eat or romp first. Both usually opted for romping after wolfing only a bite or two. Heck, you could eat any old time. Zeke unsnapped Ace's chain and sailed a Frisbee as far as he could. The one thing the Lab couldn't resist was a chance to catch or retrieve. While he went racing off to fetch, Zeke would do an arm-and-paw wrestle with Bandit who could never quite get the hang of catching or fetching. Finally, the Husky stopped to eat, and Ace decided his world would be complete with some food.

Play over, it was too late to fix a proper dinner, so Zeke settled for a bowl of cereal with banana slices and raisins tossed on. The stereo went frizzy the previous week and his new tube order still hadn't arrived, so there'd be no evening jazz concert. Reluctantly, he clicked on the idiot eye. A quick review of a made-for-TV Sunday night saccharine special and a half-dozen channel laps was enough. He fervently hoped his stereo tubes would come soon. The fire died, and he turned in.

5

When he set out to feed the dogs Monday morning, frigid air knifed Zeke the minute he opened the door. *(Not supposed to get this cold in Indiana!)* Later, Ol' Emmy vented her wrath about being left alone in the bad weather before finally wheezing and coughing to life. At least, there was one consolation—the snow was slowing to a trace. With no place to park in front of the diner, he decided to eat later and arrived at the station as DeVon was stepping from his pickup. "Tanner, if you'd leave your phone on the hook like a normal human bein', you'd know I set up a press conference at nine o'clock. S'pose you'll try to use runnin' it as an excuse to get me to buy your meal.

"That would indeed be a kindness, especially since I have no intention whatsoever of running any press conference. When I agreed I'd help you out, there wasn't a single word said about any such thing. Anyway, what's it for, and who'd come to Stony Crossing for a press conference?" "Why am *I* gettin' static? You forgettin that *you're* the one who recommended havin' press conferences? Who'd come? Lots'a people. Benson peddled the missin' hand info and the markin's on it to other news outfits besides Jim Henry's and to places your press release didn't go. Now, everbody in two hundred miles will be tryin' to find out about what they're bound and determined to call a 'cult crime.' Another reason they'd come? That damned newsfarter, Elmer Jones, made you a star last night, and everbody wants to take a look atcha."

"*What!* What was that? What about Jones? Wait a minute before you answer—I've told you ten million times, it's ev-*re*-body, not *ever*body. The same goes for your use of '*ever*-where, too."

"Correction police! Correction police are on the job! Confound it, Tanner, don'tcha never let up? I *said ever*body, and I say *everplace* and *ever* anything a'tall. Anyways, don't tell me you don't know about his editorial last night."

"I give up. What editorial are you talking about? All I know is he phoned late yesterday afternoon and acted like a jackass. I left the receiver off and went to bed early. What'd he say?"

"The usual sewage. Everbody in the wide world is out to skin the poor taxpayer, especially highly overpaid public servants such as yourself who's lost sight'a who pays your wages. You and your kind make it tough for the honest people like him to get the truth the public has a right to know. Also, no matter how hard you try to cover up a cult crime, he's gonna keep at it till he gets every last scrap'a the truth."

"Egotistical jerk! He's sore because I wouldn't kiss his patute."

"Must'a been plenty riled. Seen the *Trib*? You made it there, too, and also in a bunch'a others, I hear. How you gonna handle things?"

"Going to ignore all of them, that's what. If I've learned nothing else, it's not to get into a peeing contest with a skunk. From now on, I'm leaving the phone off the hook or getting rid of it altogether."

"Hell you are! You're gonna get an answerin' machine to screen your calls—that's what you're gonna do. Department'll spring for it if we hafta. Listen here, Zeke, I got a prime feelin' we're into somethin' a whole lot bigger'n the usual piddly dust-up—gonna need all the help I can get. You can handle a press conference better'n me. I'm more likely to tell 'em to go take a flyin' leap when they start diggin' their claws in."

DeVon's tone impressed Zeke, and he relented. "Want to give me an idea how a police press conference is held?"

"Great balls 'a fire! Those years you won the championships, you must'a held a press conference or two. Do whatcha did then."

"Well, I guess I can do it this once. You could at least tell me what information to give them about the case."

"Wise up, Tanner. When you're startin' an investigation, you don't hold a press conference to give 'em any hard *information*. You hold it to let 'em look at heroes like yourself and to show we're up to our bushy eyebrows in crime detectin'. Use the old mushroom-farm strategy—keep 'em in the dark and feed 'em bullshit. Say we're workin' on leads and make each one of 'em thinks he's gonna get the story first when we bust the case, which could be any minute now. In a way, your spat with Jones is a blessin'. It'll give the sharks somethin' to gnaw on—keep' em out from underfoot while we're gettin' on with the search."

"Remember—this is the last time for this nonsense."

Bookman ignored the edict. "Let's get to the diner for breakfast. Gotta get the blamed search goin' before long—not that we'll find much, since it's snowed so much lately."

They sat at counter stools, which sent a message to the waitress, Twyla Jean Miller, that there would be no dawdling in a booth over coffee after their breakfast. Probably meant a smaller tip, too, along with less opportunity to continue her campaign to get Zeke to pay attention to calories and cholesterol. She poured coffee for both and stony-stared Zeke as he looked her straight in the eye and ordered two scrambled eggs and bacon. Bookman added, "Make mine sausage with three eggs and a regular stack. Double hash browns, too." She didn't like that, either.

As they sipped coffee and waited for Lurinda to do her magic with the food, Dee looked Zeke up and down. "If you're gonna be the big noise for the best-dressed police department in the State, you oughta think about gettin' a haircut sometime this year. Gettin' rid'a those jeans might help, too."

"Well, thank you, *mother*! Look who's talking about jeans. When's the last time you wore anything else? As for the haircut, I don't need one—some hair has just slid down onto my neck a little. But, if you think the press won't appreciate my gorgeous locks, I'll slip into Bill Borsch's right after I finish here." *(Planned to, anyhow.)*

"You've lost track'a the days, old man. Bill closes the barbershop Mondays. Has been since shortly after you came back to town."

"Why?"

"Not altogether sure. Talk is that he needs two whole days a week to rest up from all those exercises he's been doin' this year. Been doin' lots'a other changin', includin' bein' late openin' the barbershop after his mornin' jog—not like him a'tall. He don't go to Sunday service anymore, either. Missed so many in a row, they deaconed and eldered him but it didn't get him attendin' again. Even flipped the preacher and elders the bird when they showed up at his door."

Zeke knew about "deaconing" and "eldering." Along with a large percentage of Stony Crossing's church-going residents, he was raised as a member of the church practicing it. However, he stopped attending services due to his serious misgivings about certain practices, including this one. Years ago, the elders decided members missing four consecutive Sunday services without being ill would get a reminder letter from them and the current part-time lay preacher. If that didn't do the trick, next came a visit from the preacher along with the deacons, all six of them, marching two-by-two to the backslider's door.

Should the malefactor miss more services, additional letters and another visit followed—this time from the preacher leading the elders, all twelve of them, two-by-twoing to the front door. Soon, members and non-members alike began calling the practices "deaconing" and "eldering." It was the final step before what the locals termed a "poor man's excommunication," the chronic absentee being tossed out until making a full public confession and repenting for unexcused absences and other awfulness. The practice died out years earlier, but apparently Preacher Ackerman revived it with the help of the quintessentially vapid Delbert Dove. Among the list of his flunkier duties was calling the role of members and recording the absentees immediately prior to the benediction.

Zeke also knew of Bill Borsch's man-killing workout program. At least three evenings a week, he drove over to the new fitness center at Wayne City, the HEAVEN HEALTH US CLUB. (Heaven Healths Those Who Health Themselves, their sign read.) It boasted the latest equipment modeled after giant flapping cranes and designed to inflict the same punishment as medieval torture apparatus. It also featured a sauna, tanning beds, a manicurist/masseuse and a nutrition bar.

Borsch sweated to a horsy lather, roasted himself rosy-rare in a sauna, endured a bough switching, and finished with an icy shower. Monthly, he bought health food by the case. (He gave some to Lurinda, who tried it and observed that it tasted almost as good as boiled cardboard.)

Some said Borsch was making up for four years of boozing after his wife died. Others guessed he was out to snare a young chicken. Whatever the reason for his late-blooming physical fitness mania, it was unusual to take an early morning drive, regardless of the weather or season, without seeing the barber jogging.

Twyla Jean arrived with the food and showed her displeasure by spinning the plates off to each chowhound in the manner of a poker shark dealing five-card stud. She stepped back, folded her arms and glowered at them. Zeke felt decidedly uncomfortable, but Bookman held his fork over the eggs and engaged in a brief stare-down before turning to Zeke. "Question for you, podner. If a man's talkin' way out yonder in the woods and there's no woman's there to correct him, is he still wrong?"

Twyla Jean retreated to the cash register, and the two gourmands fell to their tasks with enthusiasm. She watched and sniffed. Just you wait, her turn would come.

Their demolition of the Country Kitchen cuisine over, they downed a last shot of coffee and rose. Bookman tossed a buck tip onto the counter. Twyla Jean sniffed again—she knew it wouldn't be much.

Snow was still floating down, but the light was stronger, and a weak-kneed sun was trying to struggle through. On the way to the station, DeVon remarked, "It's gettin' lighter outside—'bout time to get the gang started on their way to Birdland. I'm thinkin' of havin' 'em search the hollows first, then the thickets. Later, a house-to-house. Listenin' to those Birdlanders bitch oughta be a load'a fun."

The collection of searchers at the station, a dozen of Bookman's men, eight volunteers, and four State Police troopers sent over by State Police Captain Mickner climbed into a small school bus borrowed for the occasion. As it was about to pull away, Roosevelt Hoover, Lurinda's kitchen assistant at the diner, drove up with three gallons of coffee and put it aboard to the cheers of the riders.

DeVon sent them on their way and went with Zeke into the station for a minute. A mob of reporters immediately besieged the chief, each trying to out-shout the others with a question. He waved a hand, "Whoa, whoa, the press conference don't start till later. Go on up to the diner and have some coffee or somethin'. Come back at 9 when our press relatin' man'll be here." Grumbling, they filed out.

Zeke murmured, "Thanks for the stretch, Stretch."

"Think nothin' of it—least I could do for somebody who's gonna be hand-feedin' those wolves in 'bout an hour. Good luck. I'm off to Birdland."

At 9 on the dot, Zeke walked into the crowded squad room. At once, everyone was shouting questions regarding his "feud" with Elmer Jones. Zeke remained silent until things quieted, then declared in a dead-calm voice, "I have nothing to say about Mr. Jones' comments."

When it became clear Zeke meant what he said about not responding to Jones, the pack soon gave up and went on with the business of the day. Similar questions were framed in about fifty different ways. Typically from the reporters: "According to my information, the markings on the hand are of a cult. Do you know which one? What exactly do they look like? Is there a photo? Can you draw us a picture? Is there a main local cult? Does your department keep track of cults operating in this area? Has there been dismembering of animals around here? Have the schools had any cult problems?"

Zeke's responses followed a standard theme. "Please, please! You seem determined to make this a cult case. There is absolutely no evidence of cult involvement."

They didn't give up easily.

Them: "You call cult markings on a severed hand *'no evidence'*?"

Zeke: "Who said they were cult markings?"

Them: "Then what are they?"

Zeke: "That's why there's a police investigation."

After the cult subject was hounded into oblivion, other obvious questions arose. Suspects? Clues? Etc., etc. Zeke stood by, patience itself, always asking if there were other questions. At last, the reporters hung it up, and "The Special Assistant for Press Ralatin" began sidling out. As he did, DeVon Bookman came in. "'Preciate everbody comin' out on such a cold day, folks. Now be sure to leave your phone number with Mr. Tanner so he can getcha the very minute we have any news. And be sure to get his personal number so you can get hold of him when necessary."

They crowded around with their numbers. Bookman waited until they were finished, then turned, motioned Zeke into his office, and closed the door. "There now, see how easy it is?"

"Oh sure, easy—easy when someone else has already cleaned up after your dog. Where do you get off with that phone number stuff? Who in blazes do you think you are!"

"Chill out, Tanner, we'll talk about it later. It'll all come out OK."

Zeke wasn't deterred. "I told you I'm through fooling around with this press conference business after today. It's only just a little after ten o'clock—what're you doing in here, anyway? Search over already?"

Once again, Bookman ignored Zeke's ultimatum. "Nope, I left Smithson in charge. They're not gonna find nothin' unless they trip over it—snow's deeper'n buffalo flop after a stampede. Hadta come in to run an errand. C'mon, I'll buy a cup."

After ordering coffee and sinkers from an unsmiling Twyla Jean, Zeke reflected, "Maybe there's not a body except in a morgue. Ever follow up on that?"

"Had Smitty phone every morgue and hospital in a hundred miles and ask 'em to do some checkin', but he got nothin'. All of 'em said no way could a hand from their shop wind up here. He's asked every police department, too—got nothin' there, either."

DeVon rose. "Gotta get back out to Birdland. Planned to have the men go at it all day, but it looks so useless, I'll probly let most of 'em leave pretty soon after noon. Only take a handful to knock on doors—no more'n a couple dozen houses out there."

The chief dropped Zeke at the station with a suggestion. "Why don'tcha go on home and do that little chore, then come back. I'll be finished with the search by then."

"What little chore? I haven't said anything about a chore."

With a "See you later, Gertrude," Bookman rolled away, leaving a puzzled Zeke staring after him. The mystery was soon solved. On the front seat of Ol' Emmy sat a box, the printing on the top informing him it was a telephone answering machine. And taped to it was a scrawled message, *Hook it up or I'll send a man to pound on your door every hour to check.*

(So this was the little chore. Some nerve!)

6

There was also a package on Zeke's porch—the new tubes for his amp. There wasn't any contest over priorities. He tossed the answering machine onto a chair in the entryway and began tube installation. Fragile rascals in place, he flipped half a dozen switches and left to fix lunch while everything warmed up.

After lunch, he drank in the gorgeous strings of Dvorak, losing track of time, awash in music as the notes faded into silence. *(It doesn't get much better than this.)* Only minutes into his reverie, some fool banged the front door. Irritated, he strode out and flung it open to Sergeant Wilson. "Chief Bookman wondered if you started puttin' in the answerin' machine. I told him probly, but he said to come over and check to be sure." His opossum grin told Zeke that Wilson was in on things.

"Go back and tell mommy I'm right in the middle of doing it."

The sergeant looked around Zeke to the unopened box on the entryway chair. "OK, I'll tell him you said you're gonna get goin' on it right away. He'll probly want me to keep checkin' back to see if you need help." Zeke blotted him out with the door, but he knocked again.

"Now what?"

"Chief said he's gonna be busy with some reglar stuff for quite a while. That'll give plenty'a time to work on the machine, so you don't hafta drop by till after gettin' her hooked up." Without bothering to answer, Zeke closed the door again. Wilson was chuckling as he stepped from the porch.

Zeke was annoyed, to put it mildly. *(Didn't promise to use the blasted thing, did I? No, I did not! Not touching it till I'm good and ready—maybe never.)* Having thought that, he took the carton with him on his way back to more music.

With Chopin as background, he battled through stubborn plastic wrap and pried the machine from its vise-like Styrofoam tomb. OK, he'd look at the instructions, but that's all he'd do. In spite of his reluctance, they began to look interesting. He fiddled with the connections, got everything plugged together, and tried recording his outgoing message. Trouble was, to talk into the built-in mike, he had to lean over just inches above it as if bobbing for apples, making him sound under considerable belt strain. Besides, he kept stumbling halfway through. Five takes later after writing it out, he managed an acceptable message.

Another CD spun to a close before curiosity overcame his resolve to ignore DeVon's request to stop in. After switching on the answering machine, he left for the station. DeVon was his usual sweet self. "Wondered how long the poutin' was gonna last."

"Can it—I'm in no mood for anything from you after your answering machine stunt. May I assume your Mounties obtained no results from the search?"

"Nothin' 'cept ten gallons'a alligator tears from the men. Guess they had a right—snow was even deeper'n I figured. Load'a questions from the house-to-house, a'course. No answers, only questions. Mostly the same old bull-feathers such as when are we gonna start protectin' the taxpayers? Just like I expected—the usual. Whole thing was a waste'a time."

"Anything new at all?"

"Nah. We've done all the routine stuff, but got nothin' worth mentionin'. I tell you, Tanner, this kind'a investigation can drive you nuts. Not even sure'a what we're dealin' with. If we could locate a body, we'd have somethin' to go on. Aw, hell with it. Let's go and grab a cup. Pie don't sound bad, either."

Monday was lemon-pie day, and Lurinda's lemon with genuine meringue was Zeke's absolute favorite in the entire world. "What time does Twyla Jean get her afternoon break, Dee?"

"Usually between 2 and 4. Why, plannin' to make a move?"

"Get real, big beak. I can't stand her chin music about a proper diet, that's all."

"She's got a thing for you and wants to protect her interest. You could do worse'n a young foxy blue-eyed blonde with a cheerleader body. Hear she works out every day."

"Bookman, you're a dirty old man, a really dirty old man."

"That's a fact, and don'tcha forget it. C'mon, let's walk—the exercise and fresh air'll clear your thinkin'."

Zeke had to admit the frosty air was a tonic. Short-lived upper, though, Twyla Jean was still on duty. He dared not even glance in the direction of the pie case. "Just coffee please, TeeJay."

"Don't give me any hypocritical innocent act—I know why you're here. Both of you are gonna die quicker and the world will be a better place." She shoved two slices of lemon pie across the counter, drew and served their coffees, then flounced off to fill the sugar dispensers.

DeVon elbowed Zeke. "Told you so, told you so. She's gotta thing for you, all right."

"Sure has an odd way of showing it. Shut up and eat your pie."

They were the only customers in the diner, so Lurinda came out of the kitchen to sit with DeVon. Zeke marveled she could be around such good food all day and still retain a figure more than a few around town admired. Not all, however, quite a few of the ladies grew pretty catty-chatty when the subject of the curvaceous, leggy redheaded Lurinda Beatty arose.

Tanner couldn't fully enjoy the pie, what with a blond-haired conscience stalking around banging the sugar shakers. After capturing the last crumb, he asked, "Well, Stretch, the pie help solve the hand mystery?"

"Don't I wish. Some daylight left—we could take a spin around the two-mile strip and see if somethin' catches our eye."

"May as well."

When they paid, Twyla Jean jabbed the register key as if stabbing an ant. No thanks for the good tip, either.

As they walked to the station, Zeke inquired, "You mentioned a two-mile strip. What's that all about?"

"Couple years ago, the town council got the county commission to agree on lettin' the council have jurisdiction over zonin' in a two-mile strip all around town. It gives the council lots'a say over what kind'a buildin' and such that's planned for out there and puts patrollin' it in my department. That's why I gotta cover most'a Birdland. Here we are. Climb in and we're off."

After a half-hour of fruitless reconnoitering, Zeke suggested, "Let's go back. I need to get home and tend the dogs."

The chief dropped him beside Ol' Emmy. "You feed those hounds better'n yourself. Notice I said *better,* not *more.*"

"Don't start."

The dogs were overjoyed, as usual. Later, with his right arm about to fall off from flinging Ace's Frisbee and his left aching from wrestling Bandit, Zeke called a halt. *(I simply must get them out for a big run as soon as I can.)*

Once inside, he mixed the usual Snake Bite and sat listening to a Cleo Laine CD. *(What a range she has!)* Two disks later, he decided to fix dinner. In the kitchen, the madly blinking answering machine demanded attention. Earlier, he turned off the PREVIEW function and ignored the sporadic ringing, letting the machine kick in after the fourth ring. He seldom answered before then. Often it was only telemarketers who's computer broke the connection if no one answered before the fourth ring. He hit PLAY, and the tape wound back several seconds. The first message went by so rapidly, he wasn't quite sure what it said. *(Oh well, I'll rewind after the last one and listen again.)* Next came the young widow Martha Mae Johannsen inviting him to dinner. *(Uh-oh.)* The rest included routine callback requests from media people interspersed with telemarketer-pest hang-ups. He had to fiddle with the REWIND button before getting the first message to play again. This time there was no mistaking what it said.

He phoned Bookman. "Better get right over here. I may have something about the investigation on the answering machine. While the chief was on the way, Zeke listened to the message several times, the obviously disguised voice sounding vaguely like one he may've heard before.

DeVon rushed in. "What's up? What's up? Sounded like you had a brain-strain."

"Nothing like that, but this is really something. Listen."

He punched PLAY to hear the message again. "Keep looking." That's all—"Keep looking."

Bookman was incredulous. "*What'n tarnation!* Let's hear that again!"

Zeke replayed it until Dee held up his hand. "Sumbitch had mush in his mouth, but I could swear I've heard that voice before. Be switched if I can place it though."

"Think I've heard it, too, but can't remember where."

After more replays, they gave up trying to identify the caller and began tossing around questions and speculations, Zeke first. "Why would anyone phone me and not the police station? What would he have said if I were home when he phoned?"

"Could be he phoned the station askin' who to talk to, and the deskman gave out your number. Reckon he would'a said the same thing if you *were* here. Had his voice disguised, so it wouldn't make any difference to him whether you answered or not. The important questions are how'd he know we haven't located a body and why's he so hot for us to find it? Don't make sense."

Zeke was perplexed about something else. "If he's so anxious for one to be found, why didn't he give a clue where it is? Assuming he knows, that is."

"No way to tell yet—could'a even been a nutso. We can't do anything about this tonight, but give me the tape. Tomorrow I'll see if Mickner's lab can do somethin' with it. So long, Gertrude, I gotta lock this tape off in the property room safe and remind the deskman to give your number to everbody callin'."

"Thanks a bunch for everything, Ethel."

7

Zeke began his morning routine but soon discovered he was out of coffee, so he was on the way to the station by 6:30. Seeing DeVon's pickup already there, he walked into the office and announced, "Citizens of Stony Crossing, would you look who's here already! Either your police chief can't sleep or it's payday."

Bookman only grunted and didn't offer a comeback. Zeke didn't push it. *(He must really be in a lousy mood this morning.)*

They went to the squad room and picked up cups of the leftover battery acid the night crew called coffee. After braving a sip, Zeke choked, "Great balls'a fire, Ethel, that's good paint thinner. What's the formula?" DeVon sat his on the desk without chancing it. Forsaking the usual banter, he plunged right in. "Dang it all, anyway. Like I said, not findin' a body is aggravatin', but not knowin' where to look next is *really* aggravatin'. Got any ideas?"

"Well, if I must do your job for you, I can't do it without real coffee. Why don't we go mug up at the diner?"

Breakfast didn't help DeVon's mood. "Damn'f I see how anything fits. The heckta-thing and numbers on the hand mean absolutely nothin' to me. Sure like to get one sliver of a clue somewhere! Hell, if I thought that runt mutt of Elizabeth Bannister's could talk, I'd be down on my hands and knees blowin' in his ear."

Zeke paused in mid-sip. "Dee, I think I just might get to see that. I believe her dog *may* be able to tell you something. Could be worth a try, anyway."

Bookman shook his head. "At last I can get the proof to putcha away—thinkin' I oughta ask a dog! All right, I'm desperate, go ahead and bobble my mind with your smarts."

"OK, I'll *boggle* your alleged mind. Her dog had to find the hand someplace close to home—too little to roam very far in the snow. If I know anything about dogs, they usually follow about the same route on their runs in order to check their territory. Why couldn't you get Mrs. Bannister to let him out and see where he goes? It's a start and probably better than anything you have."

DeVon stared silently at him for several seconds before commenting, "My daddy always reckoned a blind hog'll stumble across a kernel if it roots around long enough. Your idea's got a problem, though. Why would there be a body in the same place as the hand?"

"You're right—it's not logical. I guess using the dog isn't such a great idea."

"Whoa, I didn't say it was a *bad* idea—said it had a problem. Don't mean it's no good a'tall. Even if there's no body, there could be more parts around. Much as it pains me to say it, your idea's worth a try."

"Wow! I hadn't thought of there being more *parts.*"

"Well, podner, if there's anything I've learned in this sorry business, it's you can't go far wrong figurin' the worst things one party can do to another one."

On the way to the station, Bookman began formulating a plan. "First thing, we'll need to get the old broad to let the dog out. Next, we gotta figure how to keep up with him without scarin' him off. Might be pretty hard if he gets into the bushes or goes farther'n we think. Don't reckon we'd have to mush right along behind him, though. We could take a look at the area first and station men where somebody can see him all the time—lots easier'n mushin' and less likely to spook him away from his regular trail. Let's go scout out some likely places to plant eyeballers."

They cruised Birdland looking for locations where an officer would have a line of sight on the dog no matter where he went. They covered the section adjacent to the Bannisters', then drove past their property on Wood Thrush Lane and down the hill to where it "Tee-d" into Horse Hockey Road a couple hundred feet east of Bailey Bridge. From this spot an officer could spot the dog if it turned toward the bridge or went on into Make-Out Woods.

Altogether, DeVon pointed out seven places. "Seven men and us make nine. That oughta be enough for the pooch patrol."

"Where do you get the *us* malarkey, Great Chief? I plan to sit in the car and man the radio."

"Not a chance. But in respect for your old age and lousy physical condition, I guess you could stand next to the barricades at Sycamore and Horse Hockey so you can lean on each other. From there you can see the mutt if he goes on through Bailey Bridge and comes out the end nearest you."

"And where will Great Chief be?"

"Somebody hasta stay in a central spot to manage things."

On the way to the station, Zeke sputtered about one too many chiefs and one too few scouts on the dog-spotting detail. Bookman grinned. "I'll round up the men while you rest up, old timer."

The deskman hailed Zeke as he entered. "Messages from reporters, Mr. Tanner."

Zeke busied himself with routine callbacks until DeVon returned. "Can't go out there just yet. Nixon's cousin does maid work and cooks lunch and supper for the Bannisters. Says they don't get up hardly ever before 9, so she never goes to work much earlier'n ten. We go much sooner, we get nothin' but 'no' for an answer. I got some paperwork to finish, and Bill Mickner radioed he's comin' by. Why don'tcha get on up to the barbershop and get clipped. Your head's beginnin' to look like a half-nekkid sheep. Can't have the ee-leet at Birdland thinkin' I hire shoddy help. Barber Bill will be finished in plenty'a time. Won't take more'n a quick once around with the sheep shears."

Zeke smart-mouthed him back and left. Parking near the diner, he fancied one of Lurinda's cinnamon rolls after getting his haircut. They'd be ready pretty soon, and only one wouldn't hurt, would it?

At 8:30, the CLOSED sign was still up at the barbershop. Cupping his hands against the window to shield his eyes from the reflection, Zeke peered inside thinking maybe Bill-the-Barber Borsch came in through his rear door. No sign of him, though. (*Dang it, the sign says hours are 8:00-5:30. You'd think he could adjust his jogging so he could open on time.*) Rocking in his boots, he tried to decide whether to wait around in the snappy cold. *(Wasted trip, to heck with it.)* He turned and started off.

As he passed Maxwell's Variety Store next door, Hiram Maxwell rapped on the window with his walking stick. Zeke stopped and saw a SALE! 15% OFF! sign. Large red Christmas candles dominated the display. Maxwell was beckoning him to come inside. He often patted a person's arm or shoulder while talking and tossed out "down home" stuff the like of as "Howdy," "Welcome neighbor," and, "Y'all come back." Tourists thought him the model village merchant. The majority of townsfolk considered him a cornball and a cheapskate who'd snatch nickels from the collection plate if he thought others weren't looking.

Zeke waved and turned away, but Maxwell hurried out, caught up, and stuck out a hand. "Howdy there, Ezekial Amos."

"Morning, Mr. Maxwell."

"Oh Ezekial, you've known me long enough to forget the 'Mister'."

"If you say so."

"Let's talk a bit. What's happenin' around town?"

Zeke wanted conversation with Maxwell as much as a barroom mop across the face. He chatted only long enough to be polite, then explained, "Like to stay, but I barely had time enough for a haircut as it was. I'll catch one later."

"Pity you can't stay a mite."

"Thanks, but I must get going." Zeke unhanded himself and quick-stepped away.

Everyone in town knew Tuesday was cinnamon roll day at the diner and what time they came from the oven. Those who ate earlier returned for what they called breakfast "dessert." When Zeke entered, the tables were already filled, and only the last seat down at the end of the counter was open. Almost the minute he sat, Lurinda appeared from the kitchen bearing two trays of the mouthwatering goodies. Without a word, she left two on a tray and dished up the remainder onto plates for Twyla Jean to deal out to the waiting pack.

After making the rounds of the tables and booths, she started down the counter. Zeke could almost taste the aroma, his salivary glands shifting into overdrive to keep up with his anticipation. On came Tee-Jay, but she hadn't yet acknowledged Zeke. She knew she'd run out after serving the fellow seated right next to him. Zeke couldn't believe it. "What's going on, Twyla?"

She *knew* her turn would come. Triumphantly, she announced, "Sorry, Mr. *Bad-Diet Tanner*, we're all out of cinnamon rolls."

"This is a serious matter. You're not out—there are two more back there."

Lucinda came up. "Sorry, Zeke, they're all spoken for. You know the rules—one for the weekly sweet TeeJay allows herself, one for Roosevelt, and the rest for customers who reserve ahead. I'd have put your name in the pot, but you didn't say anything earlier."

Clearly, it was a conspiracy. Zeke paid for the coffee (no tip) and crossed the street to Miss Martha Manchester's Office Supply and Card Shop. *(May as well see if she has a replacement tape for the answering machine.)*

The Manchester store and Miss Manchester were the standards by which about everyone in Stony Crossing measured stability and integrity. The shop had been family-owned for four generations—she in command for more than half of that. To most, the store was always there and always would be. The same could be said for Miss Martha Manchester. Furthermore, if you couldn't trust her for honesty, whom could you trust for heaven's sake? Hair-bun, crocheted shawl, black Oxfords, and personally handcrafted ankle-length dresses only added to the image. Delicate in appearance and approaching 80, folks said her weight couldn't be much greater than her age. A scant few were well enough acquainted to dare call her "Martha." Never wed, it was "Miss Martha" or "Miss Manchester." After long usage, some blended "Miss Martha" into "MizMartha." Those referring to her as such included DeVon Bookman.

She appeared annoyed when Zeke asked whether she stocked answering machine tapes. "Of course. I carry everything."

He saw that she was forced to rummage around considerably before locating one that "should" fit. He paid and hastened out. (Along with so many others, he was a little awe-stricken by Miss Manchester since first grade.)

At the station, he found Bill Mickner and Dee talking about the answering machine message. The State Police captain said he'd turn it over to his crime-lab people, but about the best they could do was make a voiceprint in case they had a chance to match it to a suspect's voice later.

Bookman and Mickner shot the breeze about the case and exchanged insults about each other's ability as upholders of the law. When DeVon related the Bannister dog plan, Mickner stood. "That's it, I'm out of here. Whatever caused you to come up with such an idea may be contagious. It proves one thing, though—this department's gone to the dogs."

Bookman smiled and didn't try to top that one. The captain left and DeVon reminded, "About time to get goin'." He rounded up everyone and drove ahead with Sergeant Wilson in the back seat, the others following in black and whites. While they stayed in their cars at Sycamore and Horse Hockey, DeVon drove around Birdland and pointed out places for Wilson to station the men.

They returned to the waiting officers, and Bookman called them together. "You already know this is the pooch eyeball squad, meanin' I want somebody's beady eye on that critter every second. Cold as it is, all except the guy stationed beyond the east end'a the bridge can wait in cars. Cut cards, and we'll take the loser around through Birdland and drop him off at the edge'a Make-Out Woods before we talk to Mrs. Bannister. Don't think we oughta move the barricades to drive through the bridge and take a chance on messin' up where the dog might go. When we finish talkin' to her, I'll give Wilson the word, and he'll show everbody where to take up positions."

They cut cards from a deck Sergeant Wilson just happened to have. Strahan lost and complained it was obviously a crooked deck.

The chief drove on up Sycamore and crossed into Birdland over the iron bridge on Bumpy Butt. Turning right onto Wood Thrush Lane, they passed Bannister's mansion and drove on down the hill to where it met Horse Hockey. There, Strahan was deposited at the barricade blocking the short stretch of Horse Hockey Road leading to the east end of Bailey Bridge.

Bookman turned back toward the Bannister mansion. "Well, let's get at it. Might take more'n a little doin' to get old lady B to go for the dog deed."

8

At the Bannister's, Bookman strode up the steps past the colonnades and to the mammoth double oak doors. Repeated hammering with the ridiculously large brass knocker resulted only in a dog's yipping from inside.

"Cripes, Dee, you'd think with his money, he'd have somebody to answer the door."

"No way. He's too tight to hire more'n Nixon's cousin for maidin' and cookin'—gets other part-time help for everthing else. Even shovels his own snow sometimes."

Bookman resumed knocking. Finally, they heard locks being undone, and the door was jerked open. A hung-over Alan Bannister stood before them in pajamas and robe. "What'n hell's the *ruckus* about? *Whataya want?*"

The chief moved by Bannister into the huge room. "Alan, Zeke here has an idea that might be a big help in our investigation about the hand your dog brought home."

(Oh, that's nice—giving me all the credit.)

"Bookman, what kind of a damnfool idiot idea could be important enough to disturb us at this hour?"

"If we talk to both you and your wife, it'd save everbody's time." The way the chief put it didn't sound as if he allowed for options.

Bannister started to protest, but threw up his hands—the sooner he got it over with, the sooner he could get rid of these dumbbells. He returned wearing slacks, flannel shirt and house slippers. "Elizabeth'll be out soon as she's decent. You may as well sit." Zeke removed his coat and sat. Bookman didn't.

Broken only by Bannister's repeated early morning hacking, the silence got slicing-dense. Elizabeth Bannister finally made her entrance. She, too, was disgruntled. "Alan said you had something you wanted to bother us about."

Ordinarily, Bookman wouldn't let her remark pass without at least a short return volley, but he didn't want to give her any reason to keep her dog inside. A virtual paragon of politeness, he was. "Sorry, but we really need your help. You and your dog may be able to give us some very valuable information. He seems to be pretty smart."

Elizabeth Bannister fairly gushed, "Oh yes, he's *so* intelligent. Even as smart as he is, what makes you think he could help?"

"Plan to let him run outside today?"

"Oh, I don't think so—it's so cold. Besides, I always walk him on a leash."

"You let him run loose Sunday."

"Oh no, Alan let him out. He doesn't always do what's best for Tinkerbell." Grimacing, Alan Bannister kept still.

Bookman continued as if he hadn't heard. "Here's what we think. It's possible your dog would go about the same places he always does. What we'd do is place some men around the area so they could see where he goes. That way, we might get a line on where he found the hand, and it might lead to more clues. He'd be seen every second by one'a my men. Outside chance he'd find anything, I'll admit, but could be a big help if it worked out." If Zeke ever saw a face with "NO SALE" written on it, hers was it.

DeVon sped ahead. "You may know there's a banquet each April when we give out a Meritorious Service Award to any officers makin' outstandin' contributions. Once'n a while, we also present a Good Citizen Award to anybody who's done somethin' unusual to help the department. It's a real honor. If your dog turned up a clue, I wouldn't have any problem recommendin' an award for him *and* you. It's a big doin's, the press bein' there n'all. Zeke'll give both'a you full credit for your contributions. You do know he's the department's press relatin' man, don'tcha?" More snake oil followed.

Zeke stared. *(Great balls of fire, what a performance! He didn't swallow once nor did his nose grow a foot! Have to hand it to him.)*

Bookman stopped larding it on, and Zeke looked toward Mrs. Bannister. What a change! It appeared all DeVon needed do was be patient while she talked herself into it. "I can't believe my precious Tinkerbell could be much help. He might not even go to the same places. Still, he didn't get any exercise yesterday. Perhaps he *should* go outside for a little while. A Good Citizen Award, did you say? Well, maybe it wouldn't hurt for my precious to help out. Could I go along with him?"

"Wouldn't mind a bit," lied Bookman. "But, I think it'd be best if we kept things like they were Sunday. Weren't along then, were you?"

"I suppose you're right. When would you want him to go out?"

"Soon as I can get my men stationed. Don't turn him loose for about twenty minutes to give us time to get set up. C'mon Zeke."

As they left, Elizabeth Bannister was holding her darling doggie and cooing to him. If she noticed that Bookman made advance preparations to observe sweet-precious Tinkerbell's outing, she didn't let on.

Once outside, the chief radioed Wilson to show the men their positions. On the way to the Horse Hockey barricades, Zeke needled DeVon for buttering up Elizabeth Bannister. "What a stack of buffalo chips! How can you live with yourself? Must admit the award bit was a stroke of genius, though."

DeVon smiled thinly. He had very little hope the dog would find anything. Even if he did, it was a long time until any awards ceremony.

When he dropped off Zeke on Sycamore at the barricades, the chief informed him, "My car radio goes on the fritz now and again, so I better take the hand-held. You won't need it anyway—no chance the beast'll get near this far. Even if he does, Strahan's close enough to hear a holler, and he can radio me." Away he went, leaving Zeke alone in the cold.

As long as Zeke could remember, only one-third of the bridge roof was intact—the west end—the end nearest Sycamore Street. Sometimes snow covered the unprotected two-thirds of the bridge floor and glazed into ice when traffic packed it. This made the trip across an adventure for through travelers, but during winter Birdlanders avoided it like domestic gin. They needed to drive only a quarter-mile farther up Sycamore and cross into Birdland over the iron bridge on Oriole Way (Bumpy Butt).

Although Bailey Bridge's wooden floor still appeared fairly sound, the missing roof section and the weathered timbers to support it needed rebuilding if the floor were to survive the elements. No one worried much about that. After all, the bridge was probably due for replacement, anyway. However, attitudes changed soon after the Stony Crossing Historical Society was organized. Members discovered the bridge was one of the oldest and longest covered spans in the state, so they formed the Save The Bridge Committee. For two years now, the Committee gave thought to getting donated materials and labor to rebuild the roof.

While all the cogitation was going on, the society satisfied its restoration conscience by raising a royal fuss upon discovering any threat to "their" bridge, especially an occasional chunk splintered out by a snowplow. The town council responded to complaints with the barricade-the-bridge idea. To block traffic during snowfalls, or if snow were only predicted, street department employees placed barricades across

Horse Hockey where it joined Sycamore 100 feet or so west of the bridge. They also would place barricades the same distance from the other end.

Zeke stood at the barricades on Sycamore and squinted against the glaring sunlight while attempting to look through the bridge. Last night's snow covered the two-thirds of the bridge floor where the roof was missing. The roofed third, the end nearest Zeke, was mostly in deep shadow despite small windows in its wooden sides. *(Have a heck of a time seeing a dog starting through from the far end. Probably couldn't see him at all if he got beneath the roofed part.)* He glanced at his watch and calculated Mrs. Bannister would be letting Tinkerbell out about then.

Wait. Wait. Wait some more. Holy smokes, it seemed a long time. Quiet, too—the only sound a distant car horn. A pickup passed on Sycamore, the driver craning to see what in the world that dummy stamping around in the cold was up to. Zeke's voice broke the stillness. "Sure be nice to have a radio. At least a person could talk to someone once in a while." A foraging sparrow offered no response.

Time half-inched along with no sign of any dog. *(The little fleabag probably couldn't make it through the snow this far, even if he wanted to.)* Again, he squinted in an effort to see into the bridge.

That's when he saw the dog. Or at least something flickering in the sunlight and shadows making him think it might be a dog, a dog pawing at something. Zeke froze and stared. His mind must be playing tricks—it *couldn't* be a dog.

Hearing his own breathing, he paced cautiously forward as if needing to maintain perfect silence. He hesitated—keep going, and he'd be under the roofed part of the bridge before long. More deep breaths and forty paces later, he was about to be swallowed up in the inky interior.

Moving ever more carefully, he was no more than fifty steps from whatever he was seeing. Ten more, and there was no doubt it was a dog. *The* dog. Sir Whatitsname. He was tugging at something lying in the snow right at the junction of the unprotected area of the bridge's roadway and the part covered by the roof. Zeke squinted harder against the blinding sunlight. *(How in blazes did that dog get so far in this direction without someone spotting him? Do I go farther or yell for Strahan?)*

He decided against yelling. There was really no reason to alert Strahan, and without doubt, it would scare the bejesus out of the dog, and he might run off, no telling where. Besides, the police department's special assistant would look pretty silly if he shouted and Strahan or one of the others already spied the animal. *(What should I do?)* No answers presented themselves, so he decided no action was necessary—waiting right there was the best plan. The dog would probably soon tire of worrying around whatever held his attention. If he came toward Zeke and got by him, he'd shout the news to Strahan and try to follow. If sweetie-dog ran back the way he came, Strahan or another officer would surely spot him. Yes, watching a while was the ticket. Everything was under control.

Only, Tinkerbell didn't tire of his toy. Before long, Zeke's curiosity got the better of him, and he started edging toward the dog again. Scalp prickling, step-by-step he neared the action. Suddenly, he decided yelling for Strahan was a real good idea. In fact, so good he had a devil of a time stopping once he started. He needn't fret anymore about scaring the dog. Champion Sir Brotherington of Bostwich barely glanced in his direction and kept right on yanking at something looking very much like a sleeve covering a short length of old tree limb. A limb with dark reddish-brown stuff on the end. A limb attached to the rest of a spread-eagled outline under the fresh snow.

9

Zeke spun and bolted back toward Sycamore Street. After ten yards, he reined himself in. *(Hold on, Tanner! Whatever's under the snow isn't going anyplace.)* No longer running, but still striding rapidly, he exited the bridge before stopping, hands on knees, breathing hard. In seconds, there was the sound of a car, coming fast. He straightened and again began running through the snow toward the barricades as DeVon skidded to a stop, got out, and shouted, "Whoa, old hoss! What's the rush? Hold it! I'll be there in a second."

Zeke stopped, hands on knees again, puffing. The chief strode up. "Strahan radioed you were hollerin' your head off. I heard you all the way up there. What's up?" Special assistant Tanner lifted an arm and stabbed a finger repeatedly toward the bridge. Gulping air again, he whooshed out the dog information.

Bookman grabbed his radio and began barking orders. "All officers call in by your post number on the double." They reported at once, then he commanded, "All officers keep radio silence. Everbody except the officer at post seven stand by to be picked up. Post seven, go to the closest barricades and don't let nobody by. Turn 'em back to a county road or up the hill through Bird land. Be sure to keep an eye out for walkin' gawkers sneakin' down it, too."

Almost immediately, the others rolled up, piled out, and began asking the obvious. Bookman ordered, "All right, all right, put a cork in it—no time for yakkin'. The dog's located what's probly a body out yonder on the bridge. All except Wilson, North and Sharpel go on back to the station and go about your regular duties. And don't forget—mum's the word." A chorus of assents, and away they went.

DeVon turned and began giving assignments. "Wilson, no need to use lots'a time photographin' the scene. With the new snow, probly everthing's pretty much covered, so I'll shoot a few while you take the plain wrapper and fetch the coroner. Drop him off at the barricades, and be sure to send some evidence bags and the whiskbroom from the glove box out here with him. Then go back and find Dalton. I know for a fact he don't have a funeral today, or it'd be on our schedule. Tell him to follow you, and be certain to tell him absolutely no sirens, no overheads. After we get the body out, get on with photographin' and collectin' evidence. OK, git to gittin'. North, you stay at the barricades here at Sycamore and run off the gawkers tryin' to get onto Horse Hockey. Sharpel, go back around through Birdland and help Strahan keep the rubberheads from sneakin' down the hill from Birdland. When things slow down, come back here and help Wilson look for evidence, but tell Strahan to stay there until he's relieved. Also, Officer Sharpel, when you see your buddy, Strahan, tell him I'm expectin' a better'n average story about how the dog got by him onto the bridge without bein' seen."

"How long'll we be out here, Chief?"

"Try to getcha some relief around midnight."

Leaving Sharpel to wonder whether it was a joke, Bookman instructed, "C'mon, Zeke, let's get out there before the mutt chews him up. Take the lead, but try to follow the same track you already made."

In less time than Zeke would've liked, they arrived at the body. Bookman soundly cussed Elizabeth Bannister's little honey, but he kept at his task, whereupon DeVon grabbed Sir Diddlydog's hind legs and flipped him end-over-end. Screaming for Mamma B, he tore for home.

The chief surveyed the area around the facedown body and took photographs before beginning a closer inspection. Zeke stopped looking away and began watching in spite of his earlier aversion. As DeVon took out a notebook and started jotting, his radio squawked, "Chief, it's post seven."

"Confound it! I said keep a cork in it!"

"Yes, but the dog's owner is here and demanding to come out there. Said she was watching from up on the bluff and saw you throw him."

"Tell her it was either save his skin by tossin' him or let that big Rottweiller sneakin' across the bridge from the far side go ahead and eat him. Now get off that radio and keep off."

Wilson returned and dropped off the coroner at the barricade. Plowing toward them on stubby legs, he arrived, gave a quick greeting, whisked snow and debris from the body, then spoke as he moved about it. "White male, approximately six feet, two inches. Two hundred twenty-five pounds. Age fifty to sixty. Graying brown hair. Right hand missing—apparently severed recently. Dressed in a two-piece jogging outfit consisting of sweat-suit material. Shoes are running or jogging type. Body appears to have been exposed to extreme cold long enough to become frozen. Aside from the missing hand, no visible wounds. No evidence the crime was committed here, but the body has probably lain in this position since being placed here." After further brief inspection, the coroner added, "All right, let's turn him over."

Zeke's neck prickled. *('Let's?' That means all of us, doesn't it?)* "Doctor, I'd love to assist, but I'm not on the Turn Him Over Committee. Dalton's ambulance will be here right away, and he can help." Both ignored him.

Bookman observed, "His arms and legs are stuck out pretty stiff, we can't just roll him over. Could be froze to the ground, too. Doctor, grab an arm and I'll get the other one. Grab his feet, Zeke, and we'll turn him toward me."

Zeke still hung back as Forsythe and Bookman got into position. DeVon growled, "For God's sake, Tanner, get a move on!" Gingerly, he grasped the ankles of the corpse.

"All set, Doc? Zeke? OK, on the count'a three, lift and turn. One, two, *three!*"

Fortunately, not much effort was needed to free the body from the roadway to begin the heave-and-turn. However, as soon as it was airborne, Zeke became aware he had the trickiest end when he had to make the left-to-right, right-to-left-hand ankle transfer halfway through the exercise.

It was instantly clear why Bill Borsch's barbershop was closed today. He was easily recognizable, and horrified eyes virtually screamed the unspeakable terror he must've known while departing this vale of tears. To top it off, Zeke had the distinct impression they were staring directly at him. Shocked, his reflexes jolted him a step backward.

Bookman saw his reaction, and ever the sympathetic one, cautioned, "If you think you're gonna be sick, do it somewhere else so's not to mess up the evidence. Otherwise, bend over and take a couple deep breaths."

Zeke didn't have the will right then to reply to the chief's regard for the evidence versus him, but the advice was good. In a minute he was able to stand erect. Another minute, and his astonishment at the identity of the victim resulted in a stream of questions. "Why would a person do such a thing? Why *Bill Borsch,* of all people?" Etc., Etc.

While the coroner continued his examination, the chief answered Zeke. "Get those questions lots'a times. Outside'a tryin' to find the *whys* to help catch the doer, it's a waste'a time figurin' out reasons one citizen does nasty things to another. We just catch 'em and let the experts do the figurin'. I doubt that even *they* come up with many good answers."

Dr. Forsythe added to his earlier observations, "No visible lacerations or contusions on the face. As you can see, it's William Borsch. We'll need a positive identification, of course."

Inside Borsch's pants just below waist level was a small, partially opened red fanny-pack. Bookman crouched beside the doctor. "Let's have a look." He finished unzipping it and pulled out a thin, worn wallet. Handling it carefully, he examined its contents. "No money' a'tall. No credit cards. Not much else, either. Driver's license. Handgun permit. Health club membership card." He stood. "Very little to go on. His license and the membership card don't amount to nothin', and everbody in town's got a gun permit." Shape the wallet's in, probly not much chanc'a liftin' prints. He dropped everything into an evidence bag.

There may've been no surprises in the fanny pack, but then Forsythe pulled up the jogging-suit top to Borsch's armpits. "Great day in the morning! Would you look at that!"

There it was, the same as on the previously discovered hand. Only this heptagon was fully eight inches across. Again, the number 70 was inside. Again, it was crossed out with a broad line slashed diagonally through it. But this time, beneath the heptagon was a different set of numbers in figures more than two inches high. Instead of the originals found on the amputated hand, 1 5 3 0, these were 1 1 8 2 2. As on the hand, they were spaced widely enough apart so they wouldn't be read as only one complete number.

While they were discussing the numbers, the wail of a rapidly approaching siren could be heard. Bookman whirled. "Wilson surely must'a told him no sirens!" Dalton had ignored him and turned it on the minute he started on a run, as usual.

Clifford Dalton, "Last Dime" Dalton to most everyone, was also heartily disdained by most. He was Stony Crossing's only undertaker and the biggest gossip in town. The "Last Dime" tag was due to his reputation for flimflamming the newly bereaved into buying the most expensive caskets and services while their guilty consciences were still active, then collecting any way he could. Among many often-repeated tales was one saying it all. Trying for the last dime a family could raise, Dalton once took a pregnant cow as partial payment for one of his already exorbitant fees. When the calf died six months after it was born, he sent a bill to the destitute survivors for that part of the fee supposedly covered by the animal—*and* for it's disposal.

Stony Crossing's town council didn't want to afford a regular ambulance service, so a deal was made with Last Dime to use one of his hearses in local emergencies. He thought it a good arrangement. Complete service, so to speak—accident or illness to hospital to funeral home. Several expressed skepticism, saying they wouldn't trust that weasel not to skip the ride to the hospital altogether.

Wilson and Dalton braked to a stop at the barricades as Bookman reached them. Steaming, he jerked open the "ambulance" door. "Dalton, who in blazes you think you are! Wilson said keep that thing off!"

Dalton tried to reply, but the chief cut him off. "Don't wanna hear it. Keep on attractin' attention to my crime scenes, and I'm gonna show up at the next council meetin' with a recommendation thatcha oughta be replaced by a regular ambulance. Now hear me good! We got a situation here I don't want blabbed all over town. If anything gets back to me about your blabbin', I'm gonna do a little talkin' around town myself. Talkin' how you slip the casket-factory truck driver a buck or two for a bunch'a his company's stickers with high prices printed on 'em, then slap 'em on those caskets made'a kindlin you buy'. Got it?"

"Sure thing Chief, sure thing. You know me. My lips are sealed."

"Yeah, I know you. That's why I'm gonna tell you once more to keep your mouth shut about whatcha see here. Now back that thing you call an ambulance through the bridge. Stay on the far side and stop twenty feet short'a the body. I wanna preserve as much'a the crime scene as possible."

They loaded Borsch's body, and Bookman ordered, "Drive down around back'a the station into the garage, and we'll meetcha there. And keep that damned siren off!"

After the hearse departed, Bookman turned to Wilson, "Do any other photographin' and collect anything you think might be useful.

Sharpel will be back pretty soon to help. Take as much time as you need to finish up proper, then bring everbody back downtown."

The coroner, Zeke, and DeVon rode together to the station. On the way, Zeke was still aghast at the crime and how anyone could do such a thing.

DeVon responded, "Well, like I said before, even the experts probly don't always find good answers. But, when you can't come up with nothin' else makin' sense why certain preverts do a crime, there's always *one* reason that fits."

"That is?"

"It's *because*."

"*Because*? Because of what?"

"Because'a nothin'. Think about it, Zeke. Sometimes, there's no other way to explain somethin' screwy that happens. Stuff just happens *because*—like the biggest whale in the ocean stranglin' when it tries to swallow a grapefruit."

"Sedate him, Doctor. He's finally lost it."

"I don't know, Ezekial, he may be on to something."

"Don't either of you ever get near me again."

10

While Doctor Forsythe proceeded with a further examination of the body, Zeke and DeVon sat in his office. The chief began fiddling with his pipe. As usual when he was thinking or disturbed about something, he made the act of preparing the hoary Meerschaum into a ceremony—cleaning, scraping, blowing, filling and fiddling. The signs were all there.

"All right, chief Cruddy Calabash, what is it?"

"What is what?"

"Cut the BS, Bookman, what's on your mind?"

DeVon put down his unlit pipe. "Tell you, podner, I've been shot at, shot, gouged, kicked, stomped, cussed and clawed on this job, still the toughest things of all are the two things I gotta do next."

"They are?"

"Notifin' the next'a kin and bein' there when they identify the body. Never have figured a way to do it right—probly not any."

"You know who he is. Why must you have a relative identify him?"

"Lots'a legal reasons."

"His wife's dead. Who's the next of kin?"

"He had no kids or any other kin I can think of except MizMartha Manchester."

"Miss Manchester! I had no idea she was related to anyone alive."

"Zeke, she's his aunt. There were two sisters in the family, and they didn't visit a'tall after a squabble when they were younger. Story is, MizMartha was bein' sparked real heavy by a fella name'a Saul Borsch—a travelin' preacher, no less. MizMartha found out he was also makin' moves on her sister, and there was one helluva fracas with some'a the family takin' sides. Well, MizMartha up and goes out west. Pretty soon, the sister and the preacher married and took off for the east somewhere. Came back more'n a year later, showin' around their new baby, little Billy Borsch. Settled here and bought the old Mitchell place up on Walnut Street. I didn't know Saul Borsch, but folks say Bill was his daddy's spittin' image right down to a peculiar way'a walkin'. MizMartha didn't come home till quite a while later. Her sister and brother-in-law are both dead, but I hear MizMartha hardly ever spoke to 'em when they were alive."

"Maybe identifying him won't be so bad since she wasn't close to the family."

"Never easy, Zeke. Even if they're as far apart as south and north, you can't tell how somebody'll act. Hope her bein' so all-fired churchly will help. That's in spite'a the fact folks say she was cut out to be a church elder and spent her life bein' aggravated 'cause they wouldn't allow it—her bein' a woman." DeVon picked up his pipe. "I'll go after I finish this smoke."

"Not going to get any easier, Dee."

"Who said anything else about it gettin' easier? There's no hurry. Borsch's not goin' anywhere. Since now we know there's been a crime, we need to get crackin' on gettin' it solved. Naturally, one'a the very first things we wanna do is see if there's anything at Borsch's places maybe sheddin' some light. Both judges are out'a town, which means we can't get a search warrant yet today. Somethin' you oughta do right away, though."

"That is?"

"We can use all the stray info we can get, so whatcha better do is write a press release. Never know when some citizen might see it and phone with a good tip. Besides, we need to get the right word out before the wild tales begin. The reporter's'll start phonin' pretty soon after your release. Just answer 'em the same way as you did about the hand—promise 'em, but don't marry 'em. Use some stuff about the victim bein' a community member for a long time, n'all. Toss in about good police work in findin' him. Tell 'em we're workin' on leads and hope to have a prevert in custody pretty quick."

"Stretch, it's *pe*rvert, not *pre*vert. Want anything else in the release?"

"I *said pre*-vert. Reckon you could put in the slightest hint we're keepin' back somethin' about the victim only the perp would know. That's always good."

Zeke asked innocently, "Should I put in anything about Mrs. Bannister's doggie?"

Bookman's lip curled, but before he could answer, the coroner came from the morgue area. His further preliminary work finished, he wanted the body transferred to the county hospital in Wayne City to do a complete autopsy.

"Doc, get anything to help in the investigation?"

"Not much, DeVon. The numbers and drawing on the body appear to be made using the same liquid as those on the hand. I can't be sure yet, but I believe the hand and the body were placed outdoors about the same time. There are signs of suffocation, but we'll need to wait for the autopsy to verify the cause of death. Done anything about identifying the next of kin? Know who it might be?"

"Just tellin' Zeke I'm goin' to see MizMartha Manchester."

"Gracious, that's right! She'd be the one, sure enough. Go get her so we can get on over to Wayne City. I'll call the office and cancel appointments while you're bringing her to the station."

Chief DeVon E. Bookman, most everyone's idea of a flinty lawman, sighed, tossed his pipe aside and left to speak to one of the town's anachronisms. While he was gone, Zeke finished a short press release.

When the chief returned with Miss Manchester, it was hard to tell whether the bearer of bad tidings or their recipient took it worse. Bookman's demeanor was understandable, given his feelings about notifying the next of kin. But for someone who never even acknowledged the earthly presence of Bill Borsch, much less shown any feelings for him, Martha Manchester was displaying a profound case of grief. Ashen-faced, she leaned heavily on the chief as they entered the station. Zeke could scarcely believe this figure so well known for exuding such an aura of independence and confidence was the one he now saw.

Bookman and Dr. Forsythe escorted her in to make the identification. Minutes later, they returned. Zeke was again taken aback when Miss Manchester appeared fully composed and arrow-straight. The grief-stricken aunt was gone, and the Martha Manchester of old was once again present—head high in her usual I'm-in-charge-here manner. Bookman looked as if he'd been pounded through a knothole.

The chief placed a tape recorder on his desk, put in routine information, and turned the mike toward the coroner. He began, "Miss Martha Manchester has stated she's the only living relative of the deceased and has positively identified him as her nephew, William Borsch. She..."

Miss Manchester broke in and demanded, "Oh, get to the point, Horatio." Bookman shut off the recorder. Miss Manchester was definitely in command again. "Nothing else happened except I said I wanted his personal papers and ring. How soon can I get them?"

"Martha, there was no ring. In my earlier examination, I took note a ring was probably worn on the... (hesitating, not wanting to call attention to the severed hand)...worn by the deceased. Chief Bookman and

Mr. Tanner were both present when the examination took place, and neither saw a ring. Right, Chief? Mr. Tanner?"

Bookman answered, "There was no ring seen durin' the coroner's examination. Since then, the...(He didn't want to say it either, but he had to.)....uh, the hand's been locked here in the station, and only Dr. Forsythe has the key."

Miss Manchester looked at Zeke. "Is that the way you recall it, Ezekial Amos?"

("Ezekial Amos?") He was a first-grader again, standing before the penny-candy jar in her store again and could only nod.

Bookman added. "I do remember seein' Bill wear a ring on his right hand and thought it was strange for a right-handed person. But, I didn't notice any ring when I took a quick look in the sack Alan Bannister used for covering it. I left it locked in his car trunk, and there's no way a ring could'a been removed before I brought it into the station. We've also got Bannister's statement about what happened before I got the...hand, and there's no mention of a ring. We'll ask him again, but I think he might'a said somethin' about it."

Martha Manchester was adamant. "I simply must have that ring, I tell you! Its value isn't great—probably no more than a few hundred dollars, but it was a gift to me a long time ago. I let William wear it because he...he...well, you know, William's father died when the boy was only sixteen and he inherited nothing. I felt sorry for him and gave the ring to his mother so he could wear it. He wouldn't be without it. I think he wore it on his right hand because it fit better." She slumped and began to tremble. Zeke thought she might become distraught again, but she straightened. "Will whoever did this dreadful thing ever be captured?"

Forsythe replied gently, "Martha, everyone will do whatever's necessary to catch the perpetrator. I'm also sure the police will begin to look for your ring right away. Meantime, why don't you go home and rest? This has been a terrible strain for you."

Miss Manchester straightened even more. "Nonsense, I've a store to run. Life goes on, Horatio...at least for a little while." Turning to

Bookman, she added, "If you're going to search for the ring, shouldn't you have a description of it?"

The chief was chagrined he hadn't asked. "We certainly should. Exactly what'd it look like?"

"It was large, a man's ring of course, and had a single turquoise stone on top of a high silver setting. Somewhere I have a photograph if it would help."

"MizMartha, a picture would be a big help. How soon can you get it?"

"Certainly by this afternoon. Chief Bookman, what about obtaining his personal papers?"

"You can have 'em right after they're checked for evidence. Shouldn't take long. Probly not much'll need to be held. I'll see to it you get 'em quick as possible." He summoned an officer and instructed him to take Miss Manchester to her store. She protested only slightly.

When she left, the coroner asked, "Well now, Chief, what do you make of that?"

"Her reactions to Borsch's death, the missin' ring, or the stuff about his papers?"

"All of those."

"Reckon it hit her there was nobody left but her, even though she never had any contact with him over the years that I know of. As for the ring, I think it's a blessin' in disguise. Leastways, it gives us somethin' to start on. We can check all the jewelry stores and hockshops at the county seat in an hour or so. If she finds the photo, we can send copies all over. To follow procedure, I'll hafta ask the Bannisters if they remember anything about a ring, but I doubt there *was* any ring to see. Killer took it off before he dumped the hand and got rid of it already. About the papers, I don't have any idea what she's talkin' about. Maybe we'll know when we see some."

Zeke inquired, "Did she see the numbers and markings on her nephew?"

"No, only his face. Pondered showin' 'em to her, but she was so addlepated already, I thought it might be too much."

The chief phoned Last Dime Dalton with orders to transport Borsch to the county morgue for the autopsy, and Forsythe prepared to depart. "Gentlemen, I'll phone about the cause of death and other findings. Good luck on the ring hunt."

"Thanks, Doc. The missin' ring could be a hot clue. Gonna jump right on it. Maybe we'll get lucky."

DeVon began planning the ring search. "First thing, let's go out to Birdland and tackle the Bannisters on our way to the Wayne City hockshops. They're in another jurisdiction a'course, so I'll hafta call Jerry Milligan. He's the new chief since late last fall, and we hit it off just fine. He won't get in the way."

"It's after one o'clock, so I suppose you'll want your daily dose of meat and potatoes before we start. How you can eat right after what we saw today, I'll never know."

"Gotta keep livin, Zeke—not me on the way to the morgue. Let yourself fasten on all the bad things, and Doc'll be standin' over you one day. Got the press release out?"

"Bookman, you're some piece of work. The release is being distributed as we speak. There's also a second statement for the deskman to use when the calls start coming in."

"Good man."

After he made the call to Milligan, the chief found to his dismay all the cruisers were in use and his car was being serviced—they'd have to take Ol' Emmy. "Lord A'mighty, I hate to be seen in this rattle wagon."

"Hush your mouth, you disrespectful dog."

To Zeke's surprise, Call-me-Charlie Ackerman was just leaving the diner as they arrived. "Didn't know he ever took time to eat, much less in this den of iniquity."

"Checkin' on sinners durin' his lunch hour, I reckon. Must take all his free time from his regular job at the grocery, there bein' such a mob'a wrongdoers in Stony Crossing." DeVon ordered two turkey clubs and coffee to go—Zeke, tea and toast.

Pulling into the Bannisters' circle drive, it was obvious Bookman was into his don't-take-any-crap-from-these-mothers mode. This was confirmed by the manner in which he punished the front door. Alan Bannister opened it almost immediately. "No need to pound it down. What is it this time?"

"Will you get your wife so we can do this only once?"

"I'm right here." Neither Zeke nor DeVon had seen her sitting across the big room by the fireplace.

"What I'd like to know is, have either of you thought'a anything else about the hand the dog brought in?"

Elizabeth Bannister came over complaining on the way, "Goodness me, what more could there be to tell?"

Alan Bannister spoke up. "She's right. We talked about it, and there's nothing else."

"One question, Alan. Could either one'a you forgot about seein' a ring?"

Heatedly, Anan Bannister responded, "What the hell kind of question is that! Of course we didn't see any ring! I didn't see any ring when I covered that thing and scooped it into a sack. Bethy didn't see one, either."

Bookman turned, "Elizabeth?"

She seemed about to answer when her husband barked, "Dammit, I *told* you she didn't see any ring."

The chief asked again, "Elizabeth?"

Before Alan Bannister could fire another burst, she responded, "Everything happened so suddenly. I don't *think* there was anything, but...no, it's as Alan says—I don't remember any ring. Why are you asking, anyway?"

"There seems to be a ring missin', and I hafta ask everbody who might'a seen it."

Alan Bannister bristled, "There's one for you! Maybe we flipped a coin to see which one holds a stiff's cut-off hand while the other one twists off a ring. Bookman, what's the matter with you!"

"Nobody's even hintin' you did any such thing. When anything' a value's missin' from a victim, we hafta ask. Tracin' the ring could give us some leads."

"I'll tell you what I think about you coming in here and..."

"Alan, as Clark Grable would say, 'Frankly, my man, I don't give a crap.'" They departed to the tune of Bannister threatening to tattle to the town council.

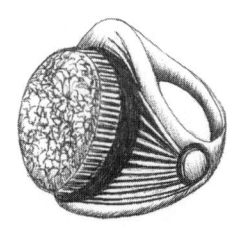

11

Leaving Bannister's, Bookman speculated, "Y'know, I got a prime hunch. If someone wanted to get rid'a that ring, he'd probly take it farther'n Wayne City—like over on the other side'a the county. Most likely place I can think of is Lefty Riggins' pawnshop in Windham. Think we'll go there first. DeVon snapped his fingers. "Forgot all about the picture. Better swing by the station and see if MizMartha's brought it in."

The chief went inside and returned with a photograph. "She brought it in not long after we left. Ring must be pretty important to her." Only a glance was needed to see that a Navajo craftsman spent more than the ordinary amount of time on this one.

The turquoise was flawless Nevada Spiderweb and the silverwork perfect. In his Western sojourns, Zeke seldom saw anything equaling it. No doubt, it was made before the "Genuine Indian Craft" machine-made fakes appeared in tourist stops in the Southwest.

On their way over to the Interstate, Zeke asked, "Notice Mrs. Bannister didn't seem so sure about not seeing a ring?"

"Yeah, but that's not unusual. Most witnesses aren't too positive'a much. Sometimes I'm suspicious when they are. Some are so anxious to be a star and get their name in the paper they see what's not there. Others see what they think you want 'em to. She was probly so shook when that pooch brought her the hand, no way she could be certain about anything."

Forty minutes later, they were visiting with Windham's chief of police, John Hawkins, as a catch-up-on-the-news and courtesy call to inform him why they needed to call on Riggins. Hawkins knew him, of course. "Ah yes, our old friend Lefty. You don't find the ring at that scoundrel's, give a shout, and we'll keep our eyes peeled.

"Much obliged, John."

Bookman guided Zeke through a maze of narrow streets until they saw the faded sign adorning the garish yellow façade heralding **LEFTY'S PAWN SHOP**, and below it, AN EASY DEAL AND AN HONEST PRICE.

"Well, Zeke, here we are at the snake's nest. Every lawman in five counties knows Lefty—crooked as fifty-miles'a mountain road and lies like a wore-out rug. But every so often, he comes up with somethin' useful, so we let him keep doin' business. Got whatcha might call a personal operatin' strategy. He comes through with what we want, we stop scarin' him to death."

"Psychology and modern criminology at work."

"Yeah, yeah, yeah."

Zeke swung into a spot directly in front of Lefty's. There was the usual come-on sign taped to the window of many pawnshops and schlock-stores—the first line reading, 50% OFF ON ALL MERCHANDISE! The second, FOR ONE WEEK ONLY! Like most, these were so shopworn Zeke wondered why Lefty didn't have them inlaid in the shiny black tile squares framing the doorway.

They walked the length of the dreary deserted shop, passing display cases and shelves crammed full of every conceivable item—some fair or better—mostly junk. Lefty Riggins, a slight, wizened-rat character, sat perched on a stool in the rear behind a chain-link divider at a combination desk/cabinet with many drawers. He pushed to close the already closed top drawer when Devon appeared. "Gooood morning, Chief, good morning!" Bookman's presence hadn't shaken Lefty too much—it was mid-afternoon. "Good to see you, Chief, but I'm kind of busy. Lots of things to do in an operation like this."

"Sure thing, Lefty. I can see that mob'a customers up front."

"Well, there's always paperwork and other stuff."

Bookman ignored the diversion attempts. "How's business? Taken in much lately?"

"Hardly anything. Things are real slow this time of year—after Christmas and all."

"Too bad about that, but if it's so slow, it'll make it all the easier to tell me whatcha *have* taken in."

"Oh, nothing you'd be interested in, Chief—only junk."

"Lefty, old buddy, I'm interested in about everthing." Bookman started around through the divider's door.

Lefty sprang to his feet. "I'd never do anything illegal, you know that."

"Sure you wouldn't, but maybe I better take a look around in case you might'a *accidentally* stepped over the traces." DeVon went on into the office.

Small as he was, Lefty Riggins looked about ready to shrink still further. What was Bookman after? Had he found out about those gold coins? Unconsciously, his eyes strayed toward the cabinet's top drawer.

The chief paused. "Well, never mind, I can always dig around later. What I'm lookin' for is a ring. Take in a ring this week? Big one with a turquoise stone?"

The pawnbroker relaxed. All the chief wanted was a lousy ring! "A ring! Why didn't you say so?"

Bookman grinned. "You were so busy tellin' me what a good citizen you are, I didn't have a chance. Now then, what about a ring like this?" He showed Lefty the photograph.

Riggins stopped relaxing. "Yeah, I got a ring something like that. On Monday, I think. Yeah, last Monday."

"Lefty, whataya think my next question's gonna be?"

"I know, I know. You're going to ask who brought it in."

"Riiiight! And the answer is?"

"What's in it for me if I say?"

"Lefty will you 'scuse me a minute? Got some rummagin' around to do back here—maybe startin' with that top drawer there."

Riggins gave up. "No big deal. You probably know who it is, anyway. What'd he do, lift it off a drunk?"

"Keep talkin, my patience is wearin' thin."

"OK, it's who you thought—Hollis Benson."

Bookman stood motionless, teeth clamped, jaw muscles taut. He took a step forward, and Lefty recoiled, seeming about ready to go into terminal shrivel. After a several-second eternity, DeVon spoke quietly. "I doubt even you'd be stupid enough to lie about somethin' like this. Get the ring and the paperwork, Riggins. Then bring everthing to me. After that, tell me exactly what Benson said when he hocked the ring."

As he handed the items to the chief, Lefty recovered enough to protest, "Who's gonna pay for that pawn?"

The chief stared at him. So much for any more questions. "Lefty, I asked what Benson said when he hocked it."

"No more than the usual—something like, 'Here's some stuff. How much? See you later.'"

"That all?...Whataya mean, the *usual*! He come in often?"

"Only once or twice a month."

Only once or twice a month! The man's a pawnin' machine! By the way, if you're entertainin' any thought'a phonin' him, you better do your dead-level best to forget it. It'd mean you and me would hafta get up close and personal. Hate to be responsible for your early retirement."

"Don't worry, Chief, don't worry. I don't need any trouble. You know I always cooperate."

"Yeah, Lefty, my man, cooperate you always do, even if it kills you. Now I wantcha to cooperate some more. Make a list'a everthing Hollis Benson's ever pawned or sold in here and mail it to me soon as it's finished. Do it *right soon*. Understand? Try to fool me and you're gonna be real sorrowful. Understand? And phone me pronto if he brings anything else in here. Understand? Lefty's head was bobbing in a great imitation of a rear-window toy dog in a good ol' boy's Chevy.

In the Blazer, Dee began unloading on "that swill-bucket Benson." Barely taking time to draw breath—spewing and spouting, he was so angry. "Never was worth a damn from the day he was whelped and never will be! Hollis Benson! The reptile some'a the town council listens to on street corners when he goes whinin' to 'em!

What makes it even worse, the sumbitch could be a good officer, but he'd rather take the short cuts. Just look at him now, the prime suspect in murder one! Either that or an accessory. It's a sure thing. Gotta be—the ring ties him right to it. There was no ring on Borsch's hand or with his body. That thievin' dog got it before the barber was offed or right after. He did it or knows who did. Wonder if somebody was in it with him—he must'a needed help. He's mink-smart enough to put those markin's on Borsch to try to fool us. He was off duty Saturday night, too."

On and on the chief barked, mile after mile. The closer to home, the more incensed he became and the more speed he demanded of Zeke. He could hardly wait to get back and put the scum where he belonged. "No, not scum—*sediment*, by damn! *Scum* at least rises to the top'a the slime."

Ol' Emmy was protesting, *"What'n hell's going on?"* Starting to vibrate and wander a little, she was. As they neared her top speed of nearly 80 mph, Zeke called Bookman's attention to their mortality and the distinct probability of Ol' Emmy expiring. He pointed out if they killed themselves, Bookman wouldn't have the pleasure of socking it to Benson. Or should Ol' Emmy pass out, his prey might escape.

Bookman eased up about the speed but didn't slow down one bit concerning Hollis Benson. "It's a sure thing—the yella-bellied low-down cur's guilty as sin. Yep, it's a sure thing if ever there was one."

Zeke was wary of sure things—made even more so by his knowledge of Bookman's usual wariness. "Dee, I know everything fits fine, but you're not sounding like the Bookman I know—the one who always warned me to keep one eye on my man and watch for a back-screen with the other. Think maybe there's any way Benson came by the ring without being involved in the Borsch murder?'

"Oh yeah, goody-goody tennis shoes—like the tooth goblin left it under his pillow. Once'n a while you may be right, but not this time, Benson bein' dirty's a *certain-sure* thing."

Zeke was still uneasy. During his years of coaching, he experienced his share of screwball events involving "sure things," but now recalled one in particular. His team lost four in a row after his star quarterback was injured, instantly turning chances for a winning season into one of break-even and job-survival. His team's final opponent of the year was unanimously considered to be possibly the worst team in recorded history and a "sure thing" pushover. The newspaper proclaimed a win was a sure thing—no way could Zeke's Bluebirds lose. (Bluebirds? The president of the school board's wife came up with that one. Maybe they were going to peck them to death?)

The game was a nightmare. Zeke's team played down to its opponent's level, and the opponents played to the top of their depths. With two minutes remaining, this continuing awfulness was broken only when Zeke's sub quarterback miraculously completed a pass of fourteen yards. It was one in a row and a distance record for him and his forgotten-how-to-block teammates.

The Cardinals (another bunch of peckers) were so startled, they let one of Zeke's fledglings flutter all the way to the two-yard line before trying to net him. In the ensuing peck-off, Zeke's bird took a wing alongside the beak, became disoriented, and winged away in the wrong direction. Hash mark to hash mark, avoiding friend and foe alike, he reeled, gasping and flopping along like a mama Killdeer pretending to be injured, decoying the fox away from her chicks, always barely out of reach.

By now, everyone on the field and in each coach's box was winded from chasing, screaming, pleading, threatening, or praying. Zeke howled for someone, *anyone,* to grab the featherhead with the football. Otherwise, **"May God strike him dead!"**

The opposing coach, appropriately garbed in red, begged his Cardinals to block for the befuddled Bluebird carrying the ball south instead of north. Meanwhile, the beleaguered birdling, who by now had run close to 150 lung-burning yards, was begging the spirits of Rockne, Lombardi and Halas to allow him to stumble the remaining twenty to the goal line.

None of those things happened due to Zeke's monster right end, Tyrone, "Typhoon" Swackhammer (5 foot-8, 167 pounds). The only certified semi-brain on the team, he was the lone contestant of the other twenty-one foul fowl on the field to pursue his teammate all the way. As they staggered across the Bluebird's own fifteen-yard line, Typhoon, seeing he couldn't catch the addled ball-toter, smartly yelled, **"*LATERAL! LATERAL!*"**

The careening Bluebird, last child in a seven-sister family, had spent a lifetime following orders. Dutifully, he spun and tossed the ball to a voice he recognized. Typhoon whirled and began the torturous journey back down the field toward his opponent's goal.

Nearing the original scrimmage line after more than 200 yards of dodging, lunging, muscle-agony, the battling Bluebird collapsed from exhaustion or tripped over a similarly depleted Cardinal, and down he flopped. The play lasted so long that time expired. The nothing-nothing tie preserved the blemished record of both teams.

Remembering the wrong-way Bluebird and the sure-thing" the game was supposed to be, Zeke's uneasiness-alarm sounded louder than ever. With a straight face, he quipped, "I agree with you one-hundred percent—he's guilty, all right. Why don't you save time and money and shoot him on sight?"

The chief was cooling down and beginning to brighten. "Tell you what—I'll talk to him first, then shoot him."

"More like it. How do you plan to get him in range?"

"He's s'posed to come in tomorrow after his suspension's over. I'll phone and tell him to stop in this afternoon to get his assignment. He'll come, all right—won't suspect a thing."

"What then?"

"Question him, read him his rights, and book him. Don't see how he can wiggle his way out'a this one."

They rode in silence until Zeke offered, "Well, there's something good to come from today."

"Name it.""

"You got the ring back for Miss Martha."

DeVon brightened further. "That's right! Only thing is, it'll probly hafta stay locked in the property room as evidence in case there's a trial, but at least she'll know it's safe." They arrived at the station as daylight was dying. The chief's demeanor also darkened once more. What he had to do was not going to be the most pleasant thing in the world. A County Sheriff's car parked in the spot reserved for the chief didn't do much for his disposition, either.

Nor were Zeke's spirits lifted when he recognized several haphazardly parked cars with PRESS stickers in front of the station. He and DeVon slipped in through the basement garage.

12

They climbed the stairs and walked swiftly down the hall to Bookman's office, but needn't have hurried. When they entered, there sat Hollis Benson. Wearing a uniform, too, although not one of the Stony Crossing PD. It was the butternut and chocolate of a county sheriff's deputy topped off with the traditional Smokey Bear hat. Benson didn't rise, just sat trying for a confident smile, his effort resulting in only a sophomoric smirk.

Chief DeVon Bookman put on his aces-in-the-hole poker face. "Hello there, Hollis. Thoughtcha weren't s'posed to come in till tomorrow. What's that you're wearin'?"

Benson could hardly wait to begin. "Sheriff Laddis offered me a good job, and I took it. Nothin' ya can do about it. Sent me over to say not to bother him any more. I'm his new chief deputy, and from here on, you'll hafta deal with me if ya want somethin' from 'im."

It came out in somewhat of a croak. Hair to toenail, he was still afraid of his former boss.

In the growing silence, back went Bookman' hat, and Zeke could swear he heard teeth grinding. By the flush on the chief's face, it looked as though he was about to perform a *pre*-mortem autopsy, *sans* anesthesia, on this snake before him. Zeke decided this was probably the right time to do something to prevent POLICE CHIEF DECAPITATES DEPUTY headlines across the country. Yes, this was definitely the time to step in. Special assistant Tanner drew a deep breath and was about to take the plunge when Bookman spoke, cool as a cucumber. "Well, congratulations on your new job, Hollis. Got yourself a new uniform and a new car n'all. That a new weapon there?"

Benson relaxed and bragged, "Oh yeah, they treat us real good over there. Don't hafta carry revolvers—got *Glocks.*"

"The hell! Lemme take a look—haven't had a chance to handle one much. Gonna hafta take any extra trainin'?"

Chief Deputy Hollis Benson bit like a famished barracuda and handed the gun to Bookman. "Nah, don't take no trainin'. Trigger pulls jist like your old S and W revolver."

DeVon took the weapon, hefted it for balance, removed the clip, and jacked the remaining shell from the chamber before placing the empty firearm on his desk. "Nice piece. By the way, sure glad you're here. I was about to phone you to come in so I could ask whether I might get some help in solvin' this little puzzle that's popped up in the investigation'a the Borsch mess."

Benson puffed up like a pouter pigeon. He was an equal, by golly! "Sure, sure, Chief. You know I always done my best to help."

"Mmm-huh. Well, the problem came up after the body was officially identified. You do know we found a body, don'tcha?"

Benson puffed up once more. "Yeah, the boys out front've been keepin' me up to date."

Bookman made a mental note to speak to "the boys out front," before continuing, "From what we found out from the person who I.D.'d the body, there's an important piece'a evidence missin'. We need to locate it so's not to spend time chasin' all over."

"What's that, Chief?"

"Seems Borsch always wore this big silver ring with a turquoise stone, one like this." He slid its photograph across the desk. "Nobody remembers seein' it on the hand, and it wasn't in his fanny pack. See anything of it durin' the big hoo-haw Sunday?"

Zeke gave Benson credit for gall. He didn't bat an eye. "Why, hell no, I didn't see no ring, and Doc Forsythe's got the only key to the cooler compartment where I put the hand."

"Why bring up the coroner?"

"Well, if there's a ring missin', somebody hadta do it."

"Think the *coroner* took it?"

"No but...."

Benson's voice trailed off as Bookman skewered him with narrowed eyes. "Hollis, I think it was taken sometime durin' Saturday."

Benson didn't flinch. "Well, I reckon if it wasn't on the hand Sunday, somebody hadta take it off before that."

"There you go. Any idea who?"

Bookman's prey swallowed hard. "None a'tall. Think *I'd* know who done it?"

"Didn't say that. Just wondered what your thinkin' might be."

DeVon began fooling with his pipe. He lit up and sat puffing, letting the silence become leaden once more before shifting gears. "Know anything about cults?"

"*Cults!* Hell no! I don't know nothin' 'bout them things." Benson leaned back in his chair, thankful Bookman was pursuing another track.

More silence, then the chief shifted again. "You know, Hollis, I wonder if somethin' about that ring might'a caused a loss'a memory on your part."

Benson went on fidget-alert, tensing forward, gravity beginning to assert itself on the sweat-beads blossoming on his forehead. He scooted back in his chair again, grabbed its arms, and sat up straight "How'd I know somethin' about a ring? If nobody seen it Sunday, how could *I*?"

Bookman's response was as smooth as cream sherry. "No, don't suppose a'body could know anything about the ring if it wasn't there Sunday—only if they saw it before Sunday. That whatcha mean?"

"A'course! It's what I been sayin'. Didn't see no ring on Sunday, so I don't know nothin' about it."

The chief was ready to spring the trap. "OK, let's go over this again. If the ring wasn't on the hand Sunday, it must'a been taken before then. So, whoever got the ring must be a hot suspect for a murder charge. Right?"

"Could be somethin' like that," Benson nasaled. "Could be lots'a things. Could be Borsch lost it somewhere. Why're ya askin' me?"

No response from Devon—he just continued to sit and eye his prey. Suddenly, the depth of his predicament began to dawn on the deputy. He rocked forward and tried meeting Bookman's eyes. No luck—his brief fling at bravado dissolved into world-class squirming.

Bookman came around the desk to tower over his quarry and slam shut his trap's steel jaws. "I don't think Borsch lost it somewhere, Hollis. I think it was pawned Monday at Lefty's up in Windham by someone signin' his name *'Hollis Benson.'* I also think I oughta say you're about half a tadpole hair from bein' booked for murder one."

Deputy Sheriff Hollis Benson recoiled and sagged. Not enough starch left to hold him erect, he swayed forward and bowed his head. Uttering small groans, he lifted his hands to cover his face and sat moaning, slowly shaking his head. *"Oh me, oh me, oh me."* On and on it went. Finally, Bookman slapped off the deputy's Smokey Bear, yanked his head up by the hair, and delivered a wicked fore and backhand across his face. "Shut up, *you worthless suck-egg-dog!* Get hold'a yourself and tell me all about offin' Borsch."

Benson cowered back in his chair, forearms crossed before his face as if expecting more of the same. "I didn't kill nobody. I *didn't!*"

"Bullshit! How do you explain the ring?"

"I got it Sunday—took it right here at the station. *Honest!*"

"Honest! Whatcha tryin' to pull? Nobody saw a ring Sunday."

"There was, I tell ya!"

Bookman returned to his chair and stared at the trembling figure. "Guess I better give your rights."

"No, Chief! Please don't do that! *Please*—ya gotta believe me! There *was* a ring I tell ya!" Benson was fairly shouting. "I took it off when we was in the cooler room—when my back was to ya—when I was puttin' the hand in the tray for Doc to examine." He turned to Zeke. "You remember when the chief told me to hurry up don'tcha? That's when I was doin' it."

DeVon snapped, "Quick thinkin', Benson—admittin' to a lower felony to get out'a a bigger one. That hound won't hunt—both Bannisters say the ring wasn't on the hand when their mutt brought it home. Just for argument, let's say your tale's true and they're wrong about there not bein' a ring. What would you done if I caughtcha takin' it?"

"I dunno. Probably used some excuse—like it fell off or I was gonna tag it for evidence or somethin'."

"No good, Benson, I think I've heard enough." The chief rose and pulled out his handcuffs just as his buzzer sounded. "Call on line one, Chief."

"*Dammit*! You know I don't take calls unless I say beforehand!"

"Yes, but Mrs. Bannister's on the phone and says it's real important. Mr. Bannister's on their other phone hollerin' we better hurry up or he'll do somethin' we won't like a'tall."

"*Crap!* Probly wants to know about her doggie award. Have her wait a second." He called an officer and instructed him to take Benson to the "box*,*" an eight-by-ten foot cubicle used as an interrogation room containing nothing but a small rectangular steel table and four steel chairs. Bolted to the table was a short sturdy chain to which was welded a pair of handcuffs. A black curtain covered the one-way mirror through which viewers in the adjacent room could view suspects without being seen.

Bookman told the officer to be sure to lock Benson in, then punched the speakerphone button. "What is it, Elizabeth? Deskman said it was important."

Alan Bannister answered, "Damn right, it's important! Think I'd be phoning otherwise? You wanted to know if we remembered anything else and now you make us wait."

DeVon ignored him and repeated, "What is it, Elizabeth?"

"You asked us if there was a ring? Well, at first I didn't think there was, but after I thought and thought, I remembered there *was* one. I was so frightened of that *thing* that I just forgot. There was one, though, with a big colored stone."

"Remember what kind'a stone?"

"Oh, I can't think of the name. You know—one of those western Indian things with a kind of greenish-blue stone—set up high in silver, I think it was."

"Elizabeth, are you absolutely sure about seein' the ring Sunday mornin', not some other time and only rememberin' it now? Swear to it in a court'a law?"

Again Alan Bannister jumped in. "Certainly she'd swear to it. She *said* she saw it, didn't she?"

"Bannister, shut up and let your wife answer for herself! I'll have a question for *you* later. Elizabeth—once more—you dead certain about seein' the ring Sunday mornin'?"

"Yes I am. I'd swear it was Sunday morning and it was on that awful thing. Where in the world could I have seen it any other time?" She paused before adding, "Chief, before I forget it, thank you for saving my Tinkerbell from that awful dog down at the bridge."

"Mmm-huh. Alan, now what I wanna know is why *you* had such a bad memory about the ring? You handled the hand more'n your wife did."

"I don't know, Bookman. How can a black cow eat green grass and give white milk that makes yellow butter?"

"That's about the kind'a half-assed answer I'd expect from you. I may have more to ask on the subject later."

The chief hung up on Bannister's bitching about public officials, etc., etc. "Sounds like her story's square. Remember how she hesitated when we asked if she saw a ring?" He sat and picked up his pipe. "You know right where findin' the ring leaves us with Benson, don'tcha? We got no case, and he'll scream his head off about police harassment."

"You still have him on theft, don't forget."

"That's a fact." He toyed with his pipe before continuing. "Zeke, I believe we can come out'a this pretty good. Let's get him back in here."

Hollis Benson looked worse than ever. He took a seat and crossed his arms protectively. Still perspiring profusely, his tie gone, shirt soaked, and sleeves rolled to the elbows.

Bookman spoke. "First the good news. There may be some truth to your story. At least I'm gonna wait a while before throwin' your wormy carcass in a cell for murder. Next, the bad news. You've admitted to grand theft in front'a me and a witness. *And*, Lefty's gonna send me a list'a everthing you've pawned. Should make for some real interestin' readin', don'tcha think? Could be a cell with your name on the door after all."

Benson's eyes were the deer-caught-in-the-headlights variety as DeVon went on, "Before I putcha inside, I want Lardass to see up close what garbage he hired."

Bookman got through to Sheriff Laddis and told him his new deputy was in his office. The laughter was so loud DeVon took the phone from his ear. Laddis said it wasn't *his* fault that Bookman didn't know a good man when he saw one and Benson was going to come in handy as a go-between for him and a certain pain-in-the-butt police chief.

Bookman began coolly enough, but ended with some heated advice. "This is Chief Pain-In-The-Butt, and your butt-pain's gonna get worse real sudden—soon as I let the word out about the county sheriff's newest deputy bein' arrested for grand theft. I'd advise you to do your damnedest to get over here." This time the clamor coming from the phone definitely wasn't laughter.

The chief sent Benson back to the box and they coffeed up while waiting for Laddis. After what must've been record time for the fifteen-mile trip, he burst in, bellow first. "*Ya miserable pile'a maggot crap! What'n hell ya think yer doin! Ain't it enough I gotta put up with your chickenshit outfit jist bein' on the planet! Where's it say you always hafta be the biggest horse apple in the pile! Whataya screwed up this time?"*

"Hostility, Sheriff, hostility," purred Bookman. "Keep on talkin' and I'm liable to start thinkin' our romance might be over. If you'll put a plug in that mule mouth for a second, I'll tell you it's not me who's buggered up. It's two sorry-ass excuses for law officers names'a Leon Laddis and Hollis Benson."

Laddis erupted again with another torrent of abuse before pausing long enough to listen. After filling him in on the details, Bookman added, "Sheriff, I'm gonna give you the straight skinny. One'a two things can happen as a result'a your bad judgment in hirin' that Benson seepage. First is, I can book your pitiful mess'a over-ripe tripe for grand theft. A'course, the press'd hafta learn how you hired a deputy already under suspension from a regular police force. Made him *chief deputy*, too. A chief deputy who got nailed for a felony right after he started wearin' the uniform'a that sheriff's department. Look real good to the voters, don'tcha think? Probly look even better to that young fella runnin' against you in the primary election this spring. Second thing that could happen is lettin' your *chief deputy* walk and go on bein' your flunky. Which sounds best?"

Laddis, no stranger to hairy situations, growled, "What's the tab?"

"My oh my, Sheriff, Sounds mighty like your suggestin' some kind'a payola. I thought a smart sheriff like yourself might come up with a good idea on his own. Somethin' like he'd keep the hell out'a the way of an outstandin' police chief. A chief who's been so kind as to have done a good favor for a smart sheriff. A really smart sheriff who might also have the good idea to keep his brand new chief deputy on the payroll and make him available to do about anything asked by an outstandin' police chief."

Laddis wasn't whipped yet. "Yes, but in a few short months, a smart sheriff could always say he found out the deputy lied on his application and pitch 'im on the fire."

"All well and good, Sheriff, but the kindly chief who did such a big favor could always say the smart sheriff was told his new chief deputy was under suspicion since way before he was hired and did nothin' about it. Be copies'a letters, a'course."

Laddis capitulated. "Aw, what the hell, win a few, lose a few. Ain't nothin' I can't live with. Jist be sure you know a certain smart sheriff's got a long memory and conivin' police chiefs can get their asses kicked."

"Oh my, Sheriff, say it ain't so. Say it ain't so—then I can sleep tonight."

The last thing they heard from Sheriff Lardass Laddis on his way out with Hollis Benson was, "No, I'm *not* gonna give your gun back! May wanna use it on ya. Even if I don't, jist remember, your skinny butt belongs to me and that great big pile'a cow do-flop back there...*ferever*! I don't hardly mind that a'tall, 'cause after I get my share, there ain't gonna be a thimbleful left fer him. Get out'a my sight, ya scrawny pissant!"

After they high-fived twice, Zeke commented, "Well now, I've seen some sides of you I never knew existed."

"Yeah? Like what?"

"I believe they call it assault and battery of a suspect. There's also blackmail or some such trivial crime, not to mention malfeasance for letting an admitted thief go free."

"All in the eye'a the behelder, my man, all in the eye'a the behelder."

Zeke let the "behelder" go. "You actually plan to ask Benson to do something sometime?"

"Same chance as a snowball in hell'a askin' anything amountin' to a hill'a rhubarb, but won't I have fun thinkin' about ol' Hollis waitin' for the other shoe to drop?"

"You're a hard man, a *real* hard man."

Bookman smiled. "A chief's gotta do what a chief's gotta do."

Zeke rose to go deal with the reporters. "You're feeling foxy about Benson and Laddis and recovering the ring, but all in all, not such a good day's work."

"The hell! I've seen lots worse. Got the ring back and Benson by the short hairs—hold theft charges over him and use 'em any way I want. Sounds pretty good to me."

"Still, you wind up with less than you had about the case."

"Meanin'?"

"Before, we thought the missing ring might lead to the killer. Now it's back to zero."

"Thank you, Mr. Gertrude Sunshine. I can stay warm with that all winter."

"Much obliged, Ethel. Keep basking in the glow while I go face that roomful of man-eaters."

13

Zeke dealt with reporters for half an hour before going home. After feeding the dogs, he entered the kitchen to a flashing answering machine and more than fifteen inquiries from media people asking him to return their calls. These were followed by several messages from local citizens who discovered he was the person to phone about the Borsch case. A few were of an inquisitive nature, several more expressing concerns a mutilating mass murderer was on the loose.

About to hit ERASE, something caused him to pause in mid-punch. The muffled voice with the last message didn't register at first. *(Only numbers? What's that all about?)* He played it twice more, listening intently. It *was* only a series of numbers, the voice pausing between each. "One...one...one...one...five."

(Could be another message concerning Borsch—better get Dee.) He caught him at the Country Kitchen amidst demolishing the Wednesday Dinner Special, a Farmer's Delight, the planet's greatest breaded

tenderloin sandwich, served with cottage fries, slaw, coffee and cobbler. "Dee, maybe you better come right over."

"Important enough to interrupt a Farmer's Delight?"

"Something on the answering machine could be about Borsch. Important enough?"

"Be right there."

"Hold it! This tape's not going anywhere. Bring me a tenderloin sandwich and pie."

While Zeke waited, he glanced through the mail. There was only the usual collection of bulk-junk. He dropped everything into the extra large basket in the front entryway placed there for such garbage. When it reached the top, he dumped it only to have it fill again as if multiplying when he wasn't looking. *(What would the world be without telemarketers and third-class mail?)*

In a few minutes, Bookman came in. Zeke played the tape while he began his sandwich. The chief listened a second time. "What'n blazes! Whataya make of it?"

"Not quite enough mayonnaise."

"The tape, smart mouth."

"Oh, that. Well, the voice sounds like one I've heard before, but I don't have the vaguest idea what it's about."

"Your stint in the Navy decodin' outfit don't help?"

"That was quite a while back. Anyhow, decoding takes time. I don't recognize the numbers series as fitting any code system, but I'll work on it. What do *you* make of the message?"

"What the numbers mean is a big question, but there's another one. What *kind'a* dude would phone? Figure it out and maybe we'll have an idea who left messages and why."

"Is it common for killers to leave them?"

"Pretty unusual, but some types'a killers might. Pry me with liquor, and I'll talk about some of 'em."

"If we're going to extend this already long day, at least we could take the drinks into the other room where it's comfortable. We can listen to music while we talk. And it's *ply*, not *pry*."

"Correction police! Correction police! Never give up, do you? Just pour, bartender."

Generous Snake Bites made and The Modern Jazz Quartet doing its velvet-smooth thing, Zeke prompted, "Get on with the types of killers who might phone."

"Well, one's a warped mother who's gotta feed his ego by murderin' so he can feel the *power.* Lots'a times, they pick the same kind'a victim. Some'a these, other lawmen call 'serial killers,' dependin' on their M.O., but I call 'em *Ego Kooks.* There's other kinds'a kooks, but Ego Kooks believe they can get away with anything, and my idea is that some of 'em liketa brag to feed their ego by thinkin' they're outfoxin' the police. One could easy be the right type for the Borsch killin'. Besides killin' to feed their ego, they phone and leave some fuzzy clues to do more feedin'."

"Then, this is the type we should be looking for?"

"Right now, I'm not sayin' nothin' for certain. Might not be an *ego* killer a'tall. This next type may have some ego kook in 'em, but I call 'em *Righteous.* Might be a *Righteous* leavin' messages as a warnin'. Don't hafta be religion freaks. It's any fool who's got the *right way* all scoped out, and you better get on board before the next comet flies 'cause it's the only way you're gonna squeak by into their idea'a paradise.

'Sometimes, Righteous hear a voice givin' orders—but not any old voice. They get orders direct from a high-level special place only they know about—sometimes backin' up their cockeyed slant on things with what the voices tell 'em. Four years ago, a Righteous head-walnut and three or four'a his lady kernels came into town and commenced preachin' their stuff outside the post office. I run 'em off when they got to botherin' folks too much, and they haven't been back since."

"Dee, you implied there are other types of killers who probably wouldn't phone. I'd like to hear about them, anyhow."

"Well, there's the *Regular* killer bunch made up'a solid citizens. Next are *Revengers* and *Romancers.* After those, it's *Addicts, Abusers* and several other kinds'a kook killers, but I doubt any'a these would be callin'." DeVon described them and added, "There's sex preverts, too, but they're not gonna phone. Neither are mob hitters or mad-dog doers." He drained his glass. "All this talkin's got me too dry to go on."

Zeke mixed him another. "Maybe this will prime the pump. Speak on, Great Chief."

"Well, there's somethin' else to ponder. With these markin's n'all, could be we're dealin' with some new kind'a killer."

"And that is?"

"You know as well as me. It's *cults*—time we start considerin' 'em. Besides the markin's on the hand, there's somethin' else maybe pointin' to 'em. Try this on. Borsch was a good-sized man and in pretty good shape. Probly there'd need to be more'n one perp to manhandle him and do the cuttin' job when he was awake. Wouldn't be easy luggin' him around when he was dead, either. There'd be enough in a cult to get it done.

"Trouble is, Zeke, I don't know enough about cult signs and sacrifices and who joins up and other stuff about 'em. You still tight with that lady friend'a yours at the university—your old blaze—the one I never met 'cause I was away in the service? You could ask her if she'd check in their big library to see if there's anything on cult markin's. Maybe phone her and drive down to talk about it—catch two birds with one stone, so to talk."

Zeke bit his tongue and let the misquotes pass. "She's no old *flame,* only a good friend. She'd probably help out. Guess I could phone if Great Chief so orders his flunky, but I see no reason to drive down."

"Great Chief so orders."

As Zeke rose to punch up the fire, he commented, "This whole thing about the markings and the messages is so *illogical.*"

"Aren't you the guy always sayin' not to make the mistake'a tryin' to put a right-thinkin' explanation on a damnfool act?"

Bookman's question touched off another round of the ongoing debate over Zeke's problem solving by A to B to C logic as opposed to the chief's often voiced detecting theory, K-I-S-S—Keep-it-Simple-Stupid.

The music stopped and their glasses were empty. Zeke was surprised when DeVon asked for another. He responded by quoting cowpoke wisdom, "Never was a horse that couldn't be rode or a rider who couldn't be throwed."

"Just keep pourin', bartender. It's been a long day with no good clues sproutin'."

Zeke mixed the drink, then asked, "What about plans for catching Borsch's killer?"

"Well, a'course we gotta fire on all fronts, startin with the routine stuff that goes on in any homicide investigation. First thing, we'll hafta toss Borsch's house and shop. Another thing is lookin' into his background. Start diggin' and you'd be surprised whatcha find."

"Know enough about his lifestyle since his wife died to think he might've become a skirt chaser? He spent a lot of time at his health club—heard anything about him scratching around in the hen house while the rooster's away?"

"Plan to put Wilson on it in the mornin'. He'll go in plainclothes—join up—act like a member. Young stud like him is more likely to get answers in a place like that. Never gave too much believin' to the gossip about Borsch tomcattin' around over there, but maybe there was a spooky-do hubby with a sharp knife. Wilson can also bird-dog around to see if the barber was mixed up in any nutso stuff."

"Blackmail?"

"Doubt there's much use in lookin' at blackmail—don't think hand-carvin' fits this kind'a crime, butcha never know. We'll check if he did any unusual bankin' business."

The chief drained the dregs of his drink and rattled the cubes for another. Zeke mixed a short one. "The bar closes after this. When there was only a hand, you mentioned something about kids being involved. Throwing out the idea now that a body's been found?"

Not thrown' nothin' out. Kids could even be mixed up in cults. Need to check if there's wierdo stuff goin' on at the high school. Gonna get Mickner to send over his cult-guy to meet with the principal."

"Plan on talking with Miss Martha?"

When there was no answer, Zeke saw that his friend was nearly asleep, but he straightened with a jerk. "Good idea, but I doubt she's got anything to tell. Don't know if Borsch ever said one word to her."

"Anything else?"

"Thinkin'a formin' a task force and puttin' Smithson in charge. Smitty's good at lots'a routine stuff. Works good with the men, too. I put him up for promotion to lieutenant three times, but the penny-pinchin' council wouldn't budget for it."

"Great Chief, why don't we talk some more about the meaning of the numbers on Borsch and the answering machine?"

Silence. Zeke looked at DeVon for his answer, then took a closer look. His last Snake Bite was already history, and he was dead to the world—sitting straight up and out like a light. Zeke went over, took his glass, toppled him sideways, head resting on a couch arm, legs sticking out like fence posts over the other. He spread a blanket over the sleeping giant and turned out the lights.

The phone rang. *(What the...!)* "Hello!"

"Zeke—Lurinda here. It's getting late, and Dee said he'd phone. He hasn't, and I'm a little worried. He there?"

"Not to fret. He's fast asleep under his blankey. From the sounds of it, I'd say he'll saw twenty logs into toothpicks before he rouses."

"Good. Zeke, as long as I have you on the phone—that new town council bunch has been giving him some flack. Think they'll try to make trouble?"

"Wouldn't worry too much about the council. He's always been pretty good at handling them. Sleep well, Lurinda."

"Thank you, Zeke. I'll save you a cinnamon roll." Zeke was so beat he flopped onto his bed for a minute's rest before undressing. In seconds he was oblivious even to the bull-elephant snores rattling the living room windows. The minute's rest lasted till six a.m.

14

Awakening at his usual time, Zeke struggled up and sat on the side of the bed. He could swear he heard various parts of his body complaining. Occasionally he joined in with an audible expression of sympathy. The living room couch rustled, and the foghorn passing as a human being blasted off. *(Criminitly! How can one person make that much racket! You'd think he'd snore himself right onto the floor. Oh well, let him sleep—probably going to need it today.)* Stretching stiff muscles one by one, he stood and snapped on the light. *(Ye gods, I slept in my clothes!)*

A shower did its best, but Zeke was still only about sixty percent after he toweled and shaved. Only then did he remember the package of fresh laundry left in the front entryway. Bare-butted, he traipsed out to retrieve it. As he passed through the living room, a raspy early-morning voice greeted him. "Praise the Lord! I've died and gone up to heaven. I'm with the angels! There's one goin' by now! Chubby little rascal, too, just like in the pictures."

Zeke grunted that DeVon looked like death on toast and not able to see *anything* through those eyes. When he returned, his guest was sitting erect, more or less, scratching here and there and griping about bad booze and a lumpy bed.

"Didn't notice dissatisfaction with the booze last night, and the bed must not've been too awful—your snoring sounded like a love-sick buffalo. Don't look like too much, either—something like a dog-food horse."

"Never felt better. Let's go get 'em!" Bookman jumped to his feet, then grabbed his head and toppled back onto the couch.

Zeke was not sympathetic. "What'd you expect? Anyone who'd throw down Snake Bites till his eyeballs turned inside out."

"Anybody ever mention what a hard man you are, Tanner? Any coffee?"

"Go shower while I make it."

"Gotta extra blade? Razor? Shavin' cream?"

"Medicine cabinet."

DeVon dog-tracked off to the shower, and looked a little less comatose when he returned. However, his head wasn't improved when Zeke told him he forgot to buy coffee. "How do I get out'a this chicken outfit? Let's go down to the diner and pound on the back door."

There was no need to knock. Lurinda was already busy getting ready for the breakfast crowd. One glance at DeVon and she guided them through the kitchen to counter stools. "Looks like you slept in those clothes, Bookman. Suppose there's no sense asking how many Snake Bites and how little sleep it took to render you into this state. One of you'd lie, and the other'd swear to it." She filled their mugs to the brim and sat the carafe between them.

Zeke picked up his cup. "Dee, you're a lawman. Is it a crime to be perfect?"

Bookman tended to his coffee and kept quiet. Twyla Jean came in, eyed the two the very same as she would any skid-row bums, sniffed, and strode by without a word. The nose tilt said it all.

DeVon, feeling better as the caffeine kicked in, poked Zeke. "I could be wrong, but it looks like womenfolk in this establishment don't approve'a somethin'. Whataya think it is?"

"Why don't you ask them?"

"May be crazy. Stupid I am not."

The early morning crowd began to drift in. Over their bacon and eggs, the chief and Zeke fielded questions. Finally, DeVon stood and rapped his glass with a spoon. Twyla Jean responded from down the counter, "The coffee's right there in front of you. A night's sleep and a gallon less booze and you could see it."

"Not coffee I want, TeeJay." DeVon rapped the glass again, harder this time, and the conversation at the tables and booths died out. "Allaya know Bill Borsch was murdered and we found him on Bailey Bridge. I don't want a bunch'a Sam Tracys on the loose playin' cop, but anything you think would be helpful, lemme know, will you?"

"OK:" "You bet." "Will do, Chief."

Zeke asked, all innocence, "Going to present them a Good Citizen's Award the same time you give one to Mrs. Bannister's doggie?"

"For that, you pay." The chief was getting back to normal.

At the station, Zeke became very busy answering calls about the case. During a rare lull, he telephoned the university. After going through a half-dozen transfers and assorted voice-mail hells, he was at last connected to Marjorie Louise Bond, a quantum leap into his past. Years ago, Marjorie Louise was a good friend, all right, but not just a *good* friend. She was a *very* good friend. In fact, she and Zeke were involved in a true college romance, and the fire flamed three years until a small spat grew into a line-in-the-sand standoff. They had a small go 'round about every other week—after all, making up was so pleasant. Only this time, each one decided to out-stubborn the other. All they proved was that they were equally bull-headed. Next thing you knew, Zeke had graduated and Marjorie Louise was married. *And*, her new chance upon one another at a shopping mall when Zeke was attending a coaching clinic at the university.

. In a coffee shop, there was some initial nervous talk including some not altogether pleasant marital history details. Zeke's former wife decided she had enough of the coaching life after five years. Without even so much as a "Dear Zeke" letter, she resigned to live on the left coast. Several years a widow, Marjorie finished her PhD, was employed by the university, advanced through the ranks, became dean, and continued to serve in that position several years now.

Afternoon joined evening, and they adjourned to Pizano's Pizza Palace. Over a large with all the trimmings, they shared a very enjoyable session doing more catching up. After pizza and beer, the conversation mellowed even more, and they parted the greatest of friends again. In the years following, an occasional letter was exchanged. Once, they enjoyed dinner during one of Zeke's infrequent trips to the area.

Marjorie's throaty voice came over the line. "Zeke Tanner! How nice! You in town?"

"Unfortunately, no. I'm calling to bum a favor."

"Fine, but there's a price. First, we catch up."

"My pleasure."

They spent a pleasant twenty minutes discussing their lives since last meeting before he briefed her about the information he wanted about cults. She promised to have someone gather the information quickly. Was there the slightest hint of disappointment in her voice when he said he'd appreciate a phone call as soon as possible? There certainly seemed more than a hint of brightening when he agreed to drive down and lunch with her after she collected the cult data.

Zeke dropped the phone into its cradle and sat looking at it. After a while, he observed aloud, "Careful, old man, a fellow looking into the past too much has his head screwed on backward."

On his way in, DeVon overheard. "When the walls start answerin' back, you got big troubles. Come and go with me to get on with tossin'

Borsch's digs. I wanna do it personal. We'll get the search warrants signed at Judge Jefferson's on the way."

While they waited in the judge's outer office, the chief briefed Zeke on his morning of putting into place plans he talked about the night before, adding, "If the killer isn't found by Monday, everbody who's been doin' anything a'tall on the case will meet to report."

"You've been busy. Anything from the coroner?"

"Phoned with more autopsy findin's. Borsch was suffocated, all right—lungs and blood evidence showed it. Time'a death was probly late Saturday night. He didn't know if Borsch had any dope in him and won't till tests come back. Marks on his ankles and wrists made it look like he could'a been tied real tight. By the way, the hand *did* come from the body. Prints from Borsch's gun permit application matched."

"That it, Great Chief?"

"Not much else except Doc found Borsch's keys on a ring down in his joggin' suit above his ankle. Must'a shook out'a his fanny pack and kept from fallin' all the way out'a the leg by the elastic in the cuff. Doc took 'em to the property room to be inventoried along with the rest'a the stuff. Doubt we'll need 'em. Borsch's house probly isn't locked. If it is, one'a the keys on my ring'll fit. Before I forget to ask—phone your *friend* at the university? Betcha couldn't wait."

"I phoned, Chief Big Beak. She agreed to get the information."

"Bet she agreed to bring it all the way up here, too."

Zeke flared, "She did no such thing." However, he conveniently forgot to mention the tentative lunch date.

"Don't know what to tell you, sports fans. His collection ranges from waitresses to college perfessors."

Before Zeke could react, Judge Jedidiah Jefferson entered. Open a dictionary to the word "judge," and there'd be a picture of Jefferson. He was Hollywood's total package, and no wonder. Handsome, tall and stately with flowing white hair and elegant mustache to match, he groomed and dressed the part. Hear him speak two baritone words and it was easy to assume he also practiced the role. There *was* this one tiny little problem—he wasn't so good at judging. However, he continued to get elected anyway because he was usually relatively harmless. Besides, the town's lawyers were making too much money to fool around with such penny-ante pursuits.

"Good morning, gentlemen. Sorry to keep you waiting, but I had to finish some dictation." The judge had no secretary, but everyone knew how to play the game.

DeVon apologized, "Know you're real busy, your honor, but we need to search Bill Borsch's house and barbershop for evidence. I'm sure you heard he was murdered."

Jefferson reacted very much as if he had *not* heard, but signed the papers Bookman handed him and asked, "Properly made out, I presume?" The chief assured him they were, and he and Zeke left after listening to another five minutes of the judge telling how busy he was.

On the way out, Bookman remarked, "Poor old guy. Gotta remind the men to pinch more chicken thieves and jaywalkers so he won't be so lonesome. Fact is, petty larceny is pretty low. I figure one big reason is the punishment'a havin' to listen to the old codger rattle on with his mottoes and Bible quotes. Makes us bring some prisoners to his office for more lecturin' two or three times durin' their ten-day sentence. They're so bored after a couple trips, most of 'em would rather be stripped and whipped in the town square. I've even had 'em volunteer for the really filthy job'a cleanin' the restrooms at the park to get out'a his lectures."

They arrived at the residence of the departed William Borsch and began their search by walking around outside the house in the trackless snow looking for the unusual and checking windows and doors. None were locked. Zeke followed Bookman through the front door. "You'd be surprised how many people still don't lock up. They're always dumb-dazed when an officer goes over and cuffs a neighbor's kid for doin' the ransackin'."

As they stood looking around the domicile of the departed barber, Zeke recalled the similarity to his parents' house. He thought that if Grant Wood had specialized in painting interiors, he surely would have included this one.

Mrs. Borsch died over four years previously. However, the many potted plants, ferns, large upright piano topped with countless photos, area rugs on hardwood floors, rocker, settee and other period pieces remained as her legacy.

Bookman knew exactly where to look. Several were places Zeke would never consider, including the back end of drawers and behind loose-fitting door frames. Aside from a monumental supply of health foods and a small pile of girlie magazines, there was nothing out of the ordinary. Even the magazines weren't of the gamiest sort.

For whatever else he may've been in the years following his wife's death, Bill was a neat housekeeper. The place was spotless and the grandfather clock current. DeVon wondered about the calendar being turned to January of the New Year. Monday, the 2nd, had a red circle around it and the notation, *Bills—P.O.* "Looks like he wanted to remind himself to get his first'a the month bill payments in the mail. Guess they'll be a little late this time."

They examined Borsch's checkbook. It was one of those large loose-like checkbooks containing only three checks per page. Everything was organized in two sections—one for his household and personal use, one for his business. Neither showed he paid any bill during the last weeks of his life, nor were there any interesting check stubs.

They continued the search until noon and found nothing appearing to be tied to the murder. "So much for the house," declared Bookman. "Don't think we missed nothin'. Once'n a while, somethin's right there and you don't see it, but I don't think so this time. Didn't see a single thing lookin' like evidence and no sign'a nothin' even close to papers MizMartha could be after, either—a will or anything else."

On the porch, the chief took out a ring of keys, chose an old-fashioned skeleton type and locked the door. "No sense leavin' an unlocked-door-invite for some amateur."

Out at the garage, he lifted the unlocked door, and they spent half an hour looking through the neatly stored tools and an assortment of items found in most everyone's garage. Borsch's car doors and trunk were unlocked, of course.

DeVon took an old .38 Colt revolver from the glove box and dropped it into a coat pocket. "At least there'll be one less piece floatin' around."

Again, they found no clues. Before they left, the chief attached POLICE LINE—DO NOT CROSS tapes across the front and garage doors. "Wouldn't be much good for stoppin' a pro, but they might help keep the kids out."

Next stop was the barbershop. They didn't have a key, so DeVon took out his ring. "Never guess how many downtown stores you can unlock with the same key. That's a throwback to the days'a Larry the Locksmith. Larry worked cheap, but he worked sloppy. Some company got him to start a campaign to get the merchants to install new dead-bolt locks, and lots of 'em did. Only thing was, Larry got in a bunch'a locks keyed alike. You know, the tumblers set so the same key fit all of 'em. Instead'a resettin' the tumblers and makin' new keys, he just slapped 'em in. Quite a few store owners didn't bother to get 'em fixed even after they found out. Larry left town pretty soon after that."

Sure enough, the first key unlocked the door. Zeke looked through the front of the shop, DeVon the rear. It was the same as at the house. Nothing suggested itself as a clue to Bill Borsch's demise.

Bookman wasn't too disappointed. "Like I more'n halfway expected." He didn't bother to put a tape across the door. "Don't think many robbers'd try to tap a barbershop."

"Hate to mention it, Stretch, but your little forays have taken us past the noon hour, and the diner's close by."

As in many downtown businesses, a black ribbon hung in the window of the Country Kitchen. Zeke remarked, "Didn't know they still hang ribbons for those who've crossed over."

"Lots'a things change slow in Stony Crossing."

The early afternoon caffeine-canines began drifting into the diner soon after the two sleuths entered and ordered lunch. The regulars heckled them mercilessly for eating a second lunch, refusing to believe their explanation about working well past noon. Even Lurinda joined in, saying she had proof they had already eaten at Jim's Truck Stop.

They could only grin and bear it. Generous portions of the daily special, chicken potpie, mashed potatoes and corn pudding helped them bear up. Apple crisp, too.

After lunch, they walked across the street to talk with Miss Martha Manchester who greeted them with the barest trace of a smile. "What can I do for you today, officers?"

Zeke started to protest he wasn't an officer when DeVon spoke up. "Ezekial Amos needs another answerin' machine tape."

(Oh sure, blame it on old Ezekial Amos.)

"My, but you must get a lot of messages, Ezekial Amos. Is the tape I sold you worn out already? Did you not care for it properly? You must learn to do that."

Zeke's ears reddened. "Yes, ma'am, but my friend here, DeVon Eugene, borrowed it and hasn't returned it." (The only thing Bookman hated more than his middle name was poison ivy up his nose.)

Miss Manchester turned to Bookman. Now it was his turn. "As I recall, it was Shakespeare who said, 'Neither a borrower nor a lender be.' I believe he may've been speaking of money, but it's good for everything. DeVon Eugene, best you return Ezekial's tape."

"Yes, ma'am, as soon as I can."

"See that you do. In the meantime, perhaps you should pay for this tape and call it a lesson for borrowing."

DeVon Eugene gritted his teeth and paid up before asking, "MizMartha, is there anything you might'a thought of to maybe help us find who did this thing to your nephew?"

She answered quickly that she couldn't think of a single thing, then asked, "Chief Bookman, have you had a chance to look for William's personal papers?"

"We're right in the middle'a doin' it, MizMartha. Shouldn't take too much longer."

Once outside, Bookman observed, "She's sure in a rush for what she's callin' 'papers'."

"Probably only wants something to remember him by, Dee."

"Could be, I reckon."

At the station, Zeke typed a short statement and gave it to the deskman with instructions to read it to anyone who phoned, then sat in his chair, thinking. It was a hectic week so far, to say the least, but events were slowing, leaving him with little to do. He swiveled to and fro, worrying the morning's search around in his mind and doodling, not seeing his work. Finally he decided to call it quits. It would be dark before long, and he wanted to give Ace and Bandit some quality time.

As he was leaving, DeVon came from his office. "Borsch's funeral's at 1:30 on Friday. We both better go—maybe we'll see somethin'. The super dicks on TV are always sayin' the criminal goes to the vic's funeral."

"Don't think so, Stretch. Don't do funerals."

"Call it in the line'a duty."

"Borsch had no immediate relatives, so there won't be too many people for Great Chief to look over by himself."

"Never can tell. I'll be by, and try to wear a clean T-shirt, will you?"

It was getting dark before the dogs let Zeke off the hook on his quality-time promise. As he walked toward the house, tiny flakes, advance guard for the overnight snowfall to come, floated gently down through the glow of the porch light.

15

Morning shower over, Zeke found he again forgot to buy coffee. *(Oh well, I'll have breakfast at the diner).* Determined to get his food regimen in order, before leaving he sat and made a list of groceries needed for a diet. *(By golly, I'm going to get on one and stick to it this time.)* Biting cold greeted him as he crunched through three inches of new snow to tend to the dogs. *(Holy Toledo – Indiana's becoming Antarctica!)*

Cussing and coughing, Ol' Emmy protested mightily, but came to life after Zeke's persistent prodding. Between home and the Country Kitchen, her heater made no difference at all, making the warmth of the diner very pleasant indeed—made even more so by the mouthwatering aroma of good food and freshly baked rolls. He sat at the counter and was about to order the origin of those delicious bouquets when the icy stare of Twyla Jean caused him to remember his diet vow. Sighing, he settled for her suggestions of a small orange juice, one boiled egg, one slice of dry wheat toast, four ounces of skim milk and coffee.

He was sipping when his breakfast, DeVon and Bill Mickner arrived simultaneously. Bracketing Zeke at the counter, they leaned toward his plate and made an exaggerated examination of the halved egg from every angle before Bookman inquired, "I say, Mr. Helms, got your detectin' spyglass along? Somethin' here on the counter in front'a Mr. Tanner needs closer inspection."

"Don't need a glass, Dr. Watson. I can see enough by the naked eye to state positively whatever it is wouldn't have lived. Its eyes are too close together."

Twyla Jean overheard. "He who laughs last, laughs best. Ignore the riffraff, Zeke. They get nasty because of what they gobble. Suppose you two chow-hogs want your regular slop."

Feigning hurt, DeVon responded, "Bricks and sticks will always wing me. You've damaged me so much, I'll need a big breakfast to heal up."

"Me too," from Mickner.

Their attempted humor in addition to Zeke's unsatisfied appetite and Bookman's tangled delivery of the "sticks and stones" saying were bad enough. However, they compounded their sins by ordering the Plowboy's Daybreak Special of apple juice, scrambled eggs and bacon, half order of biscuits and gravy, short stack and coffee. "Extra maple syrup for the pancakes, please."

Ignoring his tormentors, Zeke chewed slowly to make every bite last. He was trying to decide whether to risk a Twyla Jean lecture and order another slice of toast when DeVon asked Mickner, "Think it's a good time for our surprise?"

"Might be too much for him on an empty stomach. Maybe we should wait till he digests his mammoth breakfast."

Zeke remained silent and swore to himself he wouldn't play their game. The chief gave up. "If you're gonna beg, I guess we'll hafta tell. Go ahead, Bill."

"Oh all right. Zeke, the second tape from your answering machine? The lab boys are pretty sure the voice is different from the first."

"A second person! How certain?"

"Better than eighty percent."

"Wow, that certainly provides food for thought!"

DeVon began lathering butter onto his pancakes. "Reckon so, Zeke, but food for my belly is what I need right now."

As the two chowhounds were polishing off the remnants of their meals, Dr. Forsythe came in. "Judging from the stack of dead dishes, you three have elevated your cholesterol levels to record highs. What do you intend to do for an encore—eat Ohio? If by some miracle your brains are still functioning, can you manage to drag your bloated bodies over here and bring me up to date?" Neither Bookman nor Mickner thought it wise to answer the doctor's question about their next meal. They picked up their cups and went with Zeke to Forsythe's booth.

Twyla Jean came for the coroner's order. She also straightened him out on the number of gluttons. There were two, not three—Zeke was a good boy today. He looked righteous, but righteousness was a small reward. He was still famished.

Talk swirled idly on about the case, mostly about possible investigative priorities for the Borsch case. Zeke wasn't participating. Finally, DeVon ribbed, "Doctor, see what happens when the husky one goes without an honest breakfast? He loses his tongue."

Zeke responded, "While you two stuffed, I've been considering some ideas about the type of killer we're looking for. Before this latest evidence of two voices, we could only speculate that more than one person was involved in Borsch's murder. If there *is* a different voice on each tape, it certainly lends strong support to the theory that there were others. The other night, Great Chief described his killer types." Zeke reviewed them briefly for the coroner before continuing. "If I'm interpreting him correctly, the two most likely suspects among several types could well be his ego-motivated 'Kook' killer or his 'Righteous.' The ego-driven killer can probably be ruled out because he would likely be acting alone, and no Righteous type has been seen in town for years. If neither of these, then who? Well, a cult would have enough members to do the job, and don't forget those weird markings on Bosch. Big question is—why wouldn't any sign of cult activities be quickly observed? DeVon isn't aware of any activity, but it doesn't necessarily mean that a cult couldn't be responsible. It could be based somewhere else in the county or even in some other location in the state. If my reasoning is sound, placing the highest priority on pursuing the cult theory may indeed be the best way to proceed."

Dr. Forsythe spoke first. "Gentlemen, see what happens when one eats a modest breakfast? It keeps the mind from stagnating."

Again, DeVon wisely avoided responding to the coroner and addressed Zeke. "Whatcha say makes some sense, but we don't wanna forget other possibilities besides cults."

"Anyone see me put a gun to Bookman's head and tell him to ignore everything but cults? When I said *priority*, it implied a prioritized *list*, not the exclusion of all others."

"College smart Alex." The chief rose, put a tip on the table, slid Mickner's and his own check across and announced, "Tanner's payin' for us, Twyla Jean." They walked out to the howls of protests.

Putting off his grocery trek, Zeke drove to the station. Nothing was happening to keep him occupied, and he was about to leave to do his shopping when the deskman buzzed to say there was a phone call for a *Mr. Ezekial Tanner.*

He was surprised to hear Marjorie Louise Bond's voice. *(Bet this'll be all over the place!)* "My, but that was quick, Marjorie. Have something for me already?"

"Sorry, not yet. I called to offer a suggestion. I've spoken to Vince McElroy, head of our Sociology Department. He may be able to help you with your cult questions, and can meet with you Tuesday afternoon. OK with you? I need to tell him today. Arrive early, and we'll have lunch before the meeting."

Zeke saw immediately she wasn't giving him much chance to refuse, but he had more or less agreed to have lunch, hadn't he? "Lunch will be fine. I think it might be interesting to hear what he has to say, but I doubt I'm knowledgeable enough to ask intelligent questions of such a high powered expert."

"Fiddlesticks, consider it a date. See you, Zeke—looking forward to Tuesday."

He hung up and thought about the call. It certainly sounded as though she really meant she was anticipating a pleasurable reunion. *(What the hey, Tanner, you're imagining things. She's only being an obliging friend. Yeah, but how obliging is 'obliging?')* He put it from his mind and left to buy groceries.

Of the three grocery stores in town, two were locally owned. Zeke liked the selection at **Burkholder's Big Bargain Barn** better, especially the meat. However, Call-me-Charlie Ackerman's full-time job was assistant manager. Worse yet, Delbert Dove, the preacher's chief kiss-up and attendance-taker at the church, worked there, too. In addition to being a world-class pest about attendance, shaking the insipid little fellow's limp hand was first cousin to grasping a long expired haddock.

Each time Zeke shopped at Burkholder's, the preacher rushed up and sermonized all over him. If Ackerman were busy, Dove would come from his post behind the meat counter and deluge him with an on-the-run sermon about regular church going. Zeke might've tolerated even that if it weren't for the finnan-haddie handshakes proceeding and following it. He bypassed Burkholder's and drove farther on out to **JENSEN'S**—*55 Years Your Home Town Grocery* where he could shop in relative peace.

Placing his order at the meat counter with the third generation Jensen, Carl III, Zeke fielded the usual questions with: "Yes, sure is cold." "No, don't miss coaching a bit." "Yes, maybe we'll have an early spring." "No, nothing new on the case, but we're working on it."

Zeke whistled when he spied the prices. "Wow! Didn't want to buy the whole cow, only a few parts."

The youngest Carl Jensen displayed his best be-kind-to-you-elders smirk. "Thank you for your business, Mr. Tanner. I'm sure it'll go a long way toward paying this month's bills."

"Smart-mouth," Zeke grunted under his breath and headed for the pickles. He was only part way when it hit him. *(Bills!)* Wheeling quickly to the checkout counter, he found it manned by the second generation Jensen, Carl Jr. "I was back there and overheard the disrespectful remark my son made, Mr. Tanner. You can be sure I'll deal with him strictly about it."

(Deal with him? For Pete's sake! His son's in his mid-twenties, not in junior high.) "Oh, that's all right. I'm not upset with him."

"Nevertheless."

Zeke paid, hustled out to Ol' Emmy and coerced her back to the station. DeVon was leaning back in his chair, feet up, eyes nearly closed. For a second, Zeke thought he was asleep, but the chief was observing him beneath lowered eyelids. "Podner, from the look on your face, either you got a belly cramp or had another brain-pain from lack'a breakfast. Which?"

"Can we go back to Borsch's?"

"Right now?" Bookman asked even as his boots thumped down and he rose. On the way out, he asked, "Wanna tell me what this wild duck chase is all about?"

"Logic. It's about logic."

"Oh Lord, his brain really is starved from lack'a food. Go ahead, perfesser."

"Think about it, Stretch. You saw Borsch's calendar with the second day of the month circled? We thought it was to remind him to pay his bills. Think it could mean anything else?"

"What else besides him drawun' a circle around a date? You figure somethin' more? Comin' up with some'a your *logical*, Sherwood?"

"I say again, think about it. If Borsch drew a circle to remind him to write checks for bills and take them to the post office, there would be some bills wouldn't there? Or at least some record of payments? Everything was filed in exact order. I'm certain I saw receipts for his utilities and other bills dating back a couple months, but don't remember any he received or paid after the first days of December. You see any, Chief Eagle Eye?"

"Now you mention it, not a one. Can't figure not pickin' up on 'em bein' missin'. Remember any at the barbershop?"

"No, I don't. If they're not at either place, why are they missing, and where could they be? I know it might not mean anything. What do you think?"

"Maybe somethin', maybe nothin'. Anyhow, we better have another look. Everthing hasta be checked in a murder investigation."

Bookman unlocked Borsch's front door and went straight to the roll-top desk in the dining room. Once again, they pored through pigeonholes, drawers, and a cardboard file folder. They even checked the mailbox on the porch—nothing anywhere. As their last step, they examined Borsch's checkbook again and determined they hadn't overlooked anything the first time around—neither household nor business section showed the barber received or paid any bills during the last weeks of his life.

DeVon stood and stretched. "Well, Zeke, looks like we know for absolute certain-sure Borsch got no first'a the month bills or paid any, but knowin' that don't get us any closer to why. Don't know what it means—maybe nothin' a'tall. But it's like I said, you gotta check everthing in a murder investigation. Anyway, I think we oughta scoop up this checkbook and the rest'a the papers to hold for evidence—just in case. Then we better shoot down to the barbershop and give it the once-over again. No use bruisin' our brains till we're positive there's no bills there, either." Before leaving, they looked through Borsch's car and garage a second time. Again, they found nothing. Nor was their luck any better at the barbershop.

Once again, they worked through the noon hour. Once again, the early-afternoon coffee bunch gave them the business about eating two lunches. Over coffee, they speculated as to why they couldn't locate Borsch's bills. Bookman, as cops do everywhere during investigations, kept notes as he went along. He pulled out a worn notebook and began flipping through the pages.

Zeke watched for a while before asking, "Got the answer there?"

"No, but I think there's one more thing we need to do. I put down some'a the places Borsch sent bill payments for other months. I think it might be a real good idea to phone a couple to see whether he already sent a check durin' December. Better also call the bank to see if he used any other checkbook."

A call to the bank revealed Borsch had no additional checkbooks. Other calls revealed that he paid no bills during the month of December—not for his utilities, newspaper, medical insurance or health club. Mildred Sanford, manager of the Stony Crossing Water Company, said it wasn't unusual for Mr. Borsch's check not to come in on the first, but never more than a day or two later. "He always paid that way."

"Whataya mean, 'He always paid that way'?"

"Well, Chief Bookman, we send out the bills on the fifteenth, and they're due by the first, but lots of people send their check right on the first—lots of people." There was more than a touch of "scold" in her voice.

After the chief finished telephoning, he and Zeke worried the bills questions around until DeVon said, "Hell, we're not gettin' anyplace on this. C'mon and ride to Wayne City with me. Somebody's gotta run that Swineford kid over to the county jail to serve his 90 days for rustlin' and eatin' Paul Smith's hog. Might as well be us."

By the time the usual friendly between-cops insults were traded, a report on the Borsch killing given, the pork lover delivered for incarceration and the paperwork completed, it was near the dinner hour. DeVon suggested they have a bite before heading back. Zeke didn't argue, but jacked up his will power and ordered the diet plate.

Bookman dropped him off beside Ol' Emmy and reminded, "Don't forget to be ready for the funeral tomorrow. By that time, I'll expect you to have figured out where those missin' bills are."

16

All things considered, Zeke thought it a good day for a funeral, if there were such a thing. The lingering snow-bearing weather front finally moved out and a rare mid-winter, diamond-bright day dawned.

Zeke roughhoused with the dogs before thinking about breakfast. Arriving home so late yesterday, he put off the rest of his grocery shopping until this morning. Then he remembered the groceries left on the rear seat of Ol' Emmy all night.

The main casualties were frozen meat, milk and eggs. Fortunately, he hadn't put many perishables in his cart before the missing-bills idea struck him. The eggs were goners, of course, the bacon granite-hard. Breakfast was going to be cereal. He cut off the milk-carton top, chiseled chunks into a bowl and nuked it into skim-milk slush. Spooning it over the cereal before tossing on raisins and two canned-peach halves, he swore to get his dieting, shopping and cooking acts together.

Upon sampling his creation, he decided with a little mixing it wasn't so bad. Maybe he'd go commercial—call it "Casserole de Cereale Tanner." No coffee, though—he didn't get to it yesterday. *(By golly, I'm going to buy ten pounds next trip.)*

Listening to the stereo while house cleaning was tempting, but this was Friday already, and no matter what, he was determined to buy groceries. No way was he going to get caught in the dreaded Saturday shopping disaster. Never much fun, it was a page from purgatory on Saturdays. Shopping carts were always parked every which way blocking his aisle while their owners held their weekly reunion. Without fail, a brat alongside the cart just ahead of him was hollering up a storm for not being allowed to throw in another bag of buzzy-wuzzys. After these and many more such aggravations, Zeke regularly was forced to wait while the lady with the overloaded cart careened in front of him into the checkout lane manned by a trainee. There followed an argument over the price of every other item, causing further delay while the rookie cashier called someone to check the price of the Spud-Buds. The Cro-Magnon who finally arrived took so long to complete his mission it was obvious he had trouble making plane connections to Boise. Mrs. Shopper topped off her performance by writing a check on a bank four counties away.

Congratulating himself for avoiding Saturday at the market, Zeke crossed off the final item on his list in record time. With four bags of supplies on the kitchen table, he ignored the blinking red light of the answering machine until the food was stored. Then he skipped over the messages from reporters who evidently planned to do a follow-up on the Borsch case for their weekend editions. Finally, Bookman came on saying he'd be coming by at noon so they could eat before attending Borsch's funeral.

Zeke looked at his watch—eleven o'clock. Two minutes later, DeVon banged the door. He was in standard form. "Surely you don't figure on goin' to the funeral in those rags. How'll they know which one to bury?"

"You were supposed to be here at noon. What're you doing here already? Run out of papers to push around?"

"Somebody's gotta see to it you get presentable. Bought groceries? Remember coffee? Why don'tcha make a pot? Maybe make you less of a grouch."

Beans dumped into the grinder, Zeke asked, "Anything new?"

"Not to speak of. Coroner called. Wasn't any illegal dope in Borsch, only a trace'a somethin' they haven't got a fix on yet."

Zeke filled two king-size mugs. "Thought any more about possible suspects?"

"Your thinkin' about cults is probly solid. Hopin' by Monday's meetin' with everbody reportin', there'll be more stuff on his background. On possible nuts walkin' around, too. Come up with any new ideas about those missin' bills?"

"Nope."

After Zeke dressed for the funeral, DeVon suggested, "Let's go down and get some lunch before the funeral. Catfish today, y'know."

"Can't. You know very well I'm trying to diet. I'm fixing no-cal low-cal. Care for some?"

"Tell you what—since it looks like you're serious about starvin', I'll eat here, but none'a that rabbit-chow. Fry me a couple burgers and scare up somethin to go with 'em."

After lunch, the two Sherlocks reluctantly headed to the church. They delayed going in until the last moment, sharing as they did the opinion a corpse was the world's greatest nuisance and that the largest collection of undiluted hypocrites in captivity attended funerals.

Contrary to Zeke's prediction of a small group of mourners, the church was filled almost to overflowing. They had to take a rear pew, which was fine by them. From there they had the best view of the crowd and could make a break for the door at the earliest opportunity. Zeke hadn't the faintest notion of what they were supposed to be observing, but maybe there'd be a stranger or two of interest.

DeVon and Zeke speculated about why someone with no local relatives could possibly attract such a surprisingly large turnout. Even a few out-of-town third cousins who probably hadn't thought of the expired in twenty years were there. Zeke said perhaps funerals were something of a social event for some. Bookman thought quite a few came to congratulate themselves on not being up there in the box, others to grab a glimpse of an actual murder victim.

Beyond the question of who did in the deceased, there was a second air of mystery among the mourners. Most knew preacher Ackerman felt missing church for anything but deathbed illness was a one-way, greased-skid ticket to hell-fire. How would he handle Borsch's poor attendance record? No doubt about it, he wouldn't "preach the barber into heaven," but would he do the opposite?

He could and would, more or less. Yes, most of his life, the deceased was what many would call a "good moral man." Yes, he was a man devoted to his dear wife until she passed to the great kingdom in the sky after a lifetime of good works and regular church going. Yes, many had fond memories of the good deeds of Mr. Borsch. Yes, etc. Yes, etc. Yes, etc. But *(Ah-hah, the big 'BUT.')*, for all his good works, in his later years the departed made the mistake of many. The former brother fell into ways not found in the Good Book. No doubt, he intended, as so many do, to return to his earlier teachings and regular church attendance. But as other departed backsliders found, it was too late. It wasn't for him, H. Charles Ackerman, God's minister, to make a prediction about Bill-the-Barber's future abode. After all, the Lord is a forgiving Lord. But, it would've been ever so very much better if Mr. Borsch practiced regular church going.

On and on he rolled. With all the emphasis on regular attendance, Zeke wondered about Delbert Dove who nodded agreement at each of Call-me-Charlie's pontifications. Might Dull Delbert be asked to call the roll before the audience marched around to take a last look at the main attraction? Zeke determined not to chance it and plotted his escape.

At last the preacher wound down, and it was time for the final viewing. A blanket from the elbows downward thoughtfully covered Borsch, which no doubt disappointed some. Zeke was almost positive old lady Gibson sneaked a tug on the blanket, probably trying to cop a peek at the stray hand. He watched as each row of mourners moved toward the center aisle for their trip up front for a last look-see. When he and DeVon reached the center, they turned right instead of left and kept going toward the rear door. As far as they were concerned, they'd seen too much of Bill Borsch already.

Bookman insisted they accompany the entourage to the cemetery. All right, so it was cold, but maybe there'd be something to see. After watching the last of the mourners depart, they agreed they hadn't observed anything except about seventy-five percent of those at the church passed up the grand finale. Zeke said he had enough of crime for a while and intended to forget the whole to-do, crank up his stereo, and hibernate for the weekend.

17

Monday morning, Zeke whipped up a zesty breakfast of orange juice and inch-square, cardboard-tasting wheat-cereal things allegedly fit for human consumption. Afterwards, he bullied Ol' Emmy to life and they grumbled their way to the station. He didn't even look at the diner on the way.

About 8:30, the principles taking part in the Borsch informational meeting began drifting in, including Dr. Forsythe, Sergeant Wilson, and Bill Mickner along with his cult expert, Trooper McHenry. Sergeant Smithson and two officers assigned to him as an informal task force to help work the case came in together. Even Sheriff Leon Laddis somehow learned of the meeting and had the audacity to invite himself.

High expectations for new information soon turned to disappointment. Very little surfaced everyone didn't already know.

Additional forensic evidence confirmed Dr. Forsythe's earlier findings, including the time of death, its cause as suffocation, and that the hand was likely amputated prior to death.

Sergeant Wilson summarized his investigation at the Heaven Health Us Club. "Nothin' happenin' except the usual grab-ass goin' on in a place where people run around in underwear-lookin' stuff pretendin' it's workout gear. Don't look like Borsch was mixed up in any weird doin's or with any screwballs. Figure I'll need another month to look more into things." (Hoots and jeers erupted.) Bookman gave him until the end of the week.

Lardass Laddis asked to speak and took fifteen minutes to give a two-minute spiel about cooperating with the local "po-leece." Nothing of value, naturally. The sheriff acted as though he expected a round of applause before finally resuming his seat.

Sergeant Smithson offered bits and pieces from the task force. He hoped to have more soon.

Trooper McHenry was next. Ears perked up. Everyone there knew about the markings. "I'm only starting on this assignment and will bring Sergeant Smithson into the information loop right away. I haven't had time to do a thorough canvas of the area, but I've yet to see evidence of cults anywhere."

Bookman interjected, "What should the officers be lookin' for in the way'a signs? Do cults tag the same way as gangs?"

"Although symbols and markings spray-painted on buildings and overpasses are most often gang signs, they should also be viewed as possible evidence of cult activities. Sometimes it's hard to tell the difference. I'll pass out a pamphlet showing many of the more commonly recognized gang and cult markings, but new ones are popping up all the time. It's a good idea to check out any appearing."

Someone asked whether McHenry thought the Borsch killing was most probably cult related. "It's almost impossible to say at this time. Given Mr. Borsch's background, it seems unlikely he'd be involved with a cult, but you never know. Maybe someone is trying to make it look like a cult or gang crime to throw you off the trail. Or, it could be a message only the killer, his followers, or his targets would recognize."

The trooper answered a few more questions and concluded with, "You shouldn't think this town's too small for cults. Neither population size nor boundaries limit them. Sooner or later, most places will probably experience some activity."

The chief thanked everyone and summarized additional information, some of which was already known by the others. There was nothing out of the ordinary in Borsch's background. Charlie Harrison at the bank turned up nothing among other banks relating to transactions involving Borsch. No police jurisdiction or mental hospital offered anything relevant. No citizen stepped forward with a shred of information, good or bad. Bookman said nothing of Borsch's missing bills or of the cryptic messages left on Zeke's answering machine, reasoning it would only lead to additional needless theorizing and a loss of focus.

Letting the questions, speculations and brainstorming continue until everything was repeated at least twice, DeVon finished with, "We gotta keep pluggin'. You all know that after the first ten days, a case gets colder by the minute." Before he called a halt, he warned against concentrating too much on the cult theory while overlooking other possibilities.

Before leaving for lunch, Zeke spent the remainder of the morning preparing a press release and attending to inquiries. In his kitchen, diet dressing applied to salad and soup ready for nuking, he mulled over the pieces of the Bill-the-Barber puzzle as he ate. Part way through the salad, he gave up and picked up a magazine borrowed from a stereo store, the front cover consisting of the usual come-on headlines about new equipment. Reading down the list of new amplifiers along the left side, he couldn't see much of the bottom line, which was partially covered by the store's address label. Carefully, be began peeling it off. Something stopped him. What was unusual? He stared at the address. *(The Ultimate in Sound, P.O. Box 1253....Wait a second! 'P.O. Box?')* Leaving the remains of the salad, he went quickly to Ol' Emmy.

As he wheeled left into the intersection and onto the main drag, he was asking a lot of the old girl to beat the car approaching from the right. Making it by only a fender-whisker and ignoring the raucous horn-retort of the aggrieved driver, he "sped" toward the Country Kitchen, hoping DeVon was still at lunch. For a change, there was a space right in front. Braking as rapidly as possible, he careened across traffic into the angled parking spot. The ancient Blazer, long since incapable of performing a tire-squealing stop-and-turn, put the pursuing driver in no peril. However, he tailgated Zeke from the pullout incident and gave him another blast as he passed, as did the oncoming driver whom Zeke aced out of the parking space.

DeVon was standing at the cash register with his tab and witnessed the second incident from the diner's window. Zeke rushed in only to hear him scold, "By golly, Andretti, I knew you couldn't stand to miss the pie, but there's a law against runnin' over anybody to get here."

"Forget the bull, Bookman. Pay up and follow me to the station."

In the office, DeVon began his after-lunch pipe ceremony. "OK, Eisenhower, what's the story?"

"Stretch, the name you want is *Einstein*. When we searched Borsch's places, was there any mail?"

"Correction police are on the job! I *said* Eisensteiner. Anyway, Whataya mean, was there any mail? A'course there was—mostly junk. There weren't any bills for the month'a December, I'm sure'a that. Got any more probin' questions?"

"One. What was the address on the mail?"

"Borsch's address—you know that."

"Yes, but what was the address?"

"Dammit, Tanner, cut the crapola and spit it out."

"Some of his mail was addressed to a post office box number and not to a street address. We didn't check about a post office box. Remember, the note on his calendar was '*Bills—P.O.*' We thought it was a reminder to *mail* his bills. What if it was a reminder to go to the post office and *pick up* mail from a P.O. box?"

The chief paused, squinting at Zeke over the match he held in mid-air over his pipe. "If he had a box number, a'course he had a box. Must'a picked up his mail instead'a gettin' it delivered. Lots'a the downtown merchants do. Get their mail earlier in the day that way. He couldn't'a picked up his mail Monday, the second'a January—him bein' dead, n'all. Reckon we better see if he still had a box and if there's mail in it. You'd think he would'a gotten his bills before the first'a the month, though." The flame reached his finger, and he jerked his hand sideways. "Ouch!"

"You could call the postmaster."

Bookman tossed his pipe into the ashtray. "No, let's just go over there—too easy to get the runaround on the phone. Even if there's a box and there's mail, I doubt there'll be a clue, but we gotta check everthing."

"Won't need a warrant or something?"

"Paperwork's lots'a trouble when you're messin' with the government. I'll talk nice."

Short and slightly built, Postmaster Abel Hofstettler perched on his stool behind the customer window in the deserted post office and surveyed his domain. He's been employed there all his working years, postmaster for a dozen. After being denied a career in the military because of poor eyesight, there were only two things he wanted in life—becoming postmaster and being elected a church elder. He's proud to have achieved both. Neatness and uniformity are his personal credos, attested to by the plastic sleeve guards and pocket protectors in stiffly starched shirts, slicked down hair, and the lengthy list of employee rules posted all over the building.

Being unprofessional Abel Hofstettler simply could not abide. Therefore, DeVon knew it would take some doing to get the scrawny government man to come across concerning anything about someone else's mail. He'd probably hem and haw, reaffirming the sanctity of his high office and the patron's mail, before finally becoming somewhat cooperative. So, his immediate response to Bookman's opening question about whether Borsch had a postal box came as no surprise.

"This is a United States Postal Service post office. There are many rules and regulations governing the privacy of a patron's mail. Protecting that privacy is a sacred trust." Etc., etc.

The chief waited patiently, then asked, "Can't even tell me if Borsch had a box?"

"Well, I guess it would be all right to tell you he did."

Bookman appeared satisfied. "Much obliged for the info, Abel."

Their business apparently quickly over, DeVon chatted with the postmaster about this and that, then inquired, "Why did Borsch have a box in the first place? Wouldn't seem a barber needed to get his mail early in the day like the merchants do."

"Mr. Borsch rented a box a year or two before his wife died. She'd get forgetful and misplace the mail or lose it, so he fixed the problem by renting a box and coming to the post office for his mail. The address it came to didn't make any difference. We put everything in his box, no matter if it had his street address on it. After his wife died, Mr. Borsch just kept the box."

Bookman made as if preparing to leave. Hofstettler was clearly relieved to see the chief was going to depart without asking anything about Borsch's mail. Near the door, DeVon turned back and snapped his fingers. "By golly, I forgot to ask—isn't there apt to be mail in Borsch's box?"

The postmaster was taken off guard, but determined to evade the issue as long as possible. "I wouldn't know. One of my employees is in charge of placing mail in the boxes. After someone's passed, postal regulations say any mail sent to them is immediately returned to the sender if there's a return address. If not, there are other procedures to follow. So, Chief Bookman, any mail in Mr. Borsch's box should've been returned already. I'll certainly need to speak to my employee if he hasn't done so. It's unlikely there would be mail, anyway—Mr. Borsch got so little. He came in only every so often to pick it up, but he always came in a day or two before the first of the month. He'd pick it up one day and mail his bills the next. I'm sorry to say some box patrons who don't get very much mail only come in every few days, then put their monthly bills back in their box and don't take them out until around the first to pay them all at once. Using a United Stated Postal Service post office box as their file cabinet is not a good practice, but Mr. Borsch was one who did. Since the first fell on Sunday, no doubt Mr. Borsch came in last Saturday."

DeVon bore down. "Maybe he didn't get his mail Saturday. It was his busiest day, y'know. Lots'a times, he worked right through the noon hour, and you close at one o'clock." The chief moved right up to the window, nearly filling it. "And, maybe your man hasn't got around to returnin' Borsch's mail yet. Now then Abel, a duly authorized peace officer needs your help. S'pose you go on back there and bring everthing in Borsch's mailbox up here."

Hofstettler didn't move. Bookman stood there looking down at him. During the lengthy silence, Zeke could hear the old Regulator clock ticking. The postmaster conceded. "Oh all right, I guess I could *show* you his mail if there's any. Remember though, we can't *open* it."

"Sure thing, Abel, bring whatever there is."

Hofstettler returned with ten letters. Four looked to be glass-windowed bills and all the rest except one obviously advertisements. The exception was a plain white envelope, no return address, post-marked December 26th, and addressed to Borsch's house number.

Bookman held it up to the light. "Can't see a thing—paper inside's too thick." He turned it over and picked at the flap.

Hofstettler was just short of horrified. *"What're you doing!"* He grabbed for the letter, but the chief jerked it away. "Just checkin' to see if the envelope's sealed proper."

"Of course it is!"

"But if it's not, would it be against regulations to read a letter if it fell out?" DeVon continued to worry the flap until it was halfway un-done. "Must be a regulation that'd let a lawman read it in such a case."

"Chief Bookman, I know of no such regulation. Even if there is, which I doubt, what you're doing is illegal because the envelope's sealed tightly. Look at it, Mr. Tanner. You can see it's sealed."

"From where I'm standing, I can't really be sure one way or the other." *(Ye gods, I'm getting as bad as Bookman!)*

The flap came completely unsealed. DeVon spread and shook the envelope. A single page dropped to the floor.

The chief stooped for it and announced, "Why, look here, Mr. Postmaster, look what fell out'a this unsealed envelope. Wonder what it says." Handling it by the edges, he unfolded the sheet and stared at the contents, then held it so Zeke could see but Hofstettler couldn't. Drawn carefully was a black heptagon with a number in the middle crossed out with a diagonal stripe. However, this time the number was *68*, not the *70* on Borsch's torso. There was another difference. On his body, the numbers were 1 1 8 2 2. Here, widely spaced as they had been before, were 1 1 1 1 5.

Bookman replaced the paper in its envelope, put it in his coat pocket, and turned to leave. At the door he said to Hofstettler, "I'll return this after makin' a copy and checkin' it for prints. Meantime, let's keep this little matter to ourselves and leave your district supervisor out of it. OK?" They left to the postmaster's nervous nodding.

In the chief's office, Zeke sat drinking squad-room paint-thinner coffee and Dee loaded up for a smoke while they discussed Borsch's odd letter. A copy lay on the desk between them. With the usual, "Mum's the word," the original was handed to Sergeant Smithson to check for prints.

After a while, DeVon sighed and remarked, "To tell the truth, I was still hangin' onto the idea the stuff drawn on Borsch's parts only meant somethin' to whoever drew it or maybe it was put there to throw us off. This letter shows me it could mean other things. For instance, maybe Billy-boy could'a known what it meant, but didn't pick up the letter in time to see it. Then he got erased almost by mistake."

"By mistake?"

"The postmark's December 26th, the better part of a week before he was offed. Not knowin' he didn't pick up the letter, it could'a looked to the sender like the barber ignored what he knew was a warnin' and hadta pay." Bookman sighed. "There's only one thing wrong with such thinkin'. Could be the letter was from nutso who didn't care if Borsch knew what it meant or not."

"Then why would they bother to send the letter to him at all if they thought he wouldn't know its meaning?"

"How'n hell do I know! Nut cases don't hafta have a reason for anything."

"Great Chief, we better stop for today, or we'll start seeing little green men dropping from the ceiling. I'm out of here. I have some work to do on the stereo—tubes are still acting up. May need to go to Indy to pick up a part tomorrow. It'll give you some time to try to get your alleged brain in gear."

Bookman's buzzer complained. He listened to the phone for a second and simpered, "It's for a *Mr. Ezekial Tanner.* Somebody from the university. Who in the wide world could be calling, *Ezekial?*"

Zeke grabbed the phone. It was Marjorie Louise Bond, of course, wanting to know whether their lunch date was still on. He tried as best he could to answer without letting DeVon in on his lunch plans for the next day. The verbal needle would be rusty, an inch square, and a yard long. Zeke handed the phone back with a quick, "See you later, Ethel."

The chief had the same look he used on suspects with a suspicious story. "You bet. Say hello to the lady. Be sure to get all the dope on cults and phone me when you get back. Also, *Ezekial*, try not to eat with your fingers. College folks have a way'a frownin' on that." The door slammed on his last words.

18

The brass raised-letter nameplate proclaimed this to be the offices of Dr. M. Louise Bond, Dean. Zeke flinched at the "Dr." and "Dean." More than once on the drive down, he considered turning back. He could've made some lame excuse about an emergency or something. It would be great to see Marjorie Louise again, but he didn't want to be in a situation where she might be forced to "explain" him to any other big wheel on campus. After all, he was only an ex high school coach who hadn't gone beyond his master's degree. How would she handle the intros?

He stood outside, brushing at his sleeves and trying to straighten a balky tie knot while his imagination answered his question with the likes of, "This is Mr. Tanner. I met him a long time ago, and here he is again. He wants us to help him, poor man." (Knowing smiles from those in Armanis and Guccis.)

While Zeke considered bolting options, a figure appeared beside him and inquired, "I say, if you have no plans to use the door, mind if I do?"

The fellow was clad in loafers, jeans, elbow-patched cord sport jacket and denim shirt with the two top buttons open. He definitely looked a trifle old to be a down-in-the-pockets student, but further inspection revealed the look was carefully orchestrated and no doubt expensive.

Zeke's apprehensions were heightened by other attributes of Mr. Cool—about 6-foot-2, 180, full head of wavy hair, Vandyke beard. Hardy type, too—no topcoat. After stepping aside and offering the doorknob, Zeke sucked in his middle and followed.

Apparently Mr. Cool had the run of the place. With only a wave of the hand, he walked right by the secretary and into Dean Bond's inner office. The young lady at the computer smiled at him but didn't slow her typing as he breezed by. Things whirred and clicked. It didn't take a genius to figure the plot of a youngish, good looking, fully haired, slender specimen walking right on in as if he owned the place. What the hey, who Marjorie Louise chose as a pet was nothing to him, was it?

The secretary stopped typing and turned her smile on Zeke. "May I help you, sir?"

"My name is Tanner. I have an appointment with Dean Bond."

"Oh yes! Mr. Zeke Tanner. Dean Bond said to go in the minute you got here."

"But I saw someone go in just now. Shouldn't I wait until he's finished?"

"Oh no, that's Dr. McElroy. He's the one you're going to be meeting with."

(Drat!) Zeke thought lunch was only between Marjorie Louise and him. Mentally, he shook himself. *(Get a grip! What were you expecting, anyhow?)*

The office looked like those pictured in the business magazines stuck inside the pocket on the back of an airplane seat—lustrous dark wood, glassed-in bookcases, playing-field-size desk, leather executive chair, and the best wall-to-wall carpet. It only served to remind him how far it was from a cubicle located next to a sweat-smelling locker room and passing as a high school coach's office. That Marjorie Louise Bond looked as though she arrived minutes before from a world-class makeover didn't help. He resisted an urge to go into a fit of knot-straightening and sleeve-brushing.

"Zeke Tanner! It's been too long! Come on in here!" She strode over and gave him a big hug and kiss. Not the phony air-kiss kind, but an honest-to-gosh smooch. He was so startled, he forgot to suck in his middle.

Before he could develop a mumbled response, Marjorie Louise took his hand and towed him across the room. "I want you to meet Vince McElroy. He's the one who'll be meeting with us."

McElroy smiled broadly and tendered the used-car salesman's handshake—arm fully extended, fingers straight out, thumb sticking up. Zeke shook, much in the manner of the spelling bee runner-up congratulating the champion. "Nice to meet you," he lied.

"Same here. I'm looking forward to our session. It's always good to talk with people who are on the firing line. Sometimes we get a little overbalanced in theory, here in our sheltered world."

Try as hard as he could, Zeke couldn't interpret it as patronizing. Maybe, just maybe, this guy wouldn't be so bad after all.

After some small talk about the Borsch case, Marjorie Louise reminded, "All right, you guys, you're going to have a full session this afternoon. We're about to be late for lunch. Come on, Zeke." She led the way through the outer office. Only when she guided Zeke one direction and McElroy went another did he realize lunch was to be a twosome after all.

The Windsor Room set Zeke aback with its floor-to-ceiling wood paneling, tall stained glass windows, real table linen, waiters in starched white jackets, and all the rest. *(If this was designed to make an ex-high school coach several notches less than comfortable, it's a screaming success.)*

Everyone there appeared to be a great friend of Marjorie Louise, speaking or waving, which didn't help his sense of being a carp in a school of rainbow trout. He trailed along in her wake, following a waiter whose mission in life was apparently responding instantly to her every whim. He seated her with a flourish.

While getting his tall-backed chair in the general proximity of the table, he only bumped the diner's chair behind him twice. His was still farther away than he liked, but damned if he'd chance bumping the other guy again. They were barely settled when a starched jacket appeared with menus. Zeke glanced through the assortment of quiches and other offerings not found at the Country Kitchen.

Marjorie Louise suggested, "No hurry, Zeke. My curiosity is killing me. Tell me all about your case. What's all this about mysterious markings? Think you may have a cult in that little town killing people? What's your role in the investigation? Tell me everything. Tell me all, tell me, tell me." Leaving nothing out, Zeke related the details. She was astounded. Many questions later, Zeke said she missed her calling—she should've been a reporter.

"Well, I guess. You must be famished, let's order. The crab-stuffed flounder is very good."

"That'll be fine." Gad, he wished he could scoot a little closer. His discomfort wasn't eased when Marjorie Louise selected only soup and salad. He'd be sitting there stuffing his face while she spooned and nibbled. He recovered in the nick of time. "Sounds right to me, too. I'll have the same."

"Oh, go ahead and have the flounder."

"No—really, the salad sounds good." *(And still another lie.)* "I've begun a food program to get back in shape." (Somehow it sounded better than "diet.")

"Your shape doesn't look in terribly bad condition."

Zeke's ears reddened, and what was worse, he knew they had. Worse still, he knew she knew he knew they had. He grabbed for the oversized goblet of water, nearly tipping it over. Only the remnants of lightning reflexes saved him from a fate worse than death. (*Holy Pete! Get hold of yourself!*)

Marjorie Louise moved smoothly to the rescue, closing the menu as a signal they were ready. As if by magic, the starched jacket appeared and was informed. "Mr. Tanner is ready to order."

Quick thinking saved him from responding, "Go ahead, you first." (*That was close!*) "We'll both have the dinner salad with raspberry vinaigrette and the vichyssoise." (His least favorite soup.)

"Sure you won't have the flounder, Zeke?" He fibbed again, and the waiter departed.

After suffering cold soup, the salads arrived with dressing on the side. It featured several lettuce varieties but very little of anything else. Zeke searched for tidbits, found few, and folded oversized leaves carefully to avoid an abundance of vegetation on his fork. Of course, Marjorie had no trouble whatsoever. It made him feel even more the consummate klutz when she only dabbed her fork in the dressing before each bite after he unceremoniously spooned his over the greenery.

Zeke's only victories came when he avoided mishaps with any of the floppy ingredients or dribbling the dressing. Finally it was finished. Over coffee, he relaxed a little. Leaving too generous a tip, he paid and they strolled to Marjorie's office.

Dr. McElroy arrived, and after further brief amenities, Zeke reported the progress of the investigation to date, adding, "We're very interested in the markings, but we'd also like to get general information helpful in identifying suspects. It could assist the chief in his awareness-training program for his officers, too." He handed the professor a copy of the markings in Borsch's letter. "Do cults use anything like these?"

The professor studied it. "Afraid they don't resemble any with which I'm familiar. What I can do is keep this and do a complete search. Perhaps I may be able to help you today with the general information, though."

Zeke prepared to take notes as McElroy began. "I'll give an overview and then summarize so you can check your notes. Please keep in mind that there may be some different interpretations, but I believe what I'm about to give you is generally accepted."

More than an hour's lecture followed, interspersed with occasional questions from Zeke. In summary, McElroy ticked off the seven main points.

"One. Estimates of the number of well-organized cults in this country range from a handful to thousands. Most researchers put the figure at well over four hundred. Many are identified as social, satanic, scientific or spiritually oriented. The latest is the *cybercult* which are organized and operated through the Internet. Incidentally, members of any cult almost never use the word *'cult.'* Instead, 'group,' 'association,' 'brotherhood,' and 'family' are common.

"Two. Cult practices vary somewhat, but commonalties exist. A leader who is charismatic, controlling and manipulative dominates members. Male or female, they often sell themselves as an anointed prophet of God or some supernatural being. They have their own brand of morality and place themselves above any man-made law. Questioning anything they say is the ultimate sin.

"Three. Since leaders must have followers to survive, every conceivable field is tilled in search of recruits. Among the most fertile is the college campus. The latest, and what may be most productive in the future, is the Internet. There are many web sites related to cults. Some criticize and give beneficial information, but some are manned by wolves in sheep's clothing using well-disguised recruiting techniques. There are more and more sites using outrageous promises to attract recruits. Incidentally, you could also use the web to get additional material for your chief's awareness-training program.

"Four. Leaders employ various techniques to mold and hold novices—assisted by group members, of course. This begins with a step-by-step indoctrination, which progresses to total cultism. Gradually, the leader erases the member's concept of his former self and creates a controllable *pseudo-self.* To accomplish this, the leader must first isolate recruits from the outside world. by controlling all information. Newspapers, letters and television are severely restricted and soon banned altogether. The demand to practice continuing self-denial and confession of alleged wrongdoing is a mainstay of control and isolation. Forcing members to labor to near physical and mental exhaustion also makes isolation and indoctrination easier.

"All the while, members are being infused with the belief that everything is a struggle between *them* (outsiders) and *us*. Cults probably cannot exist without this fortress mentality. Everything *out there* is evil. Protection exists only in the group. It always comes first, and individuals must defer to it without exception. Members can only realize enlightenment, peace, and fulfillment through the group. If it's a spiritually oriented cult, salvation can only be achieved through adherence to group ideals. Actions, no matter how anti-social, sometimes illegal, are appropriate if they further group goals as defined by the leader.

"Often, members must sign over all their possessions either as a requirement for admission or later as a demonstration of submissiveness to the group and/or supernatural being. In others, members cannot achieve the next level of spirituality without additional donations.

"Five. If members stray, they are often threatened with extreme consequences, including human or supernatural intervention in their affairs and their family's. Should members actually defect, there are sometimes threats and occasionally actions taken against them or their families if the member refuses to return.

"Six. One of the most recent trends is for a cult to move into a community, perhaps a newer housing development, and exhibit no outward evidence of cult activities. They establish residence, open small businesses, and occasionally run for local public offices. I know of at least two members of cults sitting on school boards.

"Seven. One of the most important things to remember is that rarely does anyone join a cult only to be joining. They are looking for something, often a family or purpose. Cults create an instant family and purpose.

"The most vulnerable targets are those who experience a disruptive event destabilizing their emotional equilibrium. Their ability to perceive and analyze information is distorted, so they are susceptible to anything they see as helping to get their life in order. Examples of disruptive events include divorce, career changes, sudden or inexplicable death of a loved one, moving away from home, entering college, or losing a job. Curiously, even happenings viewed as positive by most can be disruptive such as sudden wealth or a job promotion. I should add that vulnerability is not always the result of spontaneous events. Disaffection can build from childhood."

McElroy thought for a moment. "Well, Zeke, that's the summary. Any more questions?"

"A couple. What's the difference between cults and religions? Sounds as though they could be pretty close."

"Good question. Among the various definitions differentiating religions and cults is one saying some *religions* may look to have cult features, but follow acceptable social practices. Conversely, *cults* may have religious features, but observe unusual, antisocial or abnormal practices."

"Could any of today's religions be classified as cults as you described them?"

"Some current religions may've been called a cult at one time and evolved to what is now considered a religion. However, in today's world, it would probably be extremely difficult for anyone to gain enough control over enough followers for it to begin acting as a true cult. I do know of one such case. In a small church in a western state, a split occurred over some minor doctrinal point, and a bloc splintered away to form its own church. Its members, already very upset, became much more threatened, and looked increasingly to their leader for relief. Before long, the group came to behave much like a cult. More questions?"

"I'll no doubt have several after some thought."

"Feel free to phone, Zeke. I wish I could've supplied an answer to your markings question. However, perhaps there was some general information you will find helpful. I hope I haven't strayed too far afield and made it a wasted trip."

"Not at all, not at all. It was more than just interesting. I've learned a lot no doubt important to the investigation."

Marjorie Louise reddened Zeke's ears again. "Don't worry about it being a wasted trip, Vince. As you may've gathered, Zeke and I are very dear friends and it gave us a chance to visit."

The professor extended his hand. Farewells over, he departed, and Zeke folded his notes and also prepared to leave. Marjorie smiled. "So soon, Ezekial? It's still early. I thought you might be able to make a day of it. I've only a few things to look after, then we could have a late afternoon coffee and chat a bit more."

He was startled, but managed, "As much as I'd like that, I promised the chief I'd be back in time to fill him in on today's meeting."

She smiled again. "Liar, liar, pants on fire. Afraid of a little coffee? Gun-shy after all these years, Ezekial?"

Red-ear time again. "No, really—God's truth." (*I wish she'd stop that smiling!*)

"Well, OK, but I won't let you off the hook without a promise. The Knicks are playing the Pacers in two weeks. I can get tickets, and I'd like to go. Can you make it? I could meet you in Indianapolis so you wouldn't need to make the extra drive here."

Zeke found you didn't have to be in imminent danger of sudden death for your life to flash before your eyes. There were lots of reasons it wasn't such a great idea, but he heard some nitwit say, "Sounds like a plan. You'll let me know the schedule?"

"Surely. Come on, I'll walk you to your car."

He was so surprised at his promise, they were halfway to Ol' Emmy before he remembered his rambling wreck. *(When she sees that heap, I won't need to worry about any basketball game. Oh well, too late now.)*

Marjorie Louise didn't bat an eye at the venerable vehicle masking as a legitimate means of transportation. He opened the door, and without one speck of hesitation, she administered what could only be described as considerably more than a good-bye peck. "So long for now, Zeke."

Somehow, he got himself under the wheel and out of the parking lot. Thirty miles up the road he achieved a semi-rational analysis of events and an equilibrium-establishing conclusion: *(Don't be a dumbass Tanner. What's past is past—let it rest in peace. Still...)* He was heading east on Interstate 70 before thoughts of *after* the game mash-mouthed him.

19

The dogs fed and watered, Zeke went inside. As usual, the message light was flashing. He ignored it and phoned the station for Bookman. "How'd you make out, Zeke? Didn't expect you back tonight. Thought maybe your old blaze might'a relit the kindlin'. Get a line on the markin's? Anything on cults?"

"Forget the old *flame* crap. That fire went out a long time ago. Got nothing on the markings, but quite a bit of general information. Any news here today?"

"Not too much on the investigation. Lefty Riggins sent the list showin' what Benson pawned or sold. Looks like the scuzball's been at it a long time. Was a little excitement, though. Fire department had a helluva fire right after lunch. Lowell Williams' place down by the old canal-barge turnaround went up like tinder. Didn't save nothin', but I doubt there was much to save. It got real run down and stood vacant for years till those hippies rented it last summer. Bet Williams is glad to see it gone."

"Showing your age, Stretch. They stopped being called 'hippies' years ago."

"Don't matter what their new names are—it hoots like a duck, it's a duck. Once hippies, always hippies."

Zeke let it go. "When do you want to talk about the cult info I brought back? Up to it right after dinner?"

"Tell you what, Zeke—we'll talk about it while we eat. How soon you goin' to the diner?"

"Nice try, but no cigar. You know darn well I'm on the diet to stay. You can join me or come over after you've finished stuffing. Eat here or eat alone."

"Much as I'd like to share your delightful cookin', I'll hafta take a rain check. Apple pie day, you know."

"You're evil, Bookman."

"That's a fact, and don't forget it. I'll come over later on one condition—no Snake Bites and no longbeard music. See you later, Slim."

Still ignoring the blinking crimson Cyclops atop the answering machine, Zeke carried his diet meal into the living room. This time the music was Duke Ellington and the big-band sax master, Johnny Hodges. He barely finishing eating before Bookman hammered.

"Well, don't beat it off the hinges, come on in."

DeVon entered, holding out a white by-the-piece foam-plastic pie container. "Here you go. Knew you couldn't live without it."

"Take it and hurt yourself real bad with it, vile person. You keep yammering about me being a few pounds over playing weight, then do your best to make me pig out."

"Here, eat it anyway." He tossed the box over. It was empty.

"Vile, Bookman, really, really vile." Zeke smashed the carton and dropped it into a wastebasket.

"Now thatcha got that out'a your system, tell me about your little excapade today. Don't leave out any'a the girl-boy parts, either."

Biting his tongue to avoid correcting "*ex*capade," Zeke got his notes and briefed the chief, answering his occasional questions. As soon as he finished, DeVon prodded, "OK, enough'a this dull bull, get to the good stuff. Don't lie to me—get propositioned?"

"Certainly not!" *(A basketball game is not a proposition, and it's none of his business, anyhow.)*

"Your ears are growin', your ears are growin'."

The phone rang, but Zeke made no move. After the fourth ring, the answering machine kicked in. "Hello, hello! You there, Zeke Tanner? Pick up, pick up, pick up."

Still Zeke sat. The voice continued, "Hello, hello! It's Charlie Norris, the fire chief. Gotta find Bookman. Pick up if you're there. Pick up, pick up."

Bookman won the race to the phone by a whisker and grabbed the receiver, which cut off the answering machine. He listened a minute. "OK." Turning to Zeke, he griped, "Charlie already left a message. Don'tcha ever check that thing? C'mon, we gotta meet him at the station."

They hurried to Bookman's pickup. "Mind telling me what this is all about, Great Chief?"

"Charlie said there's some goofy stuff about the Williams fire we might wanna know about."

Fire Chief Norris was waiting. They went into Bookman's office and closed the door. He bantered, "Mean one today, eh, Charlie. Not much fun firefightin' in this cold I'll bet, butcha gotta expect to pay the price now and again for sittin' around all year playin' checkers and eatin'."

"No fun a'tall, Dee. Water freezes 'bout as soon as it comes out'a the hose. Almost makes you wanna be a cop, but nothin' could be quite bad enough to make you do somethin' so awful."

Bookman smiled. "Whataya got?"

"Right from the start, things looked fishy. There was a nine-one-one from a pay phone reportin' the fire, but when we got there, nobody was around. It was blazin' pretty dam good by then, and we barely got through the front door before it got so bad we hadta back off. Saw enough to figure the fire started in the livin' room, but one'a the men, who went in the back door, hollered it looked like it started in the kitchen. We all know any fire startin' in more'n one place is a pretty strong sign'a arson. First thing tomorrow, I'm calllin' in the State Fire Marshall.

"Somethin' else looked funny. You'd sort'a expect at least some'a those hippies Lowell Williams rented to would'a been there, but not one of 'em was around while the place was burnin', and none showed up afterward when we were securin' things. After we got back to the firehouse, I tried hard to locate Williams. He's nowhere to be found. Strangest thing of all is out in my truck. C'mon outside and see for yourself."

In the back of the fire chief's pickup was what appeared to be the weathered top half of a Dutch-type double door. "Don't see much there, Charlie. Thought we needed a new door on the station?"

Norris reached in and lifted it on edge to reveal something painted on the underside. Bookman peered at it in the dim light, then looked more closely. "What the...!"

There was a larger version of what was becoming an all too familiar design, a two-foot-wide heptagon with the number 70 inside, again slashed diagonally with a line. Beneath were *new* numbers, 1 4 1 8. Once again, they were spaced widely apart.

Bookman glanced quickly in both directions as he dropped the door back into the pickup's bed. "Exactly where'd you come by this, and how many other people saw it?"

"After we got the fire truck and pumper back to town and secured, I went out there for a last look to see if there was any chance a spark or two might be flyin' around to light somethin' else. Y'know the old buildin' behind the house? It's got horse stalls in it with Dutch doors openin' to the outside of each one. I saw this thing on the top door'a the first stall. With all that stuff about some mysterious markin's on Bill Borsch, and 'specially since hippies lived in the house, I thought I better make sure whether the door was important. Phoned all over, but couldn't find you anywhere, so I yanked it off. Wasn't hard—the wood bein' half rotten, n'all. I finished up and finally caughtcha at Zeke's. Is this door important?"

"Hold on a minute, Charlie. "Whataya mean, 'all that stuff about mysterious markin's?' Where'd *you* hear anything about markin's? And, I asked how many other people saw this door."

"Last Dime Dalton told me. He's the only other one I know of who saw it."

"*Hell and damnation!* Last Dime Dalton! How in thunder did it come about?"

"Said he was out for a drive and happened to see my pickup. Drove up the lane and asked about the fire and was anybody hurt. Figured it was only his usual body chasin'. He saw the door and talked about the markin's bein' close to those on Borsch. The door important?"

"Con*found* it! I warned Dalton what'd happen if he blabbed. Wait'll I see him! Yeah, the door's important, all right. Drive around behind to the garage, and I'll take it there."

Down at the garage, Norris switched the doors from truck to truck. "It's all yours."

"Thanks two gazillion, Charlie. By the way, notice any tracks around where the door was?"

"Can't remember nothin' special about tracks.

Anyway, an overhang above the doors sticks out eight foot or so to keep the snow off, and there's so many tracks all around the rest'a the place there's no way to tell 'em apart."

Norris pulled away, and Bookman directed, "OK, let's go."

"Go? Go where? What about the door? Aren't you going to put it in the station?"

"Nope, gonna store it at your place till I can get it to Mickner's lab in the mornin'. Don't wanna chance some nibnose stumblin' onto it."

"It's OK to leave it with me, I guess. What do you expect the lab to find?"

"Got no idea, but it's worth a try. Could be it it'll help finger the hippies for the Borsch killin'. They're a kind'a cult, aren't they?"

"Being what you call a 'hippie' doesn't automatically make them cult members. The door could point to a cult I suppose, unless a cult is the intended target of the design."

"Happy Tanner, always the shiny cloud, ain'tcha? Maybe we'll learn more when we locate the hippies. Sure like to find Lowell Williams. Hope we don't have another killin' on our hands."

"Wow! I never thought of that!"

"Wouldn't some'a those bonehead bozos on the town council have a hooray day out'a that! Speakin'a the town council, word is they're fixin' to hold one'a their Star Closet meetin's. Probly gonna try some new way to buckshot my butt."

"Not to worry, Great Chief, they've tried plenty of times before and haven't left too many scars. What's different this time? By the way, it's Star *Chamber*, not C*loset*."

"Chamber, closet—whatever. Nothin's different, except the bunch that just got elected is like lots of 'em. Don't know the first thing you do after gettin' elected is to paint everthing and keep your mouth shut for a year. Wanna change everthing right now that's been workin' good so they can say they've done somethin'. Haven't got the sense to not take a clock in for fixin' that's tickin' and keepin' the right time. Some of 'em think they know everthing about how to do everbody's job, but couldn't do anybody's if their life depended on it. I call 'em bulls-eye bastards. Stand around doin' nothin' while somebody else's shootin' an arrow at a blank target. Then they run over and slap a bulls-eye on it anyplace they please—even if your arrow's dead center. That way they can make your shot look like anything they want.

"Couple'a this latest bunch tried to bull-batter me out'a office even before they got officially installed. If the Borsch case don't get solved pretty quick, they'll use that. There's already been talk about askin' the county prosecutor to look into the investigation. Well, it's not gonna happen. This old hound can still hunt—I gotta few cards to play."

"OK, so don't fret about it, Great Chief."

"You forgettin' you're always sayin' there never was a horse that couldn't be throwed, and a cowboy who couldn't be bucked off."

"Your quote needs a little work, but it's way too early to get agitated. The investigation's only getting a good start—don't buy trouble. Here we are. Let's get this door unloaded." They stored it in a back bedroom, and DeVon took a seat on the living room couch.

"Short Snake Bite, Stretch? We need to do some very hard thinking about why there are different numbers on the door than the others we have."

"Already said no poison tonight. We can talk about numbers till we're green in the face, but what I really wantcha to do is listen to your machine once'n a while. Who knows, the killer might'a called and confessed already."

"Could happen—everyone else has left a message." Zeke crossed into the kitchen and saw the number of calls before punching the PLAY button. *(Holy Pete, twenty-two!)*

The first twenty were from reporters interspersed with telemarketing-vermin hang-ups. *(They never stop.)* Next came Norris' call. There was a pause, and Zeke was about to hit ERASE, but there was one last message. A muffled voice dared, "If you're not afraid of fire, look at the barn."

Bookman exploded from the couch and dashed in. "Play that again. What'n hell was *that*!"

They listened several more times. Neither spoke until the chief asked, "Why you s'pose he called? Hadta know somebody'd find the door."

"My guess is he wanted to be sure *we*'d look for it right away."

After discussing this new call, Bookman sighed. "Still no answers. Now, where to? It's the same kind'a message, but it sure looks like some nut may be tryin' to play a game with us—rub our noses in it. Somethin' an ego kook would do. It is, and we're a one-headed dog back chasin' at least two tails again."

"Maybe so, but it might be too early to give up on the cult theory, don't you think?"

"S'pose so, but we can't forget to keep more'n one ball bouncin' at once. Get back to your speculatin'."

Their session lasted another hour. One question stood out. Why had no one else seen the sign on the door, what with all the firemen and onlookers milling about? Zeke thought everyone's attention was focused on the fire. DeVon figured even if anyone saw it, they probably concluded it was something the renters painted there.

"Zeke, we haven't talked much about the new numbers below the hecta-thing. Don't wanna spend all night on it, butcha got any earth-shakin' ideas about 'em?"

"No more than with the others. I played around with a code system I studied in Navy decoding school—one used in an early civilization's worship ceremonies—but didn't get anywhere. Can't seem to get a line on anything."

They thrashed the numbers question around a while longer. Finally Zeke rose and stretched. "Enough already. Get out of here. Go home and get some rest. We're not going to solve anything tonight."

"Guess you're right. See you bright'n early." A tired looking chief of police departed leaving Zeke to his numbers and music.

20

Tanner determined to exercise his right to do only what he wanted today. *(To heck with Dee's 'bright and early.')* He carried a second coffee to his listening chair, turned on the stereo to warm up, and settled back. *(Thank goodness there are no calories in coffee and music.)*

Mug emptied and halfway through the Saint-Saens *Organ Symphony*, the phone clamored. His watch showed only 8:25, so he let the answering machine do its thing. This time, it kept on ringing past the four necessary to activate the device. When it reached twelve, he decided to answer, all the while grousing about how nothing worked anymore.

(This better be good!) "Hello!"

"Sergeant Wilson, Mr. Tanner. Chief Bookman's on his way over to getcha. I think it's about those missin' hippies. He's in a big hurry, and should be there by now, your telephone takin' so long to wake you, n'all."

Before Zeke could sputter a response, sudden beating on the front door reverberated. "Sounds like the chief's there. See you later, Mr. Tanner."

He rushed over and yanked open the door. Bookman shouted, "Dammit, *COME ON!* Didn't Wilson phone?" Zeke thought of a reply, something about involuntary servitude, but he snatched his hat and coat before matching DeVon's dash to the black and white.

As they roared away, Bookman filled him in. "Charlie Norris went out to the fire scene this mornin' with the fire marshal. Just as they got there, an old painted-up van come chargin' out'a the lane and took off flyin' down the back road to the Interstate. Charlie figured it might be some'a those hippies and called the station. For once, we were lucky enough to have a car in the area. Strahan ran 'em down about a mile before they hit the main road. Had a devil of a time stoppin' 'em. I wantcha along to check out their story and maybe help with the questionin'—you bein' the cult expert. I hope we finally caught a break that ties in to Borsch's killin'."

Zeke didn't, or couldn't, say anything. The car was rocketing along at the extreme outer limits of what the narrow snowplowed road would permit, and he was giving his undivided attention to terror control. Another five minutes, and they slid to a stop behind the van and two police cars. Stony Crossing P.D's special assistant let his full weight down on the seat. *(There is a God!)*

The second car was a county sheriff's. Bookman climbed out grumbling, "Now what's that blamed fool doin' here?"

Zeke sized up the situation. *(Now we'll get two shows for the price of one.)* There would be a double feature, all right. Standing next to Strahan and arguing was Chief Deputy Hollis Benson. "Now Strahan, this here's county territory, and we got jurisdiction. Tell me what this is all about and I'll decide what to do, if anything."

Chief of Police DeVon Bookman reached the scene. "Get your worthless hide back in the ugly brown bucket'a junk you call a patrol vehicle and get out'a here! This pursuit started in our jurisdiction, and that makes it our collar. Now *git*!"

Benson was clearly still afraid of Bookman. He backpedaled toward his car, got in, and threatened, "You can bet your butt Sheriff Lard...Sheriff Laddis will hear about this. You can just bet on it!"

"Yeah, well pardon me if I don't stand here crappin' in my boots. Go on, get out'a here!" DeVon took a step toward the car. Benson spun his wheels, spraying Bookman's cruiser with sand and road salt as he gunned away.

Bookman turned to Strahan. "What was that weasel-dabble doin' here? He just stumble by?"

"No, Chief, I think he must'a monitored our frequency. Came barrelin' by and turned around. Not the first time lately a sheriff's car has butted in on a chase, but I always figured it was coincidence."

"I'll take care of it later. Whataya got here?"

"Believe it or not, there's fifteen people packed like sardines in that thing. The grand high muckity-muck, or whatever he calls himself, was drivin'. Got him in my car. Stinks like a buzzard. Gives some screwball name he had his own legally changed to. Now, it's *True* somethin'. Haven't talked to him too much, but he gives the same screwball answer to everything. Ask him a question and he babbles somethin' about followin' the most holy see-her, whoever she is. His driver's license is so beat up, it's awful hard to read. It checked out OK as best I could tell."

"Get him out here so I can have a look."

Strahan opened the door and motioned to the occupant. After a stream of unintelligible mutterings, a scraggly-bearded figure stepped onto the road. Garbed in a long, grungy, vertically striped robe of many faded colors, he rearranged a grimy turban revealing a shaved head. Palms together, he faced the four points of the compass and continued to mumble gibberish. Bookman walked over. "Knock off the bull and gimme your story."

"We are members of The Family of the Most Holy Seer and followers of his chosen disciple on earth, our Holy Leader. Most Holy

Seer holds dominion over all the planet and its creatures. We follow only his teachings. We answer only to him and Holy Leader."

The chief took another step forward. "OK fuzz-face, spit out your name and let's start gettin' some answers."

"My name is True Prophet. I am the conveyer of the teachings of the Most Holy Seer. He is everywhere, but only Holy Leader can see or speak with him."

"Let me tell you who I am," Bookman growled. "You're lookin' at the Grand Pooh-Bah of all the places you can see from where you're standin'. I speak with and for the Grandest Pooh-Bahs of 'em all, them bein' the Stony Crossing Town Council. You're gonna give me answers right now, or allaya are comin' along to the House'a the Grandest Pooh-Bahs. Get it? *Jail*, nitwit. Talk up, you dirty-hatted cue ball. Where were you and your eight-balls yesterday, and what were you runnin' from?"

True Prophet ignored the questions and began his mumbo-jumbo again. Before the chief could administer an attitude adjustment, Bill Mickner drove up. "I see you've caught our flower children. What do you have them on—dirty and disheveled?"

"Whataya doin' here, Mickner? How'n hell do *you* know who we got?"

"I'm here because my desk sergeant said you phoned saying you wanted something picked up for some lab work—he didn't know what. How do I know what's going on? Well, about three o'clock this morning, one of my troopers stopped this old painted-up VW van or its clone just outside of Greenfield. That wierdo you have there said he's the leader of the great unwashed crammed into that van—called them his 'flock.' Said they were coming from up north after some kind of all-day service. Night crew held them until they could verify their story and check the vehicle registration. Before the trooper got our cult guy out of bed to check them out, he thought he might be onto a slavery ring or something equally naughty. After all, Manson spent a lot of time no more than twenty or thirty miles from this very spot.

"After checking, our guy found that apparently the bunch is part of a collection of misfits who've been around up north for years. There are no more than three small groups—forty some all told—half men, half women, but kept separated. With no wants or warrants he could locate, the trooper let them go. Besides, he said the van stank so badly, he would've cut them loose for everything short of first-degree murder. You didn't tell me what you're going to hold them on."

DeVon's hat started toward the back of his head, keeping pace with each Mickner revelation. Then thunder and lightening erupted. "*DAMNATION*! Where's the law statin' evertime I grab for a radish danglin' in front'a me, somebody dumps an oceanload'a crap on my head! First the ring and Benson, then everthing else, and now this! *Where's the law!*"

It was only the beginning, and was some show. Most of the remaining snow around him was in danger of melting before he cooled down enough to give Strahan some orders. "Call in and get help baggin' up the head stinkweed and his buttercups. Take 'em all to County Juvy—they gotta be violatin' *somethin'* in this county—let Juvy sort it out. And, be sure to tell Wayne City I wanna keep *True Bull* on tap till we locate Lowell Williams. You can charge him with all kind'a things. For openers, I'm catchin' a real strong stink'a meth—check for runaways, too." Bookman spun on his heel. "Hell with it, I'm through here." With that, a still red-faced chief strode to his car, Zeke hustling to avoid being left behind.

Another perilous ride and they were back at the station. Last Dime Dalton came bursting into Bookman's office. "Chief! I saw Charley Norris and he said you're real mad at me. I didn't mean to say nothin', it just come out—honest! Didn't say nothin' to nobody else—honest!"

"Last Dime, you usin' that word, *honest*, sounds real peculiar."

"Chief, I didn't mean to say nothin', *honest* I didn't."

"Dalton, I really wish you'd stop usin' that *word*. Makes me suspicious'a everthing else you say." Bookman chewed on him some more before throwing him out, then turned to Mickner who entered as Last Dime was leaving. Bookman remarked, "Bill, if you hadta bring bad news, I reckon it's good to get it now. Before you came along, the hippie king was lookin' like a pretty good fit for at least the fire."

Zeke spoke up, "All is not lost, Great Chief. You still have the door from the fire, and don't forget the tape."

"Yeah. Well, maybe we got a little somethin' after all." He laid out the information about the door for Mickner who said he'd have the lab try to do something with it, then asked what tape they were talking about.

"We got another goofy answerin' machine message for your lab. I forgot to take it when I left Zeke's last night. Give him the tape, Tanner."

"Overlooking the fact you dragged me from the house without a chance to bring it with me? "

"Dang it, whataya think you're gettin' paid for? OK, you can give it to Bill when you take him by to pick up the door. The markin's surely gotta shed some light on Borsch sooner or later. Could be we'll get lucky." Returning to the case of the missing landlord, he buzzed the deskman and asked if he learned anything about the whereabouts of Lowell Williams.

"Nary a word, Chief, and we've tried about everybody and everyplace we can think of. Want we should keep lookin'?"

"Oh yeah."

DeVon commented, "Sure hope nothin's happened to Williams, but the longer he's missin', the more likely we got another murder on our hands. If there's another body, God forbid, somebody'll probly call Tanner to tell him where it is."

The three sat and discussed the Borsch murder, the fire, tape, and Williams' fate. The conclusion was unanimous that things didn't look good for Mr. Lowell Williams.

As Zeke and Mickner were leaving, Bookman's buzzer sounded. He punched the speakerphone button. "Call on one, Chief."

"Hello, Chief Bookman. Heard you were looking for me. This is Lowell Williams."

Tanner and Mickner hurried onward. Once in the patrol car, Zeke observed, "That call should help his mood, but probably not by much—True Prophet and his crowd flunking out as suspects as they did. Well, he'll get back in tune once the Borsch case is solved."

"Yes, the general heat he's taking from some councilmen added to the Borsch killing is enough to make anyone touchy."

"Bill, hope you don't mind my asking, but how did you come to know about pressure on Dee?"

They rode a block in silence before Mickner answered. "Maybe I shouldn't say anything, but I don't care—it was a pretty shoddy thing to do. A few nights ago, one of your town councilmen asked whether I'd be interested in the job. Said they were holding a meeting to force Bookman to resign. I told him in no uncertain terms I considered him a first rate chief, if a little crusty at times, and what I thought of the underhanded way they were trying to get rid of him. Also said I wouldn't take the job now or ever. Haven't given a heads-up to DeVon. Don't think they have the votes to do anything, or I would. No sense piling any more on him right now in the middle of this screwy murder case."

"I'll respect your confidence, Bill. There's been some pressure before, but he's handled it."

"Bound to wear on a man, though. It'd be great if he could get this case wrapped up soon—it's a real bummer. The trail can get awfully cold in a hurry. I'm getting this bad hunch maybe it won't be one of the quick ones."

"Sorry to hear that. Turn here. It's the last house down at the end."

Zeke got the tape and handed it to Mickner. "Hope you can do something with this."

"We got some dope from the central lab about a new technique they use to enhance voices. Maybe it'll help."

"Good. Hope they can do something with the door, too." Zeke retrieved it from the bedroom.

Mickner knelt and inspected the markings closely. "If that's not the damndest thing I ever laid eyes on. Don't know how much our lab can do with it, but we'll give it a go."

"Anything's more than we have now."

Captain Mickner departed, and Zeke ate lunch while listening to Grieg's *Concerto in A Minor*. As it neared the finale, the telephone rang. And rang. And rang. Finally, he decided it might be important. "Hello!"

A voice he didn't recognize announced, "Mr. Tanner, this is John Lawson. I don't believe we've met, but I knew your Uncle John."

(What kind of a pitch is this going to be? This is what I get for answering the phone.)

"I expect you know I was elected to the town council last November. I wonder if you could spare me the time to talk a few minutes."

Zeke said nothing. *(I know you were elected, but I'll not give you the satisfaction.)*

Lawson began, "The council is going to hold a personnel evaluation meeting, and I believe you can supply helpful information. Anything you say will be held in strictest confidence, the same as I'm sure you'll treat my call."

Zeke deduced immediately what was afoot and was furious. *(Slimy snake! Wants me to rat out DeVon. Hope I don't look that stupid!)* "What kind of information would you expect me to supply?"

"To be quite frank, council members have certain concerns about Chief Bookman. Please keep in mind no one is even *thinking* about replacing him. However, from time to time, we must make evaluations of all personnel and recommend any changes in performance if needed."

(Sneaky mother and a damnable liar to boot!)

"Mr. Tanner, we know you are an honest man who will give honest answers to honest questions. You could help both Chief Bookman and us. Since you've known him so long, you're in a good position to see whether he's showing signs of behavior changes. We'd appreciate your input."

Zeke was the essence of calm. "I think I can oblige you, Mr. Lawson. My Uncle John had a saying that may be appropriate. It went something like, 'Don't be stupid enough to try to teach a good workhorse to sing. It'll only frustrate you and annoy the horse so much it's hard to say what might happen.' I hope it helps in your deliberations."

After a prolonged silence, Zeke added, "Thank you for asking me to contribute. Goodbye."

He still hadn't calmed down when the *Concerto* ended. Not only was he still boiling about Lawson, he worked up a major concern about whether to inform DeVon about the call—hard to figure just how he'd react. Maybe it would be a good idea to talk to Lurinda. As he considered the situation, a commotion erupted on the front porch, including some galaxy-class cussing. He rushed out to find DeVon doing battle with a snow shovel left leaning against the steps where the lanky chief slipped and tripped over it. Struggling to contain his laughter, Zeke made out most Bookman's tirade. "I'm tellin' you, the (*blankity-blank-blank-bleep-bleepin'*) shovel went right for me! (*Bleep-bleepin'*) thing jumped right under me. Ain't it enough I gotta deal with every dumbass in creation! Now I got (*bleep-bleepin'*) shovels to contend with!"

While putting the shovel aside, Zeke decided right now was not the best time to mention Lawson's call, if ever. "Come in and tell Mama Tanner all about it."

Bookman glared. "Don't *you* start!"

Zeke led him into the kitchen and poured coffee. "There you are—piping hot—that should cool you off."

"Hafta be a smartass every second? Phoned a couple or three times from the diner. Got a busy signal—what else? Mickner get the door OK? Whataya plannin' this afternoon?"

Zeke let the phone comment go by. "Yes, Mickner took the door. I'm not doing anything except what I want to do—listen to music a while and maybe take Ol' Emmy in and wait for an oil change and lube. Why?"

"What I think is, we better get out a press release about the fire before the news dogs start to bayin' louder. Charlie Norris said the fire marshal released info sayin' it was suspicious, but it'd take a few days to be sure about arson. Already, two papers phoned Norris to ask about any connection to the Borsch killin'. He referred 'em to us and the deskman gave 'em your number, but they got a busy signal, too. When you gonna stop leavin' your phone off the hook?"

Again, Zeke ignored the phone comment. "I can write a release, but what is there to say?"

"Usual BS. Nothin' new on Borsch—hot on the trail, and so forth. Tell 'em some suspects were investigated—no connection to the Borsch case. C'mon, you can drive your junkyard excapee to the truck stop. I'll follow and carry you back to the station."

"Nice try, Bookman, but I'm not going to be trapped all afternoon on your slave ship. Promised myself the rest of the day to relax and unravel. Already spent too much time away from my busy calendar. And the word is *es*capee, not *ex*capee."

"Whatever. You're overworked, all right. C'mon, you can take your bolt-bucket to Jim's, then use my pickup to tote your feeble bones home after the release is finished."

At Jim's Truck Stop, the mechanic expressed surprise Ol' Emmy was still surviving. "Ain't it about time to take whatever that thing is to where old elephants go to die? Judgin' by the amount'a smoke comin' from the exhaust, callin' it *changin'* the oil in that heap's bald-faced bull. It's a *transfusion*, that's what it is. If your rusty bucket'll run that far, get it into the shop out'a sight. Leave it out front and people are liable to get the idea a wreck happened and call the cops."

Zeke smart-mouthed him back and left his faithful steed to be serviced. On the way to the station, he asked, "Anything new on the town council meeting?"

"Nah, probly the same old crap—the hate-Bookman crowd against the let-'em-alone crowd. Each bunch'll try to get the middle'a-the-roaders to vote their way. I think there's enough support to stand off the haters. You never know."

"How many of the nine are for-sure strong supporters?"

"I'll never understand why we need nine on the council for a town this size, but I'd say about a third of 'em are for and about the same against—both sides workin' on the 'tweeners. Harry Stilson's the leader'a the supporters. Some'a the others are strong, but Harry'll stand up and be counted when the goin' gets tough. Smart devil, too."

Just before they hit town, a county sheriff's car passed them, reminding Bookman to phone Sheriff Laddis about his deputies monitoring Stony Crossing police radios. Zeke accompanied an irate chief into his office and waited while he phoned the sheriff. The voice of Leon Laddis blasted through the speakerphone. **"Whataya want now?"** The chief told him in very forceful terms that his deputies better stop the policy of monitoring Stony Crossing police radios and interfering in arrests, or else!

"Bookman, it ain't agin the law in this state to listen in on your radio calls—anybody can. 'Sides, you're full'a crap. Maybe one or two'a the boys got their own scanners, but this office don't have no policy to monitor your chickenshit outfit. Why would we? You ain't got nothin' goin' on to interest a real policin' department. By the way, got the Borsch killin' solved yet?"

Bookman's face was very red and his Stetson all the way back as he lambasted Laddis for a while, concluding, "Next time I hear'a one'a those bug-brains'a yours hornin' in on our collar without bein' asked, there's gonna be a quick trip for him to our lockup for interferin' in a police investigation! Newspapers'd like that fine, I'll bet." Down went the receiver—*KA-BANG!* Zeke exited to DeVon's verbal evisceration of Laddis.

After he finished the press release and gave it to the deskman for distribution, Zeke stuck his head into Bookman's office. "You said something about a pickup?"

DeVon stepped out and handed him his keys. "Gonna be interviewin' applicants for Benson's job and probly be at it a while. Might as well go on home and get on with your loafin'. Stop in MizMartha's on your way and buy some tapes. Number'a messages you're gettin', no tellin' how many you'll hafta pass on to Mickner. Don't forget to put one in your machine. I'll phone when I'm through, and we can go get your rusted-out flivver.

"By the way, Zeke, been meanin' to ask you somethin'. I do a night patrol once'n a while to let folks get a look at me before their bedtime. It's also to stop the night shift's whinin' about 'em doin' their tough job while everbody else, includin' me a'course, gets to loll around durin' the day. Wanna go sometime?"

"Sounds like a plan. Do we wear full body armor for protection against the villains lurking about?"

"Not necessary—I'll throw my body in front'a you sometime after the fiftieth shot. I'll check the schedule and letcha know."

"OK, Ethel. See you, I'm out of here."

"Later, Gertrude."

After he endured Miss Martha Manchester's usual mini-lecture about wastefulness and thrift, she located three more tapes. On the way home, he dropped by the hay and grain elevator to chat with the owner, a Mr. Harry Stilson.

21

After breakfast, Zeke was barely into Mahler's *First* when the telephone rang. Marjorie Louise Bond's voice took him by complete surprise. Zeke! Good Morning! The officer at the police station gave me your home number. I phoned to see if we're still on for the game next week.

(Dandy, just dandy! Her second call to the station. I'll never hear the end of this.) All caution flags sprang to attention. Now was the time to get things under control—give a good reason and cancel. Then he heard some fool say, "Sure thing! Can't pass up a chance to see the Pacers and Knicks go at it." *(Help! I'm talking, and I can't shut up!)*

"Great! How about meeting a week from Saturday at the Excelsior Hotel about five? You know where that is I'm sure. We can have a bite before the game and a late supper after."

Caution flags! Caution flags! Doggone right, he knew where the "Ex" was. He also remembered several events that occurred at the old landmark years ago—better suggest someplace else. The out-of-body ignoramus answered for him again. "That'll be nifty, Marjorie." *(Nifty? Talk about your ancient!)* He could swear he heard the dean at a major university giggle.

"We're all set then. Anything new on your murder case?"

"No, nothing really new. Thought we had something going, but it didn't pan out." He related the fire story.

"I'm sure you'll catch the culprits soon. Looking forward to next week, Zeke."

(Holy Toledo! What's going on here? Is this really what it looks like, or am I a hallucinating has-been? Get a grip, Tanner—don't make a fool of yourself. It's only a basketball game.)

He spent a half-hour trying to concentrate on Mahler. *(To heck with it, might as well go to the station.)* All coated up and ready to go, he was preparing to turn on the answering machine when the phone rang. *(Nuts! Only seconds from a clean getaway!)*

"Hello, Brother Ezekial, this is Evangelist H. Charles Ackerman."

(I'll never answer this phone again!)

"Brother Ezekial, the elders went over the list of members who were good attenders but not anymore. I'm sorry to say your name's on the list. I'm sure a member that attended as good as you would like to get back in the Lord's favor. All you need to do is stand before the congregation and seek redemption for poor attendance and any other backsliding. Doing that and attending regular will get you right with God. Can I count on you to be there Sunday?"

"Frankly, Mr. Ackerman..."

"Just call me Charlie. Or Brother Ackerman would be fine. We'll look for you Sunday. Then thereafter, the elders won't need to do anything more. We'll all pray for you."

(Threatening clown—same sort of presumptuous attitude is a big reason I quit attending in the first place.)

At the office, DeVon listened to Zeke blow off steam about Ackerman's call for a while before reporting, "Got the funniest call this mornin'. MizMartha Manchester asked if we found any *documents* at Borsch's places. I asked how she knew we searched. Said she heard it somewhere—seemed awful nervous. Zeke, when she I.D.'d Borsch, and later on, she only said it was some 'personal papers' she wanted—didn't say nothin' about a *document.* Remember those things we collected for evidence from Borsch's? Wasn't much a'tall—some bills along with a few receipts, a stack'a old mail and a checkbook, but nothin' you'd call a 'document.' I'm thinkin' maybe we oughta look through it again. I asked the property man if he'd inventoried the stuff yet. A'course not, but he'd get on it. There's another thing—fire marshal told Charlie the Williams fire looks like arson for sure. Even found a burnt-up gasoline can."

Zeke was relieved he apparently wasn't going to be harassed about a woman calling the station for his home phone number. "Anything else new?"

"Nothin' a'tall. Tell you, podner, I'm startin' to take this case real personal—about ready to believe some smartasses are playin' games. First with Borsch, then the fire, it's lookin' more and more like somebody's doin' crimes practically on top of us and rubbin' our noses in it with the markin's and messages."

"Giving up on the cult theory already, Great Chief?"

"Still the best bet, I reckon, but I'm gonna take a timeout and check on some other things. Sometimes that leads to a better play. You know that."

"What's first?"

"Well, there's somethin' I been ponderin'. This day and time, we can't overlook the possibility we're dealin' with some spoiled-rotten brats lookin' for kicks from seein' how far over the line they can jump and get away with it. I'm no way near ready to point a for-sure finger at him as one'a Borsch's doers, butcha know that nephew of Alan Bannister's? The one busted for drunk and disorderly and a DUI I told you about? He'd fit the bill. Smart enough to cook up a get-even scheme, too. He's the honcho'a those two worthless pals'a his. They'd help him out, too. After I nailed him again for another DUI, he made some mighty big payback talk around town that got back to me. Took it to be the usual hot gas, but now I'm gonna dig a little deeper."

"How?"

"Gonna start with the '*O*' part of the 'M-O-M.' You know—the *opportunity* part of motive, opportunity and means to do the job. If the nephew wasn't around when the crime was goin' down, no way he could'a had the opportunity—so no way he could'a done Borsch. Some'a your 'logical,' perfesser."

"Exactly how do you intend to go about checking the nephew's opportunity?"

"Start simple by scoopin' up those two deadheads he hangs with. We've had 'em both in here for misdemeanors, and they'll figure we're on to 'em for somethin' else. We'll squeeze 'em about where they were and who they were with on the dates in question. They'll rat out their buddy in a heart blink if they think it'll keep their feet out'a the stove. Besides, if we twist 'em a little, there's a chance they'll cop to somethin' we might not even suspect 'em of. Two crows for the price'a one rock, so to speak."

Zeke sighed, but didn't correct him. "Sounds like typical Bookman strategy. When do you plan this malfeasance? I'd like the chance to be across the border."

"Nothin' illegal, just good policin'."

"If you say so, but the whole thing sounds a bit on the murky side."

"Stop cluckin', mama hen. I'm not gonna go off the deep end with the kid."

"I've got my eye on you, Ethel. Changing the subject, what's new with the town council?"

"Tonight's the night for the big personnel meetin'. Reckon I'll take the usual poundin'. Right now, I wouldn't give two hollers in hell if they tied the can to me. I'm tired 'a takin' their crap besides operatin' the department on half 'a bootstring.

"Not going to happen, Stretch. You're forgetting the town's put up with you as chief all these years. It's just like a wart on your nose.

After you live with it for some time, you become accustomed to it and might even miss it if it were gone. You're the wart on the town's nose, Dude. Folks wouldn't feel comfortable without you. Not only that, you're disregarding the fact they might even give you some credit for doing a halfway decent job. Now shut off the crocodile tears tap."

"Aw, hell with all of 'em. Let's go eat."

Soon after returning from lunch, there was a call from Stony Crossing's mayor, Denzil Ulysses Hanover. Like many small town mayors, once elected, he remained in office year after year. Not many wanted the office, anyhow—everyone knew it was a figurehead job. The town was really run by the Chamber of Commerce inner circle—usually owners of larger businesses. By and large, this group also comprised the town council.

The council remained stable with the exception of an occasional Johnny-come-lately who was nominated by a regular member and then elected. A few retirees like Alan Bannister couldn't be bothered with membership duties or the voting process anymore, but were still more than a little influential as *de facto* members.

Mayor Hanover suited his role beautifully. Years of experience as shoe clerk and stock boy at Wellman's Ready to Wear prepared him well for the office. He got to work on time and took orders with no questions asked. His re-elections were assured as long as he followed instructions to the letter. His secretary kept him from self-destruction, but it was a continuing chore.

Hanover was very short on what most consider a political necessity, a knack for remembering names. He mastered most councilmen's pretty well, but insisted on calling Bookman, "Beckleman," and had done so since they were in elementary school. When the mayor called Zeke "*Daniel* Ezekial," he assumed the confusion resulted from the books of *Ezekial* and *Daniel* being in consecutive order in the *Old Testament*. As a kid, chubby little Denny Hanover never could get his gold star for memorizing the "books" in the right sequence.

Occasionally, the town fathers commented maybe one of them should give hizzoner a little guidance about his attire. In winter, his featured garments were haphazardly buttoned shirts (no tie), trousers probably never pressed after they left the CLOSE OUTS table, and a decades-old basketball team manager's letter sweater too far gone for repair. On coldest days, he dug out a nearly buttonless overcoat with the look of a last second escapee from its trip to the town landfill. Summers, he abandoned the top half in favor of T-shirts always a trifle too short to adequately cover a well-developed abdominal overhang. Passers-by were sometimes startled to receive an accompanying naval wink when the mayor gave them one of his exaggerated waves.

The vanity license plate the mayor bolted to the front bumper of his personal car also caused some concern. It proudly proclaimed the initials of the owner of this eight-year old Ford to be D U H. In addition to the accurately implied reference to Mayor Denzil Ulysses Hanover's mental powers, the initials helped give him another title. D U H, parlayed with his bouncing belly and a proclivity for taking an early dip in the old applejack, "The Mayor" became "Duh Hangover" to many.

Hanover's voice squawked over the speakerphone. "Mornin', Beckleman. (It was afternoon.) This here's the mayor. You know, Mayor Hanover. How'rya? Good, good." (Bookman hadn't said a word.) "Phoned up for a couple reasons. Says here in the paper there's gonna be a personnel meetin' tonight right after the regular meetin'. Them personnel meetin's are secret. This kind'a stuff ain't s'posed to be in the papers. Before ya know it, everbody in creation is gonna wanna know why there's a meetin.' Even worse, they could wanna attend. Got any idea who might'a put the paper onto it? Could Daniel Ezekial a'done it?"

"Is there a personnel meetin', Denny? Can't tell you a thing. Must'a been one'a the council. They'd be the ones to ask, I guess."

When Bookman invoked the town council, Duh Hangover abandoned the subject in a hurry. "Beckleman, 'bout the other reason I phoned. Got time to come over and bring me up to date on where you're standin' on the barber's cult killin'? Wanna be sure I know everything that's goin' on so I can report it right."

"Mayor, there's not a scrap'a proof about cults bein' involved. Be more'n happy to come over and report, but I'm pretty busy with the case. I know it's a lot to ask, but could *you* come over here? I'm sure I can find time to work you in. By the way, exactly which councilmen you s'posed to report to?"

Hanover wasn't the complete fool. He knew he was in danger of wandering onto squishy soil again. "Why...uh...anybody that'd be liable to ask, Beckleman. I'm pretty busy too, but it's real important to get a report. Hafta look at my schedule. Well now, looks like I can call off an important appointment for somebody to talk to me, so I can come right over."

DeVon clicked off the speakerphone. "First rule'a combat is pick the ground you're gonna fight 'em on. Looks like Duh Hangover's got his marching orders from the council, else he never would'a phoned."

Zeke grabbed his hat and coat. "I'm out of here." As long as he could remember, he hadn't liked Hanover.

"Big coward."

"That's me."

Zeke was almost to the door when Bookman, innocence itself, asked, "Got the call from your lady friend at the university, didn'tcha? How's that goin', Ezekial Amos?"

Ezekial Amos didn't slow down to answer.

22

Bookman's day hadn't started well. Yesterday afternoon, he made a good-faith effort to inform the mayor about the progress of the murder investigation prior to the town council's personnel meeting to be held later that evening. It was a waster of time. Hanover had obviously been given a list of loaded questions to ask.

Now this morning, Duh Hangover arrived and walked in unannounced. "Beckleman, I dropped in to talk over a few things about our meetin's last night. First thing is, John Lawson got hisself elected president at the regular town council meetin'. Then at the personnel meetin' afterwards, quite a few councilmen had some pretty tough things to say about how you been runnin' the department and how ya can't get the barber's cult killin' wrapped up."

"In on the tough talk, Denny?"

"Oh, no! I wouldn't do nothin' like that."

"Mmm-huh. You're just reportin' are you? Go ahead 'n dump the rest'a the load."

Well, the council was about to vote on gettin' another chief, but Harry Stilson spoke out and asked if Lawson knew the story about the horse that couldn't sing and the state policeman that liked his job."

"What the purple hell was he talkin' about?"

"Dang'f I know. Anyhow, right away, Lawson said they wouldn't vote on nothin' right then, but maybe they could ask ya to come to a meetin' later on and talk about things."

The chief offered no response. Hanover waited for one, but didn't get it and went on. "The other thing they said was Elmer Jones wanted to get reglar reports on the barber's case right out'a the mayor's office."

"Ask Jones what hymns he wants at his funeral."

Duh Hangover stood in the silence until it dawned on him Bookman didn't intend to respond further to his last statement or anything else. "Well, see ya later, Beckleman."

"Mmm-huh."

The chief's day wasn't made any brighter by the second informational meeting for those investigating the Borsch murder, which wasn't nearly so well attended as the first and no more informative. Those who already heard there was not much new didn't bother to attend. After Bookman reviewed the evidence to date, Dr. Forsythe reported the trace of chemical substance in Borsch's blood remained unidentified and the lab was still trying to analyze it. Sergeant Wilson said he had no luck at the Heaven Health Us Club. More than one officer wanted to know what he meant by "no luck." Wilson replied he wasn't that kind of guy, of course resulting in a chorus of hoots.

Sergeant Smithson advised the group his task force efforts produced little. They were once again going over the evidence.

When they finished, John Morton, elder statesman on the force and one of the officers assigned to assist Smithson, stood and deadpanned, "Chief of Police Bookman, sir, just when is it you're gonna appear on the Elmer Jones TV show? I hear he's been featurin' you on his program again." Chuckles all around.

In spite of his less than productive morning thus far, Bookman smiled. "John, y'know that vandalism goin' on at the cemetery? Well, the council asked if I could put an officer on all-night walkin' duty out there. Think maybe I've found their man. You can trade off once in a while with the rest'a these hot dogs." He adjourned the meeting without setting a date for another. The men filed out rat-a-tat-tatting Morton with insults.

Later in the day, Zeke came in and was involved in two episodes causing DeVon to consider that perhaps the day was indeed improving. The first transpired when he dragged in the lackeys of Alan Bannister's nephew and put the heat on them about where they were on the days surrounding the Borsch murder. He got nowhere with this attempt to tie them to the case. Both insisted they and the nephew were skiing at Boyne Mountain during that time, and their story checked out. However, during the interrogation, Bookman learned the three were those who stole a great many tires from Standard Tire, and they were stored in an unused upstairs section of Alan Bannister's five-car garage. The fact that he had no knowledge whatsoever of his nephew's thievery didn't prevent Bookman from suggesting perhaps a charge of receiving stolen property might not be out of the question. Afterward, DeVon remarked, "Maybe he'll lay off me for a while."

Zeke had his own comment. "Sound's like out-and-out blackmail."

"All in the eye of the behelder, Ezekial Amos, all in the eye'a the behelder."

"That's be-*hold*-er. I told you that before."

"Yeah, yeah, yeah. Whatever."

The second episode lifting Bookman's spirits occurred during Zeke's ride-along on a night patrol. At 7:30, the chief arrived and they set out. Zeke noted a cold front was again knocking the bottom out of the thermometer.

They roamed around the town proper and to the outer edge of the council's two-mile official zoning jurisdiction. It began to snow and increased in intensity until the top safe speed was about 30 mph.

Aside from tossing Jake Walters, local candidate for International Drunk of the Decade, into the pokey for the umpteenth time, nothing much was happening. They stopped a time or two to shoot the bull with a late night businessman, but soon everyone closed due to lack of customers.

Around midnight, Bookman munched a freebie sandwich and pie at Jim's Truck Stop while the night man installed snow chains on the black and white. The sandwich and pie didn't tempt Zeke. Nothing Jim's served could.

Shortly before 1:30 a.m., DeVon decided to take one more trip around the outskirts before calling it a night. Rounding the curve by the country club, they saw taillights ahead sticking into the roadway at an odd angle. "Uh-oh, whatta we got here? What fool's out in this stuff?"

They eased to a stop behind the car, which had taken a header into the shallow drainage ditch along the narrow road. They could hear the driver gunning the engine in a futile attempt to extricate himself.

Bookman got out and went to the driver's side. After a bit, he returned and reported, "Looks to me like the clown just drove in there. Guess he thought it was the road to town and turned 'bout half-a-mile too soon. Gonna get a chain and try to pull him out. Pretty slick—might hafta call a wrecker."

He went to the trunk of the police cruiser, dug out a tow chain, and began attaching it to the two vehicles. After some cussing and grunting appropriate to the task, he gave instructions to the driver, returned and backed carefully until the chain was taut. Slowly, ever so slowly, the wayward automobile began moving. Once the errant car was back on the road, Bookman retrieved his chain and away drove the freed driver.

The chief sounded magnanimous. "Jerk smelled'a Old Rottensock. Probly should'a Breathalyzed him, but he caught a break with this weather. Didn't wanna stomp around in the cold and snow."

"Never thought I'd live to see you pass up a DUI."

"Not dead certain sure he was drunk. Besides, there's DUIs and there's DUIs."

"You'll need to translate that one for me, Ethel. Who was the driver, anyway? Someone we know?"

"Some fella name'a Lawson."

"Not *John* Lawson! *Town council president Lawson?*"

"The one and only."

"How could you ignore an opportunity to throw him into a cell?" Zeke paused, then answered his own question, "Oh, I get it. You don't arrest him and he lays off you."

"Absolutely no such thing! I don't do that stuff. Sorely tempts a'body though, don't it? Him bein' the lead hound on the town council and a church elder, it'd be a double-dip. Not countin' what the council would do, whataya reckon Call-me-Charlie would think'a one of his flock-bosses gettin' caught all drunked up?"

"If he was intoxicated, how could you let him drive? Why didn't you get his wife to drive him home?"

"Already said I wasn't for sure he was drunk. Besides, his wife couldn't."

"Why not? She polluted, too?"

"Dunno. All I know for sure is, the woman in Lawson's car was pretty oiled, all right, but she was *not* Mrs. John Lawson. She was the sweet young waitress from the country club bar. It closes at eleven o'clock on weeknights, and by my watch, it's close to two-thirty."

Approaching town, Dee began whistling. He dropped Zeke off with, "Things are lookin' up, Gertrude."

23

His head was only halfway to the pillow before Zeke was out cold. Tooling around with Bookman and pulling motorists from the ditch in the wee hours was not conducive to wakefulness. He dreamed someone was setting off bells. They stopped only to begin again seconds later. Jangle-jangle-jangle-jangle, stop. Jangle-jangle-jangle-jangle, stop.

Finally, the sleep-fog cleared enough for his brain to engage. He hadn't bothered to leave the receiver off. Now, some nut was going to keep phoning until he answered or the machine filled. He looked at the clock—7:15. Stumbling to the phone, he previewed and listened without answering.

It was DeVon, and Zeke wasn't happy to hear him. He lifted the receiver. "Why in the name of heaven are you phoning at this hour?"

"It's daylight—time to go to work. Zeke, you hear about that damned newsfarter Jones' editorial last night? In the morning *Trib*, too."

"Didn't hear—don't care. But I have this awful feeling you're going to tell me about it."

"Well, since you're beggin'. In the *Around the State* part'a his program last night, he blasted my department again about the Borsch '*cult crime.*' Said it wasn't solved because of a do-nothin' chief with a bad attitude toward taxpayers. Said the state oughta step in when there was obstruction'a justice by local officials. Damned newsfarter don't even know what obstruction is. Mentioned your name, too. What kind'a release you gonna write?"

"Thank you for sharing that with me at this ungodly hour, Bookman. For the record, I'm not going to write *anything*. Next time you get something this important, write me a letter." He broke the connection and left the receiver off.

Of course he couldn't go back to sleep. A finish-off-cold shower didn't help much, but maybe muscled-up coffee would at least get him to a halfway human stage. He trudged out to care for the dogs while it brewed. *(Is it going to snow forever?)* Slugging coffee and staring morosely out the window, he decided he might as well go to the station—stop at the diner on the way. To cap an already annoying morning, Ol' Emmy chose today to sulk. As her engine sounded as if it were grinding its last, it uttered a croupy gurgle and sputtered to what could be laughingly termed "life."

Stopping at the Country Kitchen proved a big mistake. Someone cut the Jones story from the *Trib* and taped it to the front door. His name and Bookman's were underlined. Inside, the early morning crowd rose as one and gave him a big hand. Jack Lilley, owner of the Sleepy Sheep woolens store, was, as usual, the top banana. Grabbing a sugar dispenser to use as a microphone, he rushed over to "interview" Zeke. "We have with us Mr. Ezekial Tanner. You *are* the Mr. Tanner well known for his obstruction of justice activities, are you not? Good. Tell us how you plan your obstructing. Do you have a natural talent, or does it take considerable training? Speak right into the microphone, sir."

Lilley sped ahead without allowing Zeke to respond. "That's good to hear, Mr. Tanner. Please tell our viewing audience whether you plan to write a book on the subject. You could call it *Ten Ways to Screw Justice*. Speak right into the microphone, sir." Spoons clanked on water glasses accompanying big time laughter.

Zeke grabbed the shaker/mike. "I've never been interviewed by a merchant specializing in sleepy sheep. However, I'll be glad to answer your question as soon as you fill us in on the rumors about you and that cute little curly-haired one you're always advertising."

Before he could continue, DeVon Bookman entered. Of course, the bacon and egg bunch started in on him. He exchanged banter for a minute or two before joining Zeke at the counter. "Whataya intend to do about Jones?"

"I told you before—nothing. Ignore him, and he'll stop screaming when he becomes ridiculous. It's the one thing politicians and newscasters can't stand. When people begin losing interest or cracking jokes about them harping on small potatoes, they move on to something else."

"Wouldn't give any answer a'tall?"

"That's right."

"I still think we oughta zing him."

"OK...if you want to play right into his hands."

The debate continued off and on throughout breakfast and after they went to the station until the deskman knocked and came in. "Chief, I got that stuff from Borsch's places inventoried and ready for the property room. Want the receipt stored in the checkbook filed along with it, don''tcha—instead'a with the others?"

DeVon glanced at Zeke. "Yeah, I do. First, bring everthing in here. I wanna take another look." Then, casually, "Inventory the documents?"

The officer was puzzled. "Documents? Wasn't no *documents*." He left to retrieve the items.

DeVon ham-fisted his desk. "What'n billy-blue-hell's he talkin' about? *What* receipt stored in the checkbook?' We didn't see any."

The deskman returned with envelopes containing miscellaneous papers along with Borsch's checkbook. Taped inside the front cover was an envelope marked, **RECEIPT**.

"Sure this was the only receipt in the checkbook?"

"Yeah, those pockets inside the back covers'a those big checkbooks are the same size as the back and danged easy to overlook—super tight fittin' too, but I got it out, anyhow."

"Anything interestin' in the other stuff?"

"Just inventoried it, Chief—didn't look it over good."

Bookman waved him out. "Yeah, I'll *bet* he didn't look it over good." He took the checkbook's receipt from its envelope. It was a receipt all right, but not any old receipt. It was for safety deposit box rental at the bank and dated the previous March.

Bookman sighed. "Maybe Jones is right. Maybe I'm chopped gizzard. How'd I overlook somethin' like this? Why was it in the checkbook, anyway? How'd we miss the check he wrote for it?"

"It was quite likely in the checkbook because it and the receipt were both banking business. The receipt's dated last March. We didn't look for checks that far back. "

"No excuse for not thinkin' about a safety deposit box."

"Didn't you ask the bank for information about Borsch?"

"Sure did, but there was nothin' said about a box. First, I want Harrison to explain why he didn't mention it when I asked him about Borsch's bankin'. Next, I wanna know what's in it." He reached for the phone.

Judging from what Zeke heard of Bookman's end of the conversation, he was not in the least happy with the banker's answers. He slammed down the receiver. "Bastard played dumb about the box. Said he thought I only wanted to know about Borsch's bankin' transactions. Also said it takes two keys to open a box—one the box-holder has and one the bank keeps. If the box holder's key's lost, it costs seventy-five bucks. If he's dead, then only after the next'a kin or an approved party gets a court order."

"Miss Manchester is the next of kin. Wouldn't it be pretty easy to get her involved?"

"Not takin' any chances she'll balk. We're goin' straight to Judge Jefferson's and get a court order. Jake Walters' drunk case is set for whenever somebody can get him to court, and it might as well be me. Won't take a second, and we can kill two crows with one stick." Zeke sighed.

Soon they were at the judge's with the Town Drunk Emeritus in tow. Jake made his traditional "guilty, your honor" plea and promise not to do it any more. Judge Jefferson gave him the usual stern lecture and the choice of a $50.00 fine or ten days in jail. Walters was nearly always close to broke, but somehow managed to come up with the fine after a day or so in jail. Not doing so would mean facing life sober for a little while.

DeVon put Walters in the outer office and then explained to the judge about the court order needed to authorize opening Bill Borsch's safety deposit box. It took some time for Jefferson to hunt-and-peck it out. "My secretary is off today," he apologized.

They dropped Walters off for deposit in the gray-bar hotel and headed to the bank. On the way, Zeke asked, "Did the judge *ever* have a secretary?"

"Nope, but if he did, today'd be 'er day off."

Zeke waited in the lobby while DeVon went to Harrison's office to serve the court order. In no time at all, he was back and sporting about a 7.5 reading on a ten point red-in-the-face scale. "Damn fool wouldn't honor it! Said MizMartha's attorney called twenty minutes ago sayin' she was gettin' a court order from Judge Nelson to open Borsch's deposit box—she bein' the next'a kin. I told him we had our own right here and now and Judge Jefferson'd hold him in contempt for not abidin' by it. The clown dug in his heels and said he was gonna talk to the attorney first, anyhow."

"What do you plan to do?"

"Well, the usual thing would be to go back to Judge Jefferson and get Harrison cited for contempt. I wanna ponder doin' it, though. I'd like to keep from gettin' twixt the judges if there's some other way. Meantime, after lunch we gotta go back to Borsch's and take another look for that key."

While they ate, Bookman raised questions. "Think MizMartha guessed we might'a been goin' after the box? For that matter, how'd she know there *was* a box? What could be so important she'd be gettin' a court order right now? Reckon she thinks the document she's been askin' about is in there? Only thing I can think of as bein' a *document* is a will. Reckon it could be what's she's lookin' for—her bein' the only livin' relative. Just can't figure MizMartha the kind to be so all-fired anxious to get at a will. Although, she's always been known to be pretty nickel-thrifty. Never know about folks. Zeke, *you* reckon it's a will she's after?"

"Who knows, Great Chief? Only Miss Martha can answer that and many other questions."

"I s'pose. *Whatever's* in the box, I'd like to lay hands on that key soon as I can. Be better'n havin' to get a locksmith to drill out the lock. Let's eat up and get on over to Borsch's."

They finished quickly and went to the barber's house. Oddly, the front door at Bosch's was unlocked. DeVon wasn't surprised. "Takes nothin' but a skeleton key."

When they went inside, it was obvious someone was there ahead of them. Drawers were upside down on the floor and contents strewn everywhere. Bookman was disgusted. "Just lookit this mess! Somethin' amateurs do huntin' for whatever they can steal."

Another hour's shakedown and they still came up empty. Bookman stood in the middle of the room, hands on hips. "We've seen every piece'a rat crap in this place. Let's do the garage and barbershop again and get it over with."

They searched the garage and found no key. No luck after a brief stop at the barbershop, either. Zeke remarked, "I've seen so much of Borsch's house and shop, I'm thinking of getting my mail delivered to one of them—let's go." As they departed, he asked, "Have you decided what to do about Harrison not honoring Judge Jefferson's court order?"

"Judge Nelson got Jefferson started in law school way back. He'd be awful slow about gettin' crossways'a Nelson if he could possibly help it. I'll phone the town attorney. Maybe he can stumble into a loophole so I don't hafta get untidy with Jefferson."

The attorney was not in, so DeVon left a message. They put their constitutions to the test one more time with station-house coffee while they sat and discussed the possible whereabouts of the key. Halfway to another sip of the acidic swamp water, Zeke suddenly set down his cup, then placed both hands against his temples impersonating Carnak the Great. "Oh Great Chief, All Seeing Poo-bah, I believe I may be able to shed some light on the key mystery. You must cross your heart not to do anything to hurt yourself or me when you learn how stupid we may've been."

"Not in the mood for bull. Whataya sayin?"

"The key could be right in your property room. Didn't the coroner recover a ring of keys from Borsch's jogging suit?"

Bookman was halfway around his desk almost before Zeke finished. Dashing into the property room, he jerked open the safe, pulled out the evidence packages containing Borsch's personal effects, opened the one marked "**KEYS**," and dumped them onto the table. There on the ring with the others was what was clearly a safety deposit box key with Charles Harrison's bank name stamped on it.

The chief slapped himself on the forehead. "Talk about stupid! Damn thing was right under our noses all the time!"

"Don't feel bad. The L.A. police had one of the Manson gang's murder weapons in a property room for years before they made the connection. What do you plan to do now?"

"Well, we still gotta straighten out the court order tangle. Can't wait to see Harrison's face when I whip out this key." He removed it and put it on the ring with his collection.

"All happier, Great Chief of Police Bookman, sir?"

"Told you things were lookin' up. This proves it."

"Yeah, like you knew you'd find the receipt and the key."

"My feelin's aren't always specific."

After returning the remaining keys to the safe, they chatted briefly in Bookman's office. Zeke said he was going to fall over from lack of sleep pretty soon. "I'm going home and sack out before I lie down and die right here. Don't you ever sleep?"

"Us real men don't need much."

"That why your eyes look as if they're going to start bleeding any second?"

"It's your own eyes you're lookin through. Go on home, weaklin'. See you later, Gertrude."

"Later, Ethel."

Zeke walked out back to feed his dogs before hitting the sack. Despite his bedraggled condition, he couldn't resist an at-the-ready Husky and the brown-eyed begging of a black Lab with a Frisbee in his mouth. "OK, OK, we can go at it for a few minutes."

Nearing exhaustion from Frisbee-tossing and arm-wrestling, a half-hour later Zeke called a halt—so tired he skipped dinner and went directly to bed.

24

Twelve hours sleep made a new man of Zeke. Awake before dawn, he finished the morning routine in record time and was well into a second coffee while the stereo finished Tchaikovsky's *Fifth*. In the silence following the finale, he sat immersed in pleasant reverie.

Unwilling to let well enough alone, his mental scanner flicked to the subject of the Saturday appointment with Marjorie Louise he couldn't yet bring himself to call a "date." Trying not to think too much about the schedule for *after* the game, the subject crept in, anyhow. (*Marjorie said we could have a late supper. All right, I can handle that. We'll eat, talk, and then I'll see her to her car. But, won't it be awfully late for her to drive home alone? Holy smokes, will she be staying over? So what if she does? We'll say goodnight in the lobby, and she'll go one way, me the other*). He sat up straight in his chair and shook his head. (*Get a grip, Tanner.*)

The phone rang. It was DeVon. "What's keepin' you?"

"Does the town council know how much time you spend on the phone bothering me?"

"You forget? We gotta start gettin' the court order mess straightened out."

"You don't need me for that."

"Come on down anyway. There's likely other stuff comin' up." He cut off further protests by hanging up.

Zeke's curiosity goaded him into going to the station. Bookman was still basking in the pleasure of yesterday's good news about finding the key and ignored Zeke's insults about interrupting his morning concert. The chief was also reliving his anticipation of flashing the safety deposit box key at Charlie Harrison. "Yessir, things are lookin' up." He continued his euphoria-fix a while longer before phoning the town attorney again about the court order Miss Manchester was planning to get from Judge Nelson allowing her to look into Borsch's safety deposit box.

The attorney was in. "Good morning, Chief, I was about to phone about the matter. As best as I can tell, the only options you have are to go ahead and ask Jefferson to cite Harrison for contempt or to ask Judge Nelson to hold a hearing prior to issuing Miss Manchester a court order."

"*Damnation!* There nothin' you can do?"

"Well Chief, my office probably shouldn't even be delving into this, but maybe I could check off the record with Judge Nelson about holding a hearing when she asks for the order. Want me to do that?"

"Oh yeah."

Later, all the way to lunch at the diner, the chief was still griping about lawyers and judges before relating the results of his phone call to Roseville to check on True Prophet and his bunch. "Asked the chief'a police for info about the holy ding-dong leader or whatever he goes by. They had nothin' that'd help. He's been around Roseville for about ten years. Parts'a his flock'a both men and women nutty-buddies come and go all the time, so it's pretty hard to get much of a book on any of 'em except they put goofy signs on their vans—mostly that chicken-foot thing hippies use."

Zeke chuckled. "You mean the peace symbol? It originated years ago and wasn't limited to what you call 'hippies.' Be careful or you'll show your age again, Great Chief"

"Yeah, yeah—whatever."

Twyla Jean came over, flashed a smile, and told Zeke there was a big surprise for his dessert. With a sweeping presentation fit for truffles Lurinda served it. There sat the one thing near the top of his most despised list since he was barely old enough to hold a spoon—tapioca pudding. Even worse, there was no topping. He managed a weak smile and began pushing it around in the bowl. *(Why'd they do this? Everyone knows how I just hate tapioca.)* Lurinda and Twyla Jean stood by, hinting broadly for a compliment for what they prepared especially for him. Try as he might, it was a struggle to down a quarter-teaspoonful at a time. He really loathed the stuff.

After what seemed a century to Zeke, Lurinda could stand it no longer. She broke into gales of laughter and was joined by TeeJay and DeVon. Zeke saw that the joke was on him and threatened them with his spoon, but was appeased when Lurinda set a small serving of peach cobbler before him. "See, Zeke, you get rewarded for staying on your diet."

"Maybe there'll be another if you stick to it," TeeJay added. DeVon didn't participate—too busy engulfing his over-size portion.

The cobbler crunchers lingered over coffee and exchanged barbs with the lunch crowd for a while before Lurinda rushed over to tell Bookman there was an urgent call from the station. He listened a minute, then turned to Zeke. "By golly, Tanner, I told you things were gettin' better, but this one sounds too good to be true. Guy just walked in and confessed to offin' Borsch! C'mon."

They sped to the station, the chief using lights and siren, something he rarely did. He strode up the sidewalk at a half-lope, Zeke straining to keep up.

The individual handcuffed to the table in the interrogation room, the "box," was as improbable a looking murderer as one could imagine. He was average everything—height, weight, hair, eyes, clothes and any other criterion defining the term. Zeke thought the man would be invisible in a crowd of two.

Bookman took a chair across the table from the suspect, Zeke at the end. The chief spoke calmly. "OK—before we start, let's everbody get comfortable. Somethin' I can do for you? Coffee? Soda? You smoke?"

"No thank you sir, I only want to confess and take my punishment."

"That's fine. Why don'tcha start with your name?"

"My name is Carl Thomas McPherson. I live at 3211 Northeast Tecumseh Street in Muncie, Indiana. I killed Mr. William Borsch."

Bookman waited several seconds before asking, "Mind tellin' us how you did it?"

"Why must I do that? I killed him. Isn't that enough? I want to take my punishment."

Again the chief paused. "Mr. McPherson, would you excuse us a minute?" He rose and motioned Zeke to follow him out.

Bookman sat at his desk and buzzed the deskman. "Get me Chief Monfried Anderson in Muncie."

In a minute, the Muncie chief of police came on. "Stretch Bookman, you old snakehead! In trouble again? Pinch the wrong widow? What can I do for you?"

"Monty, I leave the pinchin' up to you. They don't call you '*Claws* Anderson' for nothin'. We got this little case'a murder over here and there's a citizen in my office claimin' to be the doer. Says he's from your town."

"I know about the killing. Let me guess who's there trying to take the rap. Could it be Carl McPherson by any chance?"

Bookman slammed his palm onto the desk. "By Jehosiphat, I knew he was a phony the minute I laid eyes on him!"

Anderson laughed. "You're right on. He's known all around here as 'Confessin' Carl.' Surprised he hasn't been over to your town to confess before. He's confessed to so many crimes in these parts we're thinking of making out a standard form so he can mail his latest confession to the nearest jurisdiction. He was a student at the university until he started hearing voices of dead professors. The mental health people tried to give him some help, but it didn't do any good. These days, about the only way he gets attention is to confess."

"Might'a known! No way we're gonna have the answer to this one fall out'a the sky. Every time we get what looks like a break, it falls through." He went on to bring his fellow chief up to date on the details and progress of the Borsch investigation, finishing with, "You got any more'a these nuts hangin' in your trees, shake 'em off over there, will you?"

DeVon sent Confessin' Carl on his way, and grumbled, "By damn, Tanner, shot down again. Don't look like it was meant to be we're ever gonna catch a real break."

"How about some cheese with that whine, Mr. Gloom and Doom? What ever happened to 'Things are looking up?' Of course you're going to solve it."

"Yeah, yeah, yeah."

"I'm out of here. This down-in-the-mouth stuff may be contagious. I'm going back to my numbers and music."

Zeke arrived home to the dogs barking their usual greeting, and old lady guilt gouged him again. He walked out to their houses. "Can't take you for a big run right now, but you can have a little romp in the orchard." Once freed, they dashed off through the snow, stopping at every tree for target practice. All too soon for the dogs, he called them back. "I'll take you for a longer outing real soon, and that's a promise."

As usual, the answering machine light demanded attention. He returned several calls, then set up the kitchen table as a command post for solving the mysterious markings puzzle. Again dragging out every puzzle book and his old training manuals from Navy decoding days, he began his new attack. Almost four hours later, he was no closer to an answer than when he started.

A quick dinner, and he was back at it. For once, there was no evening jazz. Around 10, he still had no answers, but felt one might be floating just out of reach. Tomorrow he'd try again. In the silence, the basketball game "appointment" with Marjorie Louise came bubbling up. In addition to his other concerns about it, earlier in the week he allowed DeVon to pry from him the information about meeting Marjorie. Now he was kicking himself. He reined in his galloping thoughts and turned in.

25

Saturday, Zeke whiled away time until well into the afternoon before dressing for his evening. He decided to begin his trip westward to Indianapolis early. *(If Ol' Emmy throws one of her conniptions, it'll give me some time to fix the problem.)* True to her perverse nature, she purred like a kitten all the way.

(Wow! Can that be the Excelsior Hotel?) The old girl's facade was completely restored to her Victorian splendor and an adjoining self-parking garage added. He breathed a sigh of relief. Now he needn't hand over his temperamental companion to a sneering adolescent-appearing valet-parking attendant who didn't appreciate mechanical classics. Four floors up, grinding along in low gear all the way, he coaxed her into a stall.

With time to kill, he chose a seat in the lobby. It wasn't at all as he remembered. Maybe the outside had been restored, but the interior went the way of so many fine old hotels. The spacious lobby with its plush seating and pleasant sense of airiness was now a clinically sterile environment with chairs not designed for lingering, a small motel-copy check-in area, and an assortment of glitzy boutiques.

Zeke chose the chair he thought to be the least backbreaking and began his vigil. Emotions teetering between apprehension and anticipation, he tried hard for nonchalance. As the revolving door spun out guests, he eyed them quickly before turning to look at an imaginary object across the way. He wasn't having much luck with the nonchalance after the third or fourth attempt, however. *(I've been here only a few minutes, and already I'm beginning to feel like Sam Slewfoot. Maybe if I bought a newspaper, I'd be less conspicuous.)*

Through the revolving door, another guest appeared. He started to glance away again before realizing it was Marjorie Louise. *(Lord a'mighty, she's still the prettiest sight I've ever seen! Look at her—still the same gorgeous brunette—still walks as if she's floating on air. Looks about twenty-five. How does she do it?)* He rose, and she came right over and gave him a hello kiss. "Zeke! I'm glad you're early, too. The Ex has changed, but you're the same welcome sight."

He felt his ears heating up and a mumble coming on. Before his tongue could stagger around and stammer it out, she said, "Watch my bag will you? I must register. Checked in yet?"

"No, I uh..."

"Doesn't matter, I'll be right back."

(Register? Doesn't matter?) He watched her at the desk. Apprehension was definitely way out ahead of the rest of the field. She returned, followed by a bellhop. Handing him a tip, she directed, "Take my bag up please. Bring your luggage in yet, Zeke?"

"No, I uh..."

"No problem. We have oodles of time. Like to have a drink and a snack? How about Nemo's Steak House? It's still the best in town."

Zeke felt he was in a time warp. During college, Nemo's was *their* place. "Sounds like a plan," he managed.

She took his arm. "Nemo's it is. It's right on the way to the arena. Why don't we walk?"

"Sounds like a plan." *(Ye gods, is that the only thing I'm going to say all evening?)*

A block into the walk, Marjorie remarked, "Might I say, Mr. Ezekial, you're looking very dapper this evening."

Some fool he didn't know answered, "And, might I say, Mizz Marjorie, your ensemble is elegant, but suffers in light of its bearer." *(Good grief, did I say that? I better go back to ' uh.')*

"Why Zeke, you silver-tongued devil, you. I'll bet you say that to all your lady admirers."

"Yep, all four-hundred-odd of them. I can hardly keep up."

"Not the way I remember it."

Red ears and all, he followed Marjorie Louise into Nemo's. Everything else in the world might change, but the one constant was Nemo's. The iced choose-your-own-steak case, wooden floors rutted by millions of footsteps, booths equally worn, and the ancient thirty-foot bar lit with lights right out of the 1920s all virtually shouted stability. Dinner menus were non-existent. Why bother? You could have one of three cuts of steak, blood-rare to medium-well, vegetable, salad and bread of the day.

For the late afternoon munchie crowd, there were also three choices. No need for menus here, either—pick a "Number" with its chalked one-word description from the blackboard in back of the bar. **ONE—SALAD TWO—SEAFOOD THREE—COMBO**. The specific contents of each varied daily according to whatever the chef decided to include. Don't bother your waiter with questions, just pick your Number. For the after-the-game bunch, Nemo's also offered a Pacers-Burger or Deli-Delight, a mountain of shaved ham or paper-thin slices of cold sliced beef with genuine Swiss on a Kaiser—chunky jumbo dill strips and baked potato chips included.

Want to gripe or haggle? Take your business down the street to Philippe's, and don't let the doorknob hit you in the rear on the way out. Pretty rough style for a newcomer, but it worked for four generations. Rookie diners could forgive almost anything if they recovered sufficiently from the initial shock to scarf down a Nemo's steak.

Marjorie and Zeke worked themselves free of coats and grabbed a booth. A balding waiter who would never see the sunny side of fifty again strolled over. "What to drink?"

Marjorie Louise looked across. "Zeke?"

"An Orange Blossom for the lady, G and T for me."

"Zeke, you remembered. How nice."

The waiter returned with the beverages. "Decided on your Number yet?" It sounded more like a dare to refuse than a question, but Zeke rejected the challenge. "We'll chat a while first."

When they barely finished their drinks, the waiter returned. "Another?"

"Yes, please."

He brought the drinks and dared again, "Sure you don't wanna order your Number yet? You can talk and eat and drink all at the same time."

They surrendered. Marjorie ordered a "Three," Zeke a "One." Half of the fun of Nemo's was trying to guess what their selection would contain. Marjorie's was a bacon, shrimp, mushroom and onion kabob. Outstanding. Zeke's was Nemo's traditional garbage salad. Maybe no one ever succeeded in getting an accurate count of the ingredients, but however many there were on any given day, it was always delicious.

An enjoyable hour later, the early-dinner diners started drifting in, and the waiter began to toss increasingly obvious hurry-it-up stares in Zeke's direction. Finally, he suggested, "Guess we better get started for the ball-yard."

"Yes, I recall you like to watch the warm-ups, though I've never quite known why. A guy thing, I guess."

"Right, so don't try to understand it."

"Well, aren't *we* the big macho-macho? Is mighty-man going to let poor little me tag along as his servant?"

"Only as long as you stay six paces to the rear."

"Does mighty-man remember I have the tickets?"

"Then you need walk only three paces behind."

"Sure I can't get you to relent ever so slightly?" She moved closer and took his arm in a firm grasp as they left Nemo's.

"Well, OK, but if people begin to stare and make remarks, you'll have to drop back."

She was silent for a while before asking, "Zeke, have you noticed how easy it is for us? I must admit I was a wee bit nervous at first, but now feel completely at ease."

(So was I, until you mentioned it.) "It's like learning to use a typewriter. You may be a little shaky after a long layoff, but it soon comes back to you."

"Zeke Tanner, always the romantic. I don't believe I've ever been compared to a typewriter. Ah declare, Rhett, y'all still say the sweetest thangs."

"Frankly, my dear, once you have it, you always have it."

"Y'all care to define *it,* Rhett?"

"Happy to oblige, Scarlet, y'all. But, *it* has a great many forms, and when a'body has so many *its, a* goodly amount of time is necessary to define 'em all."

"Modest too. What more could a lady ask?"

"Only one of my many *its.* Well, here we are. Say something about tickets?"

She dug into her purse. "I see only one. Where could the other be?"

"No problem. Hand it over and tell me where to meet you after the game."

"As I said, always the romantic, especially when there's a basketball game." She gave him the tickets.

The contest was close for about five minutes before the Pacers starting shooting out the lights, and even the most die-hard Knickerbocker knew the outcome. Minutes from the end, Marjorie asked whether he had enough, adding, "Want to go back to Nemo's for a steak or somewhere else for a lighter meal?"

"I remember the size of Nemo's steaks. Half a sandwich would be about right. You think?"

"Sounds like a plan," she mimicked.

As usual, the place was jammed with people crowded in all the way to the door. After twenty minutes, Zeke and Marjorie moved up only two places. They were deciding whether to try another restaurant when a fellow seated half a dozen tables away stood and shouted, "Marjorie Louise! Marjorie Louise! Come on back! We'll squeeze you in. I want you to meet these people."

Somehow, he looked vaguely familiar to Zeke. Marjorie muttered under her breath, "Yes, I'll bet he could *squeeze* me in all right. Thinks he's God's gift to women, but he's only a monster octopus in human form—five hundred hands always in motion. Every time he comes to the university, I have to practice martial arts for a week beforehand."

The object of her comments wasn't about to give up. He kept shouting and looked about to come out to drag her to his table and still wouldn't stop after she waved him off and pointed to Zeke. She grimaced, "I better go back and say hello before he gets any worse. Then we'll go someplace else."

Through all of this, Zeke said nothing. Now he offered, "If you really don't want to speak to him, you needn't. We can leave."

"I'll give him a minute for the good of the university." She slipped between tables to the offensive shouter. Obviously, she was being introduced to the others at the table while the oaf moved his hand up and down her back. Just as obviously, the others were trying to crowd together to make room for her. The self-styled lady-killer now held Marjorie Louise by an arm while signaling a waiter for another chair with the other.

Zeke was at the point of intervening when she politely but firmly removed his hand, waved a quick goodbye, and returned. "Come on, let's go before I make a headline."

Once outside, they walked in silence for a few steps. The frosty air didn't lower her temperature a single degree. "I simply cannot *stand* that man. I've known him since being part of big a campaign to raise money for the university's fieldhouse expansion. He was a jerk then, but lately he's much worse—a real lecher. As I said, five hundred hands always in motion."

"Sounds like someone I could've used on defense. I thought he looked a little familiar. Anyone I should know?"

"Oh, you've probably seen him on TV in heavy makeup. He has the nightly ten o'clock news on a local station with a commentary afterward. Thinks he's a journalist, but he's not even a decent hack. I would've ignored him, but he'd find some way to knock the university."

"I assume he has a name?"

"Thought I told you. It's Elmer Jones. Don't tell me you've never heard of him."

Zeke stopped in his tracks, chuckling. Marjorie Louise whirled. "What's so funny? Think having someone paw me is *funny*! Maybe you'd like me to go back for some more massaging!"

"Simmer down, tiger. I know about the one, the only, Elmer Jones. In fact, I've spoken with him. Since you're such a big fan of his show, I'm surprised you didn't know I've been a target of his commentaries."

She readied another blast, but stopped abruptly. "What! You *know* him? Why didn't you tell me? I *never* watch his show! Why in the world were you on it?"

"Didn't say I knew him, didn't say I was *on* his show. I said I spoke with him and was a target of his commentary." He described the incidents.

Marjorie was delighted. "I'm glad *someone's* standing up to him. You're my hero, Zeke." She took his arm again and held it close.

In spite of himself, he felt an exhilarating shiver. *(Easy does it, Tanner.)* As they walked on, she suggested, "Why don't we get a bite at the hotel bar?"

"Sounds like a plan."

They ordered drinks, but got bad news from the waitress. "Sorry folks, the bar menu stops at ten. You can get room service until midnight, though."

They sat quietly, sipping their drinks, saying little. Finally, Marjorie asked, "Think we could try room service?" Without another word, they went to the elevator.

*****

As they lingered over breakfast coffee, Marjorie gazed over her cup and began, "Zeke, you were talking about the *'its'* last night? If it doesn't swell your ego too much, I can attest to the fact you haven't lost *it*. And, better still, I think *we* haven't lost it on that score. Zeke, it's been absolutely perfect. Yesterday...last night...this morning. Perhaps I shouldn't bring up something I've been thinking and chance diminishing what's happened, but here goes. It must be very, very, obvious my feelings for you still run deep. Deeper than I thought possible. Do you want to consider this only a one-nighter or maybe a same-time-next-year event? I suppose I could live with that, but perhaps we could move along slowly into a wonderful continuing relationship. Would you like to talk about it or wait a while?"

He remained silent so long she stared into her cup and sighed, "Well anyway, it was a thought."

"No, no, it's not I don't think it would be about the greatest thing ever for me. It's just that I can't envision someone who's made so much of her life..."

"Dammit, Zeke Tanner! Shut *up*!" Her cup clattered into its saucer. You think I give one *damn* about that! You think I'm so shallow I'd base my feelings for you on some stupid comparison of who did what with a career? That's what you think? Is it! Well, you're right, Tanner. You've helped me see the light. It's all based on degrees and offices." She was so mad, tears began welling up, and her speech splintered into sputters.

She drew a deep breath to continue, but Zeke reached across, clasped both her hands, and held them tightly. "Please don't speak another word. I was about to say before the explosion, I couldn't see how anyone so accomplished, and incidentally the most beautiful person I've ever known, could be so blind. How could she want to take such a big gamble? But if she did, I'd know I was the luckiest rascal who ever drew breath. I'm with you on taking it slow and easy. We're both more mature, and I think it's got a chance. Why don't we just let last night's stardust settle a little and allow what happens to happen."

She smiled and hankie-dabbed her eyes. "Look at us, Zeke. It's like the ballplayer said, 'Déjà vu all over again.' We fight, then you say the sweetest things. I don't want to get into that cycle again—it cost us too much. And you know what? I can't even remember everything the big blowup back in college was about."

"Me neither". *(Liar, liar, pants on fire!)*

"As I said, Ezekial, we're both more mature, so we surely should be able to recognize the symptoms and stop it."

(Like when I'm not pointing out you're the one who was doing all the fighting just now.)

More amenable conversation followed before Marjorie had to get back to attend an afternoon tea for a visiting scholar, but there was time for a walk. They strolled along in the sparkling sunlight, not talking much, enjoying one another's presence and nodding occasionally to churchgoers coming from the Cathedral on the Circle. They returned the greeting, probably having their own thoughts about this couple ambling along so close together and not appearing to be aware of the cold.

It was time to say goodbye. Walking to her car, nothing much needed to be said. Zeke held her for a moment and then she was gone. He didn't watch her out of sight—it was bad luck.

He took note of the spring in his step as he went to Ol' Emmy. *(There's life in the old boy yet.)* Even the antique Blazer seemed to be almost sprightly. *(Maybe it's the overnight association with the other vehicles in the garage.)*

Naturally, the dogs were overjoyed to see him. Expecting to return last night, Zeke felt guilty even though he left plenty of food and was glad he installed a heating device for their water last fall. As a reward for their patience, he allowed them a lengthy romp in the orchard.

Zeke spent the remainder of the day listening to music and contemplating the events of the past twenty-four hours—of the future, too. *(Well, take it easy and allow whatever happens to happen.)*

26

Still on cloud nine, Zeke drank coffee and puttered around Monday before eating. He decided to forego the usual pseudo-food cereal with skim-milk routine and go to the diner. Bookman was at the counter with his hay-hand breakfast. "If it isn't the wanderin' boy come home to roost."

"Can it, big beak—don't start. What is this, a second breakfast? Didn't get enough to eat the first time around?"

"Get to work at a decent time like us workin' stiffs, and you'd know why I'm late. Been ridin' the town attorney to get in touch with Judge Nelson about holdin' a court order hearin'."

"Any luck?"

`"Nah, not yet. Said he couldn't get hold of him."

Before Twyla Jean could bring Zeke's regular diet breakfast, Bookman prodded, "We gotta hurry up. Wantcha to take a look at the info we collected on those new people in that new housin' development east'a town. You know—the ones who moved here last fall to work in Bannister's paper factory. I was goin' over Wilson's reports about the health-nut club where Borsch went, and a couple of 'em are members. Had my man Hackman dig up everthing he could about everbody out there and then break it down every which way, but nothin' points to nothin.' Maybe you can see somethin' he didn't. Smithson's crew asked around and found out they do lots'a partyin' together. Could be it's only natural with most of 'em probly not knowin' many folks in town and several of 'em workin' at the same place, butcha never know. Maybe you could talk to Smitty, too."

"Thanks, but no thanks. I'm not going to hurry my breakfast, and I'm *certainly* not planning to pry into the background of citizens who aren't suspected of anything."

"Hell man, *everbody*'s a suspect. It's like eatin' those little peanuts, the ones with the husks. You grab a handful, husks and all, and rub everthing 'round and 'round between your palms till the husks come off, then blow 'em away and eat the peanuts."

Their exchanges concerning Bookman's investigative tactics continued until the chief changed the subject. "Gonna tell me about your date? Remember, this is your old bud talkin'. What's the story?"

"Let's consider the subject covered right now, anteater snout."

"Fine by me, but you're the one who started it."

"*Me!*"

"If you hadn't gone out with her, the subject would'a never come up."

"That's it! I'm going home to higher class company—my dogs, that is."

"Don't hafta be so blamed ouchy. All I asked was the details'a your personal love life."

"Which word was so tough to understand? I said the subject was closed. Here's a little gift I have for buttinskis." Zeke shoved his check across the table and left.

He spent Monday afternoon and much of Tuesday in another fruitless attempt at solving the numbers puzzle, including phoning some of his Navy decoding-unit pals—no help. He was tempted to drop a line to Marjorie, but was he rushing things? Maybe yes, maybe no. He started a note once or twice, but hesitated. It *was* too soon. Hadn't they agreed to let things simmer a while? *(Better put it off at least until the end of the week.)*

Shuffling through mail next morning, he immediately recognized Marjorie Louise's handwriting on the blue envelope. Tossing the unopened junk into the entryway basket reserved for it, he tore open her letter.

> Dear Zeke,
>
> We are too mature not to be completely honest. It's Tuesday morning, and the stardust has settled a bit. However, my thinking hasn't changed in the least. It amazes me to discover I could have such intense feelings after all this time, but I do. I'm hoping the same is true for you. If not, I will understand completely and we will remain the best of friends. Whatever happens, I shall always keep the weekend as one of my dearest memories.
>
> If you still want to let the relationship grow, I have a suggestion how we might be able to visit without interference and missing one another on the telephone. What do you think about getting a computer? It's faster than letters, and we could communicate whenever we like. I know you hoped never to deal with what you call 'confusers,' but it would be easy for you. Is it something to consider?
>
> Love,
> Marjorie

The first line threw him for a moment. He hoped the envelope wouldn't contain a "Dear Zeke" letter, but that opening line surely looked to be the start of one. Then he read the rest and smiled. *(Just like that Marjorie—never one to mince words.)*

After lunch, he tried knocking out a few items for his recently begun column, *Stony Crossing Comments*, for the *Wayne City Tribune*, but Marjorie's letter kept jumping in the way. He abandoned the column and began typing a reply.

Dear Marjorie,

>When I received your letter, I was afraid it might be bad news, but was delighted to see we share the same thoughts. I, too, am surprised at the intensity of feelings. Yes, I want to give the relationship a chance to flourish. As the song says, *Ain't That a Kick in the Head*—how about us, after this much time!
>
>As to the confuser, I suppose I could try it, but won't guarantee anything. Those devices are the products of the devil's workshop as far as I'm concerned. I always hoped to be struck by lightning before being forced to deal with the information (garbage?) age. I'm still coming to grips with the reciprocating automobile engine. Nevertheless, I will gather my courage, swallow my pride, and sneak into a confuser store—if there's one with clerks old enough to shave.
>
> Love
Zeke

He tackled his *Stony Crossing Comments* once more, only to have his reply to Marjorie keep interfering. Was it too soon to mail it? As he sat considering his question, the telephone rang. *(Heck with it, probably nothing important.)* After the fourth ring, the answering machine's PREVIEW function took over.

To his surprise, Marjorie was speaking. "Zeke, it's me. Please pick up."

It's not as if he broke any records getting to the phone or anything, but he juggled and nearly dropped the receiver grabbing for it. "Hello! Yes, I'm right here. I was just thinking of you."

"That's nice to hear. Zeke, I phoned about a letter I sent. Get it yet?"

"This morning."

"I was worried about rushing things a bit."

"Not at all, Marjorie. I even wrote a reply—wanted to tell you my thinking hadn't changed, either. But I was also concerned about rushing things."

"Oh good, I feel better. I feel great, in fact. We may be on to something. What about the computer idea?"

"Scares me to death, but I'll pull its plug if it starts bossing me around. Don't have the vaguest idea about what to buy, though."

"One of these days, maybe we could shop for one. I could help with what you need."

"You certainly can do *that*, Marjorie."

"With the *computer!*"

"Oh that, too."

"You haven't changed, Zeke Tanner. Back to the computer, the middle of the month I have both weekends free. Check your calendar and let me know which would be better."

"I can tell you right now. Let's make it the 14th. We can combine Valentine's Day and shopping. Where shall we shop?"

"It really doesn't make much difference. There are computer stores everywhere."

"OK. Marjorie, I'm delighted you called. It's great to hear your voice. Guess I won't need to send you my letter."

"Delightful to hear you, too, but please send it, anyway. Counting the days, Ezekial Amos."

"Back atcha, Marjorie Louise. See you."

"See you."

With Marjorie's call weaving in and out of his thoughts, it took all of the next hour to finish his column. After a quick read, he took it to the post office for the late out-going mail.

Following his habit, Zeke filled the evening with dinner and jazz before retiring. Two hours later, something awakened him. He became aware of Ace and Bandit interspersing grumbling and fretting with outright barking. He listened for a while, expecting them to settle down, but they kept at it. *(Looks as if they aren't going to shut up. Better take a look.)* He slipped into his robe and slippers and stepped onto the back porch into a clear night bathed in the light of a full moon. The robe afforded little protection. *(Wow, it's cold!)* "Hey guys, what's the trouble?"

Both dogs turned at his voice, but continued their fussing. They looked back into the trees, complaining under their breath again. Zeke heard a car motor running at the far edge of his property. So that was it—high school kids doing what high school kids do. The neckers and the bright night upset the dogs. "Guys, it's a school night. They'll be gone pretty soon."

No sooner did he speak than came sounds of a departing car. "OK, gentlemen, let's all try to get some sleep."

A perfunctory gripe or two, and Ace and Bandit decided order had been restored and returned to their houses. Zeke clicked up his blanket a notch and dropped off.

27

The Borsch case was at a standstill. Most of the media lost interest, so Zeke had little to do. He spent time listening to music while occupied with the number mystery—no success. Judging from this morning's snowfall still in progress, it probably wasn't going to be one of the good days. Bookman phoned earlier to say the town attorney continued to drag his feet about helping with the court order hang-up. Then there was no coffee or milk, Sunday night's snow yet to be cleared from the streets, and Ol' Emmy throwing a tantrum before he got her headed toward the diner. *(What next?)*

He stopped at his mailbox and got the answer. Buried in the usual batch of catalogs to be immediately tossed away was a letter, the return address shouting pompously: H. CHARLES ACKERMAN, EVANGELIST. It stated that the preacher had spoken with Zeke and obtained his solemn vow to attend church regularly. The preacher blessed him for doing so, but if Brother Tanner didn't follow up on his avowed promise, there would be no alternative but to recommend that formal action be taken soon. Six elders also signed as the "Membership Committee."

Disbelieving his eyes, he read the letter again. (*Dirty dog liar knows very well I made no such commitment. They try deaconing and eldering me, and they'll have a hot reception. Wonder how they'd feel about shaking off a couple of big mean dogs!*)

Zeke gunned an astounded Ol' Emmy into action so abruptly she regretted starting at all. He was going to tell off a few people! His mind raced with what he might put in a letter. (*Letter be damned, I'm gonna do this in person!*) By the time he reached Main Street, he simmered down, but not by much.

Wheeling left across both lanes, he angled into a parking space as DeVon arrived for lunch. "Old girl's actin' frisky this mornin'. Give her a talkin' to?" All he got in response was a grunt. The chief followed him into the diner and warned, "Everbody look out! Terrible Tanner's on the prowl, and he's out for blood. Keep away, he's in a real ugly mood and lookin' to drink." Still no response from Zeke. They took a seat in a booth, and Bookman coaxed, "Tell mommy all about what's caused your bloomer-bind."

After quickly recounting his other morning tribulations, Zeke blasted Ackerman and showed DeVon the letter. "I'm so angry, I can't decide what to do."

"Looks like you've hit the big time, junior. Pretty hard for me to remember when I've seen you this percolated. Best chill out a day or two so's not to go off half-cocked."

"Good advice, I suppose. OK, I'll give it a rest, but I'm not through with it. What's new at the shop?"

"Nothin', a'course."

On their way out and still steaming about Ackerman's letter, Zeke stepped into the kitchen to show it to Lurinda. "Doesn't surprise me, Zeke. I hear he's been putting really heavy heat on members he thinks need extra prodding." She glanced around to see whether DeVon was outside before continuing, "I suppose I'll be getting some kind of letter next. Ackerman was in here not long ago talking about Dee and me not being really married. *God*, don't tell him though! I'm not sure I *ever* will."

Before Zeke could respond, Bookman came rushing back in. "C'mon, Zeke! The desk just radioed that Last Dime Dalton wants an escort to the hospital. Somethin's happened at MizMartha's store."

They dashed out and saw Dalton's hearse being backed across the sidewalk toward the recessed entryway to Manchester's Office Supply and Card Shop. Racing across the street, they arrived as Last Dime was getting out. Bookman demanded, "What is it?"

"Don't know for sure, Chief. Doc Forsythe said to get here on the double. Said Miss Manchester phoned she'd come to after passin' out. Here he is now."

Dr. Forsythe hurried from his car and directed, "Get ready to transport her to the hospital at Wayne City. She's been having dizzy spells all week, and I suspect it's been light strokes. S o far, she's refused to go, but she's going this time if I have to hogtie her."

He needn't have worried about using force to place Martha Manchester into the "ambulance." Voice scarcely above a whisper, she told him she'd go, but it was a wasted trip—her time had come.

"Nonsense, Martha, you'll be fine," lied the doctor.

As they were lifting her onto the gurney, she clutched at Bookman's arm. "DeVon Eugene, please go with me to the hospital. There's something I must talk with you about. Promise me?"

"Certainly. We'll be escortin' all the way and be right with you after we get there."

Bookman's overheads and siren clearing the way, they sped off to Wayne City. He radioed the station giving their position and ordered the hospital alerted. A mile from town, a sheriff's cruiser shot by in the opposite direction. DeVon glanced at his side-view mirror. "Looked like that fool, Benson. Turnin' around. What the devil's he up to?"

Siren and lights full on, the sheriff's cruiser caught up and stayed behind Last Dime. The chief was furious. "How in blazes did he know we were goin' to the hospital? I know! The fool was monitorin' our radio frequency when the station told me about Dawson wantin' an escort. He's tryin' to horn in and play super-cop with his kiddy-car."

They flashed through traffic to the emergency room entrance. Everyone rushed to the rear of the hearse including Benson. Bookman shot him a glare, but was busy helping the hospital staff unload the patient and said nothing. Martha Manchester held onto DeVon's hand and pleaded with him again to stay right beside her—she had things she must tell him and a favor to ask. He assured her he wouldn't leave her side. But when he tried to remain with her in the ER, the white coats demanded he go away while they did their job. Miss Manchester protested weakly, giving up only when DeVon told her he'd be right outside and return soon.

Benson sat on one side of the waiting area leafing through a magazine. DeVon and Zeke took seats across the room. Some time passed, then the chief addressed Benson. "No sense in all of us stayin' around, *Chief Deputy*. You might as well go."

Before Benson could answer, Dr. Forsythe stepped out of the ER for a moment. "Looks as though Martha may be right. She's so weak I don't see how she can last much longer. She still insists on seeing you, DeVon. In a few minutes, they're going to take her up to eight-twenty-two in ICU and get her situated, then you can go up."

Benson left and Bookman sat toying with his hat while they waited. "Zeke, I gotta tell you—she's one'a those people you figure'll never die. There's always been a MizMartha Manchester. Reckon I thought there'd always be. Makes you stop and ponder, don't it?"

"Yes it does. Guess this is one more reminder."

"Yeah."

After a while, Zeke wondered, "What in the world do you suppose she wants to talk to you about?"

"Right now, I got no idea."

Finally they were permitted to go up. At the desk on the eighth floor, the nurse warned the chief, "Please don't stay longer than absolutely necessary, her condition is extremely grave. I'll show you the way. The floor nurse knows you're coming."

Before he could take a step down the long hall, the PA system began blaring, *"CODE BLUE! CODE BLUE! ROOM EIGHT TWO TWO. CODE BLUE! CODE BLUE! ROOM EIGHT TWO TWO."* White coats appeared from everywhere and ran off toward the room. One was pushing a cart loaded with all sorts of medical supplies and paraphernalia.

The elevator door opened and Dr. Forsythe burst out to Zeke's question, "What is it? What's going on?"

"Don't know," Forsythe threw over his shoulder as he hurried off, Bookman right with him. Zeke took a chair to wait. *(Never liked hospitals much, anyway—now this.)*

In only a few minutes, they came walking slowly back. DeVon shook his head. "Too late, Zeke. The nurse watchin' over her hadta step into the next room for a minute to check up on another patient. She ran back in and hit the button to call everbody when all'a MizMartha's monitorin' beeps commenced soundin', but it was too late. Nobody could'a saved her."

"That's right," Forsythe agreed. "I didn't expect her to go quite this quickly, but you can never tell."

They spoke quietly a minute or two before Bookman asked, "Doc, she's got no livin' next'a kin. Who'll take care'a the funeral arrangements and pay the bill?"

"Knowing Martha, I'd bet about anything you'll find final arrangements she made and an insurance policy in her things—a burial policy, if nothing else. She was too well organized not to have put down plans and have insurance. In any event, she's going to have a proper funeral. I promise you that, even if *I* have to make the arrangements. I'll need to speak to Last Dime. I suppose he's as good as any."

On the way out, they discussed how to proceed. Since there was no next of kin, Bookman said he'd phone the town attorney to see about the legal work necessary before looking through Miss Manchester's papers for insurance policies. They reached the door. "Well, so long, Doc. I'll be phonin' about the papers."

Neither DeVon nor Zeke had much to say on the return trip to Stony Crossing. At the station, the chief phoned the town attorney about legalities involved in looking into Miss Manchester's things. He said he wouldn't ordinarily be involved in something like this, but would check and try to move things along as fast as possible. Bookman inquired further, "Now that she's passed, what about our court order for openin' Borsch's safety deposit box? She was anxious to tell me somethin' right before she died. After ponderin' things, I'm guessin' it was about what's in that box. I wanna see what's in it as soon as possible. Might be somethin' to help with the Borsch case."

"Don't suppose there'd be any reason for Charlie Harrison not to honor it now, Chief. I'll phone Judge Nelson."

DeVon and Zeke went to Miss Manchester's store where the chief taped a **CLOSED TILL FURTHER NOTICE** sign to the door. Before leaving, he checked again to be sure the premises were properly secured.

Shortly after they returned, the town attorney phoned. "Chief, Judge Nelson said Miss Manchester's attorney hadn't asked for any court order this morning, and there was no reason for you not to present yours to Harrison again. The judge couldn't understand why he didn't honor it in the first place."

The chief grabbed his coat. "Let's get goin'—not much time before the bank locks up. Stay's open late today but it'll still be close."

Once again Bookman handed banker Harrison the court order allowing the police access to Borsch's safety deposit box, then told him Judge Nelson said Miss Manchester hadn't asked for a court order and the bank should've abided by Judge Jefferson's order. The banker examined it. "Well, since I've heard nothing from her attorney, I suppose I may be obliged to go ahead and honor this." He added (smugly, Zeke thought), "There's still one other little problem, Chief."

"Yeah? What might that be?"

"As I've already told you, the bank has only one of the two keys needed to open a box. In the absence of a second key, a locksmith will be needed to drill out the lock, and there would be the additional fee of seventy-five dollars in advance I spoke about. Even with the fee paid, it will be impossible to drill today—the locksmith will be closed. And...I probably should also phone Miss Manchester or her lawyer to be on the safe side. I don't want the bank involved in legal wrangling."

Bookman icy-eyed the banker. "No reason to stall any more, Charlie. Looks like you haven't heard that MizMartha died this afternoon."

Any further attempt at smugness fell crashing along with Charles Harrison's jaw. He could only manage an ashen-faced exclamation. "What! It can't be! I saw her only this morning! How could she be dead?"

"Well, it's true, Charlie. Guess she didn't think to notify everbody she was gonna pass on. Now I wanna see what's in the box."

Harrison regained enough composure to mutter, "There's still the problem of a second key."

It was Bookman's turn to be smug. He pulled out his key collection, ceremoniously removed the key found in Borsch's clothing, and waved it before him. "Charlie, my friend, why don't we try this little old key. My hunch is our problem is about to be solved. Without any seventy-five bucks in advance, either."

DeVon's earlier wish to see the banker's reaction to the key was granted. "Uh...uh, where'd you get that? It hasn't been located."

"Whataya mean, it's not been located?"

"Miss Martha told me she hadn't been able to find it."

"That a fact."

In silence they went into the vault. First, the banker used his key, then gestured for Bookman to try his. It worked perfectly. Without a word, Harrison opened the small door, removed the long narrow box and led them to a tiny cubicle but made no move to leave.

The chief asked, "Isn't it usual for the banker to give some privacy?"

"I thought you might want a witness."

"My witness is standin' right there—name'a Zeke Tanner. All we need is the privacy." Frowning, Harrison wheeled and left.

DeVon lifted the box's lid, took out and inspected its meager contents. "Not much here. Deeds to the barbershop and house. Car title. Couple old photos'a some young woman I don't recognize. Three little kid toys. Couple things lookin' like souvenirs—can't tell where from. Never know what somebody keeps or why. What's this?" He took a folded sheet from its long envelope.

He read it carefully, then handed it to Zeke. "We probly got an answer to the question about what *document* MizMartha was lookin' for so hard, but it's not Borsch's will. Far from it."

It was from a clinic in Albuquerque dated nearly sixty years before, and looked much like any other birth certificate—except for the baby's name. As was the custom in those days when the father of the child was unidentified, carefully lettered in the style of the era on the line for the baby's name, was only *Bastard Manchester*.

"Wow, Dee, I guess this *does* answer the question!"

"Oh Yeah. Remember I told you about MizMartha and Saul Borsch, the travelin' preacher? How they were real sweet on each other, then he started sparkin' her sister? And how pretty soon the sister run off with him out east? Remember I also said MizMartha went out west around the same time and stayed quite a while? How the preacher and the sister moved back a year or so later—married and showin' around a new baby?" Looks mighty like MizMartha was goin' out there to have Saul Borsch's baby."

"Can be no other scenario. All these years, DeVon, all these years Miss Martha stood by and saw her own child being raised by her sister. Why?"

"You know the answer. It's this town. The sisters and their family, along with the preacher, were all a party to it to hide the shame. Times may be a little bit different now, but think'a how bad it was back then."

"I guess you're right, but consider the human toll. Dee, this birth certificate being in Borsch's possession means he was also a party to all the secrecy."

"Looks like. Part'a his life, at least."

"What's your guess as to when he found out?"

"Who knows? Maybe when he got older. Maybe after both his folks died."

"Why do you suppose Miss Martha was so anxious to tell you about this?"

"Right now, my thinkin' is she figured the only place it could be was in Borsch's deposit box, and maybe found out I was tryin' to get into it. She knew she was dyin' and wanted to swear me to secrecy and get rid of what I found."

Zeke shook his head slowly. "Even on her deathbed, she simply couldn't stand the thought of the story getting out."

"That'd be my take on it."

"This could also explain why she was so upset when you told her about Borsch's murder and also why she was so anxious to get his ring. Just think about it—aring was all she had to hold onto. It's so sad. How soul-wrenching the lifetime of anguish must have been for her."

"Yeah. High price to pay for once in the haymow."

"It's more. It's a huge price to pay for intolerance."

"Guess so, perfesser. OK, let's get this stuff out'a here."

Banker Harrison's nose was still out of joint when they left. He only nodded curtly and turned away.

It was so late when they finished at the station, DeVon followed Zeke home and stopped in for a quick Snake Bite. They sat talking about Miss Martha Manchester. DeVon commented, "Zeke, somethin' comes to mind. Remember how I figured that some amateur perps trashed Bill Borsch's house searchin' it after we'd already searched? Got an idea it could'a been MizMartha lookin' for this *document*. Didn't find it and reckoned Borsch might'a kept it in a safety deposit box. May be why she was gonna get a court order. Reckon?"

"Makes sense to me."

"Another thing—would your memory go bad if this thing accidentally got too close to a match and went up in smoke?"

"Whatever are you talking about, Great Chief?"

"My thinkin' exactly." He drained his glass. "Gotta go, Gertrude. See you later."

"Later, Ethel."

Zeke sat in the stillness for a long time thinking about Miss Martha Manchester.

28

Zeke's morning's routine barely completed and only one CD later, Bookman phoned. "Come on down. Some interestin' stuff's been happenin' all at once. Besides, there's a little job you gotta get goin' on."

"I have my own jobs."

"Forget 'em, this hasta be done right away." As usual, the chief hung up before giving any additional information.

In the office, Zeke demanded, "Let me see my signature on a paper giving you permission to interrupt my morning."

"Listen first, bitch later. Early this mornin', Doc Forsythe phoned. Said Dr. Miller over at the hospital gave him a call sayin' when he went to make a final examination'a MizMartha so he could sign a death certificate, somethin' caught his attention. There was probly nothin' to it, but he wanted to talk about it. Doc's on his way there now."

"OK, spoiler of my day, what else?"

"Lefty Riggins phoned a while ago, keepin' his promise to call if Hollis Benson came in to pawn anything. Well, when he opened today, Benson was right there with a pin like women wear on their coats, a breech thing. He told Lefty it belonged to his aunt who passed last year."

"The word is *brooch*. Did Riggins take it in?"

"Nope. I think he was afraid to after our last little talk. Looked it over, though, and used the excuse he wouldn't have a market for somethin' like it in Windham. Benson's probly on his way to Indy this minute to hock it."

"You know, Stretch, I'm not positive, but I think I remember a brooch on Miss Martha's coat."

Bookman slapped the desk. "I remember that, too! *Damned dog!* He's stole from another who's passed!"

"Easy, you don't know for sure."

"Tanner, an eighteen-wheeler could run over you, and you'd thank the driver for the press job! A'course he took it. He's a thief, plain as day."

"Maybe, but won't you need proof?"

"*Maybe! Proof!* If you had as much proof the ceiling was gonna cave in the next second as we got on Benson, you'd be divin' under the desk. This time he's gonna pay!"

"OK, *OK*! You said something about a job. Assuming the highly unlikely possibility I'm going to interrupt my busy morning further, what're you talking about?"

"Zeke, somebody's gotta write MizMartha's obit."

"It certainly wouldn't be me. George Wallings at the *Clarion* would know a lot more about her."

"George's on an ice-fishin' trip in Michigan. You're elected."

"I have a better idea. She was so deeply into church affairs, why couldn't a member do it? You'll have to ask. I'm not in any mood to deal with Ackerman."

"Good idea, Gertrude. I'll call him at the grocery. S'pose he's already got wind'a MizMartha's passin'."

"Before you do that, anything else happen this morning?"

"Not much. Only other thing is, we had a little fire out back."

"A fire? Do any damage?"

"Nothin' to speak of. Burned an old paper or document or somethin'."

"I see."

Bookman phoned Call-me-Charlie who had indeed heard about Martha Manchester. The chief thought the preacher would carry on about it, but after only an abbreviated expression of sadness and agreeing to write the obituary, he passed on some information taking Bookman aback. "I know you're aware of her close ties to the church, Chief Bookman. She was the next thing to an elder, and there's no question she would've been if she'd only been a man. Our dear departed Sister Manchester left everything to the church in her will."

"*What* will?"

"Oh, she had a will, all right. Had it revised over a year ago, all proper and legal. The church has a copy. She left everything to further the Lord's work. I expect her lawyer will be doing whatever necessary to get the properties transferred right away so we can begin."

"Well, thanks for doin' the obit."

"God bless you, brother."

Bookman hung up and growled, "I'm no brother'a yours, you money-muckin' mother!"

He related the preacher's conversation to Zeke, adding, "He'd be holdin' his breath a long time before layin' a finger on MizMartha's properties if I had anything to say about it. C'mon, I gotta take a ride so I can get rid'a the taste'a that phony."

On Elm Street, they passed Hollis Benson's house, a Sheriff's patrol car parked in front. Bookman remarked, "Make my day to go right in and drag him out. He's not there, though—out in his own car. Even *he* don't have the brass jewels to drive a police vehicle when he's out doin' his theiven'."

After lunch, DeVon put his feet on his desk, fired up his pipe, and sat talking with Zeke until the deskman buzzed. "Sheriff Laddis, Chief."

Bookman's feet hit the floor as he punched the speakerphone. "Bookman."

"This here's Sheriff Laddis. Seen anything'a that no-account Benson?"

"My, how you talk, Sheriff. Can't believe you'd say such'a mean thing about your *chief deputy*."

"Cut the horse crap, Bookman. Seen 'im or ain'tcha? Been tryin' all day to raise 'im, but ain't had no luck."

"Last time I saw him was yesterday when he monitored my radio and followed our escort to the hospital. Went by his house a while ago and his patrol car's out front."

"Well, he don't answer my calls...what'n hell escort ya talkin' about? Sheriff's office don't have no report'a no escort."

"That's your story, Laddis, but I'll tell you this. If Benson don't stop buttin' his big bazoo into our business every chance he gets, me'n you are gonna have an up close and personal. Tell you somethin' else. This mornin', Lefty Riggins phoned sayin' Benson was in his place tryin' to pawn a piece'a jewelry—a woman's coat pin I'm damned near sure was stole off MizMartha Manchester at the hospital. Some dogs keep barkin' the same tune, don't they?"

Sheriff Laddis' roared reply couldn't be repeated even in a sweaty locker room after a tough loss. Mostly, it centered on observations concerning Benson's ancestry on his mother's side, adding, "Bookman, I don't wanna be seen in that two-bit station'a yours any more'n absolutely necessary, but this time I'll make an exception. Eyeball him and phone me. I'll come over and skin him alive."

"Pleasure'd be all mine, Sheriff."

Bookman got his pipe going again and leaned back, hands clasped behind his head, boots on his desk once more. "Every now and then the good guys get a chance to throw in a lick or two."

"Suppose so. However, the Borsch case is not one inch closer to being solved than it was last week."

"Always the little ray'a sunshine, ain'tcha, Tanner? You gotta look on the bright side'a life. See things your way, Ethel, and there's only horse manure. My way, you figure there's gotta be a pony around somewhere to ride. Believe we're gonna crack the Borsch case? Then we're one day closer to solvin' it."

"Is this the same guardian of the law I heard moaning and groaning about how he's never going to solve anything? This the guy?"

"All a faycade, Ezekial Amos my man, all a faycade. Just lollin' you to sleep while I get my duty done."

Zeke didn't bother to correct the mispronunciations. "If Lurinda can bottle whatever she put in your food today, her fortune's made."

"No use tryin' to lay a bummer on me, Zeke, no use a'tall. We've made it through a couple more days. Besides, what else can happen?"

Doctor Horatio Forsythe walked in with an answer. "Gentlemen, I've just come from the autopsy of Martha Manchester."

In unison: "*Autopsy!*" Bookman's boots thudded to the floor.

"Dr. Miller said something wasn't ringing right about Martha's death. He thought perhaps with my experience as coroner, I might have something to offer. Well, it didn't take long to see classic signs of suffocation."

Another duet: "*Suffocation!*"

"Yes, suffocation. Although she was obviously too weak to struggle much, there were telltale signs. To shorten the story, there appeared to be enough evidence to alert the Wayne City police chief, and he requested we take the necessary steps to proceed with an autopsy. The findings supported my earlier conclusions. In addition to the physical manifestations, there were minute foreign particles in the trachea. The preliminary blood analysis also revealed evidence of suffocation."

Bookman exclaimed, "Who! How!"

"Chief, determining *who* did it is the responsibility of law enforcement. My best speculation about *how* it was done is that a pillow was placed over her face." After a brief discussion, Forsythe departed after wishing the chief good luck.

Zeke and DeVon's discussion merry-go-rounded until the chief demanded, "OK, hold it! Enough a'ready—this's not gettin' us anyplace. Nothin' we can do from this end but help the police at Wayne City any way we can—gonna phone Chief Milligan." He finished the call and reported, "They're officially callin' it a homicide. Hospital's fit to be tied, a'course. At first, they denied it happened. Next thing, they wanted it mummed up till they finished their own investigation. Zeke, better be ready. The news dogs are gonna be all over this. Even if the crime was done over in Wayne City, there'll be plenty'a questions. Maybe it'd help if a press release said MizMartha lived here, but the crime happened over there. Mention Milligan's in charge'a the investigation, but we're gonna cooperate any way we can. Dang it, I *knew* things were goin' too good."

"Whatever became of, 'What else can happen,' oh Great Optimistic One?"

"Hush up now and go write your lies."

Bookman was right. The phone began ringing before Zeke finished the release. When he got home in late afternoon, the answering machine was blinking as though warning the populace to take cover. He ignored it, determined to finish his letter to Ackerman. However, after several fits and starts, he gave up. The events of the past two days kept invading his thoughts.

(Way too early for dinner. Might as well tend to the hellish invention.) It was filled with messages from press people asking the usual unanswerable and telemarketer nuisances. Last on the list was a voice so indistinguishable he couldn't decipher its message and quit trying.

29

Zeke walked in and tossed the latest tape on Bookman's desk. "Try on the last message for size. I listened about a dozen times, and still couldn't be sure it was anything. Didn't think you could either, so I waited until this morning to bring it in."

Bookman listened once, gave up immediately, and turned to other business. Prosecutor Barnard Mitchell was made aware Martha Manchester's death was officially designated a homicide and that she left a will. As a result, any attempt to probate it would be held up until the investigation was complete. Mitchell so notified Ackerman, Miss Manchester's lawyer, and the clerk of the court.

"Great Chief, the deskman handed me a pile of phone messages to check. But first, what's the latest on Benson or Miss Martha's brooch?"

"Nothin', but it's not too hard to figure what he's up to. Slimy thievin' reptile's pawned it in Indy and is over there spendin' the loot. Couldn'a got much for it, though—he'll be back pretty quick."

Bookman began going over the reports of patrols made by officers over the weekend. About halfway through, he took one in to Zeke. "Take a look at this."

"An attempted break-in. So?"

"Address look familiar?"

"Can't say it does. Someplace downtown. Where is it?"

"MizMartha's store, podner."

"*What!* They didn't wait long to try looting, did they?"

"Sure didn't. With some'a the kids today and so many strangers movin' in, I probly shouldn't be surprised. They didn't get in, but the report goes on to say it wasn't for lack'a tryin'. Gonna go down after a bit to take a good look for myself. Give a holler when you're done sweet talkin' the news-noses and we'll both go."

Shortly after 10, Zeke went to the chief's office. "Now's as good a time as any. About time for a coffee break anyway."

Before they could leave, Call-me-Charlie Ackerman rushed in and demanded, "Chief Bookman, what's the meaning of stopping Sister Manchester's will from being probated? She would've wanted it done as soon as possible, and now her wishes have been blocked!"

Bookman pushed his hat back. "Preacher, the law says probatin' can usually be done right away, but there's a number'a things to clear up. Besides, I'm more'n a little surprised you'd wanna start the money flowin' even before preachin' the funeral."

That gave Ackerman no pause. "Like I said, Sister Manchester would've wanted the church to begin using her worldly goods in the service of the Lord as quick as possible. When *can* I get it probated?"

The chief's hat got pushed farther back. "Officially, when the investigation is finished. Unofficially, I'd like to see it held up till God corrects your greedy deportment."

"*Blasphemy!*"

"Take it up with God when you're prayin' for speed on gettin' hold'a MizMartha's properties."

Ackerman was beside himself. "***Blasphemy!*** *Blasphemy, I say!* Blasphemers shall be smitten, sayeth the Lord!"

"Yeah, well you better pray mine takes place pretty quick. I'm gonna be doin' some prayin'a my own to find a way to keep your sticky mitts off her properties...permanent. Now, get out'a my office!"

On the way to Martha Manchester's store, Zeke chided, "You handed out pretty strong medicine to the preacher. Aren't you afraid lightning will fry you? Guess you're in the clear, though, I don't remember what he quoted as any Scripture I ever read."

"Can't afford to let every Tom, Bill and Jack bull-batter me, includin' pulpit thumpers. Here we are."

An inspection of front and rear doors proved some person or persons made aggressive attempts to break in. The deeply marred rear door showed the greatest effort was expended upon it. Even though the front was less scarred, there was little doubt it was also attacked.

DeVon was disgusted. "Plague take-ed preverts! After they tried in back and couldn't bust in, they had the guts to go at it right out here in plain sight."

"What could be so valuable in an office supply and card shop?"

"Don't take nothin much these days. You can get knocked in the head for a buck and a quarter." Bookman finished his inspection. "Ok, let's cross over and coffee up."

A black ribbon hung in the window of the Country Kitchen for Martha Manchester. They finished their coffee while answering the usual questions from the coffee crowd, and were only partly into a refill when the front door burst open. Who should come bombasting in but sheriff Leon Laddis in the (considerable) flesh.

The diner instantly fell silent. Laddis was one hundred percent disliked in Stony Crossing, and everyone knew how Chief Bookman regarded him. With the Sheriff's well-known over-the-line enforcement tactics and odious behavior, he got almost no out-county votes and barely won election even with strong Wayne City political-party backing. Rumbling through the quiet diner and right up beside the chief, he bawled, *"Might'a knowed I'd find ya at the trough.* Way I hear it, ya spend most'a your time here. For more'n just eatin', too."

Zeke slid his coffee to one side in the nick of time. DeVon spun around, jumped up and towered over the Sheriff. "Whataya mean, comin' in here bellerin' like a gelded bull, *Lardass*? Got business or just want everbody to witness your stupidity?"

In the quiet, Roosevelt Hoover's whistling could be heard coming from back in the kitchen. Laddis glanced around at the silently hostile crowd and decided not to pursue the insults—at least, not full bore and full roar. "What I wanna know, why ain'tcha been lookin' for Benson like I ast? He didn't show for the dogwatch Saturday, and still ain't come in. Patrol car's still right in front'a his house, but he ain't there—leastways, don't answer the door. Seems to me a good po-lice department would be on the ball enough so's I don't gotta come all the way over here to do the job."

Bookman took a deep breath and gritted out, "First place, you never asked me to look for him. For what it's worth, your *chief deputy* is no doubt whorin' around the big city spendin' money he got from the stolen property he hocked." (The diners' ears perked up even more.)

"Bookman, you don't know that for a fact. 'Sides, even if he did, how far can the money from that old broad's pin go? Gonna investigate 'im missin' or not?"

DeVon cooled off barely enough to offer, "If it'll get your shiftless carcass out'a my town sooner, I'll do this much'a your job. I'll go with you up to his house and try again to see if we can raise him. If he's there, he could be too wasted to answer the door. If he's not, you can come to the office and I'll make a few calls to see if we can track him a little. By the way, besides sittin' on your big butt and phonin, then comin' over here and shakin' his door, what've *you* done to find him? Anything worth mentionin'?"

"Up yours, Bookman, let's go."

Laddis was right about Benson not responding to knocking. No amount of pounding brought any reply. The chief hoisted his lanky frame through an unlocked window and emerged shortly through the front door. "No sign of him. Don't look much like he was plannin' a trip—clothes and suitcases are in a closet. Saw an awful big collection'a brand new electronical gadgets still in sealed boxes stacked all over a bedroom back there. Think he was fixin' to go into business, Sheriff?" Laddis didn't say a word.

Back at the station, Bookman's first call was to Lefty Riggins. The pawnshop owner was apprehensive. "What can I do for you, Chief? Always glad to help, always glad."

"Yeah, a'course you are, Lefty. Now help some more and tell me if you gave Benson the name'a any pawnshop in particular where he could'a pawned that pin we talked about."

"I...I'm not sure, Chief."

"Riggins, do I gotta come up there?"

"Wait a minute! I think I might've said something about one where he could take it. Yes, now I remember! The Gold Ring. That's it, The Gold Ring was the place."

"Know those people?"

"Might've met them a time or two."

"Phone 'em right now and ask if he pawned it there and how much he got for it. By the way, whataya reckon it'd bring?"

"Didn't examine it real closely Chief, but it would be worth considerably more than it cost new. Pretty good market for old-style jewelry where there are enough people around who collect it. In Indy, I'd say it would pawn out at, uh, say about four. Maybe a little more if he sold it outright."

"Only four hundred! Thoughtcha were talkin' real money."

"Not four *hundred*, Chief, four *thousand.* They'd probably take it in and send it to one'a those specialty auction houses back east. Could bring as much as twenty grand with the right bidders."

"Great balls'a fire! Get hold of 'em and phone me right back."

"Will do, Chief."

Upon hearing Lefty's information, Laddis snorted, "Four bills! We won't see that sucker till spring!"

While they waited for Lefty's call, Laddis and Bookman began talking law enforcement, and it appeared they arrived at a truce of sorts—at least enough to discuss the Manchester murder. "Bookman, I got my idea how that killin' come about. You 'member them murders right across the line in Ohio? Where some snakehead male nurse bumped off those old farts 'cause they was circlin' the drain on their way out anyway, and he wanted to put 'em out'a their misery? Who's to say this ain't the same kind'a thing? Wasn't nobody around 'cept hospital people and the old lady was pretty much a goner. All adds up."

"Got any evidence'a that?"

"No, but I talked with the sheriff over there once, and he told me they found out a lot more'a that kind'a stuff goes on than we hear about. Said there was lots'a cases of it all across the country they already proved and more they was suspicious of."

"Quite an idea, all right. Worth considerin'."

The buzzer sounded. Lefty was on the line. "Chief, I got what you wanted. They're awful nervous about it maybe being stolen. Said to tell you they made Benson identify himself and all that. I guessed pretty close to what it would pawn at. They bought it outright for forty-five. He took it all in hundreds."

"Thanks, Lefty. That's one mark on the good side for you."

"Anytime, Chief. You know I'm always glad to be of help."

Bookman hung up. "Yeah, Lefty, you're always *real* glad to help." He turned to Laddis and repeated the pawnbroker's conversation.

Bookman interrupted Laddis' verbal evisceration of Benson by asking, "Sheriff, how you gonna handle this? Gonna put out a warrant?"

"Might hafta—else we'll not likely see the yella dog around here till he's burnt up all that cash. After I finish grillin' 'im about the Manchester pin job, I wanna do some more grillin' about all them electronical do-dads in his bedroom, too."

"He's your problem, glad to say."

"Reckon so, sorry to say." Laddis heaved himself from the chair. "See ya around."

Bill Mickner came in. "Heard you have another unsolved case, Chief."

"Unsolved, yes. Mine, no. Not wishin' anything onto him, but it's over in Milligan's jurisdiction, for which I'm truly thankful. We *do* have a little somethin' for you, though. Zeke brought this in this mornin." He handed the most recent answering machine message to the captain.

"Not again!"

"It's the last one on the tape. Can't tell if it's one'a our callers or not, the voice's so fuzzied-up we can't make out anything. Thought maybe one'a your geniuses could do somethin' with it. Bill, there's another little somethin'—a missin' person—a deputy sheriff, no less. And there's the matter'a stolen and hocked jewelry for him to account for." Bookman related the Benson story and added, "There's no official warrant out on him yet, but it's only a question'a time. Any'a your overpaid, under-worked, spoiled tweetie-pie types stumble over him, we'd sort'a liketa know about it."

"I can't say I'm too surprised to hear about Benson. Don't know the man well, but I've sometimes wondered about him. "Chief, it sounds like a hotbed of tranquility around here."

"Sure is, not countin' a killin', an arson fire, and a local citizen gettin' offed in Wayne City, not to mention a thievin' and missin' deputy sheriff—all since New Years."

"That's what I said—a hotbed of tranquility."

They chatted until lunch before Zeke begged off and went home. He was still determined to finish his letter to Preacher Ackerman. After soup and salad, he carefully composed it, stating in very clear language he made no promise to him or anyone else to attend services. In addition, it left no doubt about what he thought of those who misrepresented his answers to further their own distorted ends. To make certain he wasn't misquoted again, he addressed a copy to each elder on the church's Membership Committee.

30

Martha Manchester would've been astonished at the size of the crowd attending her evening wake held at Dr. Forsythe's. Last Dime Dalton said it was the largest in memory. Next day at the funeral, the church was also packed with area residents. A few reporters swelled the ranks. As at Bill Borsch's funeral, Tanner and Bookman speculated about the big turnout. Zeke said it was because she was active in the church for so long, naturally every member attended. He also thought her demise represented the passing of an era and they felt a need to be part of the event. DeVon's idea was one he voiced at Borsch's send-off—many were attracted by the notoriety of a murder victim's services.

The audience was treated to the best of Preacher Ackerman's histrionic rhetoric. He opened what was to be a record-length eulogy by rhapsodizing about Sister Martha Manchester—layer upon layer of his finest Christian-Gone-To-Her-Just-Reward package. Sister Manchester was practically a saint, etc., etc. He described a long list of rewards she was enjoying with those who follow the teachings of the Lord—among them, streets paved with "*go-uld.*"

Thunder-clapping away, he went on to compare her to sinners and backsliders. "Sister Manchester was oh so different from many others who embrace the faith, then fall from grace and make no attempt at redemption. Never once did she stray from the straight and narrow. *Nev-ver!* Never once did she fail to attend a church service. "*Nev-ver!* Now, she's living in *eee*-ternal *glow-ry* while the unredeemed are burning forever in a lake of fire and brimstone!" Ackerman was really on a roll. He slammed his fist on the lectern. "*Fire!* I say unto you, *FIRE!*"

He was so inspirational there was a scattering of "amens" among the members. The reporters glanced at one another. This is a *funeral*?

At last, Ackerman wound down. DeVon said later there was only one reason he stopped when he did. Last Dime had warned the preacher that there was another funeral later in the afternoon at Greens Glen, and MizMartha's casket was going to be rolling back up the aisle 45 minutes after the service began whether or not Call-me-Charlie or the final viewing was finished. Zeke refused to believe it and called Bookman a cynic, but he swore it was true.

At the cemetery, the biting cold failed to noticeably curtail the preacher's final flurry. Afterward, as Doctor Forsythe walked with Zeke and DeVon to their cars. "Some service, eh, men? Ackerman was wound even a little tighter than usual. I suppose he thought these were his last shots at her and he'd make the most of it. Or, maybe gave her a special sendoff since he knew she willed her properties to the church."

Bookman stopped and turned to the doctor. "*You* knew there was a will?"

"Why, yes. Last year when I was treating her, she mentioned she was getting her affairs in order—willing her estate to the church. Not long ago in the office, she mentioned the will again and said she was in a hurry because she was meeting with her attorney to go over some things."

"Who's her attorney, Doc?"

"That new fellow who moved here recently. She started to use him instead of some lawyer in Wayne City. Why do you ask?"

"Got a question or two for him. Any idea why she didn't use Nickel-Nabber?"

"I think they had a falling out over fees, years back. You know Nesbit."

"Oh yeah."

"DeVon, while we're on the subject of her affairs, Last Dime Dalton phoned Monday and asked once more who'd be paying for the funeral. I repeated I'd guarantee the costs but wanted to see whether she had any insurance. Has the town attorney said anything about access to her papers? Would they be at the house or the store?"

"I'll ask him again, Doc. Don't know why the holdup. His usual shoe draggin, I reckon. To answer your second question, I expect she kept all her papers in the office at the store."

"Well, it'll work out sooner or later. I'll tell Last Dime he'll have to wait a while. If he gets too frantic, I'll pay him and get things sorted out later. In the unlikely event she has no burial insurance, I'll just say I've spent money on more foolish things in my lifetime."

"Haven't we all."

On the way to the station, Bookman stopped by Martha Manchester's house. "Probly wouldn't hurt to do a walk-around to see if some prevert's been doin' mischief."

Zeke waited in the car while the chief circled the house. He came back and announced, "Everthing's locked up tight, and it don't look like anybody's been here—no footprints around the house or on the porch. Saw her plants through the winda—she always liked lots'a different kind'a plants. S'pose they'll die if they don't get water."

"We'll all die if we don't get water, Dee, and we'll all die if we *do*. Does anything make much difference?"

"Ain't we on the dark side all of a sudden."

"While you were looking around, it occurred to me nothing we do, good or bad, really makes any difference. Everything winds up the same way."

"Well, Zeke, contrary to whatcha might think, I've done some thinkin' along that line. What I've come up with is what people do *does* make a difference. Like the wind, it's been makin' changes, gradual like, ever since Eve cozied up to the snake. Can't really see the wind, butcha know it's been here by the evidence—changes like soil erosion and stuff. Same thing with people. Just 'cause you can't see any changes *this very minute* that they make don't mean they're not happenin' and they're not gonna keep happenin'. Nothin' stands still as long as it's livin'. If it's not changin', it's dead."

"Interesting. Is there more?"

"I figure changes can go either way—for the better or for the worse—up or down—and if folks don't try to make *good* changes, most times things turn out for the worse all by themselves. A'body's gotta jump in and try to keep 'em from doin' that. If you're real lucky, sometimes you can see the difference you're tryin' for can happen. But, most'a the time, you just gotta keep pluggin' and doin' your damndest to do the right things to make good changes happen when the chance pops up."

"Dee, I don't quite get you. Life's only about trying to make changes? We wake up every day and think about the changes we'll make today?

"A'course not! I just told you thatcha gotta look out for the chance. Besides, there's more to it—lots more. For instance, we got no control over the weather and big stuff like that. Somebody else's pullin' those strings."

"Still sounds somewhat like you think we're the total masters of our fate. Aside from weather and other big things, we're in complete charge of everything?"

"Not a'tall. I'm sure we're not, but if *everthing* was done for us, there'd be nothin' left to do. Think'a how borin' life would be and how useless we'd be if things were too easy." DeVon paused before adding, "Maybe I don't have it *all* scoped out yet, but I can keep pluggin' away with what I got figured so far. Sometimes I keep goin' by thinkin' folks are right when they say most'a the time, life's like a movie that's not always too interestin'. There's just enough goin' on so you don't wanna leave in the middle, butcha wouldn't pay to see it again. Or maybe it's like others say, 'Life's a game you can't win, butcha still gotta keep playin' it the best you can.' I can keep churnin' with that, too."

"Perhaps, but it still seems to me that there's much more to life."

"Didn'tcha just hear me say I don't have it *all* doped out? Don't take life too serious, podner. You're never gonna get out of it alive, anyhow."

They rode in silence a while before Zeke commented, "I thank you for your thoughts. It's good to see someone's getting a handle on life."

"No need for wise-assery. I wasn't the one with his head under his wing sayin' it's a cruel, cruel world."

"Oh, no offense, DeVon. I meant it."

"Buy coffee, and I'll accept your apology. Gotta do a couple things at the office, then we'll mug up."

He phoned Martha Manchester's lawyer. "We're helpin' Chief Milligan at Wayne City with the investigation'a MizMartha Manchester's homicide, and I've got a few questions. First off, Doc Forsythe said she told him she was meetin' with you to go over some stuff. What was that all about?"

"Chief, I'd like to help, but I'm afraid any information about her falls under the umbrella of attorney-client privilege."

"Now Mr. Attorney, I don't wanna tell you your own business, but don't attorney-client privilege stop applyin' after the client's dead?"

"Not necessarily."

"Can'tcha at least tell me if you drew her a will?"

"Yes, I can tell you that."

"This is like pullin' teeth out'a a frothin' alligator. *Did* you draw her a will?"

"Yes I did."

"Notified the heirs?"

"Not yet. I'm sure she must've made arrangements with her executor to do so."

"Who'd that be?"

"I'd rather not say."

"Where's the will now?"

"I assume it is with Miss Manchester's other papers. Perhaps she had a safety deposit box."

"Already checked, and she didn't. Don'tcha have a copy?"

"I don't think I should discuss anything more about her will at this time."

"Nothin' else?"

"Not at this time."

DeVon thanked the lawyer for the information and rang off. "Which was damned little," he told the silent phone.

The town attorney phoned to say he spoke to Judge Jefferson about looking for Miss Manchester's insurance policies. The judge didn't think there'd be any problem, but had no experience in such a case and wanted his secretary to do some research.

By this time, it was too late for afternoon coffee, and they didn't want to chance the department's pot. Zeke invited, "Care to stop by the house for a coffee or a short Snake Bite later? Might even fix a snack."

"I could probly handle the coffee or a drink, but it'd take more alcohol than there is in every bottle at the Levee Tap to get me to eat that diet stuff. I must say, though, I do believe you're gainin' on your plan. Either my eyes are goin' or you're actually renderin' off a pound or two."

"I'll take that as a compliment, but if you don't eat my cooking, you don't drink my liquor. See you, Ethel."

"See you, Gertrude."

31

Police Chief Von E. Bookman wasn't in the best of moods. Elmer Jones started things off badly the previous night with his commentary, using the occasion of Martha Manchester's funeral to lambaste the town and the police force for inaction in one homicide, and now there was still another hapless victim. On and on, blah, blah, blah.

"Misleadin' newsfarter! He knows the two killin's didn't happen in the same jurisdiction." DeVon's breakfast hadn't tasted so good, either. Now he was having difficulty with a balky pipe when Bill Mickner phoned to report it was impossible to do anything with the latest answering machine tape or the sign from Lowell Williams' shed.

To add to this bilious mix, another aggravation appeared in the person of Preacher Ackerman who hastened in, not even pausing at the front desk. Apparently he wasn't too tarnished by his contact with blasphemer Bookman earlier in the week. At least not enough to prevent him from making another attempt to learn when the investigation of the Manchester murder would be concluded so he could take possession of her properties.

"Preacher, I don't have any control over the investigation, and you can thank your lucky stars it's up to the Wayne City police." Ackerman continued to stand there. "Anything else, preacher?"

"Well Chief, I've been wanting to speak to you about your friendship with Lurinda Beatty."

"*WHAT?* What'd you say?"

"Maybe this isn't a good time."

"Not now or ever, you pulpit-stompin' scroogeineezer! *Git out'a here*!"

Looking up at the suddenly standing 6 foot 9 figure with reddening face and hat pushed all the way back, the preacher made an instantaneous judgment that, no, this was absolutely not a good time. This followed by an equally prudent decision to seek a distant destination immediately, if not sooner.

Bookman was still seething and barely settled in his chair when he received a call from Elizabeth Bannister. "Chief Bookman, I'm aware that you always have a program printed for the Good Citizen Award night. I thought I should call to be sure you got my little darling dog's name spelled right."

"*Argarrrh!*" Bookman slammed down the phone, jumped up and sailed his hat toward the door with a force equaling a gold medalist Olympic discus thrower.

Unaware of DeVon's miseries, Zeke was entering the building just as Ackerman exited. The preacher hastened by without as much as a nod. At Bookman's door, a silver-belly Stetson whistled past the department's special assistant's brow. Peering around the door frame, he got a look at DeVon's countenance. "Uh-oh, see you later." He spun and crouched, poised for takeoff.

"Whoa! Wait a minute."

Feigning utmost caution, Zeke tip-toed in, then crab-sidled toward the chair farthest from the chief. "Please don't hurt me."

DeVon retrieved his hat and recounted in detail the morning's events. The more he talked, the farther back went his hat. He was especially furious about Ackerman.

(Better be sure to tell Lurinda not to even think of telling Dee that Ackerman spoke to her about not really being married. Big Chief would wring off the preacher's head in the pulpit.) Zeke smiled at his thought.

"Whatcha grinnin' about! Think all this is a laughin' matter?"

"Oh no, Great Chief," making as if to flee.

To Zeke's relief, the deskman buzzed with a phone call. The chief listened a minute, engaged in a short conversation, and hung up. "That was Jerry Milligan. He wants to do a search'a MizMartha's store and her house. Told him I'd try to fix it up, and that the judge was already lookin' into givin' us the OK to hunt for MizMartha's papers. Good guy, that Milligan. He invited us to tag along. This lets us take a look for her papers without fussin' over how to get at 'em some other way."

"Once again, citizens, your kindly police chief strikes a blow for the Constitution."

"Details."

"Ever hear, 'The devil is in the details?' Just keep skating on thin ice close to deep water."

"Ever hear'a gettin' the job done? Not gonna skate close enough to break through. We're just goin' along with Milligan as his deputies." Zeke was about to ask whether Bookman ever heard of Leavenworth prison, but gave up.

DeVon phoned Judge Jefferson and explained about Chief Milligan and the search warrant situation. "There should be no problem that I can see, Chief Bookman."

After putting the deskman to work typing search warrants for Martha Manchester's store and house, DeVon picked up a stack of forms. "Haven't even had time to go over yesterday's patrol reports." He separated the stack and tossed half to Zeke. "Here, make yourself useful as well as ugly. See anything interestin', give a holler."

"I'm not your man. What if I miss something?"

"With that nosey brain'a yours, you're not gonna miss nothin'. Pipe down and read."

Well into his stack, Zeke announced, "I do believe there may be something here worth examining."

"Even a blind hog'll root up somethin' good now and then. Lemme see."

It was Officer Dixon's report of his previous afternoon's patrol. In response to orders for increased patrols by Benson's house, he and his partner picked their way down the narrow, unpaved, and pot-holed alley behind it. The deputy's Chevy was parked away from his house and shielded from side view by the dense evergreen hedges bordering both sides of a short garage driveway to the alley. It looked as if it had been there a while, but a survey of neighbors across the alley turned up no information. The garage was padlocked, and door-knocking at the house went unanswered. There were no fresh footprints around. Several passes down the alley during the remainder of the evening yielded no sign of activity. The night shift was alerted and would give things an extra look throughout its tour.

Bookman located Officer Kenneth Johnson's dogwatch report and found an entry about checking around Benson's place. "He didn't see nothin' strange, either. Pounded on doors again around 7:30 this mornin' without gettin' an answer. Maybe we better take a look inside the garage. Don't reckon the fool would eat his gun, but he's nuts enough."

"Won't you need a search warrant?"

"Nah. The three of us'll swing by there after we take Milligan's search warrants for Jefferson's signature."

"The *three* of us?"

"Yeah, you and me and Officer Crowbar."

Zeke sighed. "Sleep well, citizens, your upholder of the Constitution is still on duty."

"Just savin' the taxpayers a little money."

Judge Jefferson glanced through the search warrants for the Manchester properties. "Enough specificity is there, Chief?" Not waiting for a reply, he signed quickly and added, "Chief, you need to bring me some wrongdoers to lecture. We must do everything in our power to correct their ways."

"You're absolutely right, Judge. I'll tend to it."

One vigorous levering and only minimum additional effort was needed from "Officer Crowbar" to gain entrance to Benson's garage. If they expected to find a body or anything else of significance, they were disappointed. Paint buckets, ladder, a rusty lawnmower, and a collection of garage-sale-to-be items were all it contained.

On the way to the station, DeVon voiced surprise at Benson's car being at his house. "Can't figure it. His patrol vehicle's parked in front, and it looks like his personal car was probly in back all the time, too. How's he gettin' around? Wonder if somebody's into his dirty dealin' with him. Gotta ponder it."

Bookman phoned Chief Milligan to report that the warrants were ready. He promised to be in Stony Crossing in thirty minutes. True to his word, Milligan and a plainclothes officer walked in with time to spare. "DeVon! Good to see you again. Shake hands with Detective Bill Larson. He's helping with the Manchester investigation."

Bookman introduced Zeke. "This here's Zeke Tanner. Fed him a time or two after he showed up at the door, and now we can't get rid of him. Been tryin' to teach him a little about writin' press releases, but he's pretty slow-brained." The visitors smiled and shook.

Greetings and the usual mutual ribbing over, Bookman asked, "Jerry, got time to take a minute and bring us up to date on MizMartha Manchester's case? We're interested a'course—her livin' here for so long n'all."

"We have almost nothing—won't take any more than a minute to tell you how far along we are. As you might expect, there were no useable prints. The pillow the doer used told us nothing. The hospital's story seems to check out. No one was along on her trip from the emergency area to her room except an orderly. As you know, after getting her situated, the nurse left the room to see to another patient and was gone for five or six minutes, tops. It being a floor for critical patients, medical personnel come and go all the time, but no one saw anything unusual. Like I said—next to nothing. I'm hoping we can pick up any sort of clue during these searches. The hospital people are getting real nervous about the public's questions, and the news hounds are starting to sound off, especially with all the publicity about that male nurse-nut over in Ohio snuffing so many patients at their hospital."

"Yeah, Lardass Laddis figured it could be the same kind'a killin', but he was only passin' gas—no evidence. Ready?"

"Let's do it. You have a key?"

"May have one that'll work."

At the Manchester store, Milligan stifled a grin when the chief took out his oversized ring of keys. "Got one here somewhere that'll fit." Four keys later, one did. They trooped through a door unlocked more than fifty years by the same person until now. DeVon looked around. "Sort'a spooky in here without MizMartha."

Zeke felt a small neck-prickle. "I know what you mean. Can't remember ever seeing the store closed except for Sundays and holidays."

"She was steady as a stone, all right."

Bookman led the others to the tiny office in the rear. There were two four-drawer file cabinets on one side and one beside a desk on the other. A quick inspection showed the first two probably contained only supplies and materials useful in operating the store. Milligan put his detective to work on those on the off chance there might be something more. The office being too small for all of them, the other three lugged all four drawers from the cabinet near the desk out onto a counter in the store. Each took a drawer and dug in.

They worked in silence until Milligan remarked, "We were right about this file cabinet containing personal papers. She even kept her will right here in her office—two copies." He put one on the pile of material already reviewed, and glanced at the other briefly before handing it to DeVon.

Bookman declared, "Yeah, Jerry, that's MizMartha all over. Don't surprise me she's got a backup." He scanned the will. "It's all here, sure enough. Left everthing to the church, and Ackerman's the executor. There's a stopper on probatin' it till your investigation is done, but it looks like he's gonna get it all—much as I hate to see it happen." He laid it beside the pile, and they resumed searching.

Next, Milligan found a letter addressed to Dr. Forsyth. It had directions for her funeral arrangements attached to an insurance burial policy for five thousand dollars naming him the beneficiary. He showed it to DeVon.

"Doc'll be glad to see this. Wonder why she didn't get it to him before she passed—never know now. Maybe she was a like the rest of us after all—put off dealin' with it for a little longer." He explained about Dr. Forsythe arranging for Martha Manchester's funeral, adding, "Looks like he came pretty close to what she wanted."

In the next folder was a regular insurance policy for a hundred thousand dollars with the church listed as the beneficiary. Bookman fumed.

Another half-hour digging through the files, and they took a break. Milligan concluded, "Doesn't look like we're going to turn up anything helpful to our investigation, but I guess it was worth a try."

While the other two were chatting about this and that during the break, Zeke idled away the time by looking through some of the papers the chiefs already finished examining and put aside. He picked up the will he thought to be the one Bookman read, glanced through it, then reread it more slowly. He was having considerable trouble believing what he was seeing. "Stretch! Look here! This second will's not just a copy of the Ackerman will at all! It's another one altogether, and it was drawn only three weeks ago. Ackerman gets nothing—it leaves everything to the Windham Woman's' Center for unwed expectant mothers."

DeVon grabbed the will. Zeke was right on all counts. "Well now, don't this paint a pretty new picture'a things. And lookit this! Doc Forsythe's the executor of this new will! That rascal—why didn't he say anything?"

"Easy does it, Dee, he may not know. There's no law saying the executor has to agree to do it or even be told when the will is drawn."

"Ain't you the legal beagle, though. How do you know?"

"I didn't learn that I was Uncle John's executor until after he died, and that was legal."

"OK, but why you reckon she changed it?"

"Well, DeVon, perhaps she wanted to give her money to something she thought would do more good."

"Maybe so, but there's another question. She was in Doc's office and talked about her will. Why didn't she tell him right then about bein' the executor?"

"Maybe she hadn't decided whom to ask. Or she could've been wary of him not accepting—thinking he wouldn't be likely to refuse after she died. Could be other reasons. What do you intend to do about the new will?"

"All I can do is notify the right people this afternoon and let them dribble the ball."

They finished about noon. As they feared, nothing was discovered appearing helpful in the Manchester murder case. Bookman offered, "Jerry, we got about the best diner in the whole country right across the street. I'll spring for lunch—my thanks for findin' somethin' to throw sand in Ackerman's greedy grabbin'."

"Never one to pass up a freebie, lead the way."

The crowd at the diner was noticeably curious about the officers accompanying their own chief. Bob Gilby shouted for the rest of them. "Finally found a replacement for ya did they, Bookman? Well, *it's about time*—thought we'd never get rid'a ya."

"Not a chance, Gilby, and you oughta be glad. This one's meaner'n a truckload'a copperheads. He'd never let your cousin keep runnin' that little moonshinin' still out in the woods behind your place." Gilby opened his mouth to reply, but thought better of it and concentrated on a spot near the ceiling. The other diners had a good laugh.

After three specials and a diet plate disposed of by the crew, Chief Milligan and his detective agreed that the Country Kitchen was worthy of DeVon's recommendation. "Don't know how we can work after all that food, but I suppose we better go do the rest of our job."

They made a quick tour of Martha Manchester's home and decided there was nothing of interest found. Bookman and Milligan exchanged "thank-yous," and the visitors departed.

At the station, Zeke took his leave. "Must be going, Ethel. I promised the dogs a run."

"OK. Later, Gertrude."

Before releasing the dogs for their chase around the orchard, Zeke brought in his mail. Atop the usual stack of useless junk was a small blue envelope. *(Oh good, it's from Marjorie.)* He dropped the rest into the junk-mail basket and opened it.

> Dear Zeke,
> Just a note to let you know I'm still on for the weekend of the 14th (Valentine's Day, remember. Get the sugar-free candy ready.) If you don't think it's bad luck, I could drive up the evening of Friday, the 13th.
> Let me know.
> Love,
> Marge

(This is one time Friday the 13th won't be bad luck. I'll drop her a line tomorrow.)

Ace, Bandit and Zeke had a high old romp'n rassle. All three boys played until late afternoon.

32

Before Zeke cranked up the stereo for the morning concert, he propped a copy of the markings and numbers on the table before him. *(If I see them every time I turn around, maybe something will pop out.)* He examined them during breakfast—still no luck.

Ol' Emmy was feeling especially cooperative this morning, starting on only the fourth try. He drove aimlessly for a while, the markings nagging him. Around 10, he entered the station as DeVon was giving Dr. Forsythe the news about him being the executor of Martha Manchester's second will. To say he was surprised was a gross understatement. "What in heaven's name am I supposed to do about this?"

"Don't think there's much to it, Doc. Every whipstitch'a her estate goes to the Windham Women's Center. Only thing you need do is see to it they get it and collect your fee."

"Fee? *What* fee?"

"Don't tell me you don't know the executor usually gets about two or three percent for doin' the job, which is about half'a what a bank would get. In this case, it's easy money."

"I couldn't take any money for doing no more than signing some papers. What happens if Ackerman contests the second will?"

"If he's half smart, he won't. If he *does* try somethin', you might hafta do a little more with lawyers, but I wouldn't sweat it."

"What's the next move on my part?"

"If it was me, I'd see Judge Jefferson about probatin' the will. If the preacher's gonna try somethin' dumb, the lawyer for the Women's Center will defend their interests." As he left, Dr. Forsythe was complaining about being given a job about which he knew nothing.

Bookman lit his pipe and reported, "Didn't wanna say nothin' to nervous up Doc right now, but Barney Mitchell—you know, the prosecutor—phoned. Said he did some checkin' with MizMartha's new attorney. Looks like he's decided to spill a few beans now that Barney's doin' the askin.' Said MizMartha wouldn't let him keep a copy of her wills, but he had his notes and, get this, he also had the deeds for her properties. Wanted him to do some figurin'. About taxes, I think he said. He wasn't done when she died, so he still had 'em. Turns out her estate could be worth way more'n a million."

"Worth more than a *million—dollars*! Miss Manchester? Did anyone ever dream it was anywhere near that much?"

"Not me for sure. She never said a word about it or showed any sign by what she spent. Probly why nobody suspected. From what the attorney said, she must'a plowed a big share'a her money into real estate. Owned a bunch'a rentals in Windham and an apartment house close to the Women's Center. Had lots'a bonds and a big chunk'a cash, too. Did her bankin' in Windham. Charlie Harrison'll be fit to be tied if he finds how much money she kept out'a his bank."

"No wonder the preacher was so anxious to get at her estate."

"I hear you."

The conversation turned to the Borsch case and continued until Zeke announced, "Enough, already. I've got a few odds and ends to wind up, then I'm out of here. If your luck holds, you'll see me this afternoon, Gertrude."

"Yeah, yeah, yeah. See you. Ethel."

At lunch, Zeke again concentrated on the drawings propped before him, reviewing the ancient civilization's ceremonial code system he tried unsuccessfully to match previously. Suddenly, he remembered another way of interpreting it and began scribbling furiously. Things were looking good, but just as it appeared the first two numbers were indicators of cosmic events, his theory collapsed. He continued to play with it to no avail. He finally gave up, put on a jazz CD, and vowed to return to code-breaking later.

A dusting of new snow greeted him when he left to return to the station. *(Probably getting ready for the basketball tournaments starting next week. Always snows a ton on the opening weekend.)*

Bookman's afternoon began with a phone call from the county prosecutor informing him word just came in that there was a state-wide warrant for True Prophet's arrest He and some male members of the Roseville bunch were wanted for physically restraining and threatening severe bodily harm to two members of the "Holy Seer's" group who wanted to escape its so-called "religion" and control. "As usual, Chief, we got the word after his release."

"Wouldn'tcha just know it," DeVon grumbled. "We had him cold pigeon—some fool's late again with the info!"

Next came a visit from some members of the town council concerned about the adverse publicity generated by Elmer Jones. Zeke entered right after they left and waited until the chief calmed down before asking, "Councilmen extra ugly?"

"Nah, not really—the usual. That damn newsfarter Elmer Jones let another one on his program last night about our unsolved *cult killin'*. A'course, the council thinks they gotta start an environment pollutin' investigation. I told 'em his BS would bring lots more tourist business, and it cooled 'em right down."

"You said True Prophet was wanted for a crime he and some *men* committed. Hr only had *girls* in his flock when you stopped them."

"Just goes to prove what I always say—you can't never figure how a nutso ticks."

The buzzer sounded. "Sheriff Laddis, Chief."

"Now what?" He grabbed the phone. "Hello!"

"Bookman, Benson still ain't showed. Seen anything of 'im?"

"Nobody's reported any sign'a activity, Sheriff, and it don't look like anybody's been around his place."

"My deputies done some checkin' with lawmen in Indy and all around Marion County, but they can't find no place a'tall he stayed or spent money."

"Tell you what, I'll talk to the guy he was always hangin' with. If he knows anything, I'll phone."

"OK, Bookman, 'preciate it."

DeVon ordered the deskman to locate Officer George Anders. In short order, he appeared. "Well, Anders, that was quick."

"I was just out back gassin' the car up and fixin' to go on patrol. What's up, Chief?"

"You're a pretty good friend'a Benson's. He's not been reportin' for duty, and Lardass is wonderin' what's goin' on."

"Chief, he wasn't what you'd call a *good* friend."

"Who you think your bullin', Anders? You're real tight with him. Got any idea where he is or not?"

"None a'tall. Don't see 'im much, now that he works for the sheriff."

"When *was* the last time you saw him?"

"Can't say for sure. A week or so ago, I guess."

"Sure you got no idea where he might be?"

"Nope. Chief, you know I'd say if I knew."

"Funny thing, Anders—Benson's car and a sheriff's patrol vehicle both bein' at his place at the same time and he's nowhere to be seen. Think somebody might be chaufferin' him around?"

"He's got women friends. Maybe one'a them."

"OK. Hear anything, lemme know."

Anders turned to leave. As he got to the door, Bookman asked, "By the way, Anders, come into money lately? Inherit some or hit the lottery or somethin'?"

The officer stopped stock-still, then slowly turned back. "Whataya mean, Chief?"

"Saw you whippin' around in a new pickup. Good lookin' vehicle. Wouldn't mind havin' one like it. Been thinkin' about tradin'. Where'd you deal? Get a good trade?"

"Aw, I been talkin' for some time with Byerly over at Wayne City. Got a pretty good deal, I guess. My old truck covered the down payment."

"Byerly, eh? Maybe I'll take'a look there myself."

After Anders left, Zeke asked, "What was that all about?"

"Can't say for certain—call it a hunch. Thought he looked shook when I asked about the truck deal. Lots'a times when a perp's done some mischief, he gets nervous and spills more'n he needs to 'cause he thinks you might be onto somethin'. Anders had no reason to throw it in about his trade-in coverin' the down payment. Looked like he could'a been queasy about me askin' questions, and it caused him to blab. On top'a that, I don't know how he could afford to buy *anything*, much less a truck. Word is he spends every dime he makes and then some. Gonna do a little checkin'." He phoned the bank. "Hello Charlie, DeVon Bookman here. I wanna ask about an account."

Charles Harrison was obviously still piqued about the Borsch safety deposit box affair. His reply was a stiff, "Official business again, I suppose?"

"Official and confidential. Did my officer, George Anders, make a good-sized deposit in the past few days?"

"I can answer without looking it up. I happened to be behind the teller when he made a deposit of thirteen one hundred-dollar bills last week. He was bragging about selling some building lots."

"Much obliged, Charlie."

DeVon's next call was to Byerly Motors, Inc. "Byerly Motors, where everyone comes to buy, bye and bye. How may I assist you?"

It was cute. Bookman *hated* "cute." "Gimme Byerly himself."

"I'm sorry, but Mr. Byerly is busy with a customer. May someone else assist you?"

"This is Chief of Police Bookman at Stony Crossing. Tell him I'll be right over there pretty quick so's he can get busy with me."

"One moment please."

"Harry Byerly here. How may I assist you?"

"Like I told your operator, this is Chief of Police Bookman at Stony Crossing. You can *assist* me by answerin' a question or two about a customer'a yours."

I'd like to help, Chief, but our customer's records are confidential."

"Rather I get your Chief Milligan to drop in and ask 'em for me?"

"Oh no, that won't be necessary. How may I assist you?"

"George Anders—A-n-d-e-r-s—is an officer on my force. He bought a truck in there this week. Did his trade-in cover the down payment?"

"Give me a minute, Chief. We sell so many trucks, I can't keep track of all the deals."

Byerly came back on. "His trade-in was about a thousand short. He had the cash with him, all in hundreds."

"Much obliged. Mum's the word."

"You bet. Happy to assist you any time, Chief."

Bookman jabbed the intercom. "Get Anders back in here!"

An obviously nervous Anders reentered. "Yeah, Chief."

Bookman rose and strode around the desk to snarl down at the foot-shorter officer. *"You lyin' reptile!"*

Anders recoiled as if struck. "Whataya mean?"

"You know damn well what I mean! You lied about the down payment on that truck. Where'd you get the extra grand for it? While you're about it, where'd you get the thirteen hundred for the bank deposit?"

Anders recovered and tried to bluff it out. "What business is that'a yours?"

The chief moved even closer. "I'll tell you, *you lyin' worm!* Hollis Benson stole some jewelry and got forty-five hundred bucks for it, all in hundreds. Whatcha deposited in hundreds along with whatcha paid Byerly in hundreds amount to about an even split. That'd probly look to a jury an awful lot like an accessory to grand theft. *That's* what business it is'a mine. Now tell me about the money and where Benson is."

Anders wilted. "Honest to God, Chief, I don't have no idea where he is. He give me the money all right, but he owed it on a boat he bought from me last summer. Honest to God!"

"That's not the same story you told at the bank. Said *you're* the one who sold some buildin' lots."

"They got it mixed up. I was talkin' about how I got it from Benson and how he come to have the money."

"Felt a need to explain it, did you?"

"Just passin' the time."

"Didn't strike you as a little peculiar he had so much cash on him?"

"Sure, but he said he sold buildin' lots his mom left 'im, and a guy paid cash."

"Give the buyer's name, did he?"

"Just a guy."

"Expect me to believe that tale? The higher you pile it, Anders, the more it stinks."

"God's truth, so help me."

Bookman returned to his chair and ordered, "Have a seat."

The shaken officer was only too glad to obey. "Believe me, I had no idea it was dirty money."

"Mmm-huh. If you had no idea, why'd you give out that phony story about the down payment? Never mind answerin'—I got a more pressin' question. What about all the electronical stuff still in sealed boxes up there in Benson's bedroom? How long you two been in business?"

"God, Chief, I don't know nothin' about that! Think I'd *steal?*"

"Well, I been checkin' the night shift patrol reports, and it looks like there's been an awful lot'a doors reported by you as bein' left unlocked at the stores that sell that kind'a stuff."

"Those doors *was* unlocked. The owners say anything was stolen?"

"You know as well as I do most of 'em consider a little pilferin' part'a the cost'a doin' business and their tough luck they left the door unlocked."

"Maybe so, but I don't know nothin' about no electronic stuff."

Bookman stood again. "You told me you hadn't seen Benson for a week and that was a lie. You lied about the pickup. Your story about the money is fishy. Got my doubts about the electronical stuff, too. You're in deep do-do, Anders. I got a special dislike for lyin' officers. It'd help a whole lot if your memory was to perk up about Benson's whereabouts."

"Nothin' to remember, 'cause I don't know where he is."

"It'd also help if you'd show me the paperwork on the boat deal."

"Ain't no paperwork—you don't always have paperwork between friends."

"While ago, you said you weren't real friendly with Benson." The silence got heavy. "OK, Anders, here's what's gonna happen. You're goin' on suspension for lyin' till I get satisfied you're givin' me the straight skinny. Then we'll go from there."

Bookman waited as if expecting Anders to say something else, but he had no more answers. Sullenly, he placed his gun and badge on the desk and left.

Zeke was astounded by the episode. "Holy Toledo! Really think he's tied in with Benson? Is there enough to suspend him?"

"There's plenty. Not only is he a proven liar to a superior officer, his money tale looks to be full'a holes. Can't tell yet if he's mixed up in Benson's nasty mischief, but it sure don't look good."

"What's next?"

"Gonna do some more checkin' on his spendin' habits. I'm real curious if those hundreds for the bank and the truck are all he got from Benson."

"You don't think..."

"I don't *think* nothin', Tanner. I'll say this, though, I'll feel a lot easier if we could locate Benson."

Zeke was speechless except for another, "Holy Toledo!"

Bookman looked at his watch. "Gotta start checkin' the follow-ups on the applicants for Benson's job, then start diggin deeper into Anders' stories."

"Fine with me. I have things to do." He went home to work on numbers. No inspiration emerged, so he wrote a note to Marjorie.

Dear Marjorie,

Sorry to delay answering, but fireworks have been popping. Will tell all when I see you. I'm looking forward to the weekend of the 14th. (The sugar-free candy is on the way.) It's the first weekend of the basketball tournaments, and there will no doubt be the traditional blizzard. If so, we can make it the following weekend.

As you suggested, I'd like you to drive up after work Friday, which will give us time to shop all day Saturday. I've checked, and there are at least ten stores in Wayne City that sell confusers. We can surely find one able to tolerate my ignorance.

Let me know.

Love,

Zeke

He drove down and dropped it into the outgoing box an hour before the afternoon deadline. Hiram Maxwell was rapping on his store window next door when Zeke left the post office, but he developed a sudden case of deafness and escaped.

33

Zeke was off in his snowstorm prediction by one week. Friday afternoon's dusting intensified into the mother of all snowstorms by noon Saturday. Sunday morning, the snow was a foot deep and showed no sign of relenting. Before noon, everything ground to a halt, even over on Interstate 70. Travelers were piled up in lobbies of motels and long-haul truckers were toughing it out in their cabs. Blowing snow buried one eighteen-wheeler so deep it was struck by a snowplow. It was the worst snow most anyone had ever seen. Over his coffee, Zeke stared out the window. *(This should shut up the old timers' talk about their blizzards.)*

Blowing and drifting continued into the wee hours of Wednesday, and by then the entire region was declared a disaster area. Between emergencies on Tuesday afternoon, Bookman phoned to keep Zeke posted on what was going on. Most of the department's time was being spent getting supplies to families or rescuing fools stupid enough to venture out to perform important tasks such as going to the video store—closed, of course. Travel was generally limited to snowmobiles, but some of the hot-rodders finally had an excuse for their built-up pickups. There was still no word on Benson. Sheriff Laddis issued a warrant for his arrest, and Officer Anders was questioned again without result. True Prophet and his "flock" hadn't been spotted.

Wednesday morning, Zeke decided he could wait no longer to phone Marjorie Louise. She was obviously disappointed about delaying their weekend shopping, but agreed it would be foolhardy to challenge the elements.

Soon after rising on Thursday, Zeke heard the welcome sound of a snowplow grinding down the street. His elation was tempered by the realization the entrance to his driveway would be piled even higher with snow and slabs of ice. Oh well, at least the plows were out.

After Mother Nature vented her spleen and again showed who was boss, the stalled storm surrendered to glorious sunshine and blew on east to continue tormenting the unfortunates in its path. Zeke finished the morning chores quickly and began shoveling. Soon, he became so warm he was forced to shuck an outer jacket. *(Can't believe I've worked up a sweat already.)* In a matter of minutes, he was stripping off another layer. He took a break and looked at the thermometer on the porch. *(Would you look at that—above freezing already!)*

As the day wore on, it was obvious Old Lady Nature wasn't finished with them after all. Following the thorough inundation of snow, she was going to melt it as rapidly as possible and drown them right out. By noon, the temperature soared to 45 degrees, and the snow was retreating in trickles. Another 10 degree rise and the trickles became rivulets. By 2:30, the rivulets were rapidly graduating to adulthood.

Friday morning, Zeke was hard put to believe what was happening. The snowstorm was halfway into local lore. The temperature stayed above freezing throughout the night. One more warm day and the streets would be bare. By noon, Zeke felt adventurous enough to make a run to the diner. After days of do-it-yourself meals, even a diet breakfast sounded good.

The Country Kitchen had been closed for three days during the snowstorm. Now it was jammed as if the regulars needed reassurance normalcy was returning. Only a counter seat was available. (*To heck with the diet, a Plowboy's Daybreak Special is going to be the reward for my backbreaking labor.*) He grabbed a menu to choose which extra side dish to order.

Twyla Jean was rushing around every which way to get orders out. After the main crowd of crumb crushers was accommodated Zeke's order still wasn't taken. At last, she came to pour his coffee. "Hello, Zeke. Chief Bookman's already been in. Made it through the storm I see. Dogs OK?"

"No problems, no problems at all. Today, I think I'll have..."

Before he could continue, TeeJay informed, "Yours will be coming right up. I saw you come in." She turned to heat up the coffee of the other elbows-on-the-counter crew.

"Wait a minute! I..."

It was no use, she was headed for the kitchen, returning all too soon with the usual diet plate. "We're all so proud of you, Zeke."

He glared at the plate of nothingness, then at Will Jones who was seated next to him doing his best to suppress a snicker. "See something funny, Jones?"

"Nothin' much there *to* see, Tanner."

Eight minutes later, Zeke was on his way to the cash register. Tee-Jay's second helping of her pride in him didn't help.

At the station, Bookman greeted him with, "Well, you had all week to get the job done on the numbers. How about it?"

"I tell you, I've looked at them until I'm seeing them in my sleep, but no luck. Going to lay off a day or two before taking another shot."

"Well, they gotta mean *somethin'*. Guess you'll get a brainshower sooner or later." The chief brought him up to date about snowstorm events.

"Sounds as though you're still up to your knees in storm stuff, Great Chief, so I'm out of here."

"I'll be caught up pretty quick. When you wanna take a break later on from your loafin', you could stop back in."

"Will do. See you later, Ethel."

"OK, Gertrude."

Driving home, Zeke was amazed at the effect of the continuing snowmelt. *(The dogs are going to get their big run soon.)*

In spite of his vow to ignore the markings a while, he couldn't put them from his mind. Perhaps one reason was the copy propped on the table where he saw it constantly. At lunch, he began to study it again. Abruptly, he reached out and turned them to the wall. *(That's better. Don't know why I didn't do it before.)* While he finished his second cup, he thought about DeVon. *(Looked tired and sounded a little down in the mouth.)* Delaying his afternoon jazz concert, he drove back to the station.

They sat analyzing the Borsch case again for an hour, arriving at nothing new. Dr. Forsythe knocked and entered. After chatting about this and that, he said, "Chief, the hospital gave me Martha Manchester's personal belongings. There wasn't very much, but they included a gold chain with William Borsch's ring on it. Question for you. I remember she was very anxious to recover that ring, but do you have any idea why she'd be wearing it as a necklace?"

"How in the world would I know anything about that?"

"Thought I'd ask, Chief, thought I'd ask. You usually know a good deal more than you let on."

"Doctor, you heard her say as much about the ring as I did."

"All right, Chief. Let me know when you have something for the coroner."

"Will do."

After the doctor left, Zeke commented, "Nice evasion, Bookman, nice evasion."

"Only doin' what I figured MizMartha would'a wanted. She must'a put the ring on the chain pretty quick after I took it back to her. Glad I got it to her when I did."

"You didn't say anything about giving it back! Until just now, I thought it was still in the property room."

"Aw, wasn't worth mentionin'."

"I don't believe you for one second. Let's hear all about it."

"Know somethin', Tanner? You gotta big beak."

"Never mind that, start talking."

"If you must know, I gave it to her a while ago—wasn't any need to hold it for evidence. Handed it to her and she took off like a shot into her office—liketa never come out. When she finally did, I could'a swore she'd been cryin'. Thanked me about a dozen times and looked like she was gonna start bawlin' again. Couldn't figure why she was carryin on about a *nephew's* ring. Reckon now we know why. Anyway, I stayed till she calmed down a little. That's all there was to it, elephant snout. Now just shut up. I said it wasn't worth mentionin'."

"Well, well, well—kindly old Police Chief Bookman. Don't blame you for not saying anything. Wouldn't do to have folks discover there's a heart somewhere under that denim jacket. Always had blind faith there might be, but I was about to abandon all hope till now."

"Just knock it off."

"Your secret is safe with me. No one would believe it anyhow. Dee, the ring business makes me very sad, but it also makes me very angry she had to live without her son."

"Things change slow in Stony Crossing, Zeke."

The deskman buzzed and announced a call from Sheriff Laddis. Zeke jumped to his feet and grabbed his coat. "I'm out of here before the eruption." He left to the sound of Bookman rasping into the phone.

After parking Ol' Emmy, he crossed the street to get his mail before going into the house. In the entryway, he flipped quickly through it. *(More junk for the wastebasket. There must be some way to shut off the flow of this stuff.)*

After a quick lick-and-a-promise straightening job, the weekly cleaning was declared finished. A full day would be needed do a complete job next week before Marjorie Louise arrived.

Stereo doing its thing, the afternoon melded blissfully into dusk and Snake Bite time. He mixed one and decided whether he should have something to stave off starvation until dinner. The only thing available was a box of rice wafers. *(Yuk!)* Accustomed as he was to ignoring the answering machine, its blinking went unnoticed until the room darkened. Now its red flashing caught his eye. The first message was the same as the one they heard the night Dee described what killer types might leave messages.

Zeke listened again, this time jotting down the numbers to be certain he counted correctly. They were the same 1 1 1 1 5, all right. He shut off the machine, removed the tape, and tossed it up and down in his hand. *(No sense calling Dee. Not a thing he can do. I'll wait till Monday.)* An hour later, he fed the dogs but passed up the usual play session with a promise of a good romp. As he walked to the house, he could feel their disappointed gaze upon him. *(All right! I'll do it tomorrow.)*

Diet dinner on the table, he turned the Borsch markings toward him and studied them. His food cooled as he tried to make some connection, finally giving up and renuking the soup. The stereo was still doing its best to entertain, but its target was too preoccupied to pay undivided attention. At the end of his favorite Art Tatum CD, he mixed another drink, much smaller, and sat at the table playing with the numbers. At 10:30, he gave up.

Saturday morning, he took a spin around Make-Out Woods to see whether enough snow melted to take the dogs for a run. Much of it was gone, but the ground was slushy and the river was at the very top of its banks. Probably every where else would be sloppy—they'd have to wait another day or two. Besides, the clouding skies were promising more rain. *(Temperature at 50 degrees with rain on the way. What kind of weather is this for the middle of February? Well, we'll pay the price—no doubt it'll snow the entire month of March.)*

34

Monday dawned gray. Last night's rain stopped around midnight, but clouds had lingered. However, a brisk southwesterly wind promised clearing skies with drying conditions, and not a moment too soon. Rocky River was beginning to crawl over the levee down by the old canal-barge turn-around.

Mid-morning, Zeke drove to the station after assuring the dogs he'd take them out later. His nearest neighbor, Call-me-Charlie Ackerman, was at his mailbox, obviously making a studied effort to avoid a greeting. *(Still pouting over my letter, I see. Good riddance.)*

Zeke handed the tape with the latest message and his written copy to DeVon. While discussing the intent of the caller and meaning of the message, he reasoned, "Zeke, maybe you keep gettin' these latest messages 'cause whoever's sendin' 'em don't know for sure we got 'em or may be ignorin' 'em. He'd figure we got the first messages about Borsch 'cause he knows we found his body. And, he'd know we got the one about the fire since he could find out easy we took the door or he heard about Last Dime Dalton's blabbin'. But, he may not have a way of knowin' about these latest ones."

"Sounds logical. You suggesting we should do something to let him, or *them*, know we're getting them?"

"Say we do. What'd be a good way?"

"The only way I can think of is the *Clarion*. George Wallings might have some ideas."

"You mean take out an ad? Somethin' like, 'Dear Mr. Caller to Zeke Tanner's answerin' machine. He's gettin' the messages, but don't know whatcha want him to do about 'em. Can you give him a hint'?"

"Not quite to such a degree, I guess. An ad in the *personals* section might do it, though."

"Might. George is back from his ice fishin' trip. Reckon we better phone him and see if he can drop in sometime later this morning."

He could do better than that—he'd be right over. Twenty minutes later, the editor/publisher of "The County's Only Locally Owned Weekly," as the *Clarion* boasted, was seated in the chief's office.

Customary greetings over, DeVon began. "George, we got a situation'a some importance—gotta be kept secret. You'll be the only one who knows it besides me'n Zeke."

"Stretch, from grade school to this very minute, ever know me to have diarrhea-mouth?"

"No offense, George, just wantcha to know how important this is."

"Call me Zipped Lip."

"OK, here's the skinny. Zeke's been gettin' nutty calls on his answerin' machine. We think somebody's tryin' to use him to get us to do somthin' and phonin' *him* 'cause they know he's the big noise for the department. The first ones were connected to findin' Borsch and the next one about Lowell Williams' fire. It'd be easy to find out we got 'em and paid attention to 'em—knowin' we found Borsch's body and somethin' at the fire, n'all. The last messages are only a set'a identical numbers, but different from those drawn on Borsch. Since we can't dope 'em out, we can't do nothin' to show proof we're gettin' 'em and are doin' somethin' about it. Reckon you heard about the stuff on Borsch—everbody else has."

"Heard some rumors."

The chief described and drew them, then went on. "Like I said, the preverts doin' the phonin' may figure they're not gettin' through or they're bein' ignored 'cause we're not doin' nothin' they can see. We been thinkin' about doin' somethin' to let 'em know we *are* gettin' the messages. Then maybe they'll leave one that'll give us a clue as to what they want."

"What'd you have in mind?"

"Thought maybe you'd have an idea or two. Zeke mentioned an ad in the *personals* column."

"Saying what?"

Zeke spoke up, "Why not put in the numbers we've been getting in the messages. The callers should be able to figure out what they'd mean."

DeVon clapped his hands. "There you go. Not a bad idea, Zeke."

Wallings inquired quietly, "Mind telling what the numbers are?"

"Not a'tall." He slid Zeke's note with the 1 1 1 1 5 across his desk. "There you are—four aces and a five spot." The editor stared at the paper.

"What's the matter, George? Cat got your tongue?"

"You're not going to believe this, but I got an anonymous typewritten letter only this morning with more than enough cash in it to run a good-sized box ad in this week's paper. It's supposed to include nothing more than those very same numbers."

"Astonished" was certainly not the word. The chief was first to react. *"The hell!"*

"That's right, I have the letter right here." Wallings pulled it from his inside pocket and started to take it from the envelope.

Bookman jumped up. "Don't touch nothin! Don't touch nothin'! We'll try to lift prints. Not likely there's any but yours, butcha can't ever tell. Here, let me get it." Handling the envelope by the edges, he cautiously shook out a single sheet and inspected it closely. "How about we keep this till we can check it for prints?"

"Sure thing. What about the box ad? OK to run it?"

"Don't see why not. Right, Zeke?"

"That's what I'd recommend, but there will be no reason to run one of ours. It would only be a repeat and might muddy the waters."

Wallings rose to leave, and the chief asked, "By the way, where's the money that was in the envelope? We could check it, too."

"Sorry, I dropped it off at the bank with the other deposits on the way over."

"Doubt it matters. Any prints probly got wiped off before it was mailed. Thanks for comin', and mum's the word about everthing, eh, George? If anybody asks suspicious questions about the ad, let us know right away, will you?"

"You bet. See you later."

Good man. See you."

After he left, DeVon turned to Zeke, "Whataya make'a that?"

"Sounds as though we're on the right track about the numbers being a message the caller wants to get out. What's your guess as to the chances of anything turning up from Wallings' readers?"

"Way things are goin', probly none. Time to eat. Goin' with me to the diner?"

"The weather looks to be clearing, and I promised the dogs a run. Better get on home."

"Wonder if them dogs realize what a catch they got when you married 'em. Brush their teeth and tuck 'em in, too?"

"Sour pears, Ethel, sour pears. See you."

"It's sour *apples,* Tanner, sour *apples.* Keep workin' on the numbers."

By early afternoon, the sun was shining. True to his promise, Zeke loaded Ace and Bandit into Ol' Emmy and set out. Too excited to sit still, they traded sides in the back seat every few seconds, afraid they'd miss something. Make-Out Woods still looked much too wet, so he went on out Sycamore Street to the partially wooded countryside near Smith's dairy farm and parked in a turn-around known to be another parking retreat of high school kids.

When he opened the rear hatch, the dogs scrambled out to race through the remaining snow patches and tear around in the field bordered by woods while burning off pent-up energy. Soon, they came roaring back for reassurance they were still his favorites.

With one hand, Zeke roughhoused Bandit and spun Ace's red Frisbee as far as he could with the other. Sometimes, he played a trick on the Lab by faking a sweeping toss of the Frisbee, then hiding it behind his back. As soon as the fake began, Ace went racing off in a mad search for the red disk. That would work a time or two until Ace caught on and waited for the real toss. Bandit usually stood by with a quizzical expression, probably wondering about the mental abilities of his buddy and their master.

After about fifteen regular tosses, Zeke faked a long throw toward the nearest thicket. Searching the open area and finding nothing, Ace began nosing around inside the tree line. In no time at all, he came out carrying what looked at a distance to be a brown Frisbee. Holding it high and wagging his tail madly, he trotted proudly back to a puzzled Zeke. *(What in the world?)*

The mystery lasted only seconds. When Ace got closer, it became a certainty he hadn't found another Frisbee. Soon, he was sitting and offering a soggy Smokey Bear hat of the type worn by the county sheriff's deputies. Zeke turned it upside down. There, stamped in the sweatband, was the faded but still legible name of the owner, Hollis Benson.

The dogs were dumbstruck when Zeke shepherded them into the Blazer before they barely began their promised long romp. The speed he demanded of Ol' Emmy as he accelerated toward town was even more amazing to her. After parking in Bookman's spot, he ripped off his jacket to cover the Smokey Bear and hurried inside. Ignoring the deskman's greeting, he ran down the hall to Bookman's office, jerked open the door, entered quickly, and pulled it closed.

The chief put down his pipe. "Well podner, I knew you loved to come to work, butcha don't need to rip the door off to get here."

Without replying, Zeke took the hat from under his coat and placed it on the desk. "Ace found this in the edge of the woods out by Smith's farm on Sycamore."

Bookman looked it over quickly and punched the intercom. "Give Wilson and North a signal three, and tell 'em to make it on the double."

His next move was to phone Sheriff Laddis. He came on, uncharacteristically affable. "What can I do fer you, Chief?"

"Tanner's dog found Benson's Smokey Bear, and we're on the way to start lookin' for him." He gave Laddis directions, locked the hat in a drawer, and grabbed his coat. "C'mon, Zeke, let's go."

"Wait a minute! I've got the dogs in Ol' Emmy."

"Confound it, come on and lead the way! May wanna turn 'em loose to help look."

By the time they reached the front of the station, Wilson and North were already coming up the sidewalk. The chief ordered, "Follow us. Use both'a your cars. No lights, no siren. Tell you what it's all about when we get there. Fire up your heap, Tanner, and lead on."

As Zeke headed for the location, he couldn't avoid thinking Ol' Emmy must be getting an enormous ego stroking, leading such important looking cousins. At Smith's farm, all except the dogs piled out. Both fixed how-could-you stares on someone they thought was their true friend.

Bookman explained the situation to the officers, then directed, "OK Zeke, take us right to where your dog found the hat."

"I believe I'll be able to show you the spot` from right here, thank you very much. Besides, someone should stay here to release Ace if you need him." Pointing, he advised, "He found it somewhere just beyond that pin oak."

"All right boys, you know what we're lookin' for. We'll start by that tree, then fan out and go on into the woods."

The search lasted only minutes. Forty feet beyond the pin oak, North found the partially snow-covered body of Hollis Benson.

The chief left North on watch and he and Wilson ran back to the cars. DeVon told Zeke, "It's Benson, all right" and ordered the sergeant, "Take a car and get the coroner. No lights, no siren. See if Bill Mickner is anywhere in the area and ask him to come out."

Sergeant Wilson appeared shaken. After all, he served on the force with Benson for a long time. The chief looked at him. "You OK?"

"Yeah, I'm OK. Want me to get Last Dime, too?"

"Not yet. It'll be a while before we're ready for him."

During the few minutes before Dr. Forsythe arrived, Bookman sat with Zeke, then removed his hat and examined it as if to somehow find some answers. "If it's true it never rains but what it gushes, we got ourselves caught in a real toad-strangler. Two killin's in Stony Crossing since New Year's. Borsch's looks pretty much like it could be a cult job—this one's got the earmarks'a robbery. Only similarity is neither of 'em is solved."

"What makes you think this one's robbery?"

"Looks like he was shot once in the back'a the head, and there's no sign of his weapon. That Glock shootin' iron would bring a good penny if the doer decides to sell it. Good bet when the coroner lets us look, we won't find a cent on him. My thinkin' is somebody got a gander at what was left'a the bundle he got from sellin' MizMartha's jewelry. Got the drop on him and cuffed him with his own cuffs, then brought him out here and offed him with his own piece. Zeke, he hadta know who it was, else how could anybody pulled it off?"

"Any suspects in mind?"

"Hate to say it, but Anders better have a good alibi. It'd be easy for him to take Benson—them bein' buddies n'all."

"I certainly *hope* he's not involved."

"*You* hope he's not involved. Whataya think *I'm* hopin'? I could believe he might be tangled up in petty larceny or receivin' money he knew wasn't totally legit, but the big *number one*? Hopin' don't cut it, though. Gotta get him in for lots more questionin', then do some more checkin'—includin' is there more hundred-dollar bills stashed somewhere?"

"Fairly confident Benson was killed right here?"

"Think so, but can't say for certain-sure. Didn't see sign'a draggin', but a'course we couldn't see nothin' even if there was tracks before. The snowstorm would'a covered 'em and the rain washed 'em out. Maybe Doc can help."

Two police cars slowed to a stop. Sergeant Wilson and Dr. Forsythe stepped from the first one, Wilson carrying a camera. State Police Captain Bill Mickner alit from the other.

"Hello, Doc. Glad you could come, Bill."

"No problem, Chief—happened to be close by."

Bookman sighed. "Doc, this is somethin' I can really do without. Benson wasn't much of a cop lately, but this is a helluva note."

For a moment, all were quiet. The coroner spoke first. "I know something of how you feel, DeVon. Never cared much for him, but this is a terrible way for any man to go."

Mickner echoed the coroner's statement, and the group started for the crime scene. Soon after, Sheriff Leon Laddis rolled to a stop. Zeke told him about the others finding Benson and where they were. He plodded off.

The dogs were very fidgety about being cooped up, but it seemed more—as though they sensed something unusual was afoot. Zeke reached back and patted them. "Easy does it fellas, we'll be going in a little while." After a great deal longer than the promised "little while," all except Officer North walked slowly toward the police vehicles and stood talking a bit before all but Bookman departed.

Several cars slowed to gawk as they passed, but as yet no one stopped. Now, two looked about ready to. DeVon hurried over and waved them on in no uncertain terms. "*Demandable buzzards*—always gotta flap around, don'tcha! Move 0n and keep goin'!" He returned and climbed in beside Zeke. "Looks like this is where the job was done, sure enough. If we can get hold of a slug, maybe we'll know for sure if he was shot with his own piece. Nowadays, all departments, even Lardass Laddis', fire every officer's weapon and keep the slug for comparison with others in case of a shootout. Appears I was right about it bein' a robbery—no money on him, and his gun's still nowhere to be found."

DeVon stared out the window. "Tough way to go, Zeke, tough way to go. Might as well head on home and drop off your dogs. Afterwards, come to the station—we'll need to get out a press release soon as possible. Lardass promised to keep a lid on things till then. Realize you're gonna be workin' like a borrowed mule again this evenin', don'tcha?"

"I know. Anything special you want in the release?"

"Nah, the usual. Dedicated officer and all that. Service record and all that. Do whatcha think. Gotta go—lot's more work to do here—won't be done for quite a while. Wilson's gone for Dalton and to round up more men to do a full-out search'a the crime scene." Another brief question or two and Zeke headed for home with his dogs.

Near town, Last Dime Dalton raced by—lights flashing, siren blaring. *(I'll bet he turns those off when he gets closer to Bookman.)*

The news of Benson's killing hit the late afternoon news only minutes before the telephone began working overtime. Zeke handled calls for almost two hours before the ringing slowed. He went home after the deskman told him Bookman was out somewhere.

Once home, Zeke got zero relief from the phone calls. They came before, during, and after he finished his dinner. Finally, he left the receiver off and mixed a Snake Bite. With only marginal success, he tried to relax with the Benny Goodman Quintet. On the ten o'clock news, Elmer Jones was again spewing forth about the small-town murder capital, blah, blah, blah. Zeke punched him off and went to bed.

35

It would be difficult for Zeke to recall a more hectic week. Thursday after lunch, he listened to CD's and thought about what had transpired so far. Of course there was the uproar following Benson's murder, including Elmer Jones' continued bleating about the mutilation murder of Borsch, the Manchester suffocation and the slaying of a policeman. He was at the top of his sensationalistic worst, including reporting all victims were from the same rural town and all the crimes unsolved. National news-noise shows also took an interest, the producers from two of them inquiring about doing a remote from Stony Crossing. The possibilities for all sorts of theatrical reporting obviously fired their imaginations. Naturally, the usual "public's right to know" nonsense was part of their pitch. Zeke pointedly discouraged them, especially after he noted the same "and-you-better-respond-immediately" demand implicit in both requests.

Ballistic tests performed on the slug removed from Benson proved he was shot with his own gun. A more complete search of the crime scene turned up a shell casing verifying the chief's earlier judgment about the killing occurring at the site. Other evidence indicated it took place several days before the body was discovered and he suffered a blow to the head. Bookman's theory that the motive was robbery seemed credible, since no money was found on the person of the slain officer. There was also evidence of what DeVon long suspected—the deputy was a doper.

Bookman grilled Officer Anders again, but got nowhere. When asked concerning a polygraph, the officer wasn't saying yes and he wasn't saying no. He stuck to his ambivalence even after the chief told him he could officially become a suspect. He hired Bo Brewster, Stony Crossing's candidate for international smarmy lawyer of the century, which ended any further attempts to get additional information. The officer wasn't held, but remained on suspension from duty. Brewster howled, and what Chief Bookman told him to do would be both difficult and painful.

Pressure on Bookman was increasing daily, with the unsolved murders, alarmed townsfolk and Elmer Jones' continued sniping supplying ammunition for criticism. Some town councilmen became ever more nervous, the thought of being the target of a national news investigation raising their anxiety level to increasingly greater heights. DeVon again calmed their fears by assuring them the publicity could bring even more tourist business to town.

As if this and other two-bit annoyances weren't enough amidst murder investigations, Bookman received a special delivery letter from Mrs. Bannister reminding him of his promise to give her darling Tinkerbell a Good Citizen Award. She also sent along the exact spelling of her precious pet's full name and his pedigree for the program. Luckily, no one else was in his office when the letter arrived.

There were further indications of Zeke's resounding fall from Preacher Ackerman's good graces. Twice in the past three days, he was at his mailbox and hurriedly turned 'a frigid shoulder when Zeke drove by. *(Still pouty-pout-pout over my letter, I see. That's just as well. As I said—good riddance.)*

Yesterday, Zeke spoke to Marjorie Louise, giving her directions to his house, afterward reminding himself that he must do a thorough cleaning job tomorrow. He didn't want it looking as though a roving band of violating Vikings used it as a base camp for a decade.

The box ad with the numbers, 1 1 1 1 5, appeared in the weekly *Clarion*, resulting in all sorts of guessing games by the Country Kitchen crowd, but no clue surfaced. Neither were there any more cryptic messages on Zeke's answering machine. However, something appearing significant occurred this very Thursday. On the way to the diner for their morning coffee break, Abraham Lincoln Smith, head gravedigger at Perpetual Rest Cemetery, flagged down DeVon.

Smith thought something looked screwy to him when he and his crew were on their way to dig Benson's grave. Someone went into the cemetery during the night before and pounded in a sign alongside Bill Borsch's grave with strange numbers on it. He figured it was only kids doing what kids do, so he yanked it out and pitched it into the trash. Then he started thinking about the numbers on Borsch and decided he better tell the chief about the sign.

Not even bothering to ask Smith where he heard about the numbers, Bookman put him in the car and sped to the cemetery to retrieve the sign, beating the trash pickup by bare minutes. Smith fished it out and handed it to Bookman. The numbers, 6 1 2 1 9, were painted in bright orange on a black background. He put it in the trunk and took the gravedigger back to his car.

Previous questions were re-run. "What in Hades was going on?" "Who?" "Why?" DeVon said he'd give the sign to Mickner to see if the paint matched the barn door paint at Lowell Williams' fire.

Zeke spent most of the afternoon working on the numbers puzzle. As usual, the old numbers made no sense, and now there was this new set. Darkness fell before he fed the dogs and promised to let them have a short orchard run.

36

Early Friday morning, Zeke renewed his vow to jump on his housecleaning. He began by sweeping, dusting, and putting things in their proper places. He was only decently into his coffee and Beethoven's *Pastoral* when DeVon phoned. "What'n blazes is keepin' you? Don'tcha know this is the day we lock up all the bad guys?"

"Your mind has finally gone. I told you about a dozen times I'm working here all day and shopping all day tomorrow. Why are you so joyful sounding? Run over some kid's pet dog?"

"Got big news! Abe Smith phoned first thing this mornin', sayin' he went over to the cemetery last night to be sure the hole they dug for Benson was covered up real good—weather-guesser said it might snow. Anyway, he caught some kids foolin' around and grabbed 'em thinkin' they might be the ones doin' the mischief out there. Maybe even the ones who left the numbers sign at Borsch's tombstone. They denied it up and down, a'course. But, get this, they admitted to bein' there night before last and seein' two guys plantin' the sign. The kids didn't get a good look and hid when they got worried the guys were gonna spot 'em.

"Abe got one'a the boys' names, and I pulled him and his parents in before breakfast. The parents liketa crapped. Kid stuck to his stories'a not bein' a devilment-doer and to spottin' the sign planters. He didn't recognize who they were, but got a gander at their vehicle before he and his buddy took off runnin' for home. Said they thought it was a dark-colored van, maybe an old Chevy, but there wasn't enough light to be sure. It's all he could remember 'cept one thing. Wanna guess what?"

"Bookman, don't you dare tell me it was the license number. I couldn't stand the shock."

"You're only gonna be about half-shocked. The kids got only the first part before high-tailin' it out'a there. It was this county's prefix number followed by an alphabet letter. The number followin' started with a two. A'course, the county prefix number only fits a gazillion cars and half of 'em's Chevy vans with a license number beginnin' with a two. The alphabet letter don't mean nothin' 'cept when the license was bought. All we gotta do is narrow 'em down to one and we got a leg up on findin' Borsch's doer and maybe the Williams' fire setter. Gonna phone the Department'a Motor Vehicles soon as they open. How about them bananas, my man!"

Zeke was thunderstruck. "I hardly know what to say. Will solving the Borsch case come down to some kids seeing an old van in the cemetery?"

"Zeke, most times the bad-asses do one stupid little thing that gets 'em or you get real lucky. Maybe this time it'll be a little'a both. Lordy mackerel, I hope so!"

"You and me both. How soon will you know something?"

"Shouldn't take long for the DMV to get a printout'a the possibles and fax it over. I'll split up the list and get several men on it. Dependin' on how many names, I don't expect we'll hafta burn too much time to get some probables sorted out. A'course, we can't run 'em all down at once, but we can ferret out a few'a the most likely to start on.

We get extra lucky, we might have a suspect later today or early tomorrow."

"Dee, this is great! Phone me as soon as you know anything, anything at all."

"Count on it. See you."

Zeke fell to his housekeeping chores with vigor, all the while thinking about DeVon's call. It would be awesome to get even one case solved, especially one as mind-benumbing as Borsch's. Then maybe they'd finally find the meaning of the markings and those phone messages.

He worked on, puzzling over the numbers on the sign. As in the past, he experienced an occasional sensation of an answer flickering across his consciousness. But, no matter how hard he screwed down his concentration, no answers were forced to the surface. Well, maybe later.

Almost two hours passed. During his sweeping and dusting he couldn't believe how he let things get in such a state. There was even a cigar butt left over from the monthly poker night. "From now on, I'm going to play *keep-up*, not *catch-up*."

The pile of magazines and other throwaway stuff in the front hallway grew even larger. Finally everything was swept or dusted. He stood in the middle of the living room contemplating the waxing and polishing yet to do. *(Holy moly, I haven't even started on the kitchen! Get going, Tanner, there's not even time for coffee.)* During a quick lunch, he phoned Bookman, but there was no real news. A few names on the list were screened, but it was only a start.

By 3:30, he finished all he intended to do on the cleaning detail except trashing the Everest of junk mail and housecleaning debris in the entryway. *(To heck with it right now—gonna have a coffee.)* As he sipped and studied the markings for the umpteenth time, Bookman phoned. "It's goin' a little slower'n I wanted. Got maybe three dozen names so far, but most of 'em can probly be ruled out."

"Anyone I know?"

"Couple. Abel Hofstettler and Hiram Maxwell are on the list, and both of 'em own vans. Only thing is, one's a newer model, and the other's light-colored. Crossed 'em off for now."

"Any good bets?"

"Zeke, ever heard'a Willis Snee? He's one worth takin' a look at. Been in jail for assault and domestic violence at least a dozen times. Tried to start one'a those survivor-nut military bunches once. Between him and some'a his cousins, there's at least five old vans. Another one's Jacob O'lean. Meaner'a stomped-on rattler and hates everbody. He's the wacko always threatenin' to pound a big bolt all way through the earth and tighten it down so's to fix everbody good. Cussed out most'a the businessmen in town—thinks they're all are out to screw him. Word is, Borsch and him went at it big-time once when the barber charged him full price for a haircut. O'lean's mostly bald, y'know."

"These are locals, Dee. Given up on Borsch's murder being a cult crime?"

"Heck no, we got names I don't recognize. Probly some could'a just moved here. Could be stolen plates, too. Gotta check everthing, don't we? Gotta rule out everthing, don't we? Don't wanna slide right by the real doer if it's not a cult, do we? No reason somebody else can't be driving an old Chevy van, is there? Always the ray'a sunshine, ain'tcha, Tanner?"

"Easy does it. I was only asking."

"Mmm-huh. Well, I'll phone as soon as we get somethin' else. Go on back to your spittin' and polishin'. Be careful not to wind up with housemaid's ankle."

"Go on back to your list-looking. Be careful not to get ear-strain. See you, Ethel."

"See you, smartass."

Zeke attacked the front entryway. Upon filling one trashcan, he lugged it outside, brought in an empty, and continued discarding the junk mail he always threw into its own basket. In his haste, he was grabbing the biggest possible handful of catalogs. Oops, too many that time! Their slick surfaces lost their grip on each other and the entire lot cascaded onto the floor. While collecting the scattered catalogs, he roundly damned every mail-order firm in the universe with every Chinese curse he could muster.

Wait a minute! What was this? A regular envelope? *(How'd that get there? M*ust*'ve been in between the catalogs.)*

Written in flowing style, there was no return address. He was about to open it when the phone interrupted. Muttering more Chinese curses aimed at its inventor, he grabbed the phone. "Hello!"

"My, aren't we the grouchy one. I intended to phone that lovable Zeke Tanner. Please excuse me, sir. I believe I've reached a wrong number."

(Marjorie Louise!) He switched from junk-mail-and-telephone-damning to sweetness-and-light in a flash. "Marjorie! I thought it was either another reporter or a flimflamming telemarketer phoning from some boiler room. You've saved them from a lifetime curse." He told her of his cleaning day topped off by the slippery catalog war going on in the entryway.

"Why, Zeke, I'm seeing a new side of you. I never dreamed you were capable of cleaning with such a vengeance."

"Just call me Mrs. Zeke."

"I phoned to let you know it may be as late as seven-thirty before I arrive. Will it be all right? I planned to leave before now, but there's a small office detail to which I must attend, darn it."

"That's OK. It'll give me more time to recover from my chores."

They chatted for a bit, reluctant to break the connection. Zeke gave her directions to his house again, and they "backatcha'd" each other on looking forward to the weekend.

Their good-byes done, Zeke sat and thought about their conversation. Something she said was sticking in his mind. What was it? A word? *What* word? He sat staring at the markings on the sheet propped on the table. A bolt of illumination flashed! Recalling Marjorie's word, he snatched a pencil and began decoding the numbers, 6 1 2 1 9. He was right! He did the same for the others. *Yes!* Excitedly, he phoned DeVon.

"Sorry, Mr. Tanner, he's out checkin' on some license plates."

"Know where?"

"No, but I'll try the radio." Zeke could hear him calling for the chief. "Sorry again, Mr. Tanner, I can't raise him. His radio's been actin' up again, but I'll keep tryin'."

"Please do, and tell him it's *extremely* important for him to contact me. You can tell him I have big news."

"Will do."

Zeke checked his calculations again. There was no mistaking it! He now knew the meaning of the markings!

While he waited for Bookman's call, he tore open the letter rescued from the junk mail and was flabbergasted. On the single sheet of paper was drawn a black heptagon with the usual diagonal line slashed through the number 68. At once he knew the meaning of an identical letter mailed to Borsch the week before his demise. How long had this letter lain in his junk basket? He got no answer from the faint postmark. He phoned the station and asked the deskman to try Bookman again. No luck.

In the darkening kitchen, Zeke sat and stewed. Still no Bookman. He decided to drive to the station and wait, but needed to feed the dogs first. While he was absorbed with the numbers, their courteous muted food requests evolved into intermittent barking. *(Listen to them! Must be extra hungry tonight.)*

As soon as he stepped onto the back porch, he had the sense of not being alone. Before he could turn to look, he was locked in a chokehold and something placed over his face. Soon, very soon, he was feeling nothing.

37

(Old Jack's dragged another dead groundhog into the yard. Looks like he's won another go-round in his war with 'em and brought his prize to mother. As usual, she don't think much of his present—not much a'tall—but she can't embarrass the old white collie by scoldin' him. Look at him standin' out there with that goofy grin—waggin' his tail off. He's so proud of his trophy, the only thing she can do is wait for a chance to throw the carcass in the garbage when he's not lookin'. Don't think it'd bother Jack much even if he saw her do it. He figures there's plenty more down by the woods. Tomorrow, he'll try his best to bring another one to the kitchen door.

(Can't spend too much time thinkin' about Jack—gotta get ready for the 4-H awards at the Johnson mansion this afternoon. Mr. Johnson owns the factory in Stony Crossing all right, but he's interested in agriculture, too. Gonna have all us winners to his mansion to get the prize *ribbons for our 4-H projects. Mine for growin' the best garden. One for best tomatoes, too.*

(The ceremony's gonna be hard on mother. She's always worryin' about what other people think. Wish she'd stop worryin' and enjoy things. What people think don't bother dad. Besides, he's known Mr. Johnson since he was too poor and raggedy to be seen at the band concerts on the Town Square. Dad says Charlie Johnson's the same man under those made-to-measure clothes as he was under worn-out overhalls, so what's all the fuss? Just 'cause he's made a fortune from inventin' some gadget used in every automobile made don't make him any different from the Charlie Johnson who useta come out here to hunt rabbits to help feed his family.

(Mr. Calhoun's gonna hand out the ribbons. He's been superintendent at the school for about a hundred years, and still scares the pants off everybody who's ever gone to Stony Crossing Public. I'm not as scared as some, 'cause I've never been called to his office. Jerry Jackson has, though, and the story he tells about it makes you wanna forget all about breakin' any one of about a million rules they got.

(The ceremony was a winner, I guess. Maggie McGraw even came and sat at my table for the refreshments. That went pretty good till Mr. Johnson patted me on the head and told how dad was the one who found Charlie Jr.'s finger he cut off in a bicycle accident. Didn't look like Maggie enjoyed the tale too awful much 'bout how the finger looked.

(Here comes dad. Got on his church suit. He's joshing with Mr. Johnson and mother looks like she's gonna drop dead from embarrassment. Why is she worryin' about what people think about dad buddy-buddying with Mr. Johnson? Don't seem to bother Mr. Johnson and sure not dad—they're havin' a ball.)

******

(Dad, the ice-skatin' party at the lake was fun. Never skated before, but it was easy to pick up. I liked the part best where Maggie McGraw kept holdin' on to keep from fallin'. Jerry told me later he

couldn't understand it, 'cause somebody told him she was a really good skater. Whatcha grinnin' about?)

******

(The final buzzer is about to go off, and we're down by one. Here I stand in front'a the center circle with the ball. Stretch is callin' for it, but they're gonna double-team him for sure if I pass it to him. Eight seconds left and I'm way out'a my range. My percentage from this distance is lower'n my hat size. Yayhoo guardin' me knows it, too—lookit him back off to cut off a drive. Four seconds! Nothing else to do but let 'er fly. Look at that! Danged if it didn't go in like it had eyes! We beat Wayne City! Sectional Tournament Champs!! How sweet it is!)

******

(Take a look at that sanctimonious clown sitting up there talking to the School Board about his precious 230-pound sweet little boy—about how he should be given another chance even though precious was trying to pull close to a rape on that little freshman cheerleader. Third try, too. It's probably going to mean my job, but no way is he back on the team. Whataya mean, 'Ezekial Amos Tanner, we're here to decide your fate?' It's the kid's fate we're talking about.)

******

(Funny place for a school board meeting. Why is it so gloomy in here? Why do they have only candlelight? Must've taken a long time to light them all. They look like those red Christmas candles Hiram Maxwell had on sale. Probably got a good buy on that many.)

******

(It's chilly. Why am I sitting out here in the middle of the room by myself? Why are those School board members sitting in rows over there to one side wearing black robes? Funny things for a board to be wearing—those hoods hide their faces, too. Can't tell how many there are—looks like an awfully big board. Hard to make out anything with it so dim in here, though. Things are kind of blurry. Why do they repeat *everything the board president says? He need to be certain they heard him? Must be taking several votes—the way they raise their right arms straight up high after he says something.)*

(What about the guy standing right there in front of me? Must be the board president—he's got the only robe with those funny figures down the front. Funny hood, too, with that skull thing.)

******

(What are these two guys beside me doing? My nose itches. Why can't I get my hand up to scratch it? Can't move my feet around, either. Hey, this is getting crampy!)

******

(The dogs are really barking. Must get them fed. Started to, but don't think I got their food. Marjorie Louise will be here pretty soon. Must get them fed before that.)

******

(Ouch! What's that for, mother? I mowed the whole yard exactly like you said.)

******

"Ouch! I don't care if you are the board president, you can't slap my face. What's that mean, 'Try not to put him under so deep this time?' **Hey! What's the idea!** Get that thing away from my face!"

******

(Wow! Must've overslept—still groggy. I see the board's still here—must be a long meeting. The president's standing there again. Better find out how long he's going to ask me to stay.) "How long are you going to keep me here?"

"**Silence!** Speak only when commanded! The entire flock has voted, and you have been found guilty of all charges. The flock's leaders are the Chosen. Their leader will read the charges the flock has found you guilty of."

('Flock? Chosen? Charges?') "What charges?" *(Am I still half-asleep? Did he really say he was going to read charges?)* "Ouch! Stop slapping me!"

"*Silence!* Speak only when commanded! You will hear the charges the flock has found you guilty of. Then the sentence will be carried out. DAMNATION TO ALL NONBELIEVERS, BROTHERS!*"*

DAMNATION TO ALL NON-BELIEVERS, HOLY LEADER!"

(Gotta get out'a here—this guy's nuts! All these guys are nuts! Can't move my arms! My legs, either! What'd he mean—the sentence will be carried out?' Hey, what're those guys doing with knives! What's the other one doing with a pillow! CAN'T MOVE! GOTTA GET OUT'A HERE!)

"Struggling won't do any good. All nonbelievers struggle. You're not even worthy of hearing the charges. The sentence will be carried out immediately. Brothers, is he conscious enough to feel the *Blades of Hades?"*

"Yes, Holy Leader, he's about like the other one."

"Carry out the sentence!"

(GOTTA GET AWAY!! Why're they grabbing my hands? What're those guys with the knives gonna do! GOTTA GET OUT'A HERE!!)

KNOCK, KNOCK, BANG, BANG, BANG.!

"POLICE! OPEN UP!"

BANG, BANG, BANG!!

"Put him under! All the way under! Then take him out the other door and load him in a van. Take him to your garage."

"YES, HOLY LEADER."

" The rest of you take off your robes and prepare to overcome the evil at the door!"

"YES, HOLY LEADER!"

BANG, BANG, CRASH!!!

(I don't understand. That looks like Stretch. Can't be—he's back in Stony-Cros.........).

"*HOLD IT RIGHT THERE, YOU FREAKS! ONE TWITCH AND YOU'RE HISTORY. YOU BUGGERS THERE BY THE DOOR—SET him DOWN. DO IT NOW!!!* GO AHEAD, I'M ITCHIN' FOR THE CHANCE!"

38

Zeke didn't believe the business about seeing a shining light when you die, but perhaps it was true after all. There was certainly one flashing directly into his eyes. Bright all around the room, too, and there was an angel all in white standing right there. *(Looks as though I must be dead, sure enough. But if I'm dead, why am I thirsty?)*

"Mr. Tanner! Wake up, Mr. Tanner! Wake up!"

(Why wouldn't an angel know my first name? The shining light went out. That mean I'm not in heaven?)

"Come on, Mr. Tanner, wake up!"

"Why?"

"You've been sleeping long enough. The doctor says I'm to wake you."

"Don't wanna—sleeping good." *(There's that shining light again. I'm dead, all right. Go away!)*

"Come on now, wake up!"

(OK, I'm awake.) "Why does an angel keep pestering me to wake if I'm dead?"

"You're not dead, and I'm not an angel, I'm a nurse." She pocketed her flashlight.

"I don't understand. Nurses don't wear white anymore."

"They still do in this hospital, believe it or not. Here, take a sip of water and let's try sitting up."

A voice boomed from across the room. "Just offer the old wart hog some food, and he'll perk right up."

(Wart hog? That's God talking? Sounds a whole lot like DeVon Bookman. You don't suppose...surely not!)

Someone else was speaking. "Zeke dear, the doctor says you'll be fine. Just do as the nurse says and try to sit up."

(Was that Marjorie Louise? Ye gods! Whoops, pardon me, God—no offense. Is Marjorie up here, too? Was it a traffic accident?)

"Let's go, Mr. Tanner. Let's get our legs over the side—it's past noon already. Time to get up and enjoy this beautiful sunny day."

(Might as well humor her—maybe she'll stop pestering me.) "OK, I guess I can give it a try. You said '*our*' legs. Gonna put yours over the side, too?"

The voice boomed again. "He's gettin' all right, his smart-assery's comin' 'round."

The second voice admonished, "Zeke! Behave yourself."

"OK, whatever you are, here we go. Oooooh, wow!"

The nurse took his shoulder and steadied him. "You're all right, Mr. Tanner. You're just not quite awake yet. The room will stop spinning in a minute. Put your head down and take deep breaths. Here, let me straighten your gown."

(Gown! Did she say 'gown?') He reached back and felt bare skin. *Now,* he was awake—w*ide* awake! Worse yet, the ox-stubborn sheet wouldn't come loose so he could wrap it all the way around him. "Gimme my clothes! Gimme my clothes!" One last jerk at the sheet, and he nearly toppled back onto the bed.

DeVon couldn't stop laughing and Marjorie Louise lost her battle to keep a straight face. The nurse eased Zeke back and raised the head of the bed. "Maybe we better take it a bit slower."

Bookman offered his usual sympathy. "Big mystery'a the day is how long you're gonna keep goldbrickin'. Lots'a work to be done."

Marjorie Louise joined in. "Yes, Zeke, everyone wants to interview you, especially Elmer Jones."

Zeke stared at them. *(I may know these people, but they're making no sense.)* "I have no idea what you're talking about. You could begin by telling me what I'm doing here."

It was Bookman's turn to stare. "You serious or playin' one'a your usual games?"

The nurse stepped to the door and motioned the chief to follow her into the hall. "The doctor said try to keep him talking and asking questions to see if he experiences any continuing memory lapse. Sometimes it takes a while for patients to remember everything after they suffer a trauma. Maybe telling him how he got here would help, then see whether he can recall anything that happened yesterday."

DeVon said it shouldn't be hard to keep big-beak Tanner asking questions, thanked her, and reentered. He had only begun speaking about events of the previous afternoon when some segments made their way into Zeke's consciousness and he interrupted, "Wait a minute! I remember, and I want to tell you who's responsible for the messages and the sign at the fire—probably for Bill Borsch's murder, too! I have it all figured out. I've been waiting to tell you, but can't reach you at the station. Where've you been?"

Bookman glanced at Marjorie. She walked to the side of the bed and took Zeke's hand. "Just take it slowly."

"But I know who's been sending the messages!"

"Just relax, Zeke. There's no hurry."

"There may be!"

Bookman added, "Zeke, old buddy, your ham sandwich's shy a slab. You don't really remember what happened last night, do you?"

"I certainly do! I talked to Marjorie and decoded the numbers right before going to feed the dogs."

"What about after that?"

"Not exactly sure. I know I was heading out to feed Ace and Bandit but woke up here. What's going on? Did the dogs get fed or not?"

DeVon assured him his dogs were OK and asked again whether he could remember anything else about the previous night. After a period of silence, Zeke abruptly began shuddering uncontrollably. Marjorie squeezed both his hands tightly and reassured him quietly until the shock of sudden further recollections of last evening's events subsided. He turned to DeVon. "Stretch, did you get *all* of them?"

"About all, Zeke, about all. Got warrants out for the rest. Some of 'em are in cells at the station, but there's so many, we hadta bring several over here to Wayne City's lockup.

"Who were under those hoods? Where'd they come from? Why *me*? I've never had anything to do with a cult in my life. Wait a minute—I remember! They called the guy out in front 'Holy Leader.' He had a different robe from those others. I'm pretty sure I know who he is. Those two guys standing there with knives—what were they going to do? What was that one with the pillow up to?"

"Slow down, Tom Tracy, slow down. I'll answer all those questions, but not until you tell us about decodin' the numbers and figurin' what they mean. Start talkin'."

Zeke endured another bout of the shakes before he could begin. "When Marjorie said...hey, just exactly when did you two get on such a chummy basis? How'd this *Marjorie* and *DeVon* stuff get started?"

"Old bud, just about the time they were cartin' your useless hide off to the hospital, this doll here comes steamin' up. Grabs me by the shirt and starts layin' down the law about findin' out what's goin' on and where they were takin' you. Couldn't get rid of her—scared me so awful bad, I hadta tell her everthing. She's been right here since they broughtcha, and I been here since sometime after midnight. Got to know one another pretty good."

"I still don't understand."

"Sport, you been sacked out dead to the world for more'n eighteen hours. Doc said whatever they used to knock you goofy caused you to sleep like a tree stump. Now, get on with tellin' about decodin' the numbers and figurin' the messages. Everthing's OK—just talk."

"Positive?" Reassured, Zeke continued. "Actually, it was a simple code. I made the mistake of expecting something more complicated. Anyhow, just after I got through talking with Marjorie on the phone, I was looking directly at the numbers propped on the kitchen table. Somehow a word she used caused that word, the messages, and the numbers to come together."

"Word? *What* word?"

"It was *vengeance*. Marjorie Louise said she didn't know I could clean house with such a *vengeance*. When I remembered her word, the numbers we found on the sign at Borsch's grave were right in front of me. Give me pencil and paper and I'll show you what I mean." He wrote the numbers, 6 1 2 1 9. "Take a look. When I saw the six, one, two, one, nine, and put them together with *vengeance*, everything fell into place. From when we were kids, do you remember when we had to memorize the books of the Bible in Vacation Bible School, then stand and recite them at Sunday night service? Same thing with certain verses from a chapter during the year? Still know the books of the New Testament?"

"Marjorie, call the nurse, he's slippin' away again. Exactly how in boomin' thunder can the *books* and *vengeance* have anything to do with Borsch?"

"Dee, does the word *Romans* mean anything to you?"

"Puttin' *Eye-talians* in Stony Crossing?"

"I'm asking again, can you remember the books of the New Testament?"

"Oughta—they drilled 'em into us enough."

"Let me hear you recite."

"I'll humor you just this one more time. Let's see, there's *Matthew, Mark, Luke, John, Acts, Romans*...wait just a minute. Is that the

Romans you're blatherin' about? What's the connection to the Borsch killin'?"

"How many books did you name? Count them."

"I'm in this deep, s'pose I'll hafta finish this silly game." DeVon ticked them off on his fingers as he counted silently. When he got to *Romans*, he stopped. "OK, six altogether. Now what?"

"Don't you see it, Dee? Romans is the *sixth* book."

"Guess I'm capable'a joinin' that together. What about it?"

"The next number is a *one*, but that doesn't decode to anything by itself. Combine it with the following number, the *two*, and what do you have?"

"One...two—*twelve*, I s'pose. OK, so now we got a six followed by a twelve. The next numbers oughta be eighteen or maybe twenty-four, I reckon, but they're not."

"No, it's nineteen."

"So somebody couldn't do 'rithmetic."

"Remember *any* Bible verses we had to recite? *Romans, twelfth chapter, nineteenth verse*, for instance. Maybe just the last line? No? It reads, 'Vengeance is mine; I will repay, saith the Lord.' That's what the numbers painted on the sign at Borsch's grave meant. How do I know for sure? Break down the other sets of numbers, and you'll see the pattern." Again, he put numbers on the pad—1 1 1 1 5. "OK, let's decode these. The first number, *one,* stands for *Matthew*, the first book of the New Testament. The next two, *one* and *one*, must be taken together to mean anything—they decode to chapter eleven. The last set, *one* and *five,* or *fifteen*, is the verse. Remember that one?"

"Go ahead. You're doin' right well for a beginner."

"It's 'He that hath ears to hear, let him hear.' I think those numbers on my answering machine and in the *Clarion* ad were meant to be a general warning to everyone. I'll tell you the rest, but I need a sip of water first."

Marjorie Louise was silent until now. "Maybe you should rest and listen to DeVon. He has news."

"Not yet! I need to tell him who's been doing the letter writing and sign making. He needs to be picked up right away!"

"But, Zeke..."

"It'll be all right, Marjorie," Bookman interrupted. "Let him keep talkin'—might be onto somethin'. Tell on, Tanner. I'm findin' this real interestin'."

"Well, when you get the first numbers decoded, all the rest are easy." Zeke wrote the numbers, 1 4 1 8, found at the Williams fire. "There are fewer of them, but they work the same way. Only *this* number *one* doesn't stand for *Matthew*. You can tell that pretty quickly by looking in that chapter—nothing fits. But, combine the first *two* numbers, the *one* and *four,* and you come up with the fourteenth book of the New Testament. Know that one, Bookman?"

"Know it all right, but I don't wanna break your winnin' streak."

"Thought not. It's *Second Thessalonians*. The next number, a *one*, is the first chapter, and the last number, an *eight*, is the verse. Want to hazard a guess as to what the first chapter, eighth verse might be about?"

"Somethin' about fire?"

"Good—you haven't forgotten *everything*. It's a command to use flaming fire to heap vengeance on those who disobey God."

"You're on a roll, Tanner. Wanna take a shot at the numbers on Borsch's hand and body?"

"A snap." Zeke wrote 1 5 3 0. "The numbers decode to *Matthew,* the first book, fifth chapter, thirtieth verse. It talks of cutting off a right hand, but it would be an extremely weird stretch of a warped mind for it to have been interpreted as anything gruesome. The author wasn't even talking about someone else. He was talking about not offending anyone—he'd cut off a hand first. There must be a connection between the verse and Borsch's hand amputation, but I don't know what it is. Anything else you'd like to know? Ask me nice."

"Your doin' pretty good with the warnin' and the vengeance part, butcha left out the other numbers on Borsch, and you haven't said a word about the seven-sided-circle heckta-thing. Got that one doped out?"

"I know exactly what it means. Take a look at this drawing of the heptagon with the numbers." Zeke drew the mysterious seven-sided figure with it's diagonal stripe crossing out the number 70, and placed I 1 8 2 2 beneath it. To one side he added, 70 x 7 = 490. "The numbers and the heptagon drawing are tied together. My guess is they were fashioned to serve as part of a standard design to be used as a warning—either before an action was taken or afterward.

"*One, one, eight, two, two* stands for *Matthew,* first book, chapter eighteen, verse twenty-two. There, the commandment is made to forgive sinners *'seventy* times seven', or four hundred ninety times. The seven-sided figure, the heptagon, is the *seven* of the Bible verse, and the number in its center is the *seventy* from the same verse." Zeke pointed to his drawing. "Get it? S*eventy* times *seven* equals *four hundred-ninety.* The heptagon design meant to be a warning to an individual *before* an action would be taken if the number crossed out by the diagonal line was less than seventy—s*ixty-eight*, for example. That number, multiplied by the heptagon's seven sides, showed the sinner had been forgiven four hundred seventy-six times, and was getting close to the biblical 'seventy times seven.' Dee, the *sixty-eight* in the heptagon sent to Borsch before he was killed? I found one just exactly like it in my junk-mail basket right before Marjorie phoned, but didn't open it till later. Anyhow, used *after* an action was taken, the number *seventy* showed all the forgiving was over and vengeance meted out. The design with the *seventy* in it like those on Borsch's hand and body then became a general warning to others. Now, don't you have anything more to ask me, Great chief?"

"Whataya expect me to ask?"

"Who killed Bill Borsch just might be a question occurring to a smart chief of police. Doesn't anything I said give you a tiny hint who it was? Maybe you think I have the numbers figured out wrong."

Marjorie Louise could stand it no longer. "Darn you, DeVon Bookman, tell him everything right this minute!"

"Tell me what?"

"Zeke, she means I already know who did Borsch and why."

"You figured out the numbers, too?"

"Nope, but when we collared the grand holy poo-bah, he spilled the beans about everthing. Couldn't stop talkin' and braggin' about who he is and what his plan is. Wouldn't explain the meanin' of the numbers and markin's, though. Every time I asked, he gave me a sappy grin and said they were his divine secret code, but everbody would know once he got goin' on weedin' out the wicked."

"All right, Bookman, I've waited long enough. I'm pretty sure I know the answer, anyway, but *w*ho do you think killed Borsch?"

"All in good time, my man, all in good time. Since it looks like some'a your marbles might'a dropped out'a the bag, reckon I'll hafta crayon a picture. Soon as I got the word yesterday you were lookin' for me, I phoned. There was no answer, as usual, so I drove to your house. Found that loopy *sixty-eight* letter on your kitchen table, the one like Borsch got, and figured somethin' naughty was up. Took a look around out back and the rest is history."

"Doggone you Dee, unravel just what *history* means, and tell me who you think is the killer."

"Fact'a history is, usin' outstandin' policin', I saved your sorry butt."

Marjorie refused to let that pass. "Zeke, the *truth* is, when he went out back, your dogs were frantic—barking and howling and trying to drag their houses out through the orchard. *Barney Fife*, here, walked out toward your storage building and saw some parked vans. He slipped up closer, heard voices, and broke open the door."

DeVon confessed. "If you must know, when I figured you were in the storage buildin' and saw all'a those vans out there behind the trees, I called for just a little back-up. For once, my radio worked. Half a dozen'a my guys showed, and Mickner and a couple'a his crew were just outside'a town. Lardass—uh-oh, pardon me, Marjorie—Sheriff Laddis and some'a his moldy bunch'a miserables got there after everthing was about over, naturally."

Marjorie Louise spoke quietly, "Zeke, DeVon broke in just as two of the gang were about to amputate your hands."

He shivered and looked at his hands. "Hold it a minute. I don't understand. They were right there on my *own property*! In the storage building? *Who were they!* How long you going to keep it a secret?"

DeVon was exasperated. "Didn'tcha never see any smoke comin' out'a the chimney? Never heard nothin'? Never see nothin' a'tall?"

"The building's quite a ways out and pretty well shielded by the orchard and evergreens. I heard a car occasionally when I didn't have the stereo cranked up, but thought it was only high school make-out artists. Saw tire tracks once, but thought the people who rented it from Nickel-Nabber before I came back to town made them. As to smoke, the building had no chimney. Uncle John only had those big propane heaters in there." Zeke paused and shook his head in disbelief. "Can't fathom how such a bunch could be operating right on my own property! How could they think no one would see their cars?"

"*You* didn't did you? One reason is that the bad guys didn't come in la bunch'a cars. They'd haul in a load'a dirty-doers in a van, drop 'em off, and go get another load so there wouldn't be lot'sa vehicles around. No need to do it yesterday, since they didn't hafta keep nothin' from you."

"A load? *Another* load? How many were involved, anyway?"

"Close to thirty."

"*Thirty!* Then I'm right! It *was* the Roseland cult that killed Borsch. The guy up front was the 'Holy Leader,' the one the True Prophet character talked about—correct?"

Neither Bookman nor Marjorie responded. Zeke was exasperated. "Well, if it wasn't them, *who* was it?"

Again, there was no response. Now, Zeke was more than just exasperated. "*Dammit,* Stretch. What's going on?"

Bookman spoke first. "Marjorie, I think he's all the way back. Got any idea a'tall where we can find a brick outhouse? Looks like we're gonna hafta drop it smack-dab onto him before he gets the picture. Zeke dummy, who's been buggin' everbody about shapin' up?"

Zeke stared. Seconds later, realization struck. "*Ackerman* was the Holy Leader in my storage building? *Ackerman* is the head of a *cult?*"

Marjorie answered, "Maybe not really a true cult yet, but they were getting there. Remember Vince McElroy telling you that in the right circumstances, a religious group could behave as a cult, especially if it were threatened? He cited the example of a church where a faction split away. I thought he meant a strong leader could control the group *leaving* a congregation. Well, I phoned him this morning and described what happened. He said it was altogether possible the group *remaining* could also look to an autocratic leader to help it survive, perhaps later drifting into cult-like behavior. From what I was able to tell him, he believes this is what may've occurred here."

Bookman elaborated, "Zeke, after we brought Ackerman in, you should'a heard him crowin' like a four-o'clock rooster about how he was fingered special to clean out the church and save the town from hell-fire. Bragged his guts out till past eleven. Didn't even want a lawyer. Said his laws weren't man-made. Here's how the whole thing went down. Right after the faction split away and started its own church, Ackerman had a big conversation with Jesus and was hand-picked to start the ball rollin' to lead the worthy to salvation. Pretty soon, he had half the congregation believin' he was divine-chosen to build a big saved flock and make everbody happy by gettin' things back like they oughta be.

"In the very beginnin', there was only one other lug nut in on things—the preacher's right-hand man. They needed group'a insiders to build on and to help plan and get things organized. Altogether, six wackos and him made seven in the first bunch. At first, Ackerman called these clowns 'The Inner Circle"—later on, the 'Chosen'. He picked mainly those who got kicked around or been made fun of all their lives—never had any real power—never been anybody important."

"Know anyone in Ackerman's 'Chosen'?"

"Oh yeah, and so do you."

"*What?*"

"It's gonna curdle your coffee plenty. Your old friend, Hiram Maxwell, was one. So was Ezra Allen Waggoner from the Bible Book Store."

"The Bible Book Store *Waggoner*? Maxwell's Variety Store M*axwell*? I can't believe it! Who else?"

"Next ones'll blow you clean out'a your socks. Ready? Our fine mayor himself, Duh Hangover! Yep, lardy little Denny Hanover."

"*No!* The *mayor*! How can that *be*?"

"Danged near impossible to believe any'a this crazy stuff, Zeke. Thought I'd come across everthing in creation, but some'a the most bumfoozlin' are others in the Chosen. Charlie Harrison, for instance. That's right, our big shot banker. Made a break for it—got away in a van and made it to the interstate with one'a Mickner's men on his tail all the way. Harrison nearly rolled the van on the entrance ramp, and once they got on the interstate, he gunned up to about a hundred. First overpass he came to, he smashed head-on. Trooper said it hadta be deliberate."

"Amazing! Amazing *and* depressing. You said Ackerman had a right-hand man in his 'Chosen' bunch. Who?"

"Figured you might'a guessed by this time. Who's been runnin' around raisin' hell—tryin' to get me fired and grabbin' for power wherever he can?"

"Not *John Lawson!*"

"The very same—church elder and town council president. Ackerman got him to come to Stony Crossing from just south'a Plymouth, then he talked some'a his cronies into movin' down here. They all lived in Maple Manor—you know, that new subdivision. We scooped 'em all up in the same litterbag. Zeke, remember the new people in town livin' out there you didn't wanna help check out? Some of 'em are part'a the bunch I'm talkin' about."

"The Constitution is still the Constitution."

"Don't forget what they was about to do to you, Goody Goody Gum Shoes."

Zeke declined to debate the constitutional issue just then. "You said there were six in Ackerman's 'Chosen', but you only talked about five. Who else?"

"You're right. I forgot to mention none other than the town blabbermouth, Last Dime Dalton. He was the one who painted the markin's on Lowell Williams' barn and set his house afire on Ackerman's orders to burn out what he called, 'those heathen sinners'."

Zeke shook his head. "Last Dime Dalton! I'd think him too much a schemer and milquetoast to get into something like this."

"He was all'a whatcha say—exactly why he *did* fit in. The only real power he got was overchargin' people when they were in a funeral bind and by drivin' his hearse flat out with the lights flashin' and the siren goin'. He knew what everbody thought of him, and this was his chance to get even and have some real power to be somebody. Goes for all the rest of 'em. Most every one was lookin' for the same things. Waggoner's old man, Jacob, booted him around like a stray cur every day of his life. Maxwell's a lot the same. His daddy never let him do nothin' but work in the store from the time he was in grade school. And he knew most'a the town thought he was an oddball."

"How does Harrison fit in? Surely he'd be seen as having power."

"Yeah, but he was power trippin', too. Already had plenty, bein' the banker n'all, but he was grabbin for more. Besides, he was a cracked-nut-survivor wierdo, too. House was plumb full'a guns and all kinds'a gear with directions for roughin' it. Must'a fit right in with Ackerman's ravin's."

"Hanover—what about him?"

"Don't hafta tell you about our mayor—he's always been a laughin' stock. First as a grade school fatty-four-eyes, then the gofer manager for our high school basketball team. And for years, he was nothin' but a *'yessir, yessir'* flunky for the town council and Chamber' a Commerce."

"Lawson?"

"Haven't learned all that much about him yet, but I'd bet most anything he crawled out'a the same pile'a slimy maggots. Put 'em with

Ackerman and you got a tickin' bomb. It's our awful bad luck they came together and went off in Stony Crossing."

"Any other church elder involved?"

"Don't think so. You might figure Abel Hofstettler would fit the bill'a what Ackerman was lookin' for. The preacher and one or two others tried approachin' him, but he was too all-fired set in his ways about followin' regulations and bein' professional. Good thing he wasn't in with 'em, or else we might'a never seen that letter to Borsch with that heckta-thing in it, and I might not'a doped out right away you were in deep cow-do when I saw the same exact thing with the *sixty-eight* in the letter on your kitchen table."

"I hear that! You said something about Ackerman having a second group."

"After he got his first group'a 'Chosen' boot-lickers together, the next thing was to sign up a bunch'a young muscle to help carry out orders. He called 'em 'The First Rank of the Brotherhood.' Another mess'a road kill. Wanna guess who was head'a that gang?"

"After all this, it could be anyone."

"Not if you thought about it a little—Hollis Benson."

"*Benson!*"

"The one and only—leadin' other skunks'a his stink."

"What other skunks?"

"How 'bout your old handshakin' pal and Ackerman's prime fetch-it, Delbert Dove? You *do* remember he was the meat man at Burkholder's, don'tcha? Another meat-cutter was in on it—the youngest Carl Jensen—the one his dad was always leanin' on. Podner, you were about to be carved up by two grocery store butchers. We already nabbed most'a the same sewer-rat crowd."

"It's all just so mind-boggling, Dee. Awfully hard to believe so many could follow Ackerman."

"He was a real spellbinder, all right. Little by little, he bent 'em into doin' anything he ordered. Even after most'a his batty bunch was locked up, they were hollerin' and carryin' on about how he'd deliver 'em."

The chief stood and stretched. "Ackerman started out simple enough, but kept snatchin' power. At first, all any church member hadta do was to promise to attend regular again—after standin' up in front'a everbody and confessin' to all their evil doin's and then repentin'. Those who didn't would be dealt with in regular ways, sometime startin' with deaconin' and elderin'. In only a couple years, he began makin' a list, addin' anybody he thought insulted him by not doin' what he wanted or did somethin' he thought was evil. Anybody who wouldn't shape up hadta be offed 'cause they were pollutin' the rest'a the membership.

"You and me were right up there. He and Lawson thought I was the head devil in stoppin' him from gettin' MizMartha's money on top'a bein' a non-attender and a blasphemer, among other things. Besides followin' what Ackerman said to do, I figure Lawson also wanted to off me 'cause I found out about his womanizen'. The preacher told me nothin's gonna change—I'm still top'a the list.

"There was a bunch'a reasons you made it, Zeke. Naturally, one big one was not attendin' church regular. Then you wrote him a wicked letter and sent copies to the church's Membership Committee. By the way, you said you couldn't hook up the connection between that 'right hand' Scripture and Borsch's hand amputation? Remember me sayin' he flipped 'em the bird when they eldered him? They cut off his birdin' hand to obey the preacher's crazy-headed readin'a that Scripture. They were gonna hack off *both* your hands 'cause you used 'em to type your letters. Must be he stretched the 'right hand' Scripture even more to include the left hand, too. Loony, just loony.

"There's other things. The preacher said you must'a also been in on helpin' to block him from gettin' MizMartha's money. Last straw was thatcha didn't toe the line in time. Never did explain it. Must'a meant before your 'seventy-times-seven' forgivin' was up. A'course you'd be easy to get to—him livin' right across the way from you n'all.

"Oh, I forgot to mention another big reason they wanted your scalp—somethin' you didn't tell me. Kind'a overlooked reportin' about Lawson's phone call pumpin' you for the goods on me, didn'tcha? Kind overlooked tellin' me about your rattin' him out to Harry Stilson, didn'tcha? Anything else your memory went dead on?"

"Ethel, you know I always have your best interest at heart."

"Got my eye on you, Gertrude."

"Dee, who else was on the list?"

"Several. Even some on the town council, includin' Harry Stilson, a'course. Lurinda made it, too—for carryin' on with me, I s'pose. Roosevelt Hoover—you know, Lurinda's kitchen assistant—was on it. Don't know why—never heard one word against him, and Ackerman wouldn't say.

"Every last one'a those who broke away from the church because'a the preacher's deportment were on it—even the women and kids. Ackerman hadn't showed the whole list to anybody. It was one'a the first things the men found when they were searchin' his house. Makes you wonder if the rest'a his nutsos had seen it, would they've gone along? Surely somebody would'a pointed out to him he couldn't get away with his plan to off so many. Don't know, though—they didn't step in to stop him from gettin' Borsch erased and you from bein' next. If they didn't object to the bigger plan, it might'a been too late for more innocent folks before we got him. I'm right prayerful we got 'em all when we did."

"Please tell me there were no more on the list."

"Well, naturally Ackerman knew that new lawyer who worked on MizMartha's will would know about a second will—might even have it in his office. Ackerman was gonna have his gang'a murderin' fools off him right away before he could talk. He was the last one on the list—put on just last week.

"Dee everything that was going on is just incredible!"

"Real weird stuff all right, Zeke."

"What's going to happen to the preacher?"

"Nothin' just yet. When he finally ran out'a gas, I laughed in his face and told him he didn't look like such a hotshot planner and his bunch looked like a gang'a extra dumbass fools who couldn't do nothin' right. He went batty as a goose and commenced to frothin' and rantin'.

You'll be happy to hear I'm a slimy tongue-shootin'-out reptile with a bitch copperhead for a mama and an overripe stinkin' skunk for a daddy. That's a right interestin' combination, don'tcha think? They got him a tied down in a rubber room at Forrest Haven. Took half a dozen officers to get a straight jacket on him."

"Will he ever be tried?"

"Don't know if they'll ever be able to. Sure hope so. Like I said, he's actin' like a crazy hee-honkin' jackass right now, but I think he could be puttin' on the whole lame-headed act—he's such a sneaky devil. Legally, I don't think for a minute he didn't know right from wrong—else why'd he try to keep his doin's so mummed up?"

"What's going to happen to the rest of them?"

"One job'a sortin' out I'm glad I don't have. There'll be a bunch'a murder ones and accessories before and after the fact. Lots'a other charges, too—for his hand-picked wackos *and* the rest'a the acorns in that crappy crop."

"Now that you have one unsolved case closed, anything new on the other one?"

"Say *one* solved? No, Ezekial Amos, my man, we got not just the one, but *both* of 'em. All *three*, if you wanna count MizMartha."

"All *three*! How so?"

"They're all three tied together."

Zeke sat bolt upright. "Ackerman had *all three* killed!"

"Not quite that. I said all three are tied together."

"What do you mean? How do you know?"

Before Bookman could answer, the nurse entered. "Time for the afternoon temps, Mr. Tanner." She was just leaving when Zeke asked, "What time this afternoon am I going to get out of here?"

"What makes you think you're going home today? The doctor says maybe tomorrow. He wants to keep an eye on you for at least another night."

Zeke began to lay down a barrage of objections, but soon learned the nurse had allies in DeVon and Marjorie. She had much the better argument. "Zeke, one more night won't hurt you. Just relax. I'll pick you up tomorrow, and we can talk or do whatever you like."

DeVon warned, "Don't know if I'd offer him that last option, Marjorie. Truth is, he's only a dirty old man on a diet."

"Maybe so, but he's my dirty old man. And haven't you noticed? His diet is beginning to show results."

Under the sheet, Zeke sucked in his middle and demanded, "OK, Bookman, get on with telling me about the other cases."

"Where do you want me to begin?"

"Who killed Miss Martha Manchester?"

"Shocks me to learn you haven't scoped that out. The doer was Benson."

"*Benson*! Why?"

"The preacher was always warnin' him and the other screwballs to be careful about keepin' their secrets—be 'specially careful around MizMartha lately. Better just stay away from her altogether. Remember how she changed her will cuttin' the church all the way out and givin' everthing to the Women's Center? When she told Ackerman, he started workin' on her to change it back, and she began havin' second thoughts. Ackerman didn't tell Benson about the will business, a'course, Then MizMartha had her stroke or whatever it was, and when he saw her bein' so anxious to talk to me, it scared him. Not knowin' Ackerman only warned 'em to stay away from her to keep 'em from doin' anything to bollix up his pitch to get her to change the wills back, Benson figured she'd got onto somethin'—figured she was gonna rat 'em out, so he up and killed her. Couldn't chance her not dyin' and talkin' to me."

"That's *awful!* How did he do it and get away?"

"Well, remember how he was underfoot all the time MizMartha was in the emergency room? He heard Doc Forsythe tell us what room they were takin' her to—eight twenty-two, I think it was. Bein' in civvies, all that reptile *chief deputy* hadta do to get by everbody was swipe a white coat. The sorry snakehead beat it up to the room, bold as copper, and hid in the closet. When the nurse hadta step into the next room for a minute, he snuffed MizMartha with a pillow. Didn't take long, the shape she was in. When her emergency monitorin' beeps started firin' off, he jumped back in the closet and stayed till things died down. Got away later still wearin' the white coat. Don't know what he would'a done if the nurse hadn't left MizMartha's room. Probly killed *her*, too, I reckon."

"Then what happened?"

"The rotten c*hief deputy* was so proud'a savin the church n'all, he went straight over to Ackerman's house to tell him the good news, but the preacher was out'a town till late the next afternoon. After the dirty low-down weasel finished hockin' MizMartha's pin on Saturday, he came back to town and paid off Anders on their boat deal. When the slinkin' hyeeny went back to Call-me-Charlie's later that afternoon, he was out in his woodshed.

"Talk about your sediment-suckers. Think about it. There was Benson, drivin' up in a sheriff's department cruiser, wearin' his lawman's uniform all ready to go on duty, and not battin' an eye while he was braggin' about killin' MizMartha. Now, a'course Call-me-Charlie had no chance'a connin' her into a will change. He grabbed a stick'a wood and knocked Benson colder'n a tuna.

"As you might figure, that caused problems. First one bein' what to do about Benson. He phoned Delbert Dove to come over, then they gagged and cuffed the *chief deputy* with his own cuffs—left him in the woodshed till after dark. Afterwards, Dove was to get help, then take him someplace out in the woods and shoot him. That left the question'a what to do about the patrol car, so they hid it in Ackerman's garage. Later that same night after Dove and another Brotherhood prevert got back from doin' the dirty deed, the brazen bastards parked it in front'a Benson's house. By the way, we found his gun in Dove's garage.

"Oh, I forgot to mention another reason you hadta go was he didn't wanna take a chance you'd seen anything from your house to make you suspicious when they were fixin' to take care'a Benson."

"Great Chief, I have some questions about Borsch's murder. For starters, why didn't he just steal Borsch's ring when they were dumping Borsch at the bridge?"

"Reckon he wouldn't be dumb enough to steal it with Ackerman's top brown-noser, Dove, right there helpin' to ditch Borsch. He would'a ratted to Ackerman for sure. No way Benson could go back later and get the ring—too risky even for a thief like him."

"Why did they amputate Borsch's hand, mark it up, and leave it with the body on the bridge? Doesn't seem logical."

"That *logical* stuff again. Ackerman was gonna freeze it and leave it somewhere else sometime as a warnin' for somebody to find, maybe even you. Right when Benson and Dove were ready to drive under the roofed part'a the bridge and dump Borsch, a street department truck pulled up on Sycamore so the men could put barricades across Horse Hockey Road to block the way to the bridge—snow bein' predicted. The body-droppers had Borsch wrapped in a tarp in Dove's car trunk. They accidentally put the hand in, too. It was close to dark already, but they got so addled at seein' the street department truck, they dumped both the hand *and* the body right where they were—just at the edge'a the roofed part—and took off. Ackerman pitched a fit when he found out about the hand and not gettin' the body all the way underneath the roof where the snow wouldn't cover it."

"Dee, if Ackerman wanted Borsch's body to be a warning, why leave him on Bailey Bridge in the first place? Might've been there quite a while before someone happened upon it."

"Way the preacher tells it, he knew snow was predicted for later that night and thought barricades blockin' travel over the bridge wouldn't be put up till the next mornin' after it snowed. Figured the street crew would be sure to find Borsch when they drove through to barricade the other end'a the bridge. Didn't expect the barricades to go up the evenin' before just because a snow was *forecast.* Except for blunderin' about when the barricadin' was gonna be done, that part wasn't such bad plannin'. Street crew almost always drives straight on through the bridge to barricade the other end of it, then back to town through Make-Out Woods. But for some reason that evenin', they decided to go all the way around through Birdland—probly to blow off the rest'a the workday before quittin' time. Who knows how many things might'a been different if only they'd drove right on through?"

"Spilled milk, Dee, spilled milk."

"S'pose so. Zeke, you been askin' lots'a questions, now I got one. I know they say this cult kind'a stuff can happen anyplace, but what is it about *Stony Crossing*, this little place, makin' it all set for Ackerman to do his mischief? How in the name'a heaven could a *religion* do such a thing?"

"Putting my somewhat limited knowledge of psychology and Professor McElroy's information together, my take on it is that this whole foul business has nothing to do with *religion*, nothing at all. It's a psychological phenomenon having everything to do with *power* and *fear of change*. Look at it this way. People in Stony Crossing lived according to a strong, well-developed moral code for over a hundred-fifty years. Along comes a mass of changes, including computers, the Internet, satellites, nuclear holocausts, TV sex, X-rated movies, AIDS, hijacking and terrorists. Also, the town is undergoing something of a transformation. All these threatened everything they lived by for decades.

"As if they weren't alarming enough, a group split from the congregation and formed its own church, threatening the remaining group's way of life, and possibly survival, even more. Ackerman instinctively knew people under stress believe what they so desperately want to believe. He told them what they wanted to hear—that things would be back to the way they once were if they only followed him. As with most zealots of any stripe, the more power his followers allowed him to seize, the more he craved, and the more off-centered he became. It's not just Stony Crossing, it could happen anywhere."

Bookman rose and gazed out the window. "What's gone on is gonna be tough on folks. Things have always changed pretty slow in Stony Crossing—most times for the best. I think this time there's gonna be some quick changes for the worse. One big one is that most'a these good people in Stony Crossing will probly never get back to trustin' anybody full out."

"Afraid so, but maybe some good will come of what's happened. In your words, I guess 'we just hafta keep pluggin'. It's still extremely hard for me to believe you or someone wouldn't have seen something was going on."

"When you were zonked out Marjorie and I talked a good bit about how that could'a happened. Figured maybe the biggest reason they got away with it's 'cause no decent person could ever even *think'a* doin' the stuff that's been goin' on, so they can't think it'a anybody else. Who in their right senses, includin' you and even me, would believe some'a the town's leadin' citizens were doin' what they did? Damned snakeheads were hidin' in plain sight, blendin' right in with the good folks who trusted 'em."

The three talked on until the nurse came to shoo out Marjorie and DeVon. "It'll soon be time for dinner, and you can talk all you want tomorrow."

Zeke protested until Marjorie Louise suggested, "His food isn't here yet. Why don't I go down to the desk and get his TV switched on? Meantime, they can chat a bit longer." The nurse was reluctant, but agreed.

When Marjorie returned, Zeke's food hadn't arrived, and he and Bookman were staring slack-jawed at the screen. The usual dressed-for-success, young needle-necked blond, national-news TV talker was standing before the Town Hall in Stony Crossing and reporting the top news story of the day. "In this pastoral community of Stony Creek, there has occurred a series of crimes so bizarre, so unbelievable, that it stretches the imagination almost beyond any limits to describe." She babbled on until the producer's voice in her earpiece finally penetrated that it was Stony *Crossing*, not *Creek*, and she hurriedly broke for yet another commercial. Afterward, she soared to even higher hyperbole. By the time she finished, Stony Crossing was the murder capital of the country. (At least the commercials lasted long enough for her to memorize the correct name of the town.)

Adding insult to injury, she continued, "...a police station groupie, Mr. Luke Tanning, and Police Chief Delmore Braken" were mentioned prominently and tagged with the false inference that both refused requests to be interviewed.

Zeke clicked to another network. It was the same, only more so. A male spouter this time. "Never in this reporter's long career has there been a case where so many of the leading citizens of a municipality have been arrested for crimes defying description." Blah, blah, blah. Again, Zeke and DeVon were featured in absentia.

Another click. Another network. Same stuff. The only thing different was a machine-gun mouth's promise to remain in Stony Crossing until every sordid detail was exposed. Apparently the others intended the same thing—in the background could be seen several large white satellite dishes mounted on trucks.

Before the program changed to less important news such as a major earthquake in Mexico and an ice storm isolating thousands in New England, the camera panned up and down a deserted Sycamore Street. Jake Walters was shuffling off on his way to the Levee Tap to begin his nightly boozing, but not another living thing was anywhere to be seen—not even a stray dog. Even the animals in Stony Crossing valued their privacy.

Zeke switched to local stations. They only repeated the networks and each other, adding the threat, "More news at six."

Zeke jabbed the idiot box into silence. "Can you beat that! Well, it'll be old news by tomorrow, and they'll all be gone."

"Ezekial Amos, my man, I don't think so. Saw all'a those flyin' saucers on the trucks, didn'tcha? Looks like you're finally gonna start earnin' your keep."

"Now wait a minute!"

"You're gonna be famous, Zeke, no doubt about it."

A food-service worker rolled a cart to the door with dinner, and Marjorie said it was their cue to go. She gave Zeke a smooch and promised to be there early next day.

"Be sure someone takes care of the dogs."

"Not to fret. I'll do it myself."

As they left, Bookman fired a final shot. "Mr. food-man, be certain he gets the diet plate, and he really likes tapioca puddin' for dessert." An ice cube narrowly missed the chief's ear and shattered against the door.

EPILOGUE

The hospital was every bit as glad to be rid of Zeke as he was to leave. His nagging began before breakfast and lasted until the doctor dismissed him at 10. Marjorie Louise sneaked him into town, and they spent the day listening to jazz and celebrating his narrow escape.

Ace and Bandit were also overjoyed. Zeke spent time with them, but retreated into the house when the industrially nosy kept driving by to catch a glimpse of the crime scene. After a while, Marjorie noticed that the rubbernecking stopped altogether. Only a while later did they learn Bookman declared the entire street a crime scene and ordered it barricaded and guarded so reporters and gawkers wouldn't bother them. Several officers remained out at the storage building, but Zeke said the only way he'd go near it again would be to burn it to the ground.

DeVon phoned twice and stopped by once, saying he wanted to bring Zeke up to date, but Marjorie had his number—he was checking on his pal. The chief brought the happy news that Ackerman's entire bunch was in jail. His parting shot was asking Zeke when he planned to move to a big city for more action.

The afternoon passed all too soon, and Marjorie had to leave but promised to return in a week for their shopping trip. As he walked her to her car, she looked at Zeke's antique Blazer and suggested that he might want to take a look at new cars as long as they were going computer shopping, anyway. He answered, "Maybe," but hoped Ol' Emmy hadn't overheard.

Soon after mixing a Snake Bite and settling back for more jazz, a knock at the front door startled him. *(Still a touch jumpy.)* He switched on the porch light and opened the door. There stood Lurinda, Twyla Jean and DeVon with about the tallest lemon meringue pie he ever laid eyes upon.

Excerpts from
JUSTICE IN STONY CROSSING
(A SEQUEL TO *MURDER IN STONY CROSSING*))
Publication date: June, 2005

Everyone in town knows Big Joe Jackson—probably most folks east of the Mississippi do. He is far and away the crookedest building contractor on the planet. Zeke Tanner's late Uncle John's description of Jackson during a court case is quoted to this day. "He's like a humped-back bull in a china store. What he can't stomp and break, he craps on." When discussing Jackson, there's no need for adjectives the likes of "vile," "lying," "cheating," "stealing," "flimflamming," "arrogant" "womanizing" or any of at least a dozen others. They are redundant—once you say "Big Joe," everyone knows the rest.

******

Sounds of a commotion at the front desk preceded footsteps pounding toward the chief's office. At the door, a man was trying to shove the deskman aside and enter. The officer had him by an arm and was trying unsuccessfully to drag him away. "*Get back here! You can't go in there!*"

The intruder shook himself free and motioned frantically for Bookman to follow. "Chief, come on! Somethin' ya gotta see! C'mon! *C'mon right now!*"

Bookman rose, "It's OK, Rogers, I'll talk to him. Take it easy Emery, take it easy. What's gotcha so bumfoozled?"

"*Just come on!*"

DeVon went around his desk and laid his hand on the man's shoulder. "Emery, take a breath. What's got hold'a you?"

The man sucked his lungs full. "I bought the contract from Joe Jackson to finish them apartments on Sycamore Street. Went up there just now to see what we needed to do before startin' work." He whirled toward the door and again beckoned wildly. "*C'mon! You gotta come on!* Joe's up there! *Joe Jackson! He's nekkid as a jaybird, and all taped up and bloody, and somebody's done whacked...!*"

"So long, Gertrude."
"See ya later, Ethel."